Dear Reader,

A funny thing happened on the way to the delivery room isn't how most women talk about the miracle of life, but the phrase perfectly fits Cheryl Anne Porter's story *Drive-By Daddy,* Harlequin Duets #21. Yes, the hero really does deliver a baby by the side of the road…but leaving mother and child behind is more difficult than he expected. Then Patricia Knoll weaves a charming tale of the eccentrics and matchmakers in a small town and the intrepid girl reporter who is trying to get herself out of Hicksville in *Calamity Jo.*

In Harlequin Duets #22 Liz Ireland returns with *The Love Police.* Sure, police officer Bill Wagner is a hunk of burning love, but that doesn't mean he has the right to interfere in Trish Peterson's love life—or does he? Then, fans of Colleen Collins will enjoy the return of Raven from *Right Chest, Wrong Name* (Love & Laughter #26). He's changed his rough and rugged image slightly…but magazine editor Liney Reed wants to pull out the *animal* in him to sell her magazine. Only problem is she finds herself far too attracted to the *primal* man he really is.

Treat yourself to a good time with Harlequin Duets.

Sincerely,

Malle Vallik

Malle Vallik
Senior Editor

Drive-By Daddy

"She looks a little like that cowboy who brought you in yesterday."

Her mother had a one-track mind. Darcy shifted…painfully…in her bed. "Oh, stop that Mother. He delivered her. He didn't father her."

"Well, I wish he had. I saw him, you know. A handsome man, with that white hat and white truck. It's all just unbelievable. And in the newspaper. See," she said, handing Darcy the folded newspaper, "big headlines. And a nice picture."

"A picture?" In her mind, Darcy again saw the camera flashes as she and her baby, wrapped in a Navajo blanket, were carried in by the cowboy whose unbuttoned chambray shirt had bared his chest to her cheek. "Dear God, I must have looked a fright."

Her mother waved her hand. "With that gorgeous cowboy in the picture, nobody will be looking at *you,* dear."

For more, turn to page 9

Calamity Jo

He didn't bother with seduction

"Shut up," Case growled, pulling her tightly against him. "Just shut up."

For once Jo obeyed, clinging to him.

With his mouth on hers, Case pulled her flush against him. Vaguely, he thought she must feel as stunned as he did, but after a moment, her hands came up to cup his jaw and her mouth ravaged his.

"You irritate the hell out of me," he murmured against her mouth.

"I...ca...an't stand you, either," she responded, wrapping her arms around his shoulders.

"You don't do what I tell you to." His lips skated across her jaw.

"You're so darned bossy." She turned her face and kissed him, wondering how he could be so delicious that she wanted to kiss him forever, and so aggravating that she wanted to kick him down the steps.

For more, turn to page 197

HARLEQUIN DUETS

ISBN 0-373-44087-1

DRIVE-BY DADDY
Copyright © 2000 by Cheryl Anne Porter

CALAMITY JO
Copyright © 2000 by Patricia Knoll

CHERYL ANNE PORTER

Drive-By Daddy

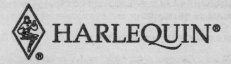

HARLEQUIN®

TORONTO • NEW YORK • LONDON
AMSTERDAM • PARIS • SYDNEY • HAMBURG
STOCKHOLM • ATHENS • TOKYO • MILAN • MADRID
PRAGUE • WARSAW • BUDAPEST • AUCKLAND

A Note from the Author

Heaven forbid you ever find yourself in Darcy Alcott's, the heroine of *Drive-By Daddy,* position. But if you do, I hope a tall, strapping cowboy like Tom Elliott happens to be driving by in his white truck. In my book, you just can't get any better than a guy like him. When I was a little girl living in Tucson, I had a thing for cowboys. I dreamt about them day and night. So I was thrilled that this book gave me the chance to do a little more "research."

I discovered that those gorgeous cowboys still exist today. They still wear white hats…and tight jeans. And yes, I probably still dream about them a little more than I should. Well, what can I say? I guess I still have a thing for cowboys....

Cheryl Anne Porter

Books by Cheryl Anne Porter

HARLEQUIN DUETS
12—PUPPY LOVE

HARLEQUIN LOVE & LAUGHTER
21—A MAN IN DEMAND
44—THE GREAT ESCAPE
63—FROM HERE TO MATERNITY

Don't miss any of our special offers. Write to us at the following address for information on our newest releases.

Harlequin Reader Service
U.S.: 3010 Walden Ave., P.O. Box 1325, Buffalo, NY 14269
Canadian: P.O. Box 609, Fort Erie, Ont. L2A 5X3

To my fiction writing class at
Hillsborough Community College in
Brandon, Florida...all of whom I know will be
checking this book to see if I've adhered to
everything I'm teaching them.

And to Mary Rodriguez, my "boss" at college, who
insists she's never met the person who can boss me.

1

"THIS IS *NOT* happening to me."

Darcy Alcott really needed to believe that. Because if she didn't, then this *was* happening to her, she *was* here alone, on a deserted stretch of southwestern Arizona highway. On a bright and steadily warming Wednesday in May. With a car that had broken down. And she was in labor. Big time labor. Baby-on-its-way labor.

"Don't panic, Darcy," she told herself, breathing fast and furiously. *Don't panic? Here I am—my baby about to make an appearance any moment and me, stuck to the tacky vinyl of the back seat of my second-hand sub-compact car. With the doors open for air. And Mom waiting on me in town for lunch. And what did I forget? The cell phone. So…don't panic? Right.*

As the full extent of her situation hit her, she came close to hyperventilating. "Oh, God, I'm panicking. I can't panic. I have to…" Her mind went blank. "What do I have to do? Keep talking. I have to keep talking. Maybe someone will come. Someone other than this baby. Maybe they'll see the open doors and the raised hood and stop. Oh. Another pain. Oh, baby, not now. You don't want to start your life with me mad at you. Please."

But baby, who was having none of it, only tried harder to make a grand entrance. Darcy's body bore down with the contraction, although she did her darned level best to breathe shallowly, to hold off the inevitable, to not help her daughter come into the world just this minute. However, two weeks early by everyone's estimation except apparently her own, baby had obviously decided to throw herself a birthday party today—before the hour was up, if that birth video Darcy and her mother/coach had suffered through in Lamaze class was to be believed.

Because according to what she'd learned from that calm, never-will-experience-labor-himself videotaped doctor and his oh-so-capable nurses, filming in the controlled setting of a hospital's delivery room... which by the way, Darcy wanted now to point out, never covered anything practical, like what to do if you were alone and in labor on a deserted highway, in both the pitcher's and the catcher's positions...she was about to become a mother. A single mother. In every sense of the word.

The pain peaked and passed. Darcy collapsed against the seat, panting and crying. Then she heard someone yell, "Please won't someone help me?" She looked around, then realized the voice was her own.

Suddenly, she heard the screech of tires, and saw a rising puff of dust and grit as a white pickup truck came to a stop. Someone was here. "Help!" Darcy cried out. "Please help me. My baby..." Her voice trailed off. *And please don't let it be some film crew. Or a passing band of ex-cons.*

Just then a long, tall shadow settled over Darcy, starting at the opened door at her feet. Not her best angle. A low whistle followed. "Sweet Jesus. Lady, you're about to have a baby."

"You think?" Darcy gasped out. Then, peeling herself off the sticky vinyl, she struggled up onto her elbows…and saw a handsome big ole white-Stetson-wearing cowboy peering in at her. "That clears everything up, doesn't it, mister? For a minute there, I thought I was— Ow, ow, ow." She shrank back against the vinyl. "Oh, no. Another…pain…help me…please…my baby."

"Yes, ma'am. Hold on. I'll help you." He pulled back and disappeared from view.

"No," Darcy whimpered, unable to move. "Come back. Don't leave me."

Then, through the glaze of her pain, her mind registered what sounded like a truck's tailgate being dropped open. Then there was silence as a few more seconds ticked by. A few minutes later, the cowboy reappeared. Only this time, he was behind her. Hatless now, his face hovering above hers, he shoved his big hands up under her shoulders, holding her. "When this pain passes, get ready to help me move you. I'm going to get you into my truck bed. I spread a blanket there for you."

Darcy shook her head, and licked at her dry lips. "No. Can't move. My baby. She's—"

"I have to move you. There's no room here. My truck's brand-new. It's clean. And I'll have more room to operate there."

Operate? A doctor word. The pain was subsiding. Darcy caught a quick breath. *Thank God…a doctor.* The world was, after all, a good place. "Are you a doctor?" she managed to say past her panting breaths.

"Relax," he told her. "Save your strength for the next pain. And no, ma'am, I'm not a doctor. I'm a rancher. Okay, here we go. One. Two.…"

A rancher? He's a rancher who's going to operate?

Why operate? What's wrong? My baby. Is something wrong with my baby?

"Three." He tugged her backwards...gently but firmly. Gasping, Darcy crabbed her feet along the seat as she reached up behind herself and grabbed at the rock-solid support of his arms. "Hurry. Faster. The pains..."

"Yes, ma'am. Let me get a hold of you. I've got to get my arm under your legs now so I can carry you. Like that. That's good. Okay, sweetheart, here we go. Ready?"

No. She wasn't ready. Not for any of this. Not labor. Not delivery. Not motherhood. "Yes," she cried out. Anything to get this ordeal over with. "Please don't leave me."

"I won't, honey. I won't leave you."

"Darcy. My name is Darcy. Not...honey."

His blue-eyed gaze met hers. He nodded his head. "Yes, ma'am. No disrespect meant...Darcy."

And then he had her in his arms and was carrying her as easily as if her pregnant weight were of no consequence to him. In only a matter of seconds—with Darcy realizing that her bare bottom was exposed to the world at large, should it care to pass by at this moment—he was settling her into his white truck's bed. He was so tall, he managed to reach in right over the fender that covered the wheel well and laid her down like a mother...okay, like a father...putting a baby in its crib.

Darcy exhaled her relief at being lain down and instantly clutched at the blanket under her, concentrating on taking deep breaths and on watching him sprint to the tailgate. In one quick movement, he hauled himself up into the grooved bed with her. Then, with his boots thudding dully against the metal of the truck deck, he stepped around her, positioning himself at her head and shoulders. "I'm going to pull you up more," he warned. "Keep your hold on that blanket."

Darcy did. Sure enough, he tugged on the brightly patterned Indian blanket's hem and effortlessly slid her farther into the bed until her head was resting against the bulkhead, at the cab's back. "This is the best I can do for you, Darcy," he told her, looking concerned. "I just wish there was some shade out here to make things easier for you."

"While I..." Darcy rasped, "just wished...there were...some drugs out here...to make things easier for me."

He chuckled. "I expect you do. Here. Raise up some." With that he levered her up and wedged another rolled blanket under her shoulders. "That ought to give you something to lean against." He stepped around her, and squatted down, all denim-covered muscle, at her feet. Lowering his gaze, he put a hand on her knee. "Bend your knees more...as far as you can. There. That's good. Now hold on to them. And keep them bent like that." He glanced up, looking into her eyes. "How're we doing?"

"Great," Darcy gasped out, feeling the onset of the next pain. "Want to...trade places?"

"Not for all the blue sky in Montana, ma'am. Easy now. Just take it as it comes." He reached up, smoothing his hand up under her maternity top and rubbing her belly. "You're doing fine, Darcy. Just breathe through it, make it easier for your baby. You say it's a girl?"

Biting at her bottom lip, with her eyes squeezed shut, Darcy nodded.

"Good for you. A daughter. But how do you know? Ultrasound? Or woman's intuition?"

The pain lessened. Darcy cried out, wanting to give up. It hurt so bad. But her body and her baby wouldn't let her. "Ultrasound," she finally sighed. "I don't…have…woman's intuition. If I did…I wouldn't…be in…this position."

The cowboy nodded. "I see. All men are slime, right?"

Darcy shook her head. "Not all. Just some." Then she remembered something. "A minute ago…in my car. You said 'operate.' Is…is everything okay? Can you tell?"

His expression clouded. "Operate?" Then it cleared. "Oh. No. I mean, yeah, everything's fine. Well, as far as I can tell. I just meant operate as in move around better."

Relieved beyond measure, Darcy exhaled. Then she thought of something else. "Have you…ever done this before?"

"More times than I care to count," he said with easy confidence. "But of course, I was helping to birth calves. I raise beef cattle."

Great. Beef cattle. And now me. Darcy's chin began quivering.

Which the cowboy obviously noticed because he changed the subject. "How'd you end up in this mess, Darcy? I mean out here on this road all alone. I figure the rest of it isn't any of my business."

Another pain began. Darcy gasped, her eyes widened, she tightened her grip on her knees. "Car trouble. Lunch. With my mother. Baby…not due…for two weeks."

The cowboy grew alert, quietly looking from

Darcy's face to the place where the action was. "Well, someone forgot to tell your daughter, I reckon. Okay, here we go. Ride it out, Darcy. That's good. Breathe. You're doing fine. You need to push?"

Her eyes now squeezed shut, her neck muscles corded with her effort, Darcy nodded and shrieked, "Yes. I need to push, dammit. That's what I'm doing. My back! My back is killing me."

Suddenly her eyes popped open. The cowboy had grabbed her arms and was—she couldn't believe it— literally pulling her to her feet, to a squatting position. "I've obviously never had a baby before, Darcy—"

"Well, neither have I, you...*man*, you!" It was the worst thing she could think to call him at this moment.

He blinked but otherwise ignored her outburst. "But I know what the Crow women say. It doesn't hurt so bad if you're squatting. It relieves some of the pain." Then, holding her steady he reached around her with his other hand and rubbed her lower back.

Blessedly, unbelievably, she did feel better in this position. But weak, tired, certain she couldn't keep this up, and wanting to be anywhere but here, Darcy leaned her weight into him, resting her forehead on his shoulder and clutching at his shirt. "I'm sorry," she sobbed. "I'm not usually this mean."

"It's okay," he soothed. "I'm not usually this help-ful."

Darcy sniffled into his shoulder. Something else, something totally inconsequential, occurred to her. "Where's your white hat?"

"In the cab."

She nodded, breathing in the clean scent of warm man and aftershave. "Like the Lone Ranger."

His hand on her back stilled. "What?"

"Your white hat. The white truck. Your being here to help me. Like the Lone Ranger."

"I'm hardly the Lone Ranger. I don't make it a habit to go around looking for damsels who need rescuing."

"Well, I'm glad you did today. You got a cell phone? Need to call my mother."

"Your mother? How about an ambulance?"

"My mother's a volunteer at the hospital. She'd get an ambulance out here."

"Makes sense. Yeah, I've got one, but not with me. Can you believe it? It's back at the hotel."

"Mine, too. At the house. Forgot it." Then Darcy felt the surging pain again and clutched at him. "Oh, no. Here comes another one. Hold me."

And he did. As her pain escalated, as it ate at the fringes of her consciousness, he talked to her…and rubbed her lower back. Darcy could only capture a few words, but she clung to them as if they were the keys to her sanity. Montana…means mountainous regions…land of blue sky…and cattle…beautiful country, Darcy…you ever been there…that's good, you're doing fine…lots of good grazing land…just here on business…can't believe he came down this road…he'd been turned around, going the wrong way, otherwise—

"Ohmigod, ohmigod, ohmigod, Cowboy—here she comes! Help me!"

"I will." And he did. Quickly but gently, he laid Darcy back on the blanket, propping her shoulders against the rolled blanket and forcing her grasping hands around her bent knees. From his shirt pocket he pulled a bandanna and quickly rolled it, finally tying a big knot in it. "Here." He stuffed it in her mouth.

"Bite down on this." She did, never taking her gaze away from his face. Sweat trickled down his temples. "Okay, Darcy, a few good, hard pushes, and we'll get your little girl out here where we can look her over."

With that, he scooted back on his knees, assumed a catcher's position, and put a hand on Darcy's knee. Then his gaze met hers. "You can do this, Darcy."

He sounded so sure. Darcy nodded, her jaw clenching around his bandanna. And then wave after wave of searing pain hit her, nearly casting her into unconsciousness. All she could hear was the cowboy's calm voice, urging her, encouraging her. All she could feel was the hard truck bed under her, the heat of the glaring sun above her. All she could do was push and breathe and groan and push again. And watch his face and listen to his voice…the Lone Ranger.

"Son of a— Here she comes, Darcy!" Excitement captured him. "Push, Darcy. Ohmigod. I've got her, Darcy. Here's her head. Breathe. Push, push. Okay, got her shoulders. She's a beauty. A ton of black hair. The hard part's over. Quit pushing…okay, I—well, I'll be damned. A baby. A whole brand-new baby! She's here, Darcy. We did it. Our little girl. Look!"

Exhausted, wringing with sweat, tired beyond belief, but elated to the point of tears, Darcy looked. Sure enough. There she was…a beautiful little pinkening-up and squalling baby girl. The child had black hair. Just like her mother's. And was mad at the world. Just like her mother. Darcy pulled the bandanna out of her mouth and reached for her daughter. "My baby. Give me my baby."

"Congratulations, Mama," he said, handing the baby to her and grinning from ear to ear. Then, and as if it were the most natural thing in the world for

him to do, he leaned over Darcy, smoothing her dampened hair back from her forehead as he kissed her
there and cupped her cheek with a warm and work-
callused hand. With his face close to hers, he said,
"You did just fine, Darcy. Just fine. Your little girl
looks just like her mama. Real beautiful."

Lost in the moment, Darcy covered his hand with
hers and then lifted it to kiss his palm. "Thank you."
The sobbing words were all she could get out as her
gaze locked with his. She saw his mouth working as
he nodded and moved back. Then she turned her complete attention to her daughter. Darcy carefully lifted
her baby until the soft, wet head was nestled in the
crook of her own neck, and whispered, "My baby. My
sweet little girl. I love you."

In the next few moments, Darcy's attention remained riveted on her child. She wiped at her, cleaning
and caressing her, looking her over, checking her color
and making sure she was breathing okay. She all but
forgot her cowboy deliverer as he worked quietly to
help her body complete the birthing process.

Once that was done, he caught her attention as he
worked his way up to her head and gently removed
the blanket from under her shoulders and wrapped it
around her waist and legs. Then, with his shadow casting Darcy in blessed shade and drawing her attention
up to him, she saw him reach into the pocket of his
jeans and pull out a pocket knife...which he opened.
Darcy's eyes widened.

"Umbilical cord," he said. "Got to cut the little
filly loose."

"Oh, God." Darcy clutched her tiny daughter
tighter.

The cowboy hunkered down beside Darcy, putting

a big, warm and strong hand on her shoulder. "I'll leave it pretty long, enough to tie it off into a knot. The doctor can clean it up later." Darcy whimpered. He squeezed her shoulder gently. "It's okay. I've done this before, Darcy."

"To calves," she blurted.

"Yep. Same principle." Very matter-of-factly, just like his answer, he opened the knife's blade and reached into a shirt pocket to pull out a match book. Darcy's eyes widened even more. "Got them at the hotel. Always pick them up even though I don't smoke. They're more of a reminder of all the places I've been. Glad I grabbed them, though. I need to sterilize the blade."

"Oh, God."

His eyebrows rose. "You can trust me. I wouldn't hurt a fly. Much less a sweet little baby." His gaze then locked with Darcy's. "Or her mama."

Darcy swallowed, nodded, and looked down, kissing her baby's head. "It'll be okay, sweetheart," she cooed. "We won't let anything happen to you." *We? Who's this we, Darcy?* She shot a look to the cowboy…and simply took a deep breath, suspending any further thoughts of him.

Thankfully—to Darcy's way of thinking—he wasn't looking at her. Instead, he'd set himself to his task, lighting the entire book of matches and running the flame back and forth under the blade. Darcy watched in horrified wonder. He intended to put that flaming-hot knife to her baby. And then she surprised herself with the realization that she trusted him to do so.

Really, really trusted him. His calm, quiet ways. His slow and sure movements. His very steadiness, like a rock, invited confidence in him. But when the matches were blown out, and the knife readied, when he reached for her daughter, turning the mewling, naked, precious little bundle over, Darcy began some mewling of her own.

The cowboy met her gaze, his blue eyes steady. "It won't hurt her. She won't feel a thing. But maybe you shouldn't watch."

Darcy liked that idea. She turned her head as he talked softly to the baby and performed this last task. "How do you know so much about this," Darcy asked, "if all you've delivered are calves?"

"I learned it from the Crow. I spent a lot of time with them when I was a boy."

Darcy rolled her head until she was looking at his square-jawed and tanned face. Bent over his task, intent on his handiwork, he was smiling at the baby. "The Crow?" she deadpanned, drawing his gaze her way. "I hope you mean the Native Americans, and not the kind that migrate in the winter."

"Well," he said, raising a hand to swipe it under his nose, as if it itched. "The Crow used to migrate in the winter, but not anymore. And I do mean the Native Americans." A slow grin now warmed his strong, weathered features. "This kind of job isn't for birds, Darcy."

She exhaled. "Imagine my relief. It's nice to know you're not crazy."

He shrugged, winking at her again. "Depends on who you ask."

"Great. Especially since I'm a little vulnerable here. And you have a knife in your hand."

His chuckle told her it would all be okay. He closed the knife, and put it down on the truck bed. "All done,

Mama.'' He gently handed the rooting, mewling baby girl back to Darcy. "We've been lucky so far. But we need to get you two into town and pronto." He made as if to stand up, bunching his muscles and bracing his hands against his bent knees.

Darcy stopped him with her hand on his chambray shirtsleeve. "Wait." He did, his eyebrows raised. Darcy looked at the cowboy, at the stranger who'd saved her life—and her baby's—the stranger with the white hat and the white truck. "Thank you. Really."

Grinning, proud, he ducked his head, nodding his you're-welcome. "Nothing to it, ma'am. Like I said, just glad I could help."

Darcy couldn't believe his humble speech. "Help? You saved us. Literally. I don't know how to repay you."

He put his hand atop hers now and gently squeezed it. His blue-eyed gaze and wide grin warmed her more than the sun above. "No need. It's payment enough for me to have been here when you needed me."

When she needed him. Darcy's chin trembled, her eyes teared up. He was the only man in her life with the exception of her now-deceased father, who'd ever been there for her when she needed him. "Well, still…thanks."

He winked at her, and released her hand as he stood. And became all business. "We need to wrap this baby girl in something before we hit the road." He began unbuttoning his shirt. "About the only thing I've got—" He pulled the shirt off, tossed it to the truck bed, and began tugging his white cotton T-shirt out of his waistband "—is my T-shirt. It's clean enough, I suppose. Probably only smells like man and sweat and dust and aftershave. What more could you want?"

What more could I want. He'd meant it to be funny. Darcy knew that. But mesmerized, lost in watching him, and holding her child close in her arms, Darcy swallowed, feeling her growing admiration of him, of his resourcefulness—not his physical presence. His kindness. Not his tanned and muscled chest. She bit at her bottom lip. Not his gorgeous smile or his blue-eyed gaze. No. Not any of those. Or even the whole mixture of them all.

Because now that she had her daughter, she was through with men. Over them. And some Montana cowboy who'd come upon her in her hour of need wasn't going to change that.

2

"I NEVER SAW the like of that navel knot your cowboy tied yesterday. Must be something they use on a ranch."

"I suppose. And he's not *my* cowboy, Mother."

Darcy watched her mother shrug. "Anyway, your 7-pound, 8-ounce daughter now has an innie navel. Dr. Harkness fixed it nice, didn't he?"

From the comfort of her hospital bed, all stitched up and still sore from yesterday's truck-bed birth, Darcy nodded as she eyed her mother. "Yes, he did. And no, I don't want to go out with Dr. Harkness."

"Well, not now. It's a little too soon."

"No. It's a little too late, Mother. Not soon. Late."

"You don't mean that."

Darcy stared at her mother. "Yes, I do. Dr. Harkness is 800 years old, if he's a day. Why don't *you* go out with him?"

Her mother pursed her lips. "I can't. I'm saving myself for Brad Pitt."

They'd had this conversation before. "Brad Pitt is too young for you, Mother."

Margie Alcott bristled in her chair next to Darcy's bed. "Well, thanks. I needed that."

Darcy sighed. "No offense meant. But admit it, Brad Pitt is even too young for me."

"Darcy, the man is in his mid-thirties. About six years older than you."

"Well," Darcy groused, crossing her arms, "he seems younger than me."

"Everybody's younger than you, honey. You're such a little old lady. Always have been. Anyway, I think you two would make a nice couple."

"Who? Brad and me? Or Dr. Harkness and me?"

A sly look came over her mother's pleasantly rounded face. "Actually, you and that cowboy."

"Here we go." Darcy threw her hands up, more to dispel her persistent thoughts about her mystery cowboy than to wave away her mother's words. Still, those she had to challenge. After all, she'd stuck herself firmly in this I-don't-need-a-man corner for the past nine months. She couldn't now, because of a chance meeting, admit that she was wrong. Darcy exhaled sharply, signaling her determination to reentrench herself in her own views. "What makes you think I need a man?"

"Well, that tiny little baby wrapped in swaddling clothes down there in the nursery, for one thing. She needs a father. You know—that nucleus family thing you hear so much about."

"Nuclear, Mother."

"Is that it? Well, it's the same thing."

"I guess." Darcy looked down at her hands and picked at a nail. Could she feel more guilty right now? It had taken her by surprise, this feeling of being alone in a way she hadn't anticipated. Could it be that she wasn't cut out to be a mother? She shook her head. No. The last thing she needed right now was to doubt herself. She couldn't, not with another life depending on her to be the adult here.

"It's not as if I'm deliberately denying my daughter a father," Darcy suddenly blurted into the silence that had settled between them. "I'm not trying to make some politically correct feminist statement here. Being a *single* mother wasn't exactly in the game plan, remember." To her distress, Darcy's chin quivered.

Her mother reached out, laying a hand on Darcy's arm. "Oh, baby, I didn't mean to upset you."

Darcy squeezed her mother's hand…and felt worse. Now she'd upset her mother too. "I know. God, Mother, the hormones. I'm all over the page with this. One second I'm mad, the next crying. Is this normal?"

Margie Alcott nodded, her smile returning. "Oh, sure it is, baby. You're a mess, and you're fine. It's all normal." Her mother squinted, as if in thought…which she promptly shared. "Well, honey, as normal as you've ever been. You always have been a little bit different, you know. Special, I like to say."

"Thanks," Darcy replied. It was moments like these that reminded Darcy that the reason her mother knew where all her buttons were and how to push them was because she'd installed them.

"Now, Darcy, don't you make that face that says I don't know what I'm talking about. Because I do."

Knowing she and her mother would never agree about Darcy needing a man in her life, she sighed and changed the subject. "Isn't your little granddaughter the sweetest thing you ever saw?"

At the mention of the baby, Margie Alcott put her hand to her bosom, and her smile turned beatific. "She's so beautiful, Darcy. I think she looks a little like that cowboy who brought you in yesterday."

Well, that hadn't worked. Here they were…back to the cowboy. Darcy shifted…painfully…in her bed.

"Oh, stop that, Mother. He delivered her. He didn't father her."

"Well, I wish he had. I saw him when he brought you in yesterday, you know. A handsome man, with that white hat and white truck. It's all just unbelievable, Darcy. And in the newspaper. You can see it for yourself right here. Big headlines. And a nice picture." She handed Darcy the folded newspaper she brought with her.

"A picture?" In her mind, Darcy again saw the camera light flashing as she and her baby, wrapped in that Indian blanket, were being carried in by the cowboy whose unbuttoned chambray shirt had bared his chest to her cheek. "Dear God. Was I covered?"

"Well, I should say so. Look for yourself. It's right there on page one."

"Page one? Great. Slow news day in Buckeye, Arizona?"

Margie Alcott puffed up sanctimoniously. "It was until you decided to deliver your baby out in the desert. I've never been so embarrassed in my whole life, Darcy. Why, it's a wonder your...*stuff* didn't get all sunburned, just hanging out there like that. What if someone had come by and seen you?"

Darcy could only stare at her mother, and fight the heat staining her cheeks. "Someone did come by and see me, Mother."

"I know. It's all there. On page one. Look at it."

Against her better judgment, Darcy finally looked. Yep, there she was. On the front page. Atop a gurney and being wheeled into surgery for stitching. The look on her face was probably the same one she'd have if she'd just escaped an alien abduction. But the accompanying picture was of her proud and grinning mother, fresh from the beauty shop, holding her new grand-baby, whose tiny little face was scrunched up in a scream. Darcy flopped the daily paper down. "Lovely. You look great, Mother."

Margie patted her silver-gray hair. "You think? Let me see that." She reached for the paper, and Darcy gave it to her, lovingly watching her mother scan the photo. "Well, I do, don't I?" Then she began turning pages, perusing them carefully. "But I'm going to get after that Vernon Fredericks. After all, he's the editor. And there's not one picture in here of your hero."

"My hero? You mean the Lone Ranger?"

Margie looked up from today's copy of the *Buckeye Bugle.* "Is that what you call him? The Lone Ranger?"

Darcy shrugged, seeing again, in her mind's eye, the man's blue eyes and hearing his calm voice. "I have to call him something. In all the excitement, I forgot to ask him his name. And then, once we got here, he just drove off."

Margie folded the paper and tossed it on the floor. "Well, who do you think he is?"

"Just some turned-around cowboy from Montana. At least, that's what he said."

Her mother pulled her chair closer. "I hope you at least thanked the man, honey. He did save your life. And your baby's."

"I know, Mother. And I did thank him."

"What'd he say to that?"

Darcy exhaled her frustration sharply. The woman wanted all the details. "He said it was nothing, as I recall."

Her mother sighed romantically. "Cowboys. They're just the most polite breed of man around."

Darcy shrugged. "I suppose."

Her mother's raised eyebrow said she'd detected something in Darcy's shrug that she didn't like. "Now, don't go blaming him for what that stupid old professor of yours did to you."

Darcy crossed her arms defensively. "Oh, you mean ask me to marry him, get me pregnant and then run off...for a second honeymoon with his wife?"

"I told you he was a married man."

"You told me nothing of the sort. You didn't even know him."

"I know his big-city kind."

"You do not. Buckeye's the only place you've ever lived. And Dad was the only man you'd ever known."

Her mother's chin rose a notch. "That may be. But I read a lot. And I watch those talk shows on TV. I've learned a few things."

What a sweet, confined little world her mother lived in—one Darcy had hated to intrude on, last Christmas at semester's end, with her own harsh reality. "I'll bet you have."

"I have. Now I've been thinking about something else, too."

"Dear God."

"Don't be disrespectful, Darcy Jean Alcott. I've been thinking about your cowboy. I think this whole thing—him being there when you needed him—is not just chance or luck. No, he was supposed to be here at that time for you. That's all there is to it. After all, his home state *is* off the beaten path."

Darcy remembered him saying the same thing yesterday. But she wasn't about to tell her mother that. "Off the beaten path? Like Buckeye, Arizona isn't? We're fifty miles southwest of nowhere, Mother."

"Hardly. Phoenix is just down the road. I swear, Darcy, you act like you left civilization when you came here from Baltimore. But anyway, what was I talking about?"

Darcy sighed. It was pointless to fight. "My screwed-up life."

"That's right." With that, Margie Alcott opened her sack lunch, arranging everything atop Darcy's bedside tray. She pulled a roast beef sandwich from a plastic bag. Darcy had to grin. It was ten-thirty in the morning. Volunteering was a hungry business.

"So. What *was* he doing down here? That cowboy, I mean."

Relentless, the woman was. Darcy could only stare at her sweet mother in her pink hospital uniform as she bit into her early lunch. "You mean besides delivering your granddaughter?"

"I do," she said, chewing. "I can't imagine." She swallowed, grabbed her soda, held it out for Darcy to pop the top, and then slurped from the can. Finally, she pointed at her daughter. "And don't you ever go off again without that cell phone, you hear me? It scared me to death yesterday when you were brought in. I don't think I could go through that again."

"I think you came through just fine, Mother. After all, you *were* front-page news." Darcy didn't have to be told how the *Buckeye Bugle* was there to get its headline. Who didn't know that Barb Fredericks's son, Vernon, was the editor? The same Barb who weekly played bridge with Darcy's mother and their two other partners in crime, Jeanette Tomlinson and Freda Smith. The bane of Buckeye. All four of them.

"Don't be silly," Margie Alcott said, crunching

now on potato chips. "That cowboy is the star. And, of course, my new granddaughter."

"And me," Darcy reminded her.

"Of course, you. I was just mentioned because I'm the one who called Barb and got Vernon on the story. It's not every day something like this happens."

"Well, certainly not to me." Darcy decided to try one last time to change the subject before her mother started her speech on how 50-year-old Vernon would make a great husband and father...if he could ever move out of his mother's house. "Have you seen the baby today?"

"Have I seen her? Is my name Margie Alcott? Of course I've seen her. I've all but conducted tours by the window that looks into the nursery. Why, she's the most beautiful child on the face of this earth. Everyone says so."

Everyone better. Darcy knew that much, knowing her mother—the social ringleader, as well as the resident bridge champ, of her group of lady friends.

Just then, her mother set down her soda and pursed her lips. This was never good. "Well? Have you named her yet? You've known for months you'd have a girl. And yet my grandchild is a day old and doesn't even have a name. 'Baby Alcott, female' it says on her little wrist ID. That's just plain awful. Everyone's calling her Louisa May. I just won't have that, Darcy. Louisa May Alcott. Why, the very idea...naming her after some dead romance writer."

Sighing, Darcy the English Lit professor reached over to the bedside table and picked up the form the nurse had left her to fill out, hoping her mother wouldn't obsess on the still-empty box marked "Father." She just couldn't bring herself to write Hank's name in the space. The very married Hank Erickson wanted nothing to do with her or his new daughter. He had two of his own with his wife, Darcy now knew. "Relax. I named her. See for yourself."

Her mother took the clipboard Darcy offered her...and read aloud. "Montana Skye Alcott." She looked up, a tremulous smile on her lips. "That's beautiful, honey. Really pretty. Little Montana." Then a knowing look claimed her grandmotherly features. "Something to do with the Montana cowboy who helped bring her into this world?"

Darcy shrugged. "I suppose. It seemed like the right thing to do, don't you think?"

"Well, I'll say I do." Margie handed back the form and looked down, swiping at some crumbs on her uniform. "Too bad you don't know what that cowboy's name is," she said with oh-so-much innocence in her voice. "Otherwise, you could put his name here in the blank place for a father."

Darcy slowly pulled herself up in her bed. "Look at me, Mother. He's not the father. *Not.* Even if I knew his name, I wouldn't do that. It's not right. Or legal."

Her mother fingered a bedside flower arrangement—one of about twenty in the room—and played with the card. "Well, we wouldn't want to do anything against the law, now would we?"

"Mother." Margie looked at Darcy, her brown eyes wide and guileless. Darcy wasn't going to fall for that. The last time she had, she'd ended up going to the senior prom with her nerdy, pimply-faced cousin Mel when her own date had stood her up—the start of a definite trend in her life, it seemed. Darcy shook her head for added emphasis. "No. We. Wouldn't. Say it with me."

Instead, Marge said, "You know, we *could* find out who he is."

"No, we can't."

"Yes, we can. Ask me how."

"No. I don't care how."

"You do, too."

Silence followed. Darcy stared at her mother. Her mother stared at her. Darcy caved. "All right. How?"

Margie smiled triumphantly. "By some of the things he left behind."

Darcy flopped the clipboard onto her bed and folded her hands together in her lap. "Like what?"

"Like that Indian blanket. And a matchbook with the name of a fancy Phoenix hotel on it. I forget which one just now. And a pocketknife with engraved initials. T.H.E. *His* initials, don't you think? Anyway, those things were all tangled up in the blanket's folds. And I have them."

Darcy remembered the knife and the matchbook. But his initials were THE? The what? Tom? Terry? Ty? Her interest quickened...before she remembered she wasn't interested. But it was too late. Her mother had noticed. *Great.* "What about them?" she was forced to ask, even as she tried hard, and failed, to sound as if she couldn't care less.

"Johnny Smith. That's what about them."

A sick feeling came over Darcy. She gripped her covering sheet in her hands. "Not Johnny. Mother, what are you thinking of doing? Don't do it. I swear—"

"Not in front of me you won't." With that, Margie Alcott stood up and collected her lunch leavings. "Now you rest easy, honey. They'll be bringing Montana in to you in a minute, I believe. And I've got to get back to work. That sweet little old lady, Mrs. Hintzel, is back in the hospital. I think she's just lonely. But I swear, that tiny stick of a woman—you know she's 87?—well, she just plain worries if I don't come around. So I'll go check on her first and then—''

"Don't practice medicine, Mother. You know how the doctors get. You're supposed to be volunteering in the admissions office. Not making patient rounds.''

Her 70-year-old mother pursed her lips. "I know what my job is, Darcy. But it doesn't hurt a thing if I visit those poor old people. I can't imagine why that young Dr. Graves can't figure out Mrs. Hintzel has something wrong with her uterus. Must be inexperience.''

Darcy sighed out her breath. "Or the fact that Mrs. Hintzel had a hysterectomy thirty years ago. You told me that the last time she was admitted.''

Margie Alcott frowned. "I see your hormones are making you testy again. I'm going to go check on Mrs. Hintzel. And then I'm going to call Johnny Smith.''

Darcy's mouth dried. Johnny Smith, bachelor son of bridge-playing Freda Smith, was also one of the small town's few policeman. The man looked like a bloodhound. But if anyone could track down a Montana cowboy…with no more information than what her mother had to give him…it would be Johnny Smith.

This was not good. For her. Or for T.H.E. Lone Ranger.

MEANWHILE, BACK AT The Ranch, an upscale hotel in Phoenix, Tom Harrison Elliott was back in his room after the morning's meeting with the land brokers who were interested in his grandfather's plot of land here.

Quickly changing clothes, Tom picked up his white Stetson, settled it low on his brow, headed for the door...and called himself a fool in love.

He stopped...as if he'd smacked into an invisible brick wall...and just stood there, staring into space as the realization washed over him. He was in love. Instantly. This was the way it happened in his family. Every one of them. One day you're just walking down the street, minding your own business, when you see that special someone and...bam, right between the eyes. In love. First-sight love. And here he'd thought the rest of his family was crazy. He'd teased his sister and cousins mercilessly about succumbing to—and believing in—the old family tradition. And now, here he was...succumbing. To two women. Well, a woman and her baby girl. Head-over-heels in love with both of them...since the moment he'd taken Darcy in his arms to lift her out of her car, and when he'd first held the baby girl in his arms.

Tom made a face. Lordy, he'd never hear the end of this once he got home. Well, he'd never hear the end of it, if there was something to report. He supposed he ought to check on the beautiful woman he knew only as Darcy to see if she'd felt anything, too. But maybe not today. After all, she'd had a baby yesterday. Might not be in a mood to think about love right now, given the wriggling consequences that she could now hold in her arms.

Take it slow, Tom, he warned himself. *One bright and shiny in-love day at a time. Give the lady some time.* Speaking of which, it was time to go. Snapping out of his reverie, Tom turned around, checking his room, then himself. He had everything he needed. Tom still couldn't believe he was doing this. He never did this. But then again, he'd never been in love before.

He'd bought flowers. A huge bunch of flowers. Pink roses, to be exact, along with something else the kindly white-haired lady in the lobby's flower shop had dubbed a beautiful baby spray. Looked like a bunch of different colored flowers in a tub-sized ceramic baby cradle, if you asked him. Pink and blue and silver balloons with streamers sprouting from all angles out of the danged thing.

But the nice lady had said it was appropriate and, since what he knew about flowers wouldn't fill a boot heel, Tom had trusted her. Signing the cards was another matter. After much thought, he signed, *Congratulations on your new daughter. Tom Harrison Elliott.* On the other one, in a moment of whimsy he now regretted—since he didn't have another card and the flower shop was closed—he'd written *Glad to have been at your coming out party, baby girl.* He'd signed it *The Lone Ranger and Silver.*

Now, that was about the dumbest thing he'd ever done. Next to buying the flowers, and getting ready to make the trip back to Buckeye to see mother and daughter. And, yes, most likely…father. Because even though one hadn't been in evidence yesterday, there had to be a father somewhere. And with Tom's luck, the man was also Darcy's husband.

Tom wasn't reassured by her lack of an engagement or wedding ring. Hell, a lot of pregnant women didn't wear them. Their fingers swelled, was his understanding. At least that's what Sam said. And his older sister ought to know. She and Luke had given him two nieces and three nephews—so far. At 37, Samantha was pregnant again.

Tom shook his head as he plucked up the flowers and put the two cards in his shirt pocket. Then he crossed the room in long-legged strides more suited to raising Montana dust and tried to convince himself that a return visit to the maternity ward in Buckeye, despite his true feelings—feelings he had no intention of acting on…today—was nothing more than a polite call. After all, with Sam and Luke doing their best to populate the entire state of Montana, there was no call for him to marry and father a child.

Fighting the fact that he'd fallen in love…fighting because reason told him there was most likely a husband.…Tom reminded himself that he was a man who liked his space. The kind of space you find out riding the range. The kind of space where you don't see another soul for days. Just you and your horse. And the mountains. And the big sky. He had no time for a family. Not when he had the ranch to run. It'd been that way for over a hundred years of Elliotts. With its thousands of acres and as many head of cattle every year to tend, it kept a man busy. It didn't give him time to think about much of anything else. Like love.

Juggling the flowers in one hand, Tom wrestled the door open and waited while it swung closed behind him. Making sure it locked, he then transferred the roses to his other hand and set off toward the bank of elevators. As much as he tried not to, he couldn't help thinking about the young woman he'd helped. He felt he knew her intimately. And he didn't mean anything disrespectful by that. No, she'd done everything she could until he got there. He could respect that…and did.

She'd seemed an intelligent sort, too, from the little bit of talking with her he'd done. Probably a woman over his head, in terms of education. Not someone to look twice at him. But, hell, no matter how he felt about her, the odds were…given that suspected husband…he wouldn't be here long enough to worry about that. Right now, he just wanted to see her—and her daughter—once more. To make sure they were really okay. And that was it.

No, it wasn't. He stopped in front of the elevators and pushed the down button. And fought the fire of need that burned at his insides like a hot branding iron. He needed to leave the woman alone. He needed to take his silly Elliott love-at-first-sight heritage and get on back to Montana. If he had a lick of sense he'd do that. But he couldn't. There was more here at stake than love. There was honor. He'd been raised to believe in the cowboy code…a life saved was a life owned. Darcy and her baby were now his responsibility in ways her husband probably wouldn't understand.

But whether or not the man understood didn't change anything for Tom. Because together, they…he and Darcy…had brought a new life safely into the world. And that new life was now his duty, too. Not just duty, either. The silly thing, the most surprising thing to Tom, was how proud he was of his part. How close he felt to that baby girl.

Son of a gun. If this wasn't instant heartache, then Tom didn't know what was. A new mother and her baby. He shook his head. He hadn't been able to think about anything else since yesterday. How afraid and yet brave Darcy'd been. How tiny and fragile the baby'd been. Tom grinned now, thinking of this morning's business meeting. More than once the bankers and developers had asked him if he was okay. He'd said yeah, that he was just tired. Then he'd asked them to repeat everything. And all because a dark-haired beauty had filled his thoughts and distracted him. He'd seen that she was a pretty woman, even despite her ordeal. Good bone structure. Nice, even teeth. Long legs. Clear eyes. Lots of curly, glossy hair that spoke of health.

The elevator bell finally dinged. The doors slid open. The car was empty. Tom stepped inside, managing...despite being flower-challenged...to press *L* for the lobby. When the doors closed and the elevator car began its quick trip down three floors, Tom suddenly realized he'd described Darcy in terms of a healthy horse. A booming laugh spilled out of him...just as the elevator reached the busy lobby and the doors opened.

All heads turned Tom's way. He instantly sobered, clearing his throat and managing to glare as he crossed the lobby and went out into the Arizona heat...trailing pink, blue and silver balloons and streamers.

Fortunately, the ride out to Buckeye wasn't an overly long one, once he cleared noontime Phoenix traffic. If it had been, the pink, blue and silver balloons and streamers...which kept floating over into his line of vision in the truck's air-conditioned cab...would have found themselves ornaments for the prickly saguaro cacti that dotted the sandy landscape. And the accompanying roses would have made a ready dinner for the Gila monsters. But as it turned out, Tom, the roses, and the beautiful baby spray made it safely to the parking lot of the Buckeye Community Hospital.

So far, so good. Tom opened the white truck's door and squinted against the heat that poured in waves over him as he scooped up the flowers from the seat.

Hitting his remote lock button and then backing out of his truck, given his floral overload, he nudged the door closed with his foot and stepped up onto the sidewalk. Glancing toward the hospital's exterior, he thought he saw a dark-haired woman, up on the second floor, quickly duck behind a curtain. Tom grinned…and wondered if the curtains would be closed in Darcy's room.

He walked through the hospital's automatic front doors, took the elevator up to the second floor without asking—he just knew that's where her room would be—and strode right up to the nurses' station. Parting the flowers, he startled the red-headed nurse, who'd had her head bent over an open chart. "Oh, I'm sorry," she said, laughing. "It's not every day I see a walking flower shop wearing a cowboy hat."

Tom grinned. "I expect not. Uhm, I'm looking for Darcy—" All he knew was her first name. "Well, I'm looking for Darcy. She had a baby girl yesterday. In the back of my truck. I brought her in."

The nurse surged to her feet. "Ohmigod, you're the Lone Ranger." She looked him up and down. "I get it. The white hat. And you drive a white truck, right?"

Tom started to answer, but was distracted by the number of hospital staff pouring out of rooms and crowding around him. Murmurs of *the Lone Ranger* and *white hat* and *saved Darcy Alcott and her baby* and *it's him* swelled around him. Tom's eyes widened. He leaned over the counter, toward the nurse. "Yes, ma'am, I drive a white truck. Isn't that what you asked me?"

"It sure is," she said. "I can't believe it, sugar. We've all been trying to figure out who you are."

Tom suddenly thought he knew how a young bull

felt when it was sent alone into the auction ring for everyone to gape at and paw over. "You have?" he asked, his mouth suddenly dry.

"We certainly have. Honey, you're a hero around these parts. Just who the heck *are* you?"

"Tom Elliott, ma'am. From Montana. Pleased to make your acquaintance. Now, would it be all right for me to see—" What had one of them said Darcy's last name was? Then, and blessedly, it came to him. "—Mrs. Alcott, please?"

"She went home already, mister."

The voice came from behind him. Tom pivoted to see a pretty Hispanic girl with a thick ponytail standing there. She smiled and repeated, "Mrs. Alcott already went home. She worked until 2:00 p.m. and then left for her bridge club meeting."

None of what this girl said made sense—even despite the corroborating nods and murmurs of the others with her. "Bridge club? She left for a bridge club meeting?" Then he focused on what else she'd said. "She *worked* today? But she just had a baby."

Tom suddenly wondered if he'd stepped into the psychiatric ward. Then one of the nurses cleared things up. "*Mrs.* Alcott is Darcy's mother. She's a volunteer here. You want Darcy...*Miss* Alcott. Well, Professor Alcott, actually."

Professor? Tom could only stare at her. What she'd said left more questions than answers. "I see. Well...Professor Alcott, then. May I see her, please?"

"Oh sure, honey. Will you look at me—standing here jawing when I should be working." She picked up a form of some sort and scanned it. "Let me check the schedule. Yep. Marty—that's the neo-natal nurse—just picked the baby up and took her back to the nursery." She put the form down and leaned toward Tom...conspiratorially. "We've got to keep a close eye on that baby—she's already got a mind of her own, as I'm sure you know." Then she straightened up and reached for the phone. "Just let me buzz Darcy's room and see if she wants a visitor."

While they waited for Darcy to pick up, Tom stared at the folks still crowded in silent wonder around him. "Howdy," he finally felt compelled to say. "How're y'all doing?"

Everyone nodded, said they were fine, glad to meet him, enjoyed the article in the paper about him, nice flowers, loved his white hat. Just as Tom was sure he'd be asked for his autograph, the nurse hung up the phone. "She says she's decent. You can go on down." She pointed to a hallway right in front of him. "Room 234. On your right."

Tom nodded his thanks. "I appreciate it, ma'am." He turned to his crowd of admirers. "Good day to you."

They variously waved, said goodbye, and began to disperse. And Tom made his escape. Only to realize he might be walking into a bigger hornet's nest than the one he'd just left behind.

And it all had to do with *Miss* Alcott and her daughter, who'd apparently been born out of wedlock. While sympathetic to Darcy's plight, and what the implications were for her, Tom still had to fight a silly grin that said there was hope. He had a chance.

3

WITH TWO PILLOWS fluffed behind her, Darcy tugged her hospital robe and then the covers around her. She smoothed the sheets as best she could, given her remaining soreness. *He's coming, he's coming, he's coming.* She folded her hands in her lap, looked toward the doorway, and pasted a smile on her face. And waited.

The curtains. Darcy's eyes widened guiltily. The curtains were still yanked closed. *Dear God.* She just knew he'd seen her standing there at the window, watching him. *Great.* Did she have time to hobble over there and open them before he—she turned back to the doorway. Her breath caught, her heart thumped excitedly.

There he stood.

Well, she assumed it was him in the doorway. All she could see was a white Stetson, a body comprised of flowers and balloons and streamers, and then long legs encased in denims...and dusty boots. The flowers parted. It was him. "Howdy, Darcy."

Her belly twitched. *Smile, Darcy.* She smiled... acted nonchalant, pleasantly surprised. "Why, hello. How nice to see you. What beautiful flowers those are." And groaned inside. *Could I sound more like the wolf in* Little Red Riding Hood? *My, what big flowers you have. Come in, dearie, and let me gobble you up.* "I wasn't expecting to see you today." *Or ever again.*

Just as she feared, his gaze riveted on the closed curtains. "You weren't? You sure about that?"

Only through sheer will did Darcy's smile and her gaze remain steady. At least with the curtains drawn he couldn't so readily see the heated blush blooming on her features. Speaking of blooms... "Oh. Come in. Please. Set down your load—the flowers. I mean the flowers."

He did. He came in, put the flowers on the bedside tray stand and pushed the wheeled cart aside. "You'll need a vase for those roses, I suspect. I should have thought of that."

"No problem," Darcy chirped. She grabbed her pitcher of ice water from the nightstand next to her and held it out. "Here. Put them in here."

His blue eyes mirrored his uncertainty. "You sure? What if you want a drink of water?"

"Oh, well, I'll just have rosewater, I guess." *Idiot, idiot, idiot.*

He unwrapped the roses, handling them awkwardly. "I've never done this before." He plunked them in the ice water. Then those blue eyes narrowed in her direction. "You okay, Darcy? You sound a little hyper."

"Hormones," she blurted. And wanted to bite her tongue off.

He nodded, completely calm and accepting. "I expect so." Then he gestured to the tacky molded-plastic chair beside the bed, as much as asking her permission to sit down. "You mind?"

"No. Please do. You made all this effort. You may as well sit a while."

And then he did, removing his Stetson, running a long-fingered hand through his black hair...Darcy watched, remembering how comforting and reassuring those hands were. Then, perching his Stetson atop his bent knee, he met her gaze. Darcy swallowed. "I hope you like roses. I didn't know—"

"The roses." She put a hand to her bosom. "Of course. I love roses. They're wonderful. Thank you. And the baby spray. It's beautiful. All those balloons and streamers. I don't know what to say."

His frowning expression considered the circus-in-a-ceramic-cradle on the bedside tray with the ice-watered roses. "Neither do I, mostly." Then he swung his attention back to her. "I'm not doing this very well, am I? Let me start over. Uhm, how are you to-day?"

Darcy, who thought he was doing just fine, didn't like herself any better for being so excited that he was here. After all, wasn't she through with men? He was just being nice, given the unusual circumstances under which their lives had collided, and wasn't the least bit interested in her, nor her in him, despite the flowers and this visit. She took a deep breath and said, "I'm fine."

He nodded, looking around the flower-littered room. "Looks like you have a heap of thoughtful friends and family. That's nice."

"Oh. Those. Well, my mother does. I don't live here anymore." She then remembered she did live here. "Well, I mean I do. For now. I'm just visiting." Visiting? She'd be here for a little over a year before she went back to Baltimore and to teaching. "Well, more than visiting, I suppose." She realized she was babbling. "And you? How about you?"

"I don't live here, either. I'm just visiting."

That wasn't what she meant, but still Darcy nodded. "You're from Montana. Yes. I remember." Could this be more awkward? Sure, it could. Some nurse could come in about now and want to check her sutures. "So. How are things in Montana?"

He nodded. "Fine."

Silence. She smiled at him, wiggled her toes, and fiddled with her fingers. *The man has seen me naked. And not in a good way.* He smiled back, looked her up and down as she sat there in her hospital bed. And no doubt remembered he'd seen her naked. "So," Darcy blurted. "What *is* your name? That has been the sixty-four-thousand-dol'ar question around here today."

"I gathered as much from the crowd at the nurses' station. It's Elliott. Tom Elliott. Pleased to meet you, Darcy Alcott." He stretched forward in the chair and offered his hand to her.

Inordinately pleased—he'd gone to the trouble, obviously, of finding out her last name—Darcy leaned over the slightest bit and took his hand, shaking it, feeling warm, firm flesh and the not-unpleasant roughness of calluses. A working man's hands. A far cry from the softness of any self-centered, lying, cheating professor types she might know. "Very pleased to meet you, Tom. Now I can quit calling you the Lone Ranger."

He chuckled...and her heart tripped over itself—and tried to jump right out of her chest so it could tackle him and lay a big smooch on his mouth...for starters. "Yeah. I got that at the nurses' station, too."

Darcy blinked. "You did? You got—" *Darcy! Knock it off. He doesn't mean he got smooched at the nurses' station. Pay attention.* She discreetly cleared her throat...and forged ahead. "Uhm, did you get to see the baby? I mean today. I know you saw her yesterday. Heck, you were the first one in the world to see her."

His smile brightened. "I hadn't thought about that. But no, I haven't seen her yet. I came straight to your room. I couldn't wait to see you. Her. You." His smile faltered, his eyes widened...as if he'd just revealed too much. Darcy felt her mouth dry. "So," he continued. "How is she? That navel get cleaned up okay?"

Still wide-eyed with wonder—he couldn't wait to see her?—she nodded. "Uhm, yes. Dr. Harkness said you did a fine job, too. He was quite impressed with that knot you tied."

"Yeah? That's a good knot, all right." Silence. "Well, since we're on the subject of names...what did you name your daughter?"

Darcy's insides melted. She took a deep breath, and confessed, "Her name is Montana Skye. Sky with an *E*."

"It is?" A smile as big as all outdoors claimed his features. He sat back in his chair. "Well, I'll be. Montana Skye. With an *E*. That's about the best name I think I've ever heard. It's perfect for such a pretty baby, too."

Darcy's cheeks heated up under his compliments. "I thought it was the least I could do, given your help. I didn't know how else to repay you. And I thought I'd never see you again to say thank-you. So I..." She exhaled and just sat there, staring at her fingers. "I hope you don't mind."

He shifted in the chair and leaned forward, plopped his Stetson at the foot of her bed. From under her eyelashes, Darcy stared at him, noting his intense blue-eyed gaze. "I don't mind at all, Darcy. In fact, I'm honored. I'm just pleased I could help. And that everything turned out so well."

"Me, too." And then she had nothing else to say. Nothing that could keep him here and talking. Which was crazy because all she really wanted was for him to go away. Because he filled this room with his presence—and made her feel small and warm and safe. All the things she couldn't afford to feel. He was from Montana. And she and her daughter would be living in Baltimore. No chance of a relationship there. Not that she wanted one anyway.

"I noticed," he said suddenly...and a little too loudly, "on the drive out here from Phoenix, that your car wasn't beside the road. I guess someone took care of that for you?"

"Yes. My mother had it towed in. It's at the garage now." Her mother. *Dear God.* "Oh, no. I need to warn you about something."

He sat up, alert, questioning. "What's that?"

"My mother. She's trying to find you."

He looked askance at her. "And yet, here I am."

"I know. But she doesn't know that. And she has your stuff. But not your name."

His frown intensified. "I don't know what—"

"That book of matches. The blanket. And your pocket knife."

Suddenly, understanding showed in his expression. "She does? That's good. I realized this morning that I didn't have my knife. I figured it'd dropped out of the truck in all the excitement. But it's mighty nice of your mother to try to get it back to me. I appreciate that."

Darcy shook her head. "No. It's *not* nice. She's not looking for you in a good way. Trust me. She's like a bloodhound. In fact, she set Johnny Smith on you. And he's a real bloodhound."

"Someone named a bloodhound Johnny Smith?"

The man wasn't getting any of this. "No. He's a policeman," Darcy explained. "He just looks like a bloodhound."

"I see." But his bewildered expression said he didn't. "Why would your mother set a policeman on me?"

"Well, not *set* one on you, I guess. You didn't do anything wrong. She means it in a good way."

"A second ago you said it was in a bad way."

"Well, a good way for her. But bad for you and me."

He stared intently at Darcy. "Now it's you and me. Bad how?"

Darcy put her hands to her steadily warming cheeks. "I am so embarrassed." She plopped her hands down to her lap. "Okay. Here we go. First things first. Despite all my babbling here, I'm a college professor. A little over a year ago I earned my doctorate in English Lit. I teach in Baltimore. I'm here with my mother until I'm back on my feet. And I'm what you'd call an unwed mother."

He nodded…calm, accepting. "Congratulations. About your doctorate, I mean. About the other…well, I thought something like that was going on, from the things you said yesterday."

Darcy recalled yesterday's labor-and-delivery tirade and nodded. "Yes. I said a lot of things, didn't I? And I apologize."

"It's okay. Hormones, like you said. My sister's had five kids. I know a little bit about that."

Darcy's eyes widened. "Five?" As he nodded his confirmation, her sore, sore, sore nether regions were screaming *Never again.* "Anyway, the you and me part," she continued. "Mother believes that my baby needs a father."

"Aah." He firmed his lips together, and glanced around the room as if trying to figure out where the closest exit was.

That hurt. But Darcy couldn't really blame him. After all, the man had no responsibility here, no relationship with her. So why else would he feel anything but trapped? But still, the last time she'd seen a similar expression, it had been on Hank's face when she'd told him she was pregnant. It was just too funny, the effect she had on men. "Don't worry. Montana already has a father. One who's not the least bit interested in her. Or in me, either. Which is how I want it, believe me. But nevertheless, she has a father. You're safe."

He stared at her. Seconds ticked by on the clock mounted on the wall behind him. His expression never changed. Darcy swallowed, felt too warm. And then too cold. Finally, he said, "I wasn't thinking that at all. Actually I was thinking of a man who didn't live up to his responsibilities. Still that was quite a speech."

Darcy raised her chin. "All that lecturing I do, no doubt."

"I suppose. But I guess it's my turn to spill my guts, right?"

Feeling a bit defensive, Darcy shrugged. "Sure. Why not? We're all friends here."

His eyebrows raised. "I sure hope we are, Darcy. I'd like that. But it's your call."

His expression radiated sincerity. And intelligence. And kindness. Three things Darcy liked in people but pretty much hadn't encountered in the men she'd chosen to have relationships with in the past. Which, she suddenly realized, said more about her than it did the men. She quirked her mouth and brushed her annoyingly curly hair back from her face. "We are, Tom. We're friends. Someone just needs to knock this chip off my shoulder, I guess."

He smiled. "It's not as bad as all that, Darcy. I imagine you're scared right now, maybe a little unsure of things. You've been through a hell of a lot, it sounds like. I can't blame you for being a little wary."

Darcy stared at this Tom Elliott, more and more convinced he was some wonderfully put-together animated robot programmed to say everything a woman wanted to hear. She felt certain she could go to a toy store and find a whole row of Tom Elliott look-alikes in bright, shiny packages. If she did, she intended to buy one for every female friend she had. "Are you always this wonderful?" she asked.

He shrugged and looked embarrassed. "No. Not usually. In fact," he said, "I expect there are some lawyers and land brokers over in Phoenix who are tacking up Wanted posters of me this minute."

"Really? Who'd you kill?"

He grinned. "Nobody yet. I'm down here on my late grandfather's business. He owned—and now I do—a piece of land outside of Phoenix that some developers are interested in. I've been looking it over." He sat up straighter and pointed at her. "As a matter of fact, I'd been looking at it when I came across you yesterday.''

"Well, thank God for your grandfather and his land, then. Or I'd have been scorpion bait. But you must have been really lost because Phoenix is a pretty good ride from here.''

He nodded. "Yeah, I know. I'd already found the land. I just wanted to take a look around a little farther out, maybe see why my granddad had hung on to it for so long. Periodically he'd have to make a trip down here and deal with some paperwork. So did my father. It was always a hassle for them. And now, it is for me, too.''

Darcy could see where this was going. "So you're thinking if you unload this land, you won't have to come back here, right?''

His gaze met hers and held. He nodded. "Pretty much. Yeah. This is my last trip here. If I sell it.''

"I see.'' Darcy suddenly felt like crying. She'd never see him again. And that bothered her. Because she felt herself really starting to like this man—this man who'd delivered another man's baby and saved her life. "So,'' she said out loud, struggling to sound conversational, "is that why they're taking out Wanted posters on you? You won't sell?''

He shrugged those broad shoulders of his. "No. I'll sell it. Just not at their price. I'm sticking around a while, letting them stew some. See how bad they want it.''

Darcy didn't know what to think. Well, she knew what she *should* be thinking. She should be hoping they made a counteroffer today, one he could accept and so he would leave. Because here she was...liking him. Really liking him. He needed to go away—and *now*. But that wasn't what she was thinking. She wanted him to stay. And that wasn't good. Or even logical.

Then she thought of something else, something she hadn't considered before. As she watched him, he reached into his white and starched Western-style shirt and pulled out two tiny envelopes. Before he could make his intentions known, Darcy blurted her belated thought. "Are you married?"

Tom Elliott froze, his hand poised in midair. Sober as a rodeo judge, he assured her, "No, ma'am. Why do you ask?"

You heard the man, Darcy—why'd you ask? "Well, I was just wondering, with all this latitude you have about staying here or going home whenever you choose…I wondered if there was someone…waiting, is all." *Lame, lame, lame.*

Cool as a mountain breeze, his neutral expression never changing, he handed her the tiny envelopes. "I meant to give you these earlier. They go with the flowers."

Darcy reached for the envelopes. His hand closed over hers making her mouth go dry. "And no, there's nobody waiting. Just some cattle and several thousand acres of land."

Darcy swallowed, then smiled…lopsidedly. "Oh. Thanks. For the cards. Not the explanation. You don't have to explain yourself to me. I—"

"I wanted to." With that, he released her hand and sat back.

He wanted to? What does that mean? Why did he want to? Is he interested? Darcy did her best to keep her expression in check as she opened the first little envelope. She could see him watching her…and wondered what he was thinking. She sure wasn't anything to look at. No makeup. In a hospital gown and robe. Her hair a fright. Her body wrung out from delivering a baby. Why, it was a wonder the man hadn't run for the hills already.

Then, as the silence stretched out, Darcy concentrated on reading each card. Finally, she looked up, grinning. "Thank you, again. And Montana's card…that's cute. The Lone Ranger and Silver. I like that."

His face actually reddened. He shifted in his chair and tried to look tough. But he failed—miserably. "It was stupid."

"No, it wasn't. I think it's cute."

"It was stupid."

"Seriously. It's not. It's cute."

"Yeah? I'm not usually so…" He seemed to be casting about for the right word.

"Stupid?" Darcy finished for him, the conspiratorial grin she wore letting him know she was joking.

He chuckled and shook his head. "I deserved that."

Darcy shook her head. The man was perfect. And would make some deserving woman a wonderful husband. Some unknown and deserving woman up in Montana…whom Darcy already hated. But that reminded her… "Hey, you want to see Montana?"

His grin died. "I already have. I live there."

"What?" Then she realized his mistake. "No. Montana Skye. Remember? My baby. You know…the one you delivered?"

He threw his hands up in the air. "Oh, hell. There's that stupid gene again." Then he sat forward and braced his hands on his knees. "Yeah. I'd love to see how that little lady cleaned up."

"Okay. We'll have to go down to the nursery." Self-consciously, she started getting off the bed, realizing she was out of shape, her ankles were still swollen and she really looked a fright. She'd probably put the man off sex for the rest of his life. Why hadn't she shaved her legs the other day?

Tom Elliott jumped up, coming to her bedside and gently gripping her arm. "Here. Let me help you. You got your land legs yet?"

His touch ignited her heart. And a few other related parts. "Yeah," Darcy said around her bottom lip…which she was biting in penance for that momentary burst of lust as her intense soreness fairly shrieked *here's why you don't need to be thinking about sex right now*. "My slippers. Can you put them right there—" He moved them in place and she slipped them on her feet. "Thanks."

She stood slowly and carefully, holding on to his rock-solid arm with one hand as she used her other to straighten out her gown and robe. His other hand covered hers on his arm.

It was a small gesture, but one so intensely intimate—especially here in the maternity ward—that Darcy looked up at him, felt her aloneness, and struggled with tears. As she straightened her robe and tried to cover her roiling emotions, she quipped, "I guess it's a little late for me to stand on decorum with you, isn't it?"

He reached out, wiping at a tear that spilled over. "You just had something on your face," he said, covering for her. Then, he ran his booted toe dramatically over the flooring. "You say this is decorum we're standing on? And here I thought it was linoleum."

The man was killing her. Darcy fought to mortar up

the bricks in her emotional wall that he kept knocking down with every kind word and thoughtful gesture. She just couldn't feel this way toward him. She just couldn't.

Then he winked at her and set them in motion...slow motion...as they headed for the opened doorway. "Come on, Darcy. Keep me from getting homesick. Show me a little bit of Montana Skye."

4

"OH, LOOK...there she is. She's so tiny and pink and sweet. I just love her so much."

"I'll bet you do." Tom smiled at the pride evident in Darcy's voice and longing expression. She'd make a great mother, he could tell. She had all the right attributes, ones he could admire. He felt qualified to draw that conclusion, too. After all, he'd observed Darcy with the baby from the first moment the little girl had come into the world. "She sure is a pretty little thing, with all that dark hair."

Darcy sighed. "I know." Then she leaned in toward him and whispered, "I think she's the prettiest baby in the whole nursery, don't you?"

Delighted with her whimsy, Tom whispered right back. "I sure do. I also think she's the *only* baby in the whole nursery."

Darcy gave a mock what-do-you-know roll of her eyes as she turned to once again stare longingly through the thick glass that separated her from her baby. "You do think she's pretty, though, right?"

Tom turned his gaze from the pink-blanket-wrapped baby in the clear plastic crib to Darcy. Memorizing her profile, he said, "I think she's beautiful."

A big smile on her face, Darcy turned his way. "Yes, she—"

She caught him staring at her. He didn't look away.

He probably should have, he knew, but he didn't. It was too late now. Darcy's expression sobered, and became one of awareness. Intense awareness. She looked away first, lowering her brown-eyed gaze to the windowsill, where she rubbed a finger along its narrow ledge. Instantly, Tom felt bad. He'd embarrassed her. That hadn't been his intention. "Darcy, I'm sorry. I didn't mean to—"

"No. It's okay." She met his gaze. "Really. I thought it was...*nice* that you'd look at me that way."

Tom tried for humor to cover this embarrassing moment of possibly unrequited attraction. "Nice, huh? The next thing I know, you'll just want to be my friend. And then I'll have to go out and shoot myself."

"Gosh, I hope not. Think of how bad I'd feel."

How nice of her...and how noncommital. Tom decided he was right—she wasn't attracted to him. He suddenly felt like the world's biggest fool. Could he have made her any more uncomfortable? "Look, I shouldn't have said anything like that, Darcy. I don't know what's wrong with me. I shouldn't be coming on to a woman who only yesterday—"

"No. It's fine. Seriously. I'm very flattered."

That only made him feel worse. "Great. I flattered you." Tom shook his head. "I need to stick with horses and cattle. Or maybe that's my problem. Maybe I've been around them too long, and I don't know how to talk to a woman—"

Darcy pressed her hand against Tom's lips, cutting off his words. "Hold on a minute, will you? Quit beating yourself up." When Tom nodded, she took her hand away and smoothed it through her black hair. "I just meant I can't believe you'd find me...attractive, is all. For heaven's sake, look at me in this hospital garb. I must look a fright.''

"A fright?'' Intensely relieved—all she'd been worried about was her appearance when here he'd been kicking himself for thinking he had his wires crossed—Tom folded his arms together over his chest and leaned a shoulder against the wall. "Not at all. Like I said, you're beautiful.''

She smiled and still managed to look embarrassed. "Must be that new-mother glow, then.''

"Could be. But I doubt if that's all it is.''

The wide-eyed, vulnerable look she sent him said she wanted to believe him...but couldn't. Tom thought he understood, given her new single-mother status. The woman had enough on her plate without him adding to her woes. But still, and feeling disappointed somehow, as if the one moment in time for them to connect had slipped away, Tom silently watched her settle her gaze on the sleeping baby in the nursery. "Anyway, I think she looks like me.''

Still leaning against the wall, Tom turned to stare through the glass with her. "I guess I'd have to agree with you since her father's not around for me to know what he looks like.''

The words were out before he could stop them.

Darcy jerked and Tom wanted to kick himself. Why had he brought up that man—the gutless son-of-a-gun who wouldn't even acknowledge his own flesh and blood? Tom shook his head, as if to say he couldn't believe his own stupidity. "Again, Darcy—I'm sorry. I didn't mean to say something that jackass stupid.''

She waved her hand. "Don't worry about it. I'm getting used to it.'' Then her eyes went big and round. "You know...everyone asks about my husband, what does he do, is he proud." She looked down. "Things like that." Then she raised her head and, dry-eyed, met his gaze. "So, it's okay. Really."

"No, it isn't. How many times have I had to apologize to you already?"

She shrugged. "Almost as many as I've had to with you."

"Well, thank God." Tom offered a shy smile. "Want to start over—again?"

Her expression brightened. "Sure."

Encouraged, Tom stuck his hand out for her to shake. "Howdy, ma'am. My name is Tom Harrison Elliott. From outside of Billings, Montana. My friends call me The Lone Ranger."

Darcy laughed...a warm, throaty sound that went all over Tom...and grasped his hand. "Hi. Pleased to meet you. My name is Darcy Jean Alcott. From Buckeye, Arizona. My friends call me Damsel in Distress."

"Is that so? Well, Damsel, that's a mighty fine baby girl you have yourself there." Without releasing Darcy's hand, which felt small and warm clasped within his, Tom nodded toward Montana Skye, who was now awake and crying heartily.

Darcy instantly sobered, pulling her hand away. A uniformed nurse came out of a backroom inside the small nursery and hurried over to pick up the baby and soothe her. Next to Tom, Darcy pressed herself against the glass and made a mewling sound that said she wanted to hold her child herself. Tom's heart went out to her, but he didn't know what to do. Just then, the nurse looked up and saw them there. Immediately she came to the window with the baby and held her up, so they could see her. Tom felt pride well in his chest and sudden emotion clog his throat. The red-faced baby's clenched fists shook with her squalling displeasure.

Darcy grabbed Tom's sleeve. "What's wrong with her?"

Tom covered her hand with his own. "I don't rightly know, Darcy. But the nurse doesn't look too worried. See? She's smiling. It must be okay, then, wouldn't you think?"

Darcy relaxed her grip on his sleeve. "I guess you're right." She slipped her hand out from under his and stuffed it in her robe pocket. Then she turned her frightened gaze his way. "What am I going to do in a day or two when you're not around to tell me these things?"

Tom put an arm around her shoulders. "You'll do fine, Darcy. It'll all come to you. You'll see. A mother's instinct, they say."

She looked unconvinced. "Oh, the famous *they*, huh? Well, then, will you leave me *their* phone number, please? Because *they're* going to get the night shift."

Tom didn't know what to say. And considering the amount of apologizing he'd already done, he settled now for patting her on the shoulder and saying, "That's the spirit. You'll be fine."

A tap on the thick, sound-insulating glass made Tom and Darcy turn toward the nurse on the other side of the window. With a puckered Montana Skye now perched in the crook of one arm, the blond nurse held up a clipboarded form, which she waved at Darcy. Then she placed it on a ledge just inside the room, and pointed to it, making writing motions with her bunched fingers.

Confused about what was going on, Tom glanced

Darcy's way...and saw her grow pale under her tanned skin. He grabbed at her arm, fearing she'd faint. "You need to sit down?"

Without looking at him, Darcy shook her head. "No. I wish that's all it was. It's just that...well, here we go again. That form she has is Montana Skye's birth certificate. The nurse wants to know the father's name."

Newly enlightened, Tom bristled in Darcy's defense. "I don't rightly believe that's any of her business."

"Well, actually it is. It's a legal thing." Darcy exhaled, sounding tired. "I suppose she's just being nice and thinks I overlooked it earlier." She looked up at Tom. Her flat brown eyes upset him. "I didn't overlook it. I just didn't know what to do. So I left that space blank."

Tom swallowed, uncomfortable with the situation. "Oh."

Then Darcy's expression became pleading, begging for understanding. "I can't put that man's name on her birth certificate, Tom. I can't. He doesn't want her. But I don't want Montana to get hurt, years from now, if she should see it blank. I don't want to lie to her, but—"

"Hold on, Darcy." On impulse, Tom reached into his back pocket. "Wait just a minute." He pulled out his wallet. "I think I can help you."

"What are you going to do—bribe the nurse?"

"No. I'm getting out my driver's license."

"Your driver's license? What—oh, wait. No. You can't." She put a restraining hand on his, covering his wallet with her long, fine fingers. "No, Tom. It's a very nice thing you want to do. But no. You've done enough.''

She was right. He knew she was. At least from her point of view. But from his, knowing that he already loved Darcy, Tom wanted nothing more than to claim this baby as his own. Because if he had anything to say about it, Montana Skye would be his. "Let me, Darcy. I want to.''

She pulled her hand back, looking earnestly into his eyes. "I know you do. And you're a very sweet man. But you *can't* do this. You're not her father. And besides, there are about a million reasons—most of them legal—why I can't allow you to do this. God knows, I won't make any child support demands on you. But you just can't. Don't you see?''

He did, but that sense of urgency still had Tom in its grip. "The only thing I see right now is your face, Darcy. And it clearly says this is eating at you. Let me help. Please. I promise you I'm thinking clearly.'' She didn't look convinced. Tom continued. "Look, you can tell Montana whatever you want, and I'll abide by it. In fact, I'll swear to you right now that I won't *ever* make any claims on her, legal or otherwise. Or on you, either.'' *None that you won't want me to,* he added to himself, all the while holding Darcy's gaze.

She still didn't budge. Tom firmed his lips together, eyed the waiting nurse—who now looked thoroughly bewildered—and turned back to Darcy. "Please. Let me. For Montana Skye's sake.''

"Her sake? Do you hear yourself?'' Before he could answer, Darcy turned to the nurse and raised an index finger, mouthing *just a minute.* The nurse nodded and smiled.

Darcy waved her thanks and then turned to Tom. "I want you to think of fifteen years from now, when she's a troubled teenager and she comes looking for you. What will you say to her? How upset do you think she's going to be with both of us when she discovers that you're *not* her father? Or what if she's sick and needs your blood or a kidney and hunts you down? What then?"

Tom's frown matched his disbelief. "Where did you come up with that stuff?"

Darcy scrubbed her hands over her face. "From life, Tom. These things happen all the time. I'm just trying to be realistic."

"Realistic? Sounds more like one of those soap operas. There're good things that could happen, too, you know."

Darcy planted her hands on her hips. "Like what?"

Tom cast around...he couldn't reveal too much about his hopes for Darcy and her daughter right now...and then he had it. "Well, like she can come spend summers with me up at my ranch, when she's old enough."

"Oh, really? And what will you tell her about why we're—you and I—not together? She'll want to know."

But they would be together, he knew that. Still, in this conversation, he was losing and had to think fast. "I'll tell her it's because her mama is the most stubborn and argumentative woman I ever met."

He was proud that he could think fast in this situation...but not well, apparently.

Darcy's expression soured. "Oh, thanks. Now it's all my fault. So there she is, a troubled teen, and you're going to belittle her mother to her. That will be helpful.''

Frustration ate at Tom. He wanted nothing more than to tell her his true feelings, but he knew that would send her scurrying off down the hall...or would, if she could scurry at this moment. ''Me? You're the one who had her for fifteen years and made her a troubled teen.''

Darcy's mouth dropped and she poked a finger at his chest. ''I did no such thing. Do you even know how hard it is to be a single mother and have to deal with a teenaged girl who—''

''Darcy.''

''Don't you Darcy me. I am not through here—''

Tom grabbed her fingers, held on to them. ''Darcy, look at me.''

She turned. ''What?''

''Why are we fighting?''

She shook her head. ''I have no idea.''

Amused now—especially since a skinny elderly gentleman had just shuffled by as fast as he could while holding his hospital gown closed with one hand and towing his IV stand along with the other...all while eyeing them as if he expected their argument to escalate momentarily into a duel with pistols...Tom said, ''Montana is a tiny baby in a newborn nursery who needs a name and that's all. It's what I'm offering. Say no, if you want. But I'm still going to set up a trust fund for her because I'd decided earlier today to do that. Somehow, I feel responsible for her.''

''A trust fund? I don't know what to say.''

''Then say yes. After all, think about it—I *did* help you bring her into the world, didn't I? Doesn't that make her even a little bit mine?'' *And you, too? You're mine.*

Darcy's gaze never wavered from his. But finally she exhaled and nodded. "All right. I think it's wrong. It's against everything I believe in—or thought I believed in. And I hope you don't live to regret this someday, but—" She gestured in a dramatic be-my-guest manner toward the waiting, smiling nurse. "Go ahead. Make her day."

An unexpected thrill raced through Tom. He'd won the moment. It was a small step, but a first step. "Thank you, Darcy." Quickly, before she could change her mind, he pulled his driver's license from his wallet and held it against the glass, at the nurse's eye level, so she could copy his name onto the form in front of her.

When the nurse signaled she was done, Tom stuffed his license into his wallet and repocketed it as he, along with Darcy, watched the nurse pantomime that she was going to change the baby's diaper. Darcy waved at her and nodded…and turned away from the window, walking slowly, stiffly back down the hall toward her room.

Tom wondered if she'd forgotten he was here. He didn't know what to do, what to say in the face of her silence. Suddenly his act of kindness seemed like just what it was—a rash one made on emotion. He never did things like this. Usually he was plodding and methodical, so slow to make a decision that he drew groans from his ranch hands and his family. Well, that certainly wasn't his problem in this instance, was it? No, he'd made up his mind and had acted on it immediately. Because he was in love.

As Tom kept pace with Darcy, but respected her

silence, he decided that maybe that's what being in love did to a man. Made him decisive. And made him do silly things. Like buy a big bunch of pink roses and a beautiful baby spray and then drive an hour to hand-deliver them…only to give a stranger's child his name at the end of the trip. Tom looked over at Darcy, noting things now like her height, the shape of her nose, her general shapelessness under the hospital's gown and robe. Yep. She was a stranger to him, and him to her.

He didn't know any of the things about her a man would normally know about a woman whose child bore his name. Things like…what it felt like to hold her, what it took to make her laugh, to make her smile. Or cry. Or to make her mad. He didn't even know her favorite flavor of ice cream. Or her favorite TV show or book. Where she'd gone to school? How would she raise Montana Skye? *Where* would she raise the little girl?

No, he didn't have any of those answers. But he did know that he had the rest of his life…and Darcy's…to find them out.

BACK IN HER room, having climbed slowly, sorely back into her bed—again with Tom's help—Darcy sat with her bottom half covered with a light blanket, her hands folded in her lap, and stared at the man who'd just…well, *fathered* her child, in essence. Looking away from him to the end of her bed where his white Stetson still rested, Darcy exhaled sharply.

The sound made him glance at her. "You okay?"

She nodded haltingly. She'd come to the decision as she'd walked back to her room that she needed to give him a way out. "Look, if you've already thought

better of putting your name on Montana's birth certificate, I can—''

He raised his hand. ''No. I'm not sorry.''

Darcy brightened. He wasn't? Then she remembered she didn't dare fall for him—not from a maternity ward bed, at any rate. This just was not good
timing. So, she raised an eyebrow, trying for skeptical.
''You look to me like you are.''

''And how's that?''

She looked him up and down. The man was perfect.
''Well, you're a little pale under your tan,'' she lied.

His gaze shifted away from her, to the roses he'd
brought. Then he resettled his gaze on her. ''Look, I
admit that what I did back there is a big thing. Huge.
But it doesn't scare me, Darcy. I won't run. And I
won't change my mind. I did it, and I'm glad.''

Pricked to her very core—could this man see all the
way into her frightened soul?—Darcy stuck to her
guns. She couldn't afford to like him any more than
she already did. Her first priority now was her daughter. She just didn't need to keep thinking of him as
good and noble and fine. But most of all, she didn't
want to let him hurt her first. And that, regrettably,
gave her only one course of action. ''Fine.'' The one
word sat him up in his chair. She snatched up the
nurse-call button.

''What are you doing?''

''I'm going to call the nurse.''

Concern edged his sky-blue eyes. ''You hurting
somewhere?''

''Not anywhere it shows.''

Tom slumped back against the chair. ''Then let me
guess. You're going to change the birth certificate,
aren't you?''

Darcy shrugged, adopting a bravado that hid her pain for her child's sake. Montana Skye was about to lose another father. "If I can. There might be a law or something that says I can't."

"But you're sure going to try, right?" He crossed his arms over his broad chest, pressing wrinkles into his crisply ironed white shirt.

Well, she'd done it now…he was angry. Still, believing she was doing the right thing, Darcy looked him up and down, trying desperately to find fault with him. "Is white the only color you wear? I mean, are you *really* all that good all the time?"

His eyes narrowed. "You trying to pick a fight with me, Darcy? You think that'll make me go away?"

Here was the opening she needed. She stabbed a pointing finger at him. "See? That's what I don't get. Make you go away? Tom, we don't have a relationship. We're essentially strangers. I shouldn't have to *make* you go away—because you shouldn't even be here. I mean, I'm thankful and all for everything you've done for me." Her heart cried out for her not to continue, but as always, she didn't listen to it. "But your work here is done, Lone Ranger."

There. She'd done it…given him nowhere to go. No way to argue. A heavy silence filled the air between them. As she held his gaze, Darcy felt triumphant…and about ready to burst into tears. Why had she been so hateful? What was wrong with her?

Tom stood up slowly. Darcy figured she was about to find out exactly what was wrong with him. "All right. You've made your point. I'll go." He walked over to the foot of her bed and snatched up his Stetson, which he carefully fitted to his head, tugging it low over his brow. Then he looked her in the eye. "Sorry to have bothered you."

Darcy didn't say anything. She couldn't. She raised her chin a notch and tried to swallow past the knotted emotion in her throat. Her heart screamed for her to stop him...but she refused to open her mouth. And so, he turned and walked out of her room. And out of her life.

He was gone. Darcy sat staring at the opened doorway to her hospital room...and listened to his every booted footfall out in the hallway until they faded. She sniffed and looked all around her at the flowers and the balloons and the cards that congratulated her and wished her well. They suddenly blurred. Darcy blinked back the tears. She'd never felt more alone.

Just then, the air-conditioning came on, blowing cold air from the vent directly onto her. As if that were the final insult, Darcy's chin dimpled and quivered. Releasing the nurse-call button, she slid down a bit in the bed and turned on her side, away from the door, drawing her knees up as much as her soreness would allow. Pulling her covers close around her, clutching a twist of the blanket in her hand, she put her other fisted hand to her mouth and bit down on a knuckle...so no one would hear her cry.

5

"WELL, HERE WE ARE, Darcy Jean, you and baby Montana home all safe and sound. Just be careful there, honey. Watch that threshold. Don't trip. I'd hate for you to drop that two-day-old baby."

"Why? Don't they bounce?"

Everyone already in the living room, as well as those people crowding in behind Darcy, froze in place and got quiet. "Good Lord, don't say things like that, Darcy," her mother scolded.

Yeah, well…she was tired. It'd been a long convoy home with the Buckeye Bridge Beauties following in their cars, all of them loaded down with the flowers and plants from Darcy's hospital room. "Well, what did you want me to say, Mother? I have no intention of dropping my baby. I would die first."

"Well, thank heavens, it's not required. I'm just nervous for you, that's all. So don't be testy. Just sit here. Freda, move that pillow for her, will you? Yes, that one. Good." Then, over her shoulder, "Close that door, can you, Barb? We'll get the flowers inside in a minute. Thanks. I know, but Darcy insisted on wearing these old maternity shorts—I just hate them—and I don't want her to catch cold."

Forget the shorts. Darcy hated being talked about like she wasn't in the room. "A cold, Mother? In Arizona? In May?"

Her cheerfully oblivious and proud mother obviously chose to ignore Darcy's questions in favor of overseeing her...with Montana in her arms...being lowered into the big, soft and overstuffed recliner—one Darcy stood no chance of getting out of without the able assistance of a construction-grade crane. "Thanks for helping, Barb," Margie Alcott said. Then she straightened up and beamed at Darcy. "There, baby. All settled. Is there anything I can get—Jeanette, hand me that afghan to put over Darcy's legs."

"I don't want the afghan—"

Jeanette Tomlinson bunched the knitted blanket around Darcy's legs. "I just love this afghan," the older woman said, a good natured twinkle lighting her blue eyes. "I've told your mama that one day I'm just going to steal it from her."

"Make that day today, will you?" Darcy coupled her words with a smile, but it was forced. Mrs. Tomlinson's eyebrows rose. And Darcy felt sorry for herself. All she wanted was to be left alone for just a bit to get to know her daughter.

But just then, Barb Fredericks leaned over Darcy and gently tugged the baby's blanket back. "Oh, she's the prettiest black-haired little girl, Darcy. Now, what state did you name her after, honey? It was something with an *M,* wasn't it? Missouri, maybe?"

Darcy stared soberly at the short, dark-haired woman whose only child was Vernon, the 50-year-old editor of *The Buckeye Bugle.* He still lived at home with her. "No. Not Missouri," Darcy corrected. "But close. Michigan."

"Darcy," came her mother's warning. "It's Montana, Barb. Montana Skye. With an *E.*"

Barb turned to her friend Margie. "With a knee? What's wrong with her knee?"

Not believing any of this, Darcy put her free hand to her forehead and rubbed. But before the ladies could get going on that tangent, a voice came from near the sofa. "Well, will you look at this. Isn't it the cutest thing?"

They all looked. Freda Smith—sitting on the over-stuffed leather sofa and rooting through the big bag of helpful gifts the hospital had bestowed on Darcy—was holding up a typical, ordinary, everyday four-ounce glass baby bottle for all to see. Looking grave and judgmental, she glanced Darcy's way. "We didn't have these when Johnny was a baby 48 years ago. All we had to use were breasts."

Amidst the collective gasps of embarrassment coming from the remaining bridge club members, Darcy...suddenly highly amused and truly loving every one of these ladies...assured Freda. "Women today still have breasts, Freda."

"But are you using them?"

Darcy couldn't resist. "Sure. Watch." She began tugging on her maternity top's buttons.

That cleared the room. The ladies bolted for the dining room around the corner, squawking about iced tea and calling home and how hot it was outside already. In the relative quiet of the abandoned living room, Darcy finally got to relax and look down at her daughter. "Your mother's a stinker, Montana. But that may be the only thing that gets us through, kiddo."

Wrapped from her head to her toes in swaddling blankets, Montana yawned and frowned and made awful faces...and dropped off to sleep. "Great," Darcy said to the otherwise empty room. "I'm such a fascinating conversationalist. I've either driven everyone away—'' She tried not to think of a tall cowboy in a white Stetson. ''—or I've put them to sleep.'' She smiled down at her tiny daughter and cooed softly, ''My lectures on Chaucer have the same effect on my students, baby girl. Yes, that's right. Your mama's boring.''

Boring? I wish. Darcy thought about her upcoming car trip to Baltimore in January, a little less than eight months away. The child-care concerns she'd have once she got there. The effect of cold weather on a baby used to Arizona warmth. The demands of her new job. The grading. The paperwork. The seemingly endless classes she had to teach. The faculty give-and-take. The trying to pull her life together after her leave-of-absence, one she'd had to take after only one year at the university. It was a miracle she still had her position there. The new apartment she'd have to find since her upstairs one in the city only had one bedroom.

It all crowded in on her now, along with the alleged independent life she was supposed to be building for herself. All that—and on the same campus as Hank Erickson. Montana's real father. Feeling defeated and overwhelmed, Darcy leaned her head back against the recliner's dense padding and closed her eyes. *Heigh-ho, Silver. Where's the real Lone Ranger when you need him?*

The doorbell rang, startling Darcy into sitting upright and staring dumbly at the closed door. From around the corner, her mother called out, ''Stay there, Darcy, I'll get it.''

Under her breath, Darcy mumbled, ''That's a good thing, Mother, because I can't get out of this chair.''

But what she was thinking, as she busied herself with rearranging Montana's soft blanket around her little face, was, *Oh, surely I didn't conjure the man up. And I mean* my *Lone Ranger. Not the Lone Ranger. Well, either Lone Ranger, actually.*

Darcy looked up when her mother rounded the corner from the dining room. Barb, Freda, and Jeanette, all holding glasses of iced tea, were close on her heels. As one, all four of them headed for the door. And they all avoided looking at Darcy. Sudden dread filled her. *Oh, this can't be good.*

"Well, I wonder who this could be," Margie Alcott chirped.

Her mother's voice, so falsely cheerful, told its own story, saying it would be just like Marjory Elaine Alcott to do exactly what she'd threatened yesterday— have Freda's son use his sheriff/bloodhound skills to track that cowboy down. Johnny Smith could do it, too. It wasn't as if Darcy'd been dumb enough to actually tell her mother that Tom Elliott had paid her a visit. But she supposed that anyone at the hospital could have done so. And probably had. They loved her mother. And were afraid of her.

So, yes, it could happen, Darcy knew. And here was the result—her mother had found the cowboy and then she'd invited him out here today. *If she did, then I have to kill her…if I can get out of this chair.*

At that point, her mother opened the door and stared outside. "Why, look. It is Vernon Fredericks. Hello." She turned to Barb, the man's mother. "Look, Barb. It is your son. Vernon. The town's most eligible bachelor. I cannot believe he is here. On this day of all days."

It was worse than Darcy'd feared. Her mother

wasn't using contractions. Darcy made a face of despair. *Oh, dear God, not Vernon Fredericks.*

"Why. What a nice surprise. Hello, son. How ever did you find me?" It was spreading. Now Barb had lost the ability to use contractions. Her stiffly repeated words sounded as if she were an amateur actor reading her lines from cue cards she'd never seen before.

Darcy slowly shook her head. *Yep. Going to have to kill them...all four of them.*

From outside, on the shaded verandah, a man's whining voice said, "But you told me to come out—"

"Why, Vernon Fredericks, you silly ass—I mean man, you silly man. Now, we did no such thing and you know it. Come in, come in." Holding her iced-tea glass out carefully, Margie Alcott snatched the skinny fellow in off the porch, closed the door behind him, and then turned him to face Darcy. "Look. Darcy's home with her new baby."

"I know. You told me she would be." He was thoroughly bewildered, that much was obvious, as he looked from one woman's face to the next. He was also balding and sweating and wearing an ill-fitting shiny suit.

Here was Bachelor Number One, Darcy had figured out. Taking pity on him—he really was a nice, if timid, man—she gave him a little wave and a smile. "Hello, Mr. Fredericks. It's nice to see you again. I enjoyed your story about me yesterday in the newspaper."

"You can call him Vernon. It's okay." This from bright-eyed, sweetly smiling Freda Smith. But the red-faced and unresponsive man himself had to be shoved forward by his mother. "Go say hello to Darcy, son. And remember to make a fuss over the baby."

Thus pushed, the older man...more than twenty

years Darcy's senior...stumbled forward across the
thick carpet and fell, landing—amidst gasps and
shouted warnings from all sides—on his knees in front
of Darcy. Startled awake by all the noise, no doubt—
and by her mother's whisking her up and out of harm's
way—Montana began screaming.

It was absolute chaos. Iced-tea glasses were plopped
down everywhere. Helping hands reached out, taking
the baby, helping Vernon to his feet, helping Darcy
struggle awkwardly out of the chair, everyone shouting and blaming each other, all—

The doorbell rang again. Everyone froze. Except
Montana, who apparently saw no reason not to continue flailing her arms and airing out her lungs. Stiff
and sore and clutching at Jeanette's arm, Darcy sought
and found her mother, who was bouncing and rocking
her granddaughter and eyeing Darcy guiltily. But
Darcy wasn't about to let her off the hook. "Would
this be Bachelor Number Two?"

Margie pursed her lips and raised her chin. "I have
no idea what you're talking about, Darcy Jean Alcott."

"Oh no?" Darcy pointed to Vernon. "Explain
him."

The doorbell rang again. Margie immediately
handed Montana off to a thrilled Freda and stalked
toward the wide entryway of her spacious ranch home.
"I have to answer the door."

And then, with everyone hushed and waiting in the
living room, she opened the door to the Arizona heat.
And just stood there. Then, planting a hand at her
waist, she said, "Well, I'll be." She turned around to
the group. "Will you look who's here? It's the Lone
Ranger."

OUT ON THE verandah, Tom pulled down the brim of his white Stetson. Yep. He should have turned around somewhere on the long sandy drive out here and gone the other way, especially when he'd seen all the cars. Hell, he shouldn't even be here. Maybe he never should have even left Phoenix. But here he was. And so was Darcy.

Tom felt like a fifth wheel. She didn't want to see him. She'd made that plain the other day in her hospital room. But now that everyone was staring at him, he didn't have any idea what to say. Except, "Howdy."

Still, no one said anything. He could hear little Montana crying. But no one moved. Tom focused on the big-haired, well-groomed older woman who'd answered the door, removing his hat and holding it in one hand, fiddling with the brim. "I'm here to see Darcy Alcott. That is, if she's up to seeing another visitor right now."

"Well, she sure enough is. Come on in. I'm her mother. You can call me Margie. Everyone else does."

Tom nodded. "Thank you, ma'am. I will." He stepped inside, and nodded to the folks facing him. "Howdy," he repeated, with a duck of his head. "I'm Tom Elliott. I—"

The room exploded with noise. "That's Tom Elliott?" "That's his name?" "He sure is tall." "And handsome." "I have to get back to the *Bugle* office." "Is he the one who stopped and—?" "Shhh, Freda. Don't say that out loud." "I have to get back to the *Bugle* office." "Yes, he is." "Well, I'll be." "He doesn't look like he's from Michigan." "Montana, Barb. Montana." "I have to get back to—"

"We know, Vernon. The *Bugle* office," Darcy said, standing up. She extricated herself from the crowd and waved him into the room. "Come in, Tom, and sit for a while. Mother, perhaps you could get him some iced tea? And maybe see Vernon out? He has to get back to the *Bugle* office. Freda, if you'll just hand me Montana, perhaps you ladies might want to get those flowers out of your cars before they wilt—the flowers, that is. Not your cars."

It apparently didn't hurt to be specific with this group. Having gotten their marching orders, everyone acted on Darcy's instructions. As Tom watched from the safety of the entryway, they crossed each other's paths and went their directed ways. Darcy got her baby back and, in the next instant, the room cleared. Doing his part, Tom opened the door and stepped aside, allowing the various ladies to pass by him, nodding at each one as they did. Some skinny older man in a shiny suit left with them. Margie Alcott headed for the kitchen.

And finally…they were alone. Tom stared at Darcy, who stood in front of an Indian-print recliner with her baby in her arms. She looked great. And tired, the poor kid. But great. Great enough to make his heart beat faster. Great enough to have him driving an hour from Phoenix, just on the off-chance that she might want to see him one more time. And now…here she was, staring at him, waiting. At a loss as to how to get the conversational ball rolling, Tom finally decided on the obvious. "I'm impressed. You really know how to clear a room."

She grinned at him. "Being a teacher makes you bossy."

"I expect it does." He nodded toward the bundle

in her arms. "Mind if I take a look at her? Or has she been pawed over enough for one day already?"

"Oh, she probably has. But I think she'd like to see you. Come sit on the sofa with us. I haven't gotten to look her over yet myself, if you can believe that."

"I saw the crowd. I can believe that."

Darcy turned to the dark-blue leather sofa to her left and sat down at one end, carefully placing her child on the middle cushion. As she did, Tom stepped into the living room and crossed it, thinking how friendly it was between them today, as if she'd never told him to go away and not come back. But she seemed pleased to see him, and he was glad for that. Really glad.

Because he couldn't keep his eyes off her. After all, this was the first time he'd seen her when she wasn't in a crisis—or in the hospital. He'd never noticed her slender, shapely legs. Or how tanned her arms were. Or how her black curly hair glimmered with red highlights as the sunlight streamed in through the big picture window behind her. How much prettier she was than the open vista he could see out there, the cactus-dotted desert, the blue sky, and the distant shadows of the dark mountains. But most of all, he noticed that her warmth and graciousness made his pulse go into overdrive. Made him feel silly and young and ready to whoop out loud.

Keeping his love-choked emotions on a tight rein, Tom carefully sat down at the sofa's other end and put his Stetson on the coffee table in front of him. He shifted slightly, turning to put an arm along the sofa's spine, as he watched Darcy unfold the baby from her receiving blankets. Then...there she was, Montana Skye Alcott, an alert, cuddly baby girl, dressed in white booties and a long thin gown with ducks on it. She waved and kicked and made faces and grinned and blinked and yawned. Tom felt his chest swell with pride. This baby was his—whether or not he could ever call himself her father.

"She's pretty cute, huh?"

Tom looked up and met Darcy's gaze as she leaned over the baby, bringing her curl-framed face very close to his. His grin faded and his gaze settled on Darcy's lips. All he'd have to do to kiss her would be to inch forward a bit... But Tom swallowed that notion and just nodded. "Yeah, she sure is. You make awfully pretty babies, Miss Alcott."

Darcy sat back, looking embarrassed. "Thank you. You want to hold her?"

Tom's heart fluttered. "I'd love to, if you think it's all right. I've held babies before. Lots of times. For Sam—"

Darcy chuckled. "It's okay Tom. I don't need a resume. I have no doubt that you're much better at this than I am." She picked her daughter up and placed the child in his arms.

Tom thought he would die from feeling the exquisite fragility of the tiny girl he held. She fit right in the crook of his arm. He couldn't breathe. He was afraid to. He might hurt her. And he couldn't believe how he was acting. He'd held lots of babies. But this was different. The baby in his arms bore his name. It was that simple. She was his. And so was her mother. Full of wonder, he looked over at Darcy...and saw the hesitant look on her face. His heart thumped. "What's wrong? Am I doing this wrong?"

Shaking her head, she put a reassuring hand on his

arm. "No." But her voice sounded tight. "You just somehow look...*right* holding her. That's all."

"You sure? I can put her down. I—"

Darcy squeezed his arm. He wanted so badly to reach over and kiss her and tell her how much he loved her, to tell her she didn't ever have to be scared or alone again. "No, Tom. You're fine. Really. I mean it."

He exhaled. "Okay. If you're sure." Then he concentrated for a moment on Montana Skye, noticing her thick dark hair. Like her mother's. Her dark eyes. Like her mother's. The baby flailed the air with her teeny little fists. Tom smiled, caught Darcy again staring at him. "She's going to give this old world a bunch of hell, you know it?"

"I fear it," Darcy told him. "And that would make her just like me, poor kid. Tilting at windmills."

"I'll bet that doesn't pay much."

"I don't know. You'd have to ask Cervantes."

And there it was. That quick, educated mind of hers. Everything about her was a turn-on, a surprise. Tom beamed at her.

But Darcy suddenly looked down at her lap and exhaled sharply. Tom sobered as he gently rubbed Montana's arm...not much bigger, it seemed, than one of his fingers. "What is it, Darcy? What's wrong?"

She looked over at him. "Everything. And none of it's your fault. And that's why...look, the other day, at the hospital...well, I just want to say I'm sorry about my behavior, Tom. I don't know what came over me. But you certainly didn't deserve it."

Tom smiled at her. And she was nice, too. Really nice. He saw the glint of gathering tears in her eyes. His chest tightened. "Don't worry about it. In fact, I probably owe you an apology, Darcy. Because you were right. I *was* sitting there in your hospital room wondering what the hell I'd just done. I mean, giving your baby my name. I never even thought about how it would be for you.''

Wiping at her eyes, she cocked her head at a questioning angle. "What do you mean...for me?''

"I mean you being an Alcott and her being an Elliott. She *will* have all those questions you brought up. I realize that now.''

"No, she won't.''

Tom frowned. "She won't?'' Acute disappointment ate at him. "Oh, I see. You changed her birth certificate, right?''

"No. I didn't. I didn't call the nurse. I just...well, I decided to have her go by Alcott. Your name's still on her birth certificate. But I thought it would be easier for her—at least, at first—if her last name was the same as mine.''

Some of Tom's disappointment eroded, but not all of it. "I see. Makes sense.''

"You don't like that, do you? You thought I'd call her Montana Elliott.''

He'd hoped she would. But he just shrugged. "Doesn't much matter if I do or don't like it. She's not my baby. She's yours. You'll do what's right for her, I expect, Darcy.''

She exhaled raggedly. "I wish I could be as sure of that as you sound.''

Tom shifted the wriggling baby in his arms and frowned. "What do you mean? You're a smart woman. Educated. You got yourself this far. You must have a good head on your shoulders.''

"Well, except for where love is concerned.''

He couldn't argue with that. But he tried. "Maybe. But that doesn't have anything to do with loving your daughter. You'll be a fine mother to Montana, and I admire that in you."

Darcy smiled, looking grateful. She started to say something else, but the front door opened and in blew the three other older ladies, their arms full of flowers...including the roses that he had brought Darcy. And then, from the other way, came Margie Alcott with that promised glass of iced tea.

Tom gently, carefully handed the baby back to Darcy and stood up, reaching for his hat. "I expect I ought to go. I don't want to overstay my welcome. And it looks like you have—"

"Oh, pooh." Margie Alcott waved at him to sit back down. "Here. You didn't even have your tea yet." She put it in his hand. "Now, sit right back down and have your visit with Darcy."

Tom looked Darcy's way, wanting her approval. "It's just easier to go along with her," she assured him. Tom grinned and sat down, only then realizing that Margie was still talking to him.

"When I get my bridge club gone—well, I suppose they'll want to be introduced to you first. Anyway, once they're gone I want you and Darcy to go into her bedroom and—"

"Mother!"

Tom didn't know where to look. Certainly not at Darcy, who was laying the baby in her receiving blankets on the sofa cushion. So he settled for taking a huge swig of the tea. He hadn't realized how thirsty he was. Or how much he genuinely liked iced tea. Enough to scrutinize it carefully for several moments.

"Oh, Darcy. I don't mean like that. For heaven's sake. I was talking about that baby crib in there."

"What about it?"

To Tom's ear, Darcy sounded downright suspicious. He chanced a peek at her. Sure enough, her eyebrows were lowered.

"Well, I never could get it all put together right."

"But you told me you had."

"I know. But there were too many parts, and I couldn't figure out where all of them went. And I didn't want you to worry. But now I'm half afraid to lay that precious baby in it for fear it'll collapse around her."

Darcy sank back against the leather sofa's thick pillows. "Oh, dear God, Mother. Don't say things like that."

"Well, it's the truth. So I thought I'd get Tom here—" She turned to him. "By the way, it's nice to meet you." All he got to do was nod before she continued. "So I thought I'd get Tom, as long as he's here, to take a look at it for us and make sure it's safe for Montana. Don't you think that's a good idea?"

Tom saw his chance and jumped in. "I think it is. I'd be glad to troubleshoot for you."

Darcy rolled her head. "Are you sure?"

"Yeah, I'm sure. I've put up a crib or two in my time before."

"You have?"

"Yeah. Remember I said Sam had five babies?"

"You know a Sam who had five babies?" That was from Margie Alcott.

Tom turned to her. "Yes, ma'am. Sam's my older sister. Samantha. She taught me a thing or two about babies and their contraptions along the way."

Margie Alcott's eyes lit up. "She did?"

"Mother. Stop it right there."

Tom looked at Darcy. "What's wrong?"

She looked tired, but she was grinning—and shaking her head. "If I were you, I wouldn't say another word, Tom."

"Why not?"

"Because if you do, you'll find yourself Eligible Bachelor Number Two."

6

DARCY SAT CROSS-LEGGED on her twin bed with her mother next to her, who cuddled a sleeping Montana in her arms. They silently, companionably watched Tom trying to wrestle into submission an ornately carved, stubbornly constructed baby crib.

From her viewpoint, though, Darcy figured—even if she didn't know him—she'd be happy to buy a ticket, climb the bleachers along with a throng of women, find her seat, eat her popcorn, and just watch him…oh, say…reconstruct a building, for example. Or put together a puzzle. Or paint a brick wall. Or rewrite, by hand, the entire phone book. Mud wrestle. It didn't matter…as long as he was naked, of course.

It was true. The man was perfectly constructed, a work of art himself. Clothes couldn't hide that, any more than she could hide, from herself, that she wanted him. Wanted him bad. *Well, who wouldn't? It's not fair. Just look at him.* The man's physique screamed *Take Me Now!*

Darcy sighed. *Great.* She'd just objectified Tom. Made him a sex object, a great body with no thoughts or personality. Well, shame on her—especially since she knew all her own arguments. She didn't want a man in her life…*yada, yada, yada. Well, not wanting a committed relationship doesn't mean I'm dead.* Nor did it mean that her libido had been stitched up along with everything else. She could still appreciate his fluid movements, his muscled legs, that broad back—another sigh escaped her. She'd better stop right now with all this wanting him, before the rest of her body caught up with her thoughts and gave her hell.

"What's all that sighing about, Darcy? Your bottom hurting?"

Darcy froze, wide-eyed. Her nails dug into her knees. His back to her, Tom made a choking sound. Slowly, ever so slowly, as if it took an act of conscious will, Darcy turned her head until she faced her mother. "No. My...*bottom's* not hurting, thank you." It was, but she wasn't admitting it.

"Well, that's good. Because it will when the numbness wears off—"

"Can we talk about something else, Mother?" Darcy counted it a victory that she got her words out without shrieking.

Margie patted Montana's back and stared at Darcy. "Now, don't get upset, honey. It'll get your hormones bubbling and then you'll be crying."

"*Now,* Mother—let's talk about something else *now.*"

"All right." Her mother looked Tom's way. "Just look at all that trouble he's having, Darcy Jean. I told you it was a nasty piece of furniture. Myself, I got a blood blister on my thumb, trying to deal with it." She held it up for inspection.

Warmed, despite herself, by her mother's past attempts with the crib, as well as by every bit of support, emotional and financial, she'd unstintingly given in the past several, trying months, Darcy hugged her mother and then eyed her own infant daughter. She rubbed a finger lovingly over the child's soft forehead. "I appreciate your war injuries, Mom. And I'm sure Tom appreciates your encouragement now.''

"I do," he said. "And I'm doing fine over here." Pieces of crib and tiny bits of necessary hardware littered the carpet around him. "Be done in a jiffy."

No, he wouldn't. That much was obvious to Darcy. Because, using one hand to hold up two ladderlike side-slats that threatened to collapse onto one another at any second, he picked up a screwdriver from the tool box Margie had presented and...lost his grip on his handiwork. The slats slowly, gracefully banged together and then backwards against the wall.

Darcy jumped at the sound and felt her mother do the same. She glanced at her baby. Surprisingly, Montana slept on. Darcy exchanged a what-do-you-know look with her mother. Then she heard Tom mutter something under his breath—something, no doubt, that was probably best left unheard. Darcy took pity on the man. "You don't have to do this, Tom. I'm sure you hadn't planned to sign up for crib construction when Mom had you tracked down and told you to come out here today."

Tom turned to her. So did her mother. They spoke as one. "What do you mean—"

"Darcy Jean, I never—"

"She didn't—"

"I went to the hospital—"

"He went to the hospital—"

"—and they gave me directions—"

"—and they gave him directions out here—"

"I hope you don't mind—"

"They're not supposed to do that—"

"Never mind." As amused as she was overwhelmed with their denials, Darcy held up a hand.

"Okay, I'm sorry." She turned to her mother. "You really didn't coerce him into coming out here?"

"She didn't."

Darcy's heart took a thrilling leap as she turned to Tom. "She didn't?"

His blue eyes regarded her sincerely. "No. Like I said, I came out here because I wanted to. I went to the hospital, where I was told you'd just left. Then the nurse at the desk gave me directions here. She said she wasn't supposed to do that, but me being who I am and seeing how I'd helped deliver Montana...well, you know the rest."

"Yes. I read about it in the newspaper," Darcy said drolly. "Didn't I, Mother?"

The older woman's eyes widened...guiltily. But she recovered beautifully. "Do y'all smell something that's soured?" She bent over the sleeping infant in her arms and sniffed at her. "Phew. I think this child has christened her diaper." She stood up. "I'll just take her in the living room and change her there where all that stuff—" She began her retreat from the room. "—they gave you at the hospital is and then I'll—" She exited the room and took a sharp turn to her left, heading up the hallway. "—do something else, I don't know what. It'll come to me."

Darcy waited a moment, giving her mother a chance to leave, and then turned to Tom. "Is she a piece of work, or what?"

"Museum quality," he assured her, adding a wink to his words.

"She means well. Underneath that busybody exterior is a heart of gold. Even if she does go a bit far sometimes." Warmed by his wink, and itching to stroke his face, his jaw, his neck...Darcy felt self-conscious now that she was alone with him in her bedroom, knowing he'd sought her out on his own. That knowledge had done nothing to settle her reawakening libido.

Hunkered down on a knee, with a screwdriver in his hand, looking like an open invitation, Tom smiled back at her. "She goes a bit far? You're talking about me being Bachelor Number Two, right?"

Darcy put her hands to her suddenly too-warm cheeks. "You poor man. Yes. She thinks I need a man and Montana needs a father. Well, one who wants to stick around, I should say."

Tom regarded her silently. Darcy thought maybe he was going to declare himself. An accompanying thrill raced through her, one she couldn't quite put a name to. Good thrill or bad thrill? But Tom saved her from having to explore that feeling. "I see. So who was Bachelor Number One? That skinny man in the shiny suit?"

"You mean Vernon?" Darcy laughed. "You make him sound like a mobster. Which is probably the most exotic thing that's ever been said about him. But yes. Vernon. Who lives with his mother."

Tom seemed to be enjoying Darcy's discomfort a little too much. "Any other competition I should know about?"

"Unfortunately, I won't know until she trots them by. But for now it's just you and Vernon."

"Good. I think I can take him." Tom's gaze slowly traveled over her face. "How're you doing, Darcy? I mean really."

The genuine concern in his voice disconcerted her. "We're not talking about my bottom again, are we?"

Amusement sparked in his eyes. "No. But we can, if you like."

She shook her head. "I don't like."

"I didn't think so. But what I meant was...you look tired."

"Great." Darcy made an ineffectual swipe at her hair, trying in vain to brush back her tangle of shoulder-length curls. "Will the day ever come when I look presentable again?"

"You look just fine right now."

Darcy scoffed. "Yeah, me and my leftover maternity clothes. Yuck." She pulled at them. "And I look tired, too, remember?"

"I didn't mean anything by it. Hell, you have every right to be tired. You just had a baby a few days ago...well, I guess you know that."

Darcy dramatically shifted her stitched-up nether-region on her bed. "Good. We're back to my bottom. Finally." Then, belatedly, she realized how that sounded and to whom she was speaking. The man had been right there and had seen everything. "I mean, I..." She gave up. "Oh, the heck with it. You're right. I am tired. Very tired. It's been an exhausting day so far. For me and for Montana."

"I expect it has. It's hot outside. That'll sap your strength. And then there was that long drive out here. You probably could both use a good nap about now."

Something inside Darcy grew soft. Had there ever been a more sympathetic soul on the face of the earth than this man? Just his way of talking, so slow and calm, and his constant concern for her, was enough to make her want to crawl into his lap. And put her arms around him and her cheek against his chest so she could hear his heart beating and then just lay there against him and soak up—

"Darcy? Did you hear me?"

Blinking, embarrassed, she snapped back to the moment. "Oh. No. I'm sorry. I didn't. What did you say?"

"I said I closed the deal today on my grandfather's land."

Darcy froze. She felt as if she'd just been slapped. "Oh, you did? Well…that's great. Good for you. I guess that means…you'll be going home soon."

Distractedly twisting and turning the screwdriver around in his hand, he stared her way and nodded. "It does."

Darcy looked down at her lap. She couldn't imagine why the thought of him leaving upset her so much. But it did. It made her want to cry and left her feeling alone and scared. Immediately, she chastised herself for being so silly. She looked up at him. He was studying her. Darcy tried a smile, but it wouldn't quite hold. "So. When are you leaving?"

"I don't know. There are some details to see to and some papers to be drawn up and signed. I figure about the middle of next week."

This was Friday. "Wow. As soon as that?"

"Yep. As soon as that." He casually tossed the screwdriver into the tool box. It clanked against several other metal pieces and sounded unusually loud to Darcy. She watched Tom turn back to putting the crib together. "I got a good price for the land. The developers want to turn it into a golf course."

"Well, you can't have too many of those out here in the desert."

Tom turned and eyed her. "You don't approve?"

A shrug accompanied Darcy's words. "I don't have an opinion either way. It's your land. Well, it *was* your land."

"It was. Now it's Montana's."

Darcy snapped upright, her soreness and tiredness forgotten. "Montana's? I hope you mean the state of."

He shook his head. "No. Your Montana. All the corporation's land payments, her share of the profits, everything…it will all come to her. That's the trust fund I told you about. Oh, and you're the conservator. You'll have to sign some papers."

"I have to—?" Darcy realized she was shaking her head. "You shouldn't have done that, Tom."

He frowned. "Why? It's only a simple matter of paperwork."

"I'm not talking about that. I'm talking about the money. I can't even begin to imagine the amount."

"Well, it's a lot all right. Up into seven figures. To begin with."

Darcy had difficulty swallowing. Words would not come out of her mouth, no matter how hard she tried to form them. She couldn't believe it. Tom had just changed her life forever, and he acted as if he had no idea that he had. Why, the magnitude alone of the gift he'd just bestowed was mind-boggling. So why wasn't she happy? Well, because this gift, if she accepted it, obligated her and Montana to him forever. Forever. And the part of her that remembered her fiasco of a relationship with Montana's real father reminded her that this could be a complication. That his gift might be a claim on her and Montana—even after he'd promised at the hospital that he wouldn't make any. But how could she refuse it, either? The gift was for

Montana, not her. Could she deny her daughter this wealth?

Darcy simply wasn't sure how she felt about any of this. So she sat and stared at Tom, certain she could feel each and every nerve ending tingling inside her. Finally, another thought came to her. "But you can't, Tom. Your family. What about your family? What will they say?"

He shrugged. "The only family I have to consider is my sister. I ran it by her. Not that I had to. The land is mine. But still, she's happy with what I'm doing."

"That's awfully generous of her."

"That's how she is."

"Well, I like her already. But what about *your* future children? That land was their legacy, too."

"If I have any kids down the road, they'll have plenty of legacy." Then he grinned, obviously trying for lightness. "Try not to worry so much, Darcy. I want this for you and Montana. I thought you'd be happy."

Darcy put a be-still-my-heart hand to her chest. "Happy? Tom, I'm reeling. It's a good thing I'm already sitting down. That's just so much money. I don't—"

Tom waved off her concern. "Oh, hell, it's not that big a deal. And it's not like we're going to give it to Montana when she's two years old. I set it up for you to draw regularly on the interest and to determine when she's ready to take the reins herself. Who better than her mama to know that?"

Darcy could only stare at this man. "Wow. You put a lot of trust in me."

He smiled warmly. "I don't think it's misplaced. You appear to be the honorable type to me." With that, he stretched up to his full height and turned to inspect his handiwork, running his hands over the crib's wood and jiggling it to make certain of its sturdiness. Apparently satisfied, he then hefted the baby mattress into the crib, lowered it onto the boxspring and wedged it down tightly into position. "There. All done."

Watching him, drinking in his handsome masculine profile, and lingering over the lines of his tall, long-muscled body, Darcy had to remind herself to take a breath. "Why are you doing this?"

He looked her way. "The crib? Your mother asked me to—"

"Not the crib, Tom. The trust fund. I mean, I can't believe you. You act as if you've just given Montana a little toy…and not a Phoenix *golf course,* for crying out loud."

"Well, it's not a golf course yet. But it will be. And I didn't sell the land. Just gave the developers a long-term lease. So the money and the profits will keep rolling in. Ought to be a nice little college fund for Montana by the time she reaches eighteen."

Darcy couldn't decide if he was humble or arrogant. "Tom, by the time she's eighteen, with that kind of money, she can *buy* her own nice little college. In Europe."

"I suppose she could, if she chooses to. I admit that. But it's just a simple land deal."

"And the Rocky Mountains are just a bunch of hills."

He frowned at her. "You really aren't happy about this, are you?"

"Happy? I don't know. But I *am* overwhelmed, I'll say that much. I mean, it's like you're Elvis and you're giving away Cadillacs to startled strangers who never had any hope of owning one.''

Tom shifted his position, suddenly looking uncomfortable. ''Well, it sounds downright arrogant of me when you put it like that.''

She knew better. ''I don't think you're arrogant. Maybe...overly generous. But this gift of yours still changes everything for me, Tom. Everything. Where I'll live. What I'll do. How I'll raise Montana. How I'll instill in her a humility and respect that should go along with such riches. And if I should even sign the papers. Things like that. Do you understand?''

He nodded, still looking thoughtful and...could it be?...proud of her. ''Now see there? What you just said tells me I did the right thing, that I judged you correctly. Most people wouldn't even hesitate. They'd jump on that money right off. But not you. You worry about the right things, Darcy. You're a good person. And you'll raise Montana just fine.''

Darcy made a self-deprecating sound. ''I wish I had as much confidence in me as you do, Tom.''

''It'll come. But, hell, Darcy, I never meant for the trust fund to give you such fits. It was just a sudden brainstorm during one of my meetings yesterday. I only wanted to do something nice. For you and Montana.''

Darcy chuckled. ''Tom, a big bag of disposable diapers would have been something nice for me and Montana.''

He stood alert. ''You need some? I'll go to the—''

''No, Tom. I don't need any. Well, I do. No, Montana does—or at least, she will soon, if Mom doesn't quit changing her every ten minutes. But you don't have to do that. It's not your place.''

His expression sobered. He looked hurt. "I know I don't have any place here, Darcy. I just want to..." His words trailed off. He exhaled and looked down at his boots.

"You want to what, Tom?"

He looked up at her, surprising her with the fierce longing evident in his eyes. "I don't know what I want, Darcy. I promise you, though, I'm not some crackpot millionaire who goes around throwing his money at folks. I've never done anything like this before."

Darcy folded her hands together in her lap. "I believe you. Tom, you are the sweetest man I've ever met. But your timing is just all wrong."

"How so?"

How so, indeed. "I don't mean to cause you any trouble legally with your land deal, Tom. And what you did was the most wonderful thing that I've ever heard of. It's the stuff of dreams."

He crossed his arms over his chest. "But?"

"*But* I'm not going to sign those papers. I just can't let you do this."

His blue eyes glinted. "Why not?"

"Because I would have no way of explaining it— or you—to Montana. It's the same argument we had in the hospital over putting your name on her birth certificate. What would I tell her when she asks me who you *are?* Or *why* you would do such a thing? She'll want to know."

"Well, just tell her, then. Would that be so awful? I mean, hell, I'm not the father who abandoned her. I'm the one trying to help her."

Darcy sat there, stunned. Insult warred with anger

inside her. "*You're* the one trying to help her? What about me?"

Tom's expression bled to an apology. "Oh, hell, Darcy, I'm sorry. I didn't mean it that way."

Tears sprang to Darcy's eyes, tears that played on every insecurity she had about parenting Montana alone. "Yes, you did. You meant it. Just like my mother's friends with all their advice and their bachelor sons. Apparently no one thinks I can raise my child by myself."

Tom covered the distance between them. He hunkered down in front of her, taking her hands in his. "Darcy, you know that's not true. I already told you different. You're overreacting here."

Darcy looked into his sincere, blue eyes, and felt awful. "Am I?" She pulled a hand free and rubbed at her temple. "I could be, Tom. I don't know. God, these hormones of mine. One minute I'm up, the next down. I'm either crying or sleeping or depressed." She flopped her hand down to her lap. "Even Montana hates me. I don't blame her."

Tom instantly took her hand again and squeezed it affectionately. "She does not. She'll love you best in all the world, Darcy. All her life, she'll only have one mama. And that's you."

"And that's what scares me, Tom. I could completely screw her up."

"You won't. Because you love her. And every decision you make, you'll make with Montana in mind."

Darcy stared at the man in front of her...and finally understood. "Either I'm Cinderella and you're my fairy godmother. Or you have twelve kids you haven't told me about, and have learned to be this wise the hard way."

Grinning, he shook his head. "Neither. I just—well, I just care, Darcy."

She didn't know what to say to that. She'd meant it when she said she wanted to raise her daughter on her own. Or at least be alone for a while with her. But Darcy couldn't help but realize, even with her hands in his, even with her childbirth-battered body already responding to his nearness, what an eye-opener this conversation was. Apparently, despite the nice things he'd said, when it came right down to it, not even this man—a stranger to her—thought her capable of raising her child without his help—or his money.

Do I really come across as that pathetic? She feared she did. *Well, no more.* Darcy squeezed Tom's hands and smiled. "Tom, I appreciate everything you're trying to do here. I really do. But I have to decline your generous offer. See, it's important to me to know that *I'll* be the one providing for my daughter. Whether it's diapers or a college fund, *I* want to provide it. And—" Darcy took a deep breath as she set about cutting off her nose to spite her face. "—not you or anyone else."

Tom came to his feet and looked down at her. "I understand your feelings, Darcy. And I have to respect them."

Darcy's chin came up...and a tear spilled over, one that begged her to reconsider. But she couldn't afford to listen. Because if she did, she'd be in Tom's arms in a heartbeat...and she'd lose all respect for herself. "Thank you," was all she managed to get out as her throat constricted.

Still, Tom stood there...as if rooted to the spot. Like storm clouds passing rapidly over a desert, some emotion flickered across his features...and then was gone.

Finally, he exhaled sharply. "Well, then, this is good-bye, Darcy. Take care. I wish you the best of everything, you and Montana." With that, he walked out of her bedroom.

As soon as he left, Darcy looked up to the ceiling, willing away the ever-present tears that lurked in her eyes of late. *I can do this,* she told the overhead fan. *I can.*

"I CAN'T DO this." Darcy threw her hands up. She'd already ruined four disposable diapers, trying to fit them to Montana's tiny hips.

The problem was, the child had too many moving parts and was built like a frog. And the diapers! Forget them. If Darcy didn't fold them in half, they were up to Montana's neck. *Or* if she did successfully get the diaper on, the baby would draw her legs up, catch her tiny feet in the folds, straighten her legs...and yank the diaper off her body. *Or* the tabs wouldn't stick. Even if they did, when Darcy picked her daughter up, no matter how carefully she held her, the darned thing eventually slid off. And once already, as soon as Darcy had gotten the obnoxious thing taped just right, Montana had, well, soiled it. Soiled it good.

And now, on this bright Sunday afternoon, Darcy was in a lather. Sweaty, exhausted from a lack of sleep and needing a bath, she was ready to throw in the towel. Montana—who hated her, Darcy was sure of it—was crying...no doubt, over her mother's inadequacies. Darcy, in turn, wanted her own mother, who stood next to her. "Could she be more helpless? And these diapers! Are you sure they're the newborn size? I swear they'd fit a pony. And how am I supposed to keep that hideous navel-thing dry and exposed to the air, Mother? It's been four days, and I still can't even do one single thing right—''

"Darcy. Stop it." Margie took a hold of Darcy's arm. "You're getting yourself in a state. And that won't do you or your daughter any good."

Darcy's chin trembled. Her mother immediately wrapped her in an embrace. "It's okay, baby. What you're feeling is normal. All new mothers go through this. I sure did. I was certain that I'd break you or forget where I'd left you. I swear, the only time you didn't cry was when your daddy was holding you. Then, when things got to their worst point, it never failed that my mother, bless her heart, would choose right then to call and ask me something crazy, like had I remembered to feed you that day."

Darcy pulled back and swiped at the tears on her cheeks. Her mother had never shared such things with her. Of course, there'd been no need before now. But still, they made her feel better. "Grandma would do that?"

"You bet. I was sure I was the worst mother in the history of the world."

Darcy impulsively hugged her mother tightly. "You were not. You were—and still are—the best mother ever. I love you."

After a moment, her mother tugged herself out of Darcy's embrace. Looking about ready to cry herself, Margie eyed the baby in the crib. Darcy did, too...and swore Montana glared back suspiciously. Her mother turned to go. "Well, I'll just leave you to it, honey."

Darcy grabbed at her mother's bright pullover top. "No. Don't go. Please? I'm scared. And she hates me."

Her mother pulled the fabric from Darcy's clutches.

"Now, Darcy, she does not. She's just picking up on your agitation. Forget the diaper. Just hold her. That's all she wants."

"She does?" Darcy pivoted to look at her daughter just lying there naked in the crib. Montana churned her legs and chewed on a fist. "How do you know that?"

"Because that's what all babies want. You can't spoil them by loving them. Well, not at this age. Later on, yes. But not now. You'll know when it's too much."

Darcy stared at her mother. "Did I miss a meeting of the mother's club or something? Where do women learn all this stuff?" She clutched her mother's arm. "Look at me. I teach college, for God's sake. But I can't do this. I thought I could, but I can't. I suck at motherhood. And Montana knows it. And she hates me. What am I going to do?"

Margie pursed her lips. That was never good. "Why don't you let me see to this baby while you go get a shower and some sleep. That's what you need. Montana will be okay for three or four hours since you just nursed her. So, go on now and don't argue with me."

A bath and some sleep. It was heaven. And Darcy wasn't arguing. She knew she was at the end of her rope emotionally. And she also knew, as she trailed off to the bathroom and listened to her mother cooing at Montana, that in most families, one with a caring husband...someone, say, like Tom Elliott...it would be him taking over instead of her 70-year-old mother. Her mother was her backup and her support...when it should have been the husband. The husband that Darcy didn't have. *Or want,* she reminded herself.

DARCY SUDDENLY jerked awake. Lying there, blinking and staring at the ceiling, she couldn't immediately figure out what had awakened her. Sighing, still bone-weary, she struggled to a sitting position. She pushed her hair back from her face, and suddenly realized something else. She couldn't remember what day it was. Or why she smelled so good and was sleeping during the day. Or where everyone was. *Everyone?*

The baby! Gasping, Darcy put a hand to her mouth and darted a glance over at the crib. Empty. Then she searched her memory…and came up with it. *Oh, right. Mom has the baby.* Slumping with relief, she glanced at the digital clock on the bedside table. It was after 6:00 p.m. Why, she'd slept for three hours. And this was Sunday.

Feeling a bit guilty, and thinking her poor mother could probably use some help about now, since it was close to suppertime, Darcy pulled herself up and stood beside her bed, tugging at her knee-length cotton nightshirt to straighten it around her. As she did, she winced, feeling the tight fullness in her bra-bound breasts, which reminded her that it was also Montana's suppertime. Thus motivated, she set off for the living room. The house sure was quiet, she suddenly realized. *Maybe Mom and Montana are sleeping.*

Thinking of her mother's daily afternoon nap, Darcy

suddenly felt guilty. *Oh, the poor thing. If she needed to lie down, she could've just put the baby back in her crib.* That was the only safe place for her since you just never knew, her mother had said, when a baby would take a notion to roll over for the first time and fall on the floor. Remembering the nightmares that scenario had given her, Darcy told herself, *Well, before they go leaping headfirst off sofas, maybe babies ought to have the decency to send up warning flares to alert unsuspecting adults as to their intentions.*

Okay, that sounds good on paper, Darcy now conceded as she turned into the living room, *but the odds of actually getting an infant to use flares—*

"Son of a—" Darcy stopped cold. "What *are* you doing here, Tom?"

Looking cool and crisp in his starched chambray shirt and black denims, with his white Stetson perched next to him on a cushion, Tom Elliott sat on the couch, holding the contentedly sleeping Montana. With an intent stare probably more suited to counting grazing cattle out on an open plain, he scrutinized Darcy, looking her up and down. Then he hefted the sleeping baby in his arms. "Well, as you can see, I'm baby-sitting."

Suddenly feeling all warm and giddy inside, Darcy took stock of her appearance and wanted to die. She looked around. He was right. Because her mother was nowhere to be seen. "Where's my mother?"

"I tied her up and threw her down the basement stairs."

Darcy raised an eyebrow at him and narrowed her eyes. "We don't have a basement."

He raised an eyebrow. "Well then, I guess we should start over."

"Okay. Could you please tell me where my mother is?" she asked sarcastically.

"That's better. She went to the store."

Now, that was even more appalling. "The store? It's after six o'clock, and the nearest store is fifteen miles away. Why?"

"Well, I don't know. I guess that's just where they built it."

Darcy pursed her lips. "Not that. I mean what did she go to the store for? Or do you know?"

"I do. She went for diapers."

"Diapers? I thought we had bags of them."

"I couldn't tell you what 'we' have," Tom said pleasantly enough.

Darcy put a hand to her waist. "Well, why didn't you go for her, then? She's seventy years old, you know."

"I offered. I told her I didn't mind—"

Darcy waved a hand at him. "Never mind. Let's try this again. What *are* you doing here? And don't say baby-sitting. I know that. And don't say one word about the way I look, either. Or about how I've been sleeping while my aged mother was left to tend my child. Or about that land and the trust-fund thing. Or how you drove by and delivered my baby, and then put your name on her birth certificate. Anything but that."

Tom stared at her. "Well, that leaves politics or religion. But in polite society, you're not supposed to talk about such things."

Darcy puffed up. "So you're saying I'm not being polite, right?"

Tom frowned. "No. That wouldn't be polite of me, now would it?"

"No. It wouldn't. So don't."

"I won't." Silence followed. "You'd like to tell me where to go right now, wouldn't you?"

Darcy nodded. "I have. Twice. But obviously it doesn't take with you."

He grinned. "You'd think you'd quit trying, wouldn't you?" He then turned his attention back to Montana, smoothing her downy hair.

Darcy stood where she was, not quite believing the moment or her life. She couldn't believe how irresistibly good-looking and wonderful he was. Just being around him made her heart thump wildly and her knees go weak. And all she'd done was act obnoxious to him every time they met. And in return? The man seemed to take it all in stride, barely noticing her behavior. How could he be so unflappable?

Was it just his personality? Maybe it was that good old cowboy code. Most likely, it was because she didn't affect him like he did her. A disheartening thought, but a logical conclusion. The man simply felt responsible for Montana, obviously loved babies, and maybe enjoyed his hero notoriety a bit. Darcy watched him smile down at her daughter and rub a fingertip gently across her tiny forehead. *A wonderfully kind and generous man. But trouble, nonetheless. Heartache trouble. For me.*

Tom chose that moment to look up at her. "Why don't you come sit down a spell? Your daughter will be waking up in a minute, I expect, and she'll want her mama."

Darcy slumped. "Not that she has any choice, the poor kid. She hates me, but I am the chuck wagon. Still, thanks, I think I will sit down." Darcy headed for the plush Indian-print rocker/recliner on the other side of the sofa. Exercising extreme caution in lowering herself onto the upholstered seat, she finally got herself comfortable and looked over at Tom. "What?"

"Nothing. I just wondered how you're doing."

"You always ask me that."

"I always want to know."

"Why?"

He shrugged, shifting Montana in his arms. The baby stirred...then slowly slumped back into her sleep. Tom sought Darcy's gaze. "Why? Because I care, I suppose."

"About what?"

He chuckled, then sighed—an all-right-we'll-play-it-your-way sound—and looked her right in the eyes. "About you. I care about you. I want to know that you're okay. How you feel. What you think. Things like that."

"Why?" Darcy couldn't stop herself. Nor would she allow herself to feel anything for him, at least any more than she already felt. Because if she did, she'd leap into his lap and beg to be held in his arms, in much the same way he was holding her daughter.

"You're a hard customer, Darcy Jean Alcott."

Her eyebrows raised. "So now it's Darcy Jean. You've been talking to my mother."

"No. Well, yeah, I have. But you told me that was your middle name, while you were in the hospital. After our first fight."

"Our first fight? Do you hear yourself? You make it sound like some kind of modern relationship milestone you'd read about in *Cosmo*."

"You're talking about that woman's magazine, right? Don't look so surprised. My sister reads it. Along with her older daughter, Alex. Geri—that's

G-E-R-I—is too young yet. She's the baby. Or will be until Sam delivers sometime in late August.''

"Your sister Sam has daughters named Alex and Geri? How enlightened. I like that. Does she have sons?"

He nodded. "Yep. Three."

"Joan and Tara and Susan, I hope."

He grinned. "Good guesses. Her husband's name is Marion."

"Well I guess that was alright for John Wayne, but I have a feeling you're pulling my leg." Darcy fought a grin. This was not good. He was so much darned fun. She needed to keep reminding herself that she'd told him she wasn't interested in having a relationship. "Seriously. What's his name?"

"Luke. And the boys are Matthew, Mark, and John."

"Clever. A biblical theme. I get it."

"Yep. But what about you? You've got 49 more states to go. You intend to cover them all?"

Darcy frowned…then she got it. "Oh, I see. Montana. The states. Sure. Why not? Can't you just see a kid named New Hampshire?"

"Or twins named South Dakota and North Dakota."

Darcy stared at him. This was fun, but, boy, were they only treading water here. Again, it was her fault that nothing went below the surface. After all, she was the one who'd refused to discuss anything relevant between them. So it was up to her to open those areas…if she ever hoped for any resolution to their dilemma. *Dilemma?*

Tom sat up straighter. "Why the frown? You hurting somewhere?"

An immediate blush stained Darcy's cheeks. "No. I'm not hurting *somewhere*. I was just thinking of our dilemma."

"We have a dilemma?"

"Well, that's what I was trying to decide. I don't know. Maybe we do, maybe we don't. I mean, I did tell you I'm not going to sign those papers, right?"

He didn't even blink. "That you did. And more."

Darcy lowered her gaze a second, appropriately guilty for having as much as told him to go away and never come back two days ago. She looked back up, changing the subject. "So, did your land deal go sour after that, or what? I was afraid my refusal might cause you some legal hassles."

"No hassle. Not yet, anyway."

Then…she knew. "You didn't change it yet, did you?"

He shook his head. "I couldn't. That was Friday afternoon when you said you wouldn't sign. Can't meet with them again until tomorrow."

That made sense. But still, feeling as if there were a trap here she couldn't see, Darcy nodded and answered warily. "Oh yeah, right. I see."

Tom just smiled…and nodded.

Darcy exhaled sharply. "Dammit, Tom, are you going to meet with them tomorrow and change it, or not?"

He looked at her as if she'd just sprouted wings. "You mean the land deal in Montana's favor?"

"Of course." Darcy waited. He didn't say anything. "Well?" she prompted, and then quickly added, "And don't say 'well what.'"

His eyes narrowed. "You always dictate people's responses for them?"

"Only when I have to. When they're being elusive. Or evasive."

"And you think that's what I'm doing?"

Darcy crossed her arms. "Right now? Yes."

"You think I came out here today, after everything that was said Friday, just so I could evade issues between us?"

There it was...the talk they needed to have. "All right. Fine. You didn't. What *are* the issues, Tom?"

The doorbell rang. Montana jerked awake, stiffened, and immediately began screaming. Tom's eyes widened. He suddenly looked awkward holding the baby as he patted and bounced her and Darcy struggled out of the recliner.

"Let me get it, Darcy. You take Montana. She probably wants you anyway."

But by then, Darcy was on her feet and didn't particularly relish the prospect of sitting down again so soon. "No, she doesn't. She hates me. I'll get the door. Just walk around with her and pat her." As Tom got up and headed down the hallway, Darcy started for the door. "It's probably Mom. She'll do that sometimes—ring the doorbell—when she has her hands full.

"Although why she just doesn't come in through the garage, I'll never—" she continued under her breath. Stepping carefully across the tiled floor, she opened the door. "—Johnny Smith! What are you doing here?"

Outside in the warm Arizona evening, Sheriff Johnny Smith stood there soberly in uniform and doffed his hard-brimmed hat. "Evening, Miz Alcott. I'm afraid I've got some bad news for you. It's about your mama—"

"WHAT THE HELL happened?" Numbing fright raced through Tom. All he knew was he was holding Darcy's hungry, crying infant daughter. And some big hound-dog-faced policeman was holding Montana's limp and unconscious mother. And the two of them, Tom and the cop, seemed to be frozen with surprise as they faced each other in the Alcotts' hallway.

"Who're you?" the police officer asked first…yelling over the baby's cries.

"I'm Tom Elliott. Who are you?" Tom carefully put Montana to his shoulder and patted her back…which only made her madder and louder.

"Sheriff Smith," the other man yelled even louder. "I'm the law around these parts. What're you doing here, Mr. Elliott?"

"I'm holding up Montana Skye." Tom saw the man's questioning look, so he explained. "The baby. Montana's her name." When Sheriff Smith—Tom now recalled he was the bloodhound Darcy had warned him about in the hospital—nodded, Tom threw the man's question back at him. "What are *you* doing here?"

The sheriff looked down at Darcy's limp body in his arms. Tom didn't like it one bit, either, that the man's hands were on her, whether or not in an official capacity. "I guess I'm holding Miz Alcott."

"I see that. What happened to her?"

"She fainted."

"That was my guess. Did she hit her head on the tiled floor?"

"No. I caught her first."

Relief coursed through Tom. "Well, good. But do you know *why* she fainted?"

"What's wrong with the baby?"

Frustration ate at Tom. It was as if they were having two different conversations. "She's hungry, and her mama is unconscious. I suggest you get Darcy to the couch and see if you can wake her up. Otherwise, one of us—me or you—is going to have to figure out how to feed this child."

The sheriff's face turned beet-red. He immediately headed for the couch, handling Darcy as if she were made of glass. Tom's eyes narrowed as he wondered at Johnny Smith's sudden appearance here this evening. Was the police officer Bachelor Number Three? *Most likely,* Tom decided, before quickly turning his thoughts back to Darcy. Why had she fainted? Had she jumped out of the chair too quickly?

That was logical. But still, he was worried, more than he'd ever been in his life. And he was really beginning to sweat from the sheer force of Montana's protestations, which showed no sign of letting up. The eight-pound baby girl had to be eighty percent lungs. His hand on her diapered bottom, even through the receiving blanket, was suddenly wet and warm. *And twenty percent water,* he added resignedly to himself.

Diapers and tears would have to wait a minute. Because all Tom could do right now was follow Officer Johnny to the couch and watch him decorously lay Darcy out flat. The policeman then gingerly straightened her nightshirt over her body and began patting her hand.

Tom took over. "Bend her knees up. And take the throw pillow out from under her head and put it under her legs."

Johnny Smith gave Tom the same look he probably would have if Tom had suggested they undress her and take pictures of her. "It's for the blood flow to her brain," Tom quickly explained...before he found himself in handcuffs. "Her head needs to be lower than her feet. Trust me. It'll work."

"It better." Johnny eyed Tom a moment more but then set about doing as he had instructed.

"That's it. We'll wait a minute and see if she comes around." Tom once again rearranged his grip on the wet and—blessedly—now softly mewling baby. *Poor kid.* "In the meantime, Sheriff, what happened back there at the door? Did Darcy just seem dizzy all of a sudden? Or did you say something to her?"

Johnny Smith removed his hat and scratched at his balding head. "Well, I don't know about dizzy. But I did say something to her. I said I had some bad news, that it was about her mother—"

"Her mother?" Tom froze...and then felt weak. "What about her mother? What happened?"

"Nothing that I know of. Is she here?" Johnny Smith made a slow visual sweep of the room.

Tom rocked the softly hiccuping Montana...anything to keep his hands busy so one of them didn't just take a notion to pop the cop upside the head. "No, she's not home," Tom responded. "Don't you think she'd be right here yelling at us, if she was?"

Johnny looked very sad. "I believe so."

Tom nodded. "So do I. And what do you mean...nothing's happened to Mrs. Alcott that *you* know of? How else could you have bad news about her—which, I expect, is what made Darcy pass out."

The man nodded slowly. "I see your point. But she passed out before I could finish. I was just going to tell her that I had bad news about her mother's wanting me to track down that cowboy who delivered Miz Alcott here's baby.''

Tom stilled. His gaze went to his white Stetson that the officer had to have moved himself from the couch to the coffee table. Montana suddenly flailed her tiny fists and tried to nuzzle Tom's neck. He switched her to a cradle hold on his arm. "What kind of bad news?"

"I haven't been able to find him. Is that your white truck outside?"

"Yes." Tom had nothing to hide. But still, he wanted to see what this bloodhound of a policeman might be able to surmise on his own...especially considering the suspect was standing right here in front of him, that is.

Johnny Smith again nodded, apparently digesting Tom's affirmative reply. Then he pointed to Tom's white Stetson. "That yours?"

"Yes." This was getting interesting. Thankfully, Montana chose that moment to find her fist, which she promptly stuffed into her mouth and began gnawing on. Into the blessed silence between them, Tom exhaled raggedly. "You think, Officer, that we could do all this interrogating after we get mother and daughter back together again? This baby's hungry."

The policeman jumped up. "Gotcha. I'll get some water for Darcy. Maybe that'll wake her up."

"Only if you throw it in her face. Otherwise, she'll choke. Maybe you ought to—'' Tom eyed the man. He was probably a good policeman, but he hadn't a clue when it came to females. Tom stepped over to Johnny and plopped Montana in his arms. "Here. Hold her."

Johnny drew in his breath and then held the baby

out from him, away from his now stained uniform shirt. "She's wet."

"I know. It just doesn't get any better than this, does it, Johnny? The only way this situation could be worse would be if—"

"*The great good Lord in heaven.* What's going on in here? What's wrong with Darcy? What did you two do?"

Tom turned with Johnny. Sure enough, the front door was open. And right there in the entryway stood Tom's definition of worse...Margie Alcott armed with a huge bag of diapers. Tom instantly pointed to Johnny. "He did it."

Narrow-eyed, Margie turned on the policeman. His eyes widened and his jowls waggled with his head-shaking denial. "I never did any such thing. All I did was come out here, like you asked me to—"

"Johnny Smith, don't you tell a lie right in front of me. I never asked you to come out here today, now did I?"

"No ma'am. But you did ask me to investigate that cowboy—"

"I did not." Every last one of Margie Alcott's feathers were ruffled. She shot a look at Tom, then despite her reddening cheeks, she continued with her tirade. "You quit your storytelling and get to the point, you hear me Johnny Smith? And you leave me out of this."

"Yes, ma'am. Well, I came out here, even though you didn't ask me to, just so I could tell you what you didn't ask me to find out. And instead, I find this here *stranger* with the baby—"

"Oh, that's enough. Quit your babbling. And Tom's no stranger." Margie tossed down the diapers and her oversize purse and made a beeline for the couch and her daughter. "In fact, he's the cowboy who delivered Montana Skye. Why, in my book he's practically that baby's daddy."

Johnny's eyes widened as he stared at Tom...who smiled and smugly waved howdy.

Margie lovingly ran her hand over Darcy's face. Then she turned to Johnny. "Now, hand me my grandbaby." He did. "Oh, for the love of—she is soaked through. And look at the poor tiny little thing, reduced to gnawing on her own fist." She turned to the two men. "Can't I be gone for more than an hour without you men—" Her gaze again lit upon her Sleeping Beauty of a daughter just lying there on the leather couch. "And what *is* wrong with my own child?"

Tom pointed again at Johnny. "He did that, too."

"I did not," was Johnny's instant denial.

"Johnny Smith, just what *did* you do? Don't make me call your mother."

As Johnny attempted to come up with an answer, all Tom could think was *Goodbye, Bachelor Number Three*. But in the next instant, he realized that Margie Alcott was now talking to him.

"—in the kitchen and wet a rag, Tom. Are you listening to me? Good. Go get a wet rag and wipe Darcy's face and neck with it. That ought to bring her around. I'll go change my sweet precious grandbaby's diaper. It's a good thing I bought more." On her way to the bedroom, Margie stopped her cooing at her granddaughter long enough to take Johnny Smith to task one last time. "You caused all this. So if Darcy doesn't come around in a minute or so, then you're going to be taking the lot of us—lights, siren and all— right to the hospital. You hear me?"

The big policeman turned his hat around and around in his hands. "Yes, ma'am. But do we have to tell my mother about this? I won't ever hear the end of it, if you do."

"Well, of course I have to, Walter John Smith. I don't keep any secrets from Freda. Your mother is my best friend. Or one of them, anyway." She started past him but stopped again. "And when I do talk to her, I need to have my story straight. So tell me again what it is you said you came out here for."

The man looked absolutely sheepish. "Well, I came out here to tell you that I...well, that I—" He suddenly pulled himself up to his full height and pointed the long arm of the law at Tom. "—that I found *him.*"

Feeling a little guilty, Tom decided to give the poor guy a break. "Like the man said, Margie, here I am." He met Johnny's rounded eyes. The officer's expression clearly related *Thank you, man.* Tom nodded to him and then turned to Mrs. Alcott. "It's true. He found me here, saved Darcy from hitting her head on the tiled floor, and even safely held a wet baby."

Apparently his words settled a few of Margie's feathers. "Well, I guess that's about all I could ask of him, then. Except *he* can go get that wet rag. Tom, you sit with Darcy. I think she's beginning to come around."

Tom nodded, started to move toward Darcy, but got skewered in place by Margie's next words. "And then, young man—" She narrowed her eyes at him. "—you and I are going to have a little talk, too."

8

HOLDING MONTANA in her arms, Darcy sat out back on the porch swing with Tom at dusk on Monday, the next evening. The Arizona sun hung low and heavy over the horizon and bathed the sky in reds, yellows, and pinks. Lengthening shadows fell across the desert. The cactus seemed so close and the mountains so far. It was a beautiful sight, one that warmed Darcy, one she never tired of—one she'd hungered for when she'd lived in Baltimore.

After a year of this vista, she wondered, how would she ever be able to give it up again? This moment, with just the three of them—a gentle wind blowing and Tom rocking them slowly back and forth—had to be the dictionary definition of contentment.

Darcy smiled as she looked down at Montana. Covered lightly by a cotton swaddling blanket, the baby blinked and sighed and looked the world over as her tiny fists flailed in the air. A surge of pure love for the little girl who'd changed her life rushed through Darcy.

"She looks just like her mama, doesn't she?"

Warmed by his sentiment, by his very nearness, but feeling very undesirable in an old pair of "fat" pants, a.k.a. loose shorts with an elastic waistband, and a V-necked pink T-shirt, Darcy darted a glance Tom's way, saw that wide grin of his that she could drown in, and then focused on Montana. "Yes. Poor kid."

"Poor kid? Hardly." Tom suddenly shifted his weight on the seat, inadvertently causing the swing to sway crazily. "Oops. Hold on."

Darcy did—and found herself hugged up tightly against Tom's side. She felt unnerved and giddy in the same breath. But once he corrected the swing's motion, Darcy immediately started talking, mainly to cover her own self-consciousness. "So. There's just one thing I still don't understand about yesterday afternoon."

"Only one?" Tom stretched, pushing his booted foot against the ground…this time stopping the swing from moving altogether. "I can think of about ten things I still don't get." He relaxed. The swing took up its swaying motion again…and Tom winked at her. "I just hope you're not one of them."

Darcy stared at him. He did? He hoped he…*got* her? In what sense? She just didn't know. And she wasn't sure if she wanted to know. But with him all but molded to her right side, an arm flung loosely around her shoulders and resting more against her flesh than the wooden swing's back, Darcy could feel the heat of his body tempting her, drawing her in… Hatless now, his black hair gleamed in the day's waning light. The wordless moments ticked by.

But just then, Montana yawned so wide she made a squeaky noise. This gave Tom and Darcy the perfect opportunity to make a fuss of the baby and to chuckle over her innocent antics. Then, with the tension broken, Darcy felt more comfortable broaching the subject uppermost on her mind. "So, Tom, tell me why you're staying with us now. And don't make me have to fight to get a straight answer from you. You and your 'strong silent type' ways. I think you've been watching too many Westerns.''

He grinned. "You think I'm the strong silent type?''

Darcy's embarrassment mounted. "That is so *not* the question, Tom Elliott. Now quit trying to put me off.'' With her cheeks heating up, Darcy looked out over the desert. It was easier than facing him...especially since his face was about three inches from her own right now. "All I know was last night, once I came to—'' Now she looked up at him. "—by the way, I will never forgive Johnny Smith for scaring me like that.''

Tom shook his head. "I won't, either. But we need to ease up on the poor guy. He has more women problems than anyone I've ever known.''

Darcy frowned her disbelief. "Johnny? Women problems? Those are two words I never expected to find in the same sentence with his name.''

"It's true, though. His mother. Your mother. You. Women problems.''

"How am I a problem for him? I mean, my mother and his own I get.''

Tom chuckled. "Well, that makes one of us, then.''

And once again, he hadn't answered her question. That was so like him. And then it occurred to Darcy that in only a few short days, she knew Tom well enough to draw a conclusion on what was typical behavior for him. Now, wasn't that interesting? And disconcerting....

"Well, anyway,'' she said, deciding to get the conversation back on track and away from where her thoughts had wandered, "last night I went back to the bedroom to nurse Montana and when I came out, you were gone. Then a little over two hours later, you were back and all checked out of your hotel. And you're still here. Now how did *that* happen? And please be specific."

"Yes, ma'am." Tom laughed at her...in a good-natured way, one that surprisingly didn't make her feel defensive. "But you'd think you'd have asked me that before now. After all, I've been here a whole day." His voice, to Darcy, sounded lazy and content, like some big...well, Tom-cat completely satisfied with himself.

"I beg to differ. Your belongings have been here. But you haven't." She left it at that, a pregnant silence, hoping to get him to volunteer more information than she'd been able to drag out of him so far.

"Well, that's true enough. I had that business in Phoenix to see to."

Bingo. "Taking care of that land deal and the trust-fund thing, right?"

"Yep. Had to do some legal wrangling. But it's all taken care of now. You happy about that?"

"Yes, I am." She *was* happy, wasn't she?

Tom searched her expression. "You sure?"

Darcy pulled back some. "Of course I'm sure. Why wouldn't I be sure—or happy? I am happy. It's what I wanted."

He nodded...slowly, thoughtfully. "Was it?"

Darcy firmed her lips. "I just said it was."

Tom raised a placating hand. "All right. Good. It's done."

"Then, fine. It must have been quite the paperwork battle because you were gone most of the day." The words were out before she could stop them. He'd know that she'd missed him. And her voice...could it have sounded more pouty? Clearing her throat, she tried for a more normal tone of voice. "Anyway, Tom, how come you decided to stay here?"

"Two words. Your mother."

Darcy chuckled. "Who didn't know that."

"I hear you. But your mama said—" He took a deep breath. "—if she couldn't even be gone to the store for an hour and leave you and the baby here by yourselves without a couple of good-for-nothing men—and those were her words, believe me—making you pass out and leaving the baby in a wet diaper and screaming for her supper, then by golly, I could just plant my butt out here and help watch over things before the place was run over with tomcats on the prowl." He exhaled loudly. "There. Whew."

Darcy stared at him. "My mother said that— about…dear God…tomcats on the prowl?" He nodded. Darcy wanted to die. "I am personally going to kill her."

"Well, don't do it on my watch. I don't want her mad at me."

Darcy pulled back and just looked at him—a great big muscled cowboy of about six feet and two hundred pounds. "Are you afraid of my tiny slip of a mother?"

Tom frowned. "I certainly am. Aren't you?"

Darcy made a scoffing sound. "Well, of course I am. Everyone is. Even Johnny Smith is—and he's armed."

"Ah. Johnny." For some reason, Tom grinned…and Darcy melted. This was so *not* good, his effect on her. "Bachelor Number Three."

Darcy pulled back. "Bachelor Number Three? Johnny?" Her frown deepened as she adjusted the baby more comfortably in her arms. "Oh, no. You think so?"

"Yep. I do. Women problems, like I said earlier."

Darcy again searched Tom's grinning face and narrowed her eyes. "The idea of a parade of Buckeye's finest bachelors really amuses you, doesn't it?"

His blue eyes danced. "I have to say it does. Personally, I think Johnny's a better prospect than that other one. What's his name?"

"Vernon," Darcy supplied.

"Oh, yeah. Vernon." Another chuckle, but no further comment.

Darcy desperately wanted to ask Tom if he considered himself a prospect. But she didn't because, for one thing, it would sound...well, desperate. And for another, she didn't want a man in her life, right? *Right.* So why did she have to meet Tom now? Why did he have to be the one to stop and deliver Montana? It just wasn't fair. He was so handsome. And warm and caring. And funny. *And sexy.*

"*So*, Tom—" She denied that his nearness unhinged her. "So, Tom," she said again, barely able to make eye contact with him. "You never did answer my question yesterday."

He pulled back a bit. "You'll have to be more specific. I've slept since then."

And, boy, was she aware of that...that he'd slept in the guest bedroom next to hers. What was she going to do if he stayed much longer? She'd be completely ga-ga over him by then. And that was another thing. Where were all those new mother hormones when she needed them? The ones where a woman didn't feel sexual attraction for a man? The ones that made her focus exclusively on her child? Not that she'd ignored

Montana for even a second. She hadn't. No, she just hadn't expected to be interested in men—any men. But once again, Tom proved her wrong. *Great.*

She shook her head, trying to remember what she was going to ask him, when the sliding glass door behind them opened. That could only be one person. Sure enough, Margie Alcott sang out, "Yoo-hoo! I came to get the baby and change her diaper."

"She's dry, Mother," Darcy called over her shoulder.

Her mother came out on the porch and put her hands on her hips. Then she dramatically nodded her head in Tom's direction. As if he weren't sitting right there and couldn't see the broad hint Margie was giving her daughter. Darcy couldn't resist. "What does that mean, Mom? That head-shake thing?"

Margie patted at her gray hair and did her best to look nonchalant. "It doesn't mean a thing, Darcy Jean Alcott." Then she reached in and scooped the startled baby up from Darcy's arms. "Did you nurse her?"

Tom made a strangled noise and Darcy's face flamed. "Yes, Mom. Right out here in front of Tom. Of course I did."

Cuddling her tiny granddaughter, Margie gave Darcy the look that said "Mind your manners, young lady." "I meant before you came out here. So don't you be peevish like that. Now, you two can sit out here and bake all night if you want to. But I'm going to take this child in before she gets sunburned."

"Sunburned?" Stung—did her mother really think she'd let her daughter get sunburned?—Darcy pivoted on the seat to see Margie's retreating figure. "I only brought her out ten minutes ago. The sun was already going down, and I had the blanket over her—"

"Darcy?" Tom put his hand on her bare arm.

She turned. "I wouldn't let her get sunburned, Tom."

"I know that. And so does she. She's just being a grandmother."

"A grandmother? I'll never know how my having a baby made my mother grand." Darcy slumped in the swing. Behind her, the patio doors slid closed. Darcy shook her head, and felt close to tears. "I swear, Tom, I can't seem to do anything right with that child."

"I think you can, Darcy. I think—"

"—even Mom's friends came out today and were telling me their horror stories. Freda even asked me if I'd remembered to feed Montana." Darcy's expression intensified. "To *feed* her, Tom—"

"And you had, right? You'd fed her?"

She nodded, and continued with her rantings, not really internalizing Tom's supportive words. "They were saying awful things—like I wasn't to poke my finger into the soft spot on top of Montana's head or her brain would leak out." Horrified, Darcy covered her face with her hands and spoke through her fingers. "Dear God, now I'm worried that I might just accidentally do it." She lowered her hands and let Tom see her bereft expression. "Look at me. I'm afraid I'll drop her or forget to feed her or change her. I might even forget where I put her—"

"No, you won't, Darcy."

"But I could—"

"But you *won't*, Darcy." He pivoted and captured her arms, forcing her to look at him. "Have you heard one thing I've said? You won't forget to do anything you need to do for Montana. You won't. Because you're a good mother, and you love your baby. And that's all there is to it. The rest of it will follow with experience."

Darcy wanted to believe him. She really did. "You promise?"

He nodded. "Yes. Sam told me she had the same fears with her first baby. And I expect your mother and all those other ladies felt the same way about themselves with their kids when they came along."

Darcy thought about that. "Well, that's true. Mom did say something like that the other day. And Jeanette—one of Mom's friends, you met her the other day—never had children. So what does she know?"

"Well, maybe a lot. You pick things up along the way—"

Darcy's expression fell.

Tom changed course in midsentence. "—but you're right. What does she know? If you can't rope a calf, you shouldn't go around telling those folks who're trying to learn how they should be doing it, right?"

On board with this idea, Darcy blurted, "Right." Then she frowned. "What?"

"I don't know," Tom assured her. "But it sure sounded good—and that's what I want you to realize, Darcy. You'll be a good mother. You'll make mistakes, I'm sure. But your heart is in the right place. I believe in you, Darcy."

And that was when Darcy finally heard him. Instantly, her heart filled with emotion. She stared at him, memorizing his features. He believed in her. He really did. He thought she could do this. Before she could put her emotional guard up, she said what she was thinking. "Has anyone ever told you what a great guy you are, Tom Elliott?"

Tom looked embarrassed and released her arms. "Not lately."

Still feeling the impression of his touch on her bare skin, Darcy turned in the swing. "Well, you are. You've made me feel much better." She looked over at him now and smiled her thanks.

Tom nonchalantly put his arm around her shoulders again, this time, gently rubbing her upper arm in an intimate gesture that had Darcy's skin tingling. "Well, good," he said. "Then my work here is done."

Darcy's breath caught. She didn't like the final tone of his last words. Stretching her bare legs out, she pretended to contemplate her sandals. "So. Your work here is done, huh? Does that mean it's 'Heigh-ho, Silver, and away'?"

"Heigh-ho, Silver, and—? Oh, I get it. The Lone Ranger." He chuckled. "No. Not *all* my good deeds here are done. Still got a few to attend to."

Darcy exhaled the breath she hadn't realized she'd been holding. "Oh. Well…good. Like what?"

"Oh, like all the things out here that your mama wants me to see to. As long as I'm here anyway, she says."

Darcy stared at him. "Great. My mother's made you her ranch hand. I told you she was a piece of work."

"That you did. And yet I didn't run, did I?"

His expression was so intense, so full of unspoken emotion that Darcy had to look away. She swallowed. What was he leading up to here? "No," she said quietly. "You didn't. But you don't strike me as a man who would run."

He nodded. "That's good to know."

Darcy shot him a shy glance. "You should have run, though. A smart man would have."

"Well, I never have been accused of being too smart."

"I'll bet you have."

He shrugged. "Maybe once or twice. Not enough for me to believe it."

After that, the moments stretched out silently. The sun continued to sink beyond the horizon. The evening sky darkened and cast its shadows. The gentle breeze stilled. All around her, Darcy felt warmth and contentment. She wondered—and worried—about what degree these good feelings welling up inside her were a result of the nearness of the man who sat so quietly to her right. She looked over at him.

He was staring at her. Or contemplating her profile was more like it. When Darcy caught his attention, he didn't look away. She saw the yearning in his eyes and had to look down. Drawing circles on the porch, with her sandaled toe, Darcy said, "Why are you looking at me like that?"

"Like what?"

She met his gaze. "Like you..." Words failed her. She took a breath and started over. "Like you...I don't know...like you care." Hearing herself, she sat up straighter. "That sounded like I was in junior-high school again, didn't it? Almost as bad as passing a note in class that says—"

"Check here if you like me?"

Darcy grinned. "I see you've gotten one of those."

"Gotten and sent."

"Really? I wouldn't have figured you for a sender."

"No? Hmm. I need to work on that."

"On what? Showing your feelings?"

"My feelings? Is that what you meant?"

"Yeah. What'd you mean?"

"I meant my note-passing skill."

"You did not."

"Did, too."

Darcy fought a smile. He was so charming. And funny. Quiet. Intense. Confident. Steady. Strong. Intelligent. Handsome. A girl could really fall hard for him. *Whoa!* "So, Tom," she blurted, desperate for anything to say. "What do you think my mother's up to now?"

Surprising the life out of Darcy, Tom leaned over until he could whisper in her ear. "I think she came to get the baby purely as an excuse to let us be alone out here." Having said that…and having caused goose bumps to break out on Darcy's flesh…he started to pull back.

But Darcy surprised him—and herself—by stopping him. She put a hand to his clean-shaven cheek, encountering warm, taut skin and a strong jaw. Then locking his gaze with hers as they both acknowledged the moment, she captured his lips and put everything she had into kissing him.

It was the middle of the night. Tom lay awake, his hands clasped behind his head, listening to the muted sounds coming through the wall. Darcy was up again with Montana. The baby's mewling little cries and Darcy's crooning brought a tender smile to Tom's face. He shifted until he could see the digital clock beside the bed. Three forty-five a.m. They'd last been awake at midnight. "Whew. Poor kid," he muttered, thinking of Darcy. She'd be exhausted tomorrow. Well, later on today, was more like it.

Unable to stop himself, Tom threw the covers back and got out of bed. He reached for his jeans and pulled them on, working the button fly until it was closed. Then he shrugged into a white T-shirt and, barefoot, quietly crossed the room and opened the door. Only then, when he stood on the room's threshold did he hesitate and question himself. He had to admit that he had no idea what he thought he was doing or even why.

All he knew was…he wanted to see Darcy. In the middle of the night. With her child. As if they were his family. He felt so outside their world, so isolated from them. And after Darcy's kiss this evening, he couldn't stand that. She'd burned him with her touch. He'd known she would, as sure as if she'd branded him. She made him, for the first time in his adult life, want to belong. To be a part of a family. One of his own.

Of course he was a part of Sam's family. She was his sister, after all. But she and Luke and their kids lived across the state from him. He didn't see them that much. Until now, the few times a year he saw Sam and her brood—his only remaining family—had been enough. But no longer. Now he wanted more.

Like hell, Elliott. You don't just want more. You want Darcy.

"Yes, I do," Tom whispered into the darkness. "I want Darcy." He didn't let it get any farther than that in his mind. Because if he did, he knew reason would set in. And right now, in the middle of the night, with his body still burning from her kiss, from her touch, and craving just the sight of her, the last thing Tom intended to listen to was reason. He knew what it would tell him—the reason she'd as much as jumped up and fled after kissing him was because she'd regretted it. It had been a whim, or she'd been taken by the moment. And that was all.

Like hell, it was. He rounded the corner into the hallway and took the few steps he needed to put him in the opened doorway of the room Darcy shared with her daughter. And there they were. Tom's breath caught, his knees felt weak. He leaned against the doorjamb and crossed his arms over his chest. He felt as if someone had punched him in the gut, so powerful was the emotional impact of the scene before him. Darcy hadn't seen him yet, but she would at any moment. All she had to do was look up...look up from nursing her daughter.

Tom had never seen such an intensely satisfying sight before. But this moment, one he knew he had no right to witness, was incredibly beautiful. There Darcy sat, in a padded rocking chair, bathed in the muted golden light of a bedside lamp. She gently rocked the chair as she held her daughter to her breast and sang softly to her. Darcy's black hair tumbled around her pale face and fell against her long white nightgown. Tom knew right then he'd never forget this sight as long as he lived. Never.

Darcy looked up. The song died on her lips. Her expression sobered. Tom jerked upright, away from the wall. "I'm sorry—"

Darcy shushed him, a finger to her lips. She then pointed to Montana and mouthed *She's asleep.* Feeling foolish already, Tom started backing up, his hands held out as if to again say he was sorry. But to his surprise, Darcy motioned him into the room. Tom stopped...and then mouthed back *You sure?* She smiled and nodded, again waving him in. Tom approached with reverence…and trepidation. He didn't know what to do. He knew what he wanted to do, but didn't know if he should. He wanted to hunker down on the floor next to Darcy's chair, and he wanted to watch her feed her child, a baby he felt in his heart was truly his own.

But in the end what he did was stand awkwardly next to Darcy and just stare down at the two of them. He smiled and put a hand out, only to withdraw it. Then he scratched his head.

"It's okay," Darcy whispered, taking his hand and tugging him down beside her. "Come see her."

Even as thrilled as he was by her invitation, Tom felt really awkward. He knew that in the daylight, Darcy wouldn't have allowed this familiarity. After all, her breast was exposed…except for the part that Montana still had a hold of. But here in the darkness, it was, as Darcy'd said, okay. Tom hunkered down, resting an arm along the rocker's arm. Every breath he took enveloped him in the scent of warm woman. Tom wasn't sure he could catch a breath, let alone a good deep one.

"She's beautiful," he finally whispered to Darcy, trapping her tender gaze with his own. His fingers ached to touch the baby, but he didn't want to wake her. More than that, he wanted to touch Darcy's cheek and tell her *she* was beautiful.

But Darcy had made herself plain about her current hurt feelings towards men. He didn't blame her. The last thing he needed to do, then, was to declare himself to her. Like a skittish foal, she'd shy away even further from him. Tom thought he was mature enough to understand that he shouldn't read too much into her kiss earlier or make too much of the tenderness of this moment right here. She had her moments of weakness—she was allowed them. Tom just wished he could be here for every one of them.

But the truth was, he wouldn't be. She'd rejected his trust fund. She'd almost rejected his offer of a name. She felt threatened by all the well-meaning advice on child rearing she'd received by her mother and her mother's friends. And she'd certainly already had a craw-full of Johnny Smith and Vernon Whatever-his-name-is trailing after her.

Tom didn't want to add his name to the notches on her belt. She didn't want him or anyone else. That much was obvious. So all he could do was soak up what he could of her and Montana...and then be on his way. As early as Wednesday. Less than two days from now.

9

BEHIND TOM, the door from the kitchen out into the garage opened and closed. "Did you get in touch with your foreman up there in Montana?"

Halfway up a ladder, Tom turned from putting the finishing touches on the automatic door opener he was installing. There stood Margie Alcott. "Yep. Thanks. He said things were going smooth, that they hardly missed me. He also said I should take my time here."

"Smart man." Dressed to the nines in a flowered blouse and stretchy-looking pants, with heavy gold jewelry dripping off her, Margie patted down her hair. "And did you tell him you would?"

A look...and a grin...passed between them. The old gal wanted him to hang around and court her daughter. "Well, I told him my time here pretty much depended on your hospitality."

Margie waved. "Don't fret yourself over that. We're pleased to have you here."

"Well, *you* are. I'm not so sure about your daughter, though."

"Now, Tom, you're not having second thoughts, are you?"

Tom frowned. "Some. I wouldn't want to force myself—"

"Oh, pooh. I'm the one who asked you to stay on here."

"Yes, ma'am, I know. And that's why I think I—"

"Quit thinking so much. Darcy's as thrilled as I am to have you here."

Tom raised an eyebrow. "You think she knows she's thrilled?"

"Of course she does. Well, she might. Maybe. Anyway, don't you worry about that. Now, tell me how upsetting it was to find out your place up in Montana can run just fine without you."

Tom realized Margie was purposely changing the subject on him, but he allowed it. After all, Darcy was the one he should talk to about how she felt having him around, not her mother. So he good-naturedly answered the question put to him. "Not disconcerting at all. I like to think my holdings can do that because of good management on my part."

Margie shrugged. "Maybe. Or maybe it's because a bunch of cattle just don't need constant supervising. After all, what have they got to do but stand out in the pasture and eat? It's not like they're passing laws, you know."

Tom chuckled. What a pistol she was. "Well, I can't argue with that, Margie." With a screwdriver gripped in his fist, he braced his hand against his thigh and looked her up and down. "You look mighty nice today. Where're you off to?"

She made a face. "Oh, I've got to go into the hospital for a bit. Some of those old setting hens have their britches in a wad."

Tom bit back his mirth. "Is that so? Over what?"

"Oh, over the schedule I made up of their hours. You know—to cover my absence since I'm needed here with Darcy and the baby for a few weeks. But I swear, if I—as the head volunteer—don't go straighten it out, they'll pluck the feathers right out of each other. And who wants to see that?''

"Well, not me, for one." A surge of friendly warmth for this older woman washed over him. "I don't know what they'd do without you, Margie."

She nodded soberly. "I've told Darcy the same thing." But then she became all business. "Well, after that, I've got the bridge club meeting at Barb's. And I need to buy Montana some more diapers. Oh, yeah— I made y'all some lunch, so that's taken care of. Right now, Darcy's bathing the baby. Well, as much as you can bathe one until that nasty navel thing falls off. Anyway, it's her first time to handle Montana's bath on her own, but I think she's ready. It'll do her good. And I'm not expecting any company, so it should be a quiet day out here. Don't you fuss none about supper, either. I expect to be back in time for that. Although, I think I'll just pick up some pizzas. Nobody'll probably feel much like cooking. And how about you? You need anything from town? Shaving cream or the like?''

Tom had been so caught up in nodding in time with her monologue that it took him a second to realize he'd been asked a question. "Oh. No. But thanks anyway." He was secretly glad that the Buckeye Bridge Beauties, as Darcy had told him they were called, weren't meeting here today. Because that was about the last thing Darcy needed—another dose of horror stories. "You go on and have a good time. I'll have this done in a bit. And when you get home—'' He turned to pat the motor casing he'd just mounted to the garage ceiling. "—you'll be in business."

Margie brimmed with happiness. "Well, won't that be great? I swear, neither me nor Darcy can get that heavy door up sometimes. It's just so nice to have a man around the house to do these things. You know, a frail widow like myself has to pay a man to come out and do these chores.''

Tom didn't think there was anything the least bit frail about Margie Alcott, but he wisely kept that observation to himself. ''Well, I don't mind earning my keep by helping out. Seems like there's plenty of work here to go around.''

''That's the truth.'' Then Margie Alcott stepped up closer to the ladder and her expression again sobered. ''I guess I ought to tell you, Tom, that I think Darcy is beginning to suspect the real reason you're out here. And I don't just mean in the garage, either.''

''Is that so? And what is it you think she suspects?''

A pure conspirator now, Margie looked over her shoulder at the house and then stepped up onto the first rung of the ladder. Tom found himself leaning down toward her. This had to be good. ''I think she suspects,'' Margie, whispered, ''that you're staying with us to make her…you know.''

Tom shook his head and whispered back, ''No, I don't know.''

Margie smacked at his denim-covered calf. ''Yes, you do. Don't make me say it.''

''Well, you're going to have to because I don't know what you mean.''

''Oh, Tom.'' She was clearly incensed with him. ''You know. Fall in love.''

Tom's eyebrows rose. ''Is that what I'm doing? I'm supposed to be trying to make Darcy fall in love with me?''

Margie stepped down off the ladder and frowned up at him. ''Well, you better be. Why else would I have you staying here, except to give you two time to get to know each other? But if *you* don't even know, then this is just awful, and my plan won't work."

Her plan? Sensing trouble—a whole lot of trouble—Tom came down the ladder and faced the tiny but formidable Margie Alcott. "And what plan is that?"

"Now you're talking." All smiles, Margie snatched up a clean rag from the workbench and held it out to him.

"Thanks." Tom took it and tossed the screwdriver back into the opened tool chest. Using the rag to wipe the grease off his hands, he then repeated, "And what plan is that?"

"The one where you and Darcy get married."

Tom's hands stilled. So did his breathing. "Me and Darcy? We get married...in your plan?"

"Well, of course. How many times do I have to tell you? That's the reason you're here—so you can be close to her. And so she can see that you're the man for her."

"Well, I am flattered. And I do have my own feelings about Darcy, which is why I agreed to stick around. But, now that I think about it, I don't think your daughter wants a man in her life right now."

Margie waved that away. "Oh, pooh. Of course she does. She just doesn't know it. Besides, everyone knows the cure for falling out of the saddle is to get back on the horse. You're a cowboy. You ought to know that."

Tom had no idea how to answer that. Or if there was even anything there to be answered.

But Margie again took up the slack. "Now, wait just a minute. You didn't really believe what I said the other evening about you staying out here for my sake, now did you?'' Margie pulled herself up to her full height...of about five feet two inches. ''You think I'm in the habit of taking in every stray cowboy that drives by? I'm not that kind of a woman.''

''Hold on. I never thought you were. But I don't think your daughter is, either. And no matter how I might feel about this situation—and by the way, you haven't even asked me how I feel.''

''I know how you feel. But go ahead...tell me. How do you feel?''

Feeling devilish, Tom frowned. ''I don't know.''

Margie gasped. ''You don't? You really don't?''

''Well, maybe I do.''

''Maybe you do...good? Or maybe you do...bad?''

Tom thought about that...and felt the butterflies start up in his stomach. There was no sense teasing Margie. He grinned down at her. ''Good.''

Excited again, Margie gripped his hand. ''Oh, Tom, I'm so—''

''Hold on, again.'' Tom covered her hand with his. ''As I was saying, I suspect your daughter might have something to say about your plan, don't you think?''

Margie instantly retrieved her hand and waved it at him. ''I don't have to *think*. I know. Just like I knew with you the first time I saw you.''

''Now, Margie, how can you know? Maybe you can guess—''

''No, that's not what I mean. I mean...*I know* what she thinks. Because I just asked her...after I told her.''

Tom's insides chilled. ''Told her what?''

Margie looked everywhere but at him. ''My plan. Well, I said it was your plan, too. Otherwise, she might not go along with it so readily. Or at all.''

Frozen in place, Tom stared at the sweetly insane

woman in front of him. "Look at me, Margie." She did, her brown eyes wide and guileless. Tom wasn't the least bit fooled. "You told Darcy…that I'm staying here at your place?—" Margie nodded. "—in the hopes of…making her fall in love with me?" She kept nodding. "So we can get married?" Another nod…and a beatific smile. "And you told her I'm in on this plan of yours?"

"Well, of course, I did. Because you *are* in on the plan. Honey, you're the other half of it."

"Oh, hell." He meant that. He stared at the closed door of the house—and then down at Margie the Destroyer. Only then did he take note of the big fabric purse and the car keys she'd pulled out of it. "Oh, no. You're not leaving *me* here with her."

"Why, I sure am." Margie Alcott grinned and stepped around him. "You two need to chat…son."

Son? Tom pivoted to see her retreat. "Wait a minute, Margie. What did she say when you told her about this plan of…ours?"

Margie rattled her car keys over her head. "She said plenty. Go ask her."

Ask her? Son of a gun. Tom ran a hand over his mouth. *Speaking of guns…* he called after Margie, "Well, at least tell me this—is she armed?"

INSIDE, ALREADY dressed herself and just stepping out of the private bath attached to her bedroom, Darcy was armed with her freshly bathed daughter. The infant's damp and curling dark hair stood straight up…*like baby-monkey fuzz,* Darcy decided, her heart swelling with love for her tiny, helpless child. For her part, Montana stared wide-eyed at the world. No doubt, she was just glad to see it. Obviously, that whole notion of a sponge bath—with only her nervous mother in attendance and not Grandma's steadying hand there for help—had given her a lot to think about.

Crossing her bedroom, making for the twin bed where she'd already lain out everything she'd need to dress Montana, Darcy looked over to see Tom, uncustomarily dusty and greasy, already standing in the opened doorway to her bedroom. Her heart jumped over itself...and pitter-pattered sadly, given what her mother'd told her only a bit ago about his plans—that he was leaving tomorrow, that he'd confessed to Margie that he had a girlfriend up in Billings and needed to get home. Darcy somehow managed to keep all that off her face as she said, "Hi. You startled me."

"I'm sorry. I didn't mean to."

His words were a slow drawl that skittered over Darcy's flesh. Somehow, there seemed to be so much more packed into his simple words than what he actually said. With their every exchange, she felt more and more aware of the undercurrent of want and need between them, one that tugged her relentlessly in his direction. She'd thought that he felt it, too. But she supposed now that she'd been wrong.

Forcing her gaze away from his blue eyes, she took in his appearance. "It's a little different to see you like this. You're always so neat."

A frown crossed his face. "I am?"

"You are. At least, all the times I've seen you."

He nodded, thoughtfully. "Yeah, I guess that's true enough. Back home, I'm usually a lot dirtier than this."

Back home. Where you'll be headed tomorrow. To that woman. Darcy couldn't even call him a two-timer, since she didn't have, or want, a relationship with him.

But she could call him a liar—he'd told her he had no one back home. Darcy's chin came up defensively...jealously. "I can see that. I guess you don't have to dress up for cattle...or for anyone else."

He shrugged, his gaze never leaving her face. "That's true enough."

Darcy found, despite everything she'd just learned, she couldn't look away from him, couldn't stop wanting him. "So," she said, for the sake of the conversation, "what does Mother have you doing?"

Silence met her question...silence and a serious stare packing a huge undercurrent. "You mean just now? Or in the larger sense?"

"Well, just now, I suppose. I didn't know there *was* a larger sense."

"Okay. I just installed an automatic garage-door opener." He leaned against the doorjamb, crossing his arms over his chest.

"Oh, good. Thank you. We need one."

"That's what your mama said. I'm happy to oblige."

*Are you?...*Darcy wanted to yell. *You make me care, when I never wanted to, and then you up and leave—for another woman you said you didn't have? You call that obliging?* Hurting inside, but denying it, and still somehow maintaining an air of outward calm, Darcy gently laid her daughter on the twin bed, again marked Tom's steady stare, and swiped at her nose. "What? Is there something on my nose?"

Tom shook his head. "No. There's nothing on your nose. You're fine."

"Oh, I am, huh?" Darcy wouldn't even look at him as she tucked her long hair behind her ears and then unwrapped the towel from around her baby. *I'm so fine that you can't wait to leave tomorrow. You give up your hotel room, come out here and sleep one room away from me. You're here morning, noon, and night—for two days. I'm just starting to really care about you, and then you leave for another woman—after installing a garage-door opener. Fine.* She leaned over Montana, quickly and gently diapering her daughter before the baby caught a chill. "That's one man's opinion, I suppose. About my being fine, that is."

"It's probably all men's opinions, where you're concerned."

Darcy made a scoffing sound. "I hardly think so."

"I don't."

Fighting for calm—she didn't want to communicate her agitation to the baby and make her cry—Darcy did the simplest thing she could. She remained quiet, essentially ignoring Tom as she dressed Montana in a clean infant gown and then wrapped her in a cotton receiving blanket. Only then, when she could pick her baby up again and settle her in her arms, did she turn to him. He'd remained as silent as she had. "Tom, is there something specific on your mind?"

He pulled away from the jamb. "I'm sorry. Am I keeping you from doing something?"

"No, I didn't mean that. I just…well, it's the way you're looking at me. As if you have something to say that you don't want to. Or as if you're waiting for *me* to say something you don't want to hear. I don't know which." Well, there. She'd brought it up. Now he could say *I have to get a shower and pack because I'm leaving tomorrow—after driving into your life and delivering your child and then giving her my name and setting her up a trust fund that leaves you both fabu-*

lously wealthy—or did for a few days since you said you didn't want it and so I changed it. And oh, by the way, I really do have a woman up in Montana. He could say all that.

But he didn't. He didn't say a thing. Darcy exhaled and, without looking away from him, put Montana to her shoulder and kissed her daughter's sweet-smelling little head. "Well?"

"I don't blame you for being mad, Darcy. You have every right to be."

Darcy froze. Did he know that her mother had told Darcy the truth? That had to be it. Darcy swallowed the gathering emotion in her throat and told herself she was being ridiculous. It wasn't as if she loved the man. "Mad? Why would I be mad? You don't owe me anything."

"I didn't think I did, either. I never looked at it as owing you anything."

Well, that hurt. "Well then, good." Darcy struggled not to show a thing on her face as she cradled Montana and stared at Tom...and waited.

After a moment, he said, "I thought you'd have something more to say to me."

"You did? Like what?"

"That's just it. I don't know."

Darcy quirked her mouth. "Boy, we're getting nowhere fast. I'll give you a clue, if you'll give me one."

Tom ran a hand through his hair. "All right. Your mother."

Darcy rolled her eyes. "Great. I already said I was clueless. And now you want me to figure out what she's up to?"

"No. I guess I'm just waiting for your reaction to

her telling you about her grand plan for the two of us.''

That stopped her. ''The two of us? You and her? Or me and you? And what grand plan?''

Tom stared at her. ''You don't know, do you?''

She shook her head. ''I don't.''

''I'll be damned. Darcy, are you saying your mother didn't come in here this morning, while I was out working in the garage, and tell you that she—?'' He ran a hand through his hair again. ''I'll be damned, Darcy. She didn't tell you anything, did she?''

''Oh, she told me a lot.'' Pride kicked in and Darcy raised her chin. ''About the woman you love up in Billings.''

Tom looked stunned. ''What? A woman up in Billings? And I'm supposed to love her?''

Her eyes widening, Darcy's heart thudded dully in her chest. ''You don't?''

Now Tom chuckled. ''Hell, no. I don't know her, so how can I love her?''

''Well, that would make it hard.''

''I can't believe your mother told you that. That little stinker. She set us both up. She thought I'd come in here and spill my guts and that you'd be jealous and—'' He stopped. ''You *were,* weren't you?''

Darcy's mouth dried. She licked at her lips. ''I was what?''

''Jealous…when you thought I had a woman up in Billings.''

Darcy looked everywhere but at him…. ''First tell me what you were supposed to come in here and spill your guts about to me.''

He crossed his arms over his chest. ''I don't think so. You first.''

Darcy's gaze met Tom's…and held. She wanted so much to tell him— *Tell him what exactly, Darcy? That you think you might care about him, but you don't know, so could he stick around until you make up your mind sometime in the next several months?* Oh, this was so silly. They were all adults here. Except for Montana. "Just tell me this much…are you leaving tomorrow?"

He shrugged. "Do you want me to?"

Darcy exhaled. Confession time. And time to test her convictions. If she said no…then she had to admit, even to herself, that she cared. If she said yes…well, darn it, he'd leave. And just thinking about how she'd feel if he was gone told her everything she needed to know. Well, that made it simple, then, didn't it? Darcy slumped and, exposing her vulnerability, whispered, "I don't want you to leave, Tom. I wish I did. But I don't."

Tom's silence again met her words. Darcy was almost afraid to look up. She hadn't exactly given him a ringing endorsement. Finally, she chanced a glance at him. "Well?"

"You wish you did but you don't? What does that mean?"

Darcy exhaled, glanced down at Montana, and saw she was asleep. "Let me lay her down first and then we'll talk, okay?"

"All right. I'll get a quick shower and meet you in the living room."

Darcy nodded her agreement, started to turn away, but suddenly pivoted back to face Tom. He hadn't moved. He'd been watching her. Before she could lose her nerve, Darcy blurted out her feelings. "I really am glad you're here." He smiled. She rushed on. "And I really don't want you to leave. Well, tomorrow anyway. I mean, I guess you'll have to leave sometime, won't you?''

His blue eyes bored into hers. "Yeah. Sometime. Sometime soon.''

10

DARCY WONDERED if she was worrying too much about her much-needed talk with Tom. Talk? It felt more like *Gunfight at the OK Corral.* A real showdown. And, boy, was her stomach full of butterflies to prove it. Still, never one to relish confrontations, Darcy gave Tom plenty of time to shower and change.

In the meantime, she had all she could do to keep her hands occupied. Because they itched to get into the bathroom where Tom was...all naked, wet, and gorgeous. They wanted nothing more than to show him exactly how jealous she'd been of that other woman. Darcy rolled her eyes at herself. Obviously single-motherhood hadn't taught her anything. And so, she poured her frustrated energies into cleaning her own bathroom, into gathering the laundry together, and then into brushing her hair and inspecting her face in front of the mirror over the sink.

She looked from side to side at her reflection and ran her fingers over her cheeks. No makeup. *Great.* Should she put some on? She decided that would be too obvious. He'd already seen her, so he'd know she'd fussed after the fact. Well, what about her clothes, then? She looked down at herself...at her mauve T-shirt and drawstring-waist shorts. Should she change? No. Again, he'd know.

Great. Fine. So, I'll just go tell this wonderful man

that I don't want him to step out of my life—all while looking like roadkill. Oh, well, if my appearance hasn't already sent him screaming down the driveway, then nothing will.

Giving up on herself, Darcy stepped away from the mirror and gathered the laundry left over from her own shower and from Montana's bath. But suddenly she stopped, belatedly realizing what she'd been thinking. She didn't want Tom to step out of her life? Since when? What happened to all that *I never want another man in my life again* stuff?

After all, she'd known Tom for less than a week. But he'd been there for practically every hour of that week and, yes, they'd met under some quick-bonding circumstances. So maybe she felt as if she knew him better than she probably did.

But still, those circumstances had tested and exposed his true colors, as well as her own. There was nothing like a crisis to bring out the best and the worst in people...her worst, his best. The situation had brought out more than personality traits. It had also produced her daughter. Literally. That thought brought Darcy back to the moment. With her arms full of damp towels and baby clothes, she slumped.

Montana. That's who she needed to concentrate on. Her daughter. And not some gorgeous stranger, who would be leaving one day soon. Darcy's thoughts turned cynical... *Didn't they all?* Yes. And that was the last thing she needed—another broken heart.

There. Everything was in perspective now. Suddenly, Darcy felt better. She squared her shoulders and marched through the house. She dumped her laundry, sorted it, put in a load...all while smiling at this new and reassuring conviction inside her regarding her pri-

orities in life. Moments later, she headed for the living
room and her appointment with Tom. She could handle this.

He came into the room, just as she rounded in from
the kitchen. He saw her at the exact moment she saw
him. She stopped cold, struck anew by the force of
her attraction to him. She knew what he was seeing—
an unkempt new mother with no makeup, ratty clothes,
and limp hair.

But she wondered if he had any idea how he looked
in his clean denims and a white Western-cut shirt, the
sleeves rolled up a turn or two. Darcy took in his black
and shining hair, his electric-blue eyes, his broad
shoulders, his muscled chest—and wanted to cry.

I was wrong. I can't handle this. He was the nicest
guy she'd ever met. He seemed to love Montana and
somehow to feel a genuine responsibility toward her
where none actually existed. All that, and to the tune
of several million dollars. Now, how endearing and
mind-boggling was that? *Extremely.* Darcy sighed, and
had to chuckle.

"What's so funny?" Tom asked her. "Is my shirt
buttoned wrong?"

"No. You look fine."

"Thanks." He advanced into the living room. "So
do you. As always."

"I do not." Darcy walked toward him. "But thanks,
anyway."

He sat on the leather couch situated in front of the
picture window. "You're welcome, anyway."

Darcy sat at the other end of the couch...about as
relaxed as she'd felt in high school when she'd been
called into the principal's office for questioning about
that suspicious orange-dye-in-the-school-fountain in-

cident. Her gaze skittered away from Tom's. "So. Tom."

"So. Darcy."

She glanced over at him. Saw him staring at her and waiting—for exactly what, she didn't know. "Could this be more awkward?"

Tom nodded. "Sure. We could both be naked."

A burst of laughter escaped Darcy. Embarrassed laughter. "It would only be fair. You've already seen me as close to naked as it gets. But not in a good way."

"That's true."

Thanks. Darcy shied away from the whole naked issue. "Well, how about this for awkward? The house could be on fire."

"Or your hair."

Her hand went to her hair. "It's not, is it?"

Tom looked her over. "Doesn't seem to be."

Finally relaxing some, Darcy decided that, this being her home, it pretty much made her the hostess for this little soiree. So again...she ought to say something first. "Can we do anything but skirt the issues here?"

"I don't look good in a skirt—don't ask me how I know—so I'll go first. Just tell me why you don't want me to leave tomorrow. Tell me why you don't want that trust fund in Montana's name. Tell me why you think you have to do everything yourself."

Then, suddenly, surprisingly, he leaned toward her and reached out, gently cupping her chin as he drew her nearer. Darcy's heart pounded, her breathing became ragged. Tom edged over...and he kissed her. With a tremendous amount of passion and caring. With a longing that had his arms around her and had Darcy melting into him and putting all her suppressed passion into returning the kiss. The feel of his mouth on hers, of his hands on her, just burned her.

Then he broke their kiss and pulled back. With his voice low and husky, he said, ''That was a pretty honest kiss, Darcy. Tell me you don't want me.''

Swallowing, Darcy could only stare at him. Finally, after a moment or two, she recovered and drew back, pulling away from his touch. ''This changes nothing, Tom. A kiss is just a kiss.''

''I think it's more than that. I saw your face in your bedroom when you thought I had another woman. You didn't like it one bit.''

Even trapped, Darcy wouldn't come clean. ''I was just confused.''.

''That wasn't confusion I saw.''

''Then what was it?''

''Hurt.''

Stung, her lips pinched together, Darcy inhaled deeply. Boy, he pulled no punches. Well, neither did she. ''Whatever. Tell me what Mom said she'd told me about you.''

''That I was here to make you fall in love with me and marry me.''

A brilliant heat suffused Darcy's cheeks. ''I see I'm going to have to kill my mother.''

Tom reached out again, this time taking Darcy's hand and holding it, squeezing it gently. ''No need. She's not completely wrong.''

''She's not? Completely?''

Tom shook his head. ''No. Look, Darcy, I know I shouldn't push you like I do. I just feel I have to. I never know when your mother will pop in and bring half the population of Buckeye with her. Or when Montana will wake up and need you. Or when the place will be overrun with long-in-the-tooth eligible bachelors.''

Darcy exhaled and looked at her hand in his. All but lost, it was. And that was just how she felt...unless Tom was close. "Well, I can't argue with you there. That's a pretty fair assessment of the past week."

"Yep. And since that's the case, can you try to give me what answers you can?"

Darcy's tummy churned. "I'll do my best," she said quietly. This was too important to rush. *Too important to rush?* So there was her answer. She looked over at Tom, who was now sitting back with one arm stretched out along the sofa's spine...and chickened out. "First you tell me why you feel you have the right to ask me for those answers."

"What right?" Tom's frowning expression told its own story. He sat forward on the couch and folded his hands together. "I don't suppose I have *any* rights here, Darcy. Not if you don't think so."

Darcy slumped, feeling terrible. *Could I be a bigger jerk?* "You know, Tom, this is silly." He looked over at her, his expression somber. "Seriously." Sudden conviction spurred her on. "It is. You have every right to ask. I mean that. All I need to do is look at Montana to know who you are and what you stand for. You're the only man in my life, except my father, who hasn't cut and run at the first sign of difficulty."

"That's not my way," he said quietly. "I wouldn't ever do that to you."

"I know," she answered, just as quietly. "And that's what is important to me—that I *know* you wouldn't do that." Really warming to her subject now, she turned slightly on the couch, resting a leg atop a leather cushion. "You've been *by* my side and *on* my side since the moment I met you. You've done nothing but be kind and offer reassurances—''

"I'm starting to get embarrassed."

"Well, just wait. I'm not through singing your praises."

His eyebrows rose. "You're going to sing?"

"I might. Anyway, you've done more than stand by me and say encouraging things, Tom. You've *done* things. Everything from bringing Montana into the world almost a week ago...to putting up that garage-door opener for my mother an hour ago. And in between, there've been flowers and visits and an offer of a trust fund and even your name—your *name,* Tom. I just don't know what to make of you."

His grin, a shy, endearing one, all but melted Darcy's bones. "Pretty terrific, aren't I?"

Darcy smiled back at him, thinking—maybe fearing—she loved this man already. After one week—it couldn't be love. It had to be muddled hormones. "Great. Now you're Tom Terrific. Had enough of being the Lone Ranger?"

Tom's expression turned serious. He crossed an ankle over his opposite knee. As always, he spoke slowly, with a drawl that gave the impression every word was well thought out. "Yes. Actually, I am tired of being the Lone Ranger, Darcy. I want more than what I have. And I don't mean money. See, for the last few years, since my father passed away, I'd about decided that my ranch and my solitary life up in Montana would be all I—''

"Solitary? Look at you. I would have thought there'd be women crawling all over you every time you stepped out of the house." The words were out of Darcy's mouth before she could stop them. Her face heated up again.

But Tom managed a grin. "Thank you. But it's not like that. I'm not in town much, and I don't go looking when I am. Still, I've known women, of course. Came close in my early twenties, right out of college, to getting married. But she didn't like the chances I took on the rodeo circuit. I can't blame her." Tom's blue eyes bored into Darcy's. "Guess she just wasn't the right one."

Darcy's breath caught. "I guess not." As the silence between them stretched out, she tried hard to think what it was he'd been saying before she'd interrupted him. Then it came to her. "So, your solitary life has lost some of its attraction for you."

"Yes. And it's because of you that I know that."

Darcy swallowed. "Me?"

"Yep. You've shown me there's more."

"I have? Define more."

Tom pulled back and stared at her. "Yes, professor. But I didn't realize this was going to be a test."

Darcy slumped, even though the giddy feeling in her belly notched upward. "I'm sorry. Go ahead." Then she looked at her watch. "But you'd better hurry. Montana could wake up at any moment. Or Mother could walk through that door—"

"And bring the entire town, a brass band, and a circus with elephants in with her, right?"

"Right. All that, and a preacher." She couldn't believe she'd said it. But outwardly, she played it cool. Especially since she didn't want a wedding. She'd already made her peace with living life on her own. When he didn't say anything, Darcy blurted out, "All right. My turn.'' She twisted her fingers together. ''I know how you feel about Montana—''

''I love Montana enough to give her my name.'' He was dead serious.

Darcy stilled. ''I know. But, you see, you came along at a time in my life when I'd already decided that I'd go it alone.''

''I see. But for me, you came along at a time in my life when I'd decided I didn't want to go it alone any longer.''

It sounded to Darcy that Tom was getting close to declaring himself. And that made her jumpy and edgy. Trying to lighten the moment, she said, ''So what you're saying is, you were looking for someone and there I was? Stranded on the side of the road and in labor?''

He smiled. ''Yep. All my life, that's exactly how I pictured it would happen.''

''I bet.'' She got quiet as she digested everything he'd essentially confessed...that he cared, that he'd been looking, that it was her he'd been looking for. Wasn't that what she was hearing? She thought so. So she decided to try again to make him understand where she was coming from. ''I'm happy for you, Tom, that you've decided to find someone. I really am. But me? I'm not good with relationships. I fall for the wrong guys. I get hurt. I hurt them.''

''I don't hurt easily. I went to college on a rodeo scholarship. Bull-riding.''

''Ouch. You are tough. But what I meant was—''

''That blackhearted son-of-a-gun who's Montana's biological father shook up your whole world and left you high and dry at a time in your life when you were at your most vulnerable. Now you're thinking you're better off alone. You're a modern woman, and you don't need all the heartache and the uncertainty that comes from a relationship with a man who's most likely from some other planet, anyway."

"Wow." Darcy slumped against the sofa's back. "You weren't kidding. You do read *Cosmo*."

"Told you. Winters are long up north. Come about mid-January, you find yourself reaching for anything to read."

"I'm impressed."

Tom quirked his head. "Is that so? Enough to *say* you care about me? Maybe enough to kiss *me* after you do?"

Darcy's throat went dry. She swallowed. She licked her lips. She inhaled. She exhaled. She ran out of things to do. "But we did just kiss."

"We did. At my instigation. And we're still just talking in circles here. I need you to say outright that you care about me, Darcy. Because I'm not hearing anything yet from you to keep me here. If you can't say it, for whatever reason, I'll leave tomorrow."

Darcy frowned. "Why is this all on me? What about you? I haven't heard the first word from you about…caring."

"Fair enough. I love you, Darcy. I want to make a life with you and Montana. Your turn."

She stared at him. Her mind whirled. She'd been through too much, she was still off balance, they were going too fast. She'd declared her independence too publicly too many times lately to just back down now—especially since she'd only known this man one week. This man who fired her senses, a man she respected. But if she took the plunge this quickly—again—what did it say about her? She was tired of the old Darcy. She wanted to be more thoughtful, more mature. She wanted time. "I need time."

"Either you know or you don't. Either you feel it or you don't."

This was unfair. "I've only known you a week, Tom."

"I've only known you a week, Darcy. Yet I know I love you."

"Well, I'm not you." Feeling trapped, Darcy began searching for excuses. "I have another person here to think of."

"So do I. I have two. You and Montana."

"No, get your own. Those are my two. Me and Montana."

"Okay. But I still need you to give me something, Darcy. Anything to keep me here."

Already in a state of elevated emotion, Darcy broke down. "I don't respond well to ultimatums."

Tom looked her in the eye. "You can't say it, can you?"

Darcy's chin came up. "I could. But I won't. Not until *I'm* ready."

Tom shifted his position on the sofa. "It sounds to me as if you're getting up on a high horse, Darcy."

"Oh, another warning? Right here in my own living room?"

"Your mother's living room."

That reminder didn't sit well, either. "Why, thank you. I'd forgotten that. Yes, this is my mother's house, isn't it? And you are *her* invited guest, aren't you? Point taken." She stood up. "Now, if you'll excuse me, I believe I hear *my* daughter crying."

Tom stood up, too. "Darcy, please. I didn't mean to upset you."

Darcy put a hand to her chest. "Upset? Me? I'm not upset. I just hear my daughter crying. Excuse me." She turned away and stalked toward the bedroom.

From behind her Tom called, "Will you wait a minute, please? She's not crying, Darcy. I don't hear a thing."

"Well, you will when I wake her up." Darcy was even with the entryway.

Just then the front door burst open.

In blew Margie Alcott, a huge bundle of plastic-bagged disposable diapers dangling from her hand. "Guess what was on sale? I just came back to drop them off before I— What's wrong, honey?"

"Nothing, Mother. But your plan didn't work. We know the truth."

"Well, where are you going?"

Over her shoulder, as she turned down the hallway, Darcy called out, "I'm not going anywhere. But Tom was just leaving."

THAT EVENING, once Margie was inside with two of her friends fussing over Montana—and fussing at him for letting the situation between him and Darcy go sour—Tom got his nerve up enough to go look for Darcy. He found her outside in the swing. At the first sight of her, his knees weakened and his heart fluttered. She was so damned beautiful, sitting there and reading a magazine.

Cosmopolitan. Point taken.

Tom almost went back inside and said to hell with it. But he didn't. He couldn't. It was already too late for him. And she knew it because he'd said it. Well, he'd give it one more chance. And then, if she still didn't care, he could leave knowing he'd tried everything. "Darcy?"

"What?" She didn't look up from the glossy pages. Tom bit back a sudden grin. She wasn't giving him an inch. No one had to tell him that Montana, in turn, with all this Alcott blood flowing through her veins, would be gorgeous and hell-on-wheels when she grew up. "I was wondering if you'd consent to take a ride with me."

Darcy turned a page and folded the magazine back. "You can stop wondering. Because I won't."

Tom exhaled. "I'd be pleased if you would. There's something I'd like to show you, something that's real special to me."

"Oh, really?" Her voice dripped with sarcasm. "Well, I've already seen one. Dozens, in fact. And if you ask me, they all look alike."

Tom squirmed uncomfortably. "What exactly are you talking about?"

Darcy finally looked up, crumpling her magazine and flopping it down on her lap. "Golf courses. Isn't that where you wanted to take me?"

"Well, yes, it is. But how'd you know?"

"Good guess. What did you think I was talking about?"

"Same thing." Relief coursed through Tom. "Golf courses."

Darcy eyed him suspiciously. "I'll bet."

Tom was seized by a sudden desire to grab her up and swing her around, hugging and kissing her silly. But he wisely didn't give in to that impulse. For one thing, she was still pretty delicate following the birth of her daughter. And for another, he remained convinced she'd claw his eyes out if he so much as tried.

But still, he couldn't get over the sight of her. Damn, she was pretty. She had on a white sundress and white sandals. Her long, dark hair shone like a halo around her face in the evening's light behind her.

But more than her looks attracted him. He respected her, her intellect, her education, her making her own way, and most especially, her commitment to her daughter…in a day and age when a woman had other choices. Even her loving tolerance of her mother's antics—not to mention the entire town's, endeared her to him. He wondered if she knew just what a treasure she was. If she didn't, maybe it was his job to tell her.

"You're staring. Was there something else you wanted, Tom?"

A loaded question, if he'd ever heard one. And it came at a time when he was almost at the end of his rope. He was tired of being a gentleman, of suppressing his less than lofty thoughts of her. His urges just seemed sacrilegious, with her being such a new mother, but tell that to his itchy hands and body. He couldn't resist allowing himself a suggestive grin…because there was something downright sexy about her, even with all this tension between them. Hell, he didn't even think she was really all that mad. Nor did he think she wanted him to leave. She just wanted convincing. Even her mother said so—and so did Jeanette and Freda.

"I see that grin, cowboy. Don't go there," she warned.

"All right. But it's not exactly a golf course yet. I want you to see the land."

"I'm sure it's nice. But I can't leave for that long. I have to be here for Montana."

"Your mama said you fed her just before you came

out here. And right now, Montana Skye has three little grandmothers inside with her. She'll be fine for a few hours.''

"Three? Who's here?"

"Mrs. Smith and Mrs. Tomlinson came by."

Darcy wrinkled her nose. "Great. Freda and Jeanette. Just what I need—more warnings about how I'm going to damage my child for life."

In the face of this common enemy—Tom had already had his fifteen minutes under the gun—he pressed his case. "They couldn't get to you if you weren't here. Ride with me out to the land. We'll be back before you know it."

Darcy squinted up at him. "I don't want to see the land. All I want is to see your luggage in the back of your pickup and your taillights as you drive off."

That did it. He'd been nice up to now, but no more. Tom walked around the swing and was about to sit down—right on Darcy's legs. At the last second, she pulled her feet up and, holding onto the swing's chain, righted herself. "What do you think you're doing?"

Tom braced his feet on the ground, too, effectively stopping the swing's motion. "I'm trying to get you to talk to me, Darcy. It's just plain silly for you to be behaving this way."

"You mean like a child? Is that what you're thinking?"

A retort rode Tom's lips, one that would most likely silence her. She probably deserved it, too. But he had another choice. "No. I was thinking how beautiful you are. And stubborn. And proud. And smart. And I was thinking how much I love and respect everything about you.''

Darcy just stared at him. Her chin trembled, her cheeks reddened and her eyes filled with tears. Then she burst out crying.

11

"Wow. This certainly is a beautiful piece of land, Tom. It sort of brings home that phrase 'as far as the eye can see.' No wonder the developers want to put a golf course here. Gorgeous." Standing off to the side of the highway that led to Phoenix, Darcy looked out on the open desert. The starkly beautiful vista, with its shifting sands and yellow dunes and saguaro cacti, was breathtaking, especially in the evening sun.

"Yeah. My grandfather loved this place. One of the stipulations of the deal I made is the developers have to name the course after him."

Her heart touched by his thoughtful ways, Darcy looked up at Tom. "That was nice."

Tom shrugged. "Seemed like the thing to do."

"I agree," she said quietly. "So what's his name? What will this place be called?"

"The Jack Randolph Elliott Golf Course."

"That's quite a mouthful. Probably over time, it'll come to be called Jack's Place, or something like that, don't you think?"

Tom chuckled. "I don't suppose that'd be so bad. Sounds homey. He'd like that. He had a way of making folks feel welcome."

He's not the only one, Darcy thought as she stared, transfixed, up at the tall, handsome man at her side. Right then she decided it was time to get some things straight between them. "Look, Tom, I'm sorry about my outburst at home. You said some really nice things. I just think my hormones are still amok."

To her surprise, Tom put his arm around her shoulders. "No need to be sorry, Darcy. I'm the one who should be saying that. It's not like I can't see you've got a lot on your plate right now. All I've done is add to your problems."

"I don't see it that way at all, Tom."

"It's true. I'm the one who should be apologizing."

"For what?" She didn't like his tone. It sounded like he was saying goodbye. That stopped her. Wasn't that what she wanted...for him to leave? For her and her baby to go back east to Baltimore, the two of them against the world? Yes, how brave and modern and challenging. And scary. And lonely. But she'd be damned if she'd make a commitment to Tom based on fear. It had to be for love, and nothing else. "You haven't done anything you need to apologize for."

"Yes, I have. I've got places I could be, things I could be doing. I sure as hell don't need to inflict myself on you at this delicate time in your life."

But I want you to inflict yourself on me. Further surprise. Was there something going on inside her that she wasn't in touch with—like her true feelings? Darcy began to look inside herself for the answer. "I hate feeling delicate. I'll be glad when I'm back to being my true self."

Tom's hand squeezed her sun-warmed flesh. "You mean this isn't the real you I'm talking to right now?"

He was teasing her. She liked that. "No. I'm usually stubborn and growling for a fight. I cry a lot and look terrible. Unlike now."

Tom laughed, and took her hand. A thrill raced over

Darcy's skin, sending electric sparks throughout her body. Only belatedly did she realize he was talking to her—and leading her somewhere.

"Come over here to this big rock and let me lift you up on it. I want you to get the full effect of the view, and I'll point out some things of interest."

Feeling her pregnant weight still hanging on to her body, Darcy pulled back. "I might be too heavy for you."

"Hell, Darcy, my right leg weighs more than you." And he proved it by easily swinging her up onto the rock's smoothly rounded top. "You okay? Did I make you dizzy?"

A loaded question. Darcy just shook her head. "No. I'm fine."

Tom reached up to put his arm protectively around her waist. Darcy's throat went dry…and it had nothing to do with the heat. Almost shyly, she rested her hand atop his shoulder…just for balance. "So. What did you want to show me?"

He pointed to the distant purple-hazed mountains as he described what she was seeing and what the developers intended to do. "There, to the right, behind that stand of saguaros—which they're to leave in place—will be the clubhouse. And over there, they intend to…"

He continued talking, but Darcy only listened with half an ear. Inside her, turmoil raged. He just completely upset her. Everything about him. His touch. His kindness. His intelligence. His calm steadiness when she needed it the most. It just wasn't fair. She didn't want a relationship right now. Her whole life was up in the air, and here he was, making things more of a mess for her. And stealing her heart.

She glanced at him as he spoke of sand traps and water hazards. So handsome. And intelligent. And kind and sexy and bedeviling and...gosh, how she loved him. Darcy would have fallen off the rock she was standing on if his arm hadn't still been around her. *I love him?* Swept away with a sudden giddiness, Darcy turned to Tom. "Kiss me, Tom."

"And over there, I—what did you say?"

"Kiss me."

"Right here, right now? You want me to kiss you?"

"Yes. It's not negotiable. Kiss me."

"Why?"

"You don't want to?"

"Hell, yes, I want to."

"Then what are you waiting for?"

His blue eyes narrowed. "Why *now*, Darcy? Why not earlier when I wanted you to kiss me?"

Darcy wondered if it had taken this much dickering to come up with the settlement terms that ended World War II. His reaction depressed her. Maybe she was wrong. Maybe she didn't feel love. She thought she'd loved Hank, too—which made her track record in not recognizing it perfect. "Never mind."

Tom reached up and swung her down from the rock, but he didn't release her once she stood firmly on the ground. Still clinging to him, Darcy stared up at him. He shook his head. "I don't want to never mind. Because this is the talk we've needed to have for days. And I aim to have it now. Why do you think I brought you out here?"

Darcy shrugged.

"To get you away from your home and all the demands on your attention there. So we could be truly alone and talk. And so you couldn't walk away from me.''

"I see. Silly me. I thought it was to get a little fresh air.'' She sounded calm enough. But inside she was feeling vulnerable...and was shaking with trepidation over how this talk would end. It would either be good or bad—and she still hadn't defined for herself which was good and which was bad. Tom staying. Or Tom leaving.

"What's going on inside you, Darcy? Right now. This minute. What're you thinking about? I've been standing here holding you in my arms and you're a million miles away. Sometimes I think you care about me, and sometimes I think you don't even know I'm here. What do you want me to do?''

Darcy blinked. "Kiss me.''

"No.''

She came close to stomping her foot in frustration. "Why not?''

"Because I want to talk first about our feelings for each other. Because I think you're full of doubts. And no kiss is going to take them away.''

Darcy frowned. "Tom, you have *got* to quit reading women's magazines. It's supposed to be *me* who wants to talk about feelings and *you* who wants to get physical.''

"Ready when you are.''

Weren't men supposed to be afraid of commitment? Not this one. The man had no doubts about himself or his feelings. He just spoke from his heart. How unsettling, in this day and age. Darcy pulled herself out of his arms and turned her back to him. She needed a moment to regroup. Then she abruptly turned, again facing him, and saw he'd bent a knee and hooked his thumbs in his denims' front pockets. His whole demeanor screamed aloof.

"Tom, I've only known you a week. What am I supposed to do—throw myself at you and declare my undying love?"

"If that's what you feel, yes," he snapped. But then his glare softened. "It'd be nice, too, Darcy. Real nice, if you did."

She stood there, still feeling the repercussions of her experience with Hank. "I can't do that—again. I leaped once before, without giving it time…and look where I landed. A single mother. I love my daughter. I'd do it all over again, too, if in the end I could have her, Tom. I think you know that. But now that I do have her, I can't be that irresponsible ever again."

Tom fiddled with his hat's brim and quirked his mouth. "And loving me would be irresponsible? Is that what you're saying?"

"Is it? I don't know." After all, she'd thought she loved Hank, too. And had only several months ago, been trying to commit to a life with him, just as Tom was standing here now, urging her to do. Had there been a different outcome with Hank, the bald truth was she wouldn't even be standing here now with Tom. No, she'd be married to Hank and her mother would be visiting her in Baltimore to meet her new granddaughter.

So, what did it all mean? Well, it meant she was right to hesitate, right to wonder if love was, after all, enough. And here she was, too…wondering if she knew her own mind. Or could trust her own heart. After all, she'd been so wrong about Hank.

"I don't know, either, Darcy. All I know is what I feel. I've never chased after a woman the way I've pursued you. I've never hung around and made a nuisance, if not a complete jackass, of myself like I've done with you. I've sure as hell never given my name to a woman's child before—or offered her millions of dollars. And I've never been a handyman, not even for folks I've known all my life. So, what does all that say to you?''

She looked away from him and tipped her sandaled toes through the sand. ''It says you're acting outside the bounds of your normal behavior.''

''Hell, so do folks who turn into werewolves during a full moon.''

She looked up at him. ''All right. It says you care, dammit.''

''I more than care. I love you. And that seems to do nothing but make you mad.''

That was just too much for Darcy. Her frustration bubbled over. ''Yes, it does—if you're going to push me. Why today? Tonight? Why can't I have more time? Is the world suddenly going to end, and I just didn't get the memo?''

''Nothing like that, Darcy. Maybe I'm the one who's wrong here. You see, in my family, we fall in love at first sight. It's a curse—as you can see. We don't know who we want until we see her. Or him, in my sister's case. But once we know, we go after the one we want. At a full gallop. Sam all but lassoed Luke. But what I feel for you gives me this sense of urgency. I'm afraid to let you think about it too long. The moment could pass. The opening could close.''

Darcy's smile was a sad one. ''I understand what you're saying, Tom, and you make some good points. I just don't know if I'm capable of risking my heart again so soon. Hank Erickson—he's Montana's father—really did a number on me. Do you know what I mean?''

Looking grim, Tom settled his Stetson on his head. ''Yep. I understand. You need time, and I don't have it. I'm not doing you any good here. It's time to go. My business is conducted. I have interests and holdings there that need my attention, so I'll just get myself on back to Montana.'' He chuckled...not a humorous sound, more of a resigned one. ''I guess I need to get you back to Montana, too. The baby, that is.''

''Yes.'' The time for them had passed. She heard it in his voice. With her heart breaking, Darcy still hedged. ''But it's not like you can't call or write. Or visit again. I mean we can still communicate and give each other some more time. After all, we do live in the age of technology. Oh, I have it—do you e-mail?''

''I do.''

''Well, see there?'' She forced a brightness she didn't feel into her words. ''Even if you're in Billings and I'm here, or in Baltimore next winter, it will be like we're in the same room.''

His expression sobered, telling her plainly enough that after tomorrow they'd never see each other again. She hoped she was reading him wrong. Then he said, ''I think it'd be best if we went back to Buckeye now, Darcy. I think I should clear out of your house tonight and get a hotel room.''

Darcy's heart sank. She'd been right—the moment for them had passed. Time had moved forward. They hadn't connected. And it was so darned sad...and needless. Darcy wanted nothing more than to shout that she loved him, that she wanted him in her life. But none of that would come out of her mouth.

"Maybe that's a good idea," she finally said. "I'm sure Montana is missing me about now."

Ever the gentleman, Tom took her arm and guided her back to his white pickup. "That's what my foreman said this morning when I talked to him on the phone. Montana is missing me."

"MONTANA? You're going back to Montana—tonight?"

Tom interrupted his packing to face Margie Alcott who, with her two cronies, crowded into the doorway of the Alcott guest bedroom. "No, ma'am, not tonight. I'll just go into Phoenix for the night, then I'll get an early start tomorrow."

"Why are you leaving?"

Tom looked to the little lady who'd spoken. He believed it was Mrs. Tomlinson. "Well, ma'am, I don't live here. I have a ranch up in Billings I need to get back to."

"Is that so?" the next and third Buckeye Beauty asked. This was Mrs. Smith, to the best of his recollection. "You taking Darcy with you? She loves you, you know."

Tom stared at the three blue-haired bridge-playing Musketeers and then looked down at his folded clothes, spread across the bed. "No, ma'am, I don't know that. And neither does she."

"Oh, lizard spit—she does, too. She knows. She's just not telling you, son. I know my daughter. And she's playing hard to get."

Tom chuckled. "Well, she plays a good game of it, Margie, I'll give her that." He tucked a belt and some socks into his leather suitcase.

The three ladies came into the room and stood by

the bed. And began unpacking. "You going to give up that easily?" Margie challenged, stuffing his rolled-up socks into the crook of one of her arms.

Tom took the socks from her, and a shirt and pants from another of the ladies, and put them back into his suitcase. "I am. I don't stay where I'm not wanted."

"I want you."

Mrs. Tomlinson and Mrs. Smith gasped at their bold friend. "Oh, hush, you two. I want him for Darcy." She took the same shirt and pants back out of the suitcase that Tom had just repacked and this time, she held them to her chest…all while pointing a finger at Tom. "I handpicked you for Darcy, and I don't like losing."

"We don't, either," the other two women said…and began unpacking in earnest. "We like you."

"Margie, Freda…look," Jeanette said. She held up a pair of Tom's underwear by the waistband. "He wears boxers. You know what that means."

The women turned wide-eyed expressions Tom's way. He, though, had no idea what it meant—and he sure as hell didn't want to hear it from them. He snatched his boxers away from Jeanette and planted his hands atop the remainder of his clothes. "Now stop that. I've tried everything I know and Darcy still—"

"You tried everything? You sure? Did you kiss her?"

"Freda! That's personal." Margie turned to Tom. "Did you?"

Before Tom could say a word, Jeanette…Mrs. Tomlinson…cut in. "I bet he's a good kisser."

Before Tom could protest, Freda…Mrs.

Smith...said, "Well, you just know he is. Look at the man. He's beautiful." She turned her sweet little face up to him. "Are you good in bed? Maybe that's the problem."

Tom nearly died of embarrassment. Margie came to his rescue...sort of. "For heaven's sake, Freda, what kind of a question is that? Darcy just had a baby a week ago. Besides, look at the way the man fills out his blue jeans. Of course he's good in bed." She turned to Tom. "Tell her, son."

All Tom knew was if this discussion of his sexual prowess continued with these three grandmotherly types, he'd never want sex again...or be capable of performing. "I would appreciate it if—"

"Oh, I know." Freda put her hand on Tom's arm. "Let me see your thumb."

"My thumb?"

"Yes. Just pick one and show it to me."

"Freda, what are you up to?"

The frail little blue-haired woman turned to Margie. "I was just remembering something that Barb told me the other day. She said you can look at a man's thumb and tell the size of his—"

"That's enough," Tom bellowed...tucking his thumbs into his palms. "Now, listen to me, all of you." They stood there next to each other, like three little bluebirds on a limb. "I'm going to finish my packing—in peace. And alone, if you don't mind. And then, I'm going to leave, okay?" They nodded their heads in unison. "Good." He turned to Margie Alcott. "I want to thank you for your hospitality. I just wish I had more time to fix some other things around here for you."

"Me, too," she sniffed, her chin quivering. "Especially my daughter."

Tom steeled himself against feeling sorry for her—and against falling into her trap. "Well, it wasn't meant to be. And I'm sorry for that. You're—" He included all three ladies now. "—all really nice, and I appreciate your friendship. But things just didn't work out. And I need to go." He looked from one woman to the other. They stared mutely, forlornly, back at him. Tom exhaled sharply, feeling like a heel. "We're all agreed on that? No tricks, no tears, nothing like that? You'll just let me go?" *And not try to hogtie me?* He wouldn't put it past them.

The three ladies exchanged glances and nods. Tom feared some silent form of communication had just taken place…one that didn't bode well for him. Then, Margie said, brightly, "Well, goodbye, Tom. It was nice to have met you." She stuck her bejeweled hand out for him to shake. He did. The other two ladies followed suit.

This was too easy. Tom was highly suspicious…especially when they filed out, single-file. In sync, they turned right once they were out of his room. The direction of Darcy's room, where she was with the baby.

Oh, no. Oh, yes.

"Come on," he heard Margie whisper. "Let's go work on Darcy."

12

WEDNESDAY morning progressed like any other beautiful May day in sunny Phoenix. Birds sang. A soft breeze blew. The air smelled fresh and sweet with promise. But out in Buckeye it was anything but sunny.

Last night, without a word, Tom had packed up and left for a hotel, exactly as he'd said he would. When she'd finally come out of her room after being assailed by her mother, Freda and Jeanette to get up and stop that man...he'd been gone.

And now, as she relaxed in the shower, with instructions from her understanding mother to take her time and pamper herself while she watched Montana, Darcy quirked her mouth. Tom Elliott was a man of his word, she'd give him that much. But where was he now, she wondered. No doubt he was already on the road and headed in the direction of his Rocking E Ranch outside of Billings, Montana. *Heigh-ho, Silver,* was Darcy's frustrated thought. Then something else struck her. That was pretty much all she knew about him. He had a ranch. And an older sister named Sam who had five kids. And a deceased grandfather who'd left him land outside of Phoenix.

In one whole week of being with him nearly every minute, that was all she knew? Well, she recounted a few other things, like he'd gone to college on a rodeo scholarship, both of his parents were deceased, and he was fabulously wealthy. But there was something else—something much more important—she knew about him. Darcy stood still in the shower, allowing the warm water to rain down on her…so she could tell herself the wetness on her cheeks wasn't from tears. Yes, she knew something else. He loved her. How much? Enough to leave if she couldn't admit to having the same feelings for him.

Well…darn him. Maybe he wasn't the Lone Ranger, after all. Maybe he was just doggoned Dudley Do-Right. And wasn't that just like a man? Once you have them pegged, off they go and do something wonderful. You couldn't trust them. Darcy'd always known that.

So, now she'd gotten her wish, Darcy admitted as she rinsed the lather off her body and turned off the water. Her life now consisted of her and her daughter against the world. Under those conditions, Darcy couldn't exactly call her life loveless, now could she? She stepped out of the shower and began toweling off. No, she had a loving mother and a tiny daughter whom she loved very much…even if she remained convinced that Montana hated her.

Still, taking care of Montana Skye—*Great. Now I'll think about Tom every time I say my daughter's name*—would stave off her sense of loss and her loneliness for a while. That was true. But it wasn't fair to Montana, who would grow up and leave one day to pursue her own life. Just as Darcy now realized she'd done, leaving *her* mother here alone.

That was quite the revelation. Staring into the fogged bathroom mirror, Darcy realized she'd never given much thought to how that had made her already-

widowed mother feel. Not that Darcy had been callous
back then, just young and wanting some adventure.
But not once had her mother tried to hold her back.
No, she'd given her daughter the gift of wings when
it was time to go. And Darcy had to do the same thing
for Montana.

Wow. Only now, Darcy realized, could she see her
mother for the wonderful person she was. Not just a
parent, but a woman who had hopes and dreams and
goals, like anyone else. What a moment. It was quite
a surprise for Darcy to consciously realize that she
wasn't such a bad person and to acknowledge exactly
who was responsible for the state of her wonderful-
ness. Her parents. Even more staggering was the realization that if they hadn't been her parents but her
neighbors, she'd still like them.

So there it was. *Life goes on.* She needed to get her
own life in order and be responsible for her own happiness. Because her daughter would one day…it being
the natural order of the world…leave to find her own
path in life. It was true then, wasn't it, that saying
about what goes around comes around?

Having ordered the universe to her own satisfaction,
Darcy toweled herself off and dressed. Leaving the
steamy room, and feeling more like her old self than
she had in months…even if her heart was broken over
Tom's leaving—all because she couldn't open her stupid mouth and say *I love you*—she started down the
hallway toward the living room.

She just couldn't wait, this being Montana's one-
week birthday, to tell her mother everything she was
feeling. And to tell her how happy she was inside herself. Well, relatively happy, Darcy admitted, slowing
her pace some. Yes, Tom was gone. Yes, she did love

him but she'd blown it. But yes, she'd go on bravely and alone, her head held high, to forge a new life for herself, one that would allow her daughter to grow up to be the beautiful butterfly that she would one day be—

Darcy stopped short...and stared. She put her hands to her waist, which was beginning somewhat to redefine itself. The living room. It looked like a baby-furniture and party-supply store had exploded and its merchandise had landed artfully in her mother's living room. Colorful baby stuff littered the room. And speaking of the room...it was empty. "What is all this?" Darcy called out...to no one in particular.

Margie Alcott came flying out of the kitchen. She all but skidded to a stop in front of Darcy and smiled...guiltily. "Oh, Darcy, you're through already." She looked her up and down. "You look great, sweetheart. I have always loved that blouse on you. But maybe with those shorts you ought to go shave your legs."

Darcy automatically looked down at her legs and then up at her mother. "I don't need to shave my legs."

"All right, sweetie. You know best." Then, smoothing her hands down an apron tied over her purple polyester pants, Darcy's mother smiled and chirped, "What do you think? The room looks pretty, huh?"

Darcy blinked. "Pretty? It looks like...*a lot.* Mother, what's going on?"

Margie beamed. "I just knew you'd be happy, honey."

"Happy? But there are balloons and streamers and flowers and punch and cake and presents and...*stuff* everywhere. I don't get it. How did you do this? *When* did you do this?''

"Well, obviously while you were in the shower, honey."

Darcy could only stare at her excited mother. "By yourself? While I was in the shower? The whole thing? When I went back to the bathroom, none of this stuff was—wait a minute. Where's Montana?''

Her mother threw her arms up as she shrieked, "Surprise!"

Darcy jumped back a step, a hand to her chest. Her mother'd gone mad. She'd heard of this before. Desert fever. People just suddenly and for no discernible reason went nuts. They—

About 400 people—or so it seemed—suddenly popped up from behind every piece of furniture and house plant, all whooping and yelling. "Surprise, Darcy! Ha-ha. Bet we fooled you, huh? Wow, we really got her. Look how shocked she is. She can't even say anything. Hoo-boy, she doesn't look like she just had a baby a week ago, does she? Surprise!''

The suddenness of their cheerful attack had Darcy clutching at the nearest wall for support. It was too early…about 10:00 a.m. And it was a weekday. Why weren't people at work? She turned to the obvious culprit, the one who should have known that Darcy wanted nothing more than…on this day especially, when one week ago she'd had her baby and had met Tom, who was now gone—to be alone. Her mother.

Darcy found her amongst the happy, milling throng comprised of her neighbors, Darcy's own high school friends, her mother's friends, a few local politicians, and about half the general population of Buckeye, Arizona. She grabbed her mother's arm and pulled her aside. "What is going on?"

"Why, baby, can't you tell? A party."

"I know that, Mother. But...*why?* Why today?"

Her mother smoothed a lock of Darcy's hair back and inspected her face. "Look at you. You have on makeup, and you've fixed your hair. You look so pretty."

"Thank you. Now—" Darcy waved her hand around to indicate the crowd. "—explain, please."

Margie exhaled, lending exasperation to the sound. "Darcy Jean Alcott, I thought that was obvious. It's a baby shower-slash-birthday party for Montana Skye. She's a week old today."

Darcy nodded. "She is. And *where* is she, Mother?"

With growing horror, Darcy watched the look of confusion come over Margie's face as she looked everywhere but at her daughter. "Oh, I don't know," she said airily, "she's here somewhere."

"She's—" The words wouldn't come out on the first try. Darcy put a hand to her throat. "She's here *somewhere*, Mother?"

"Shhh, honey. You'll upset our guests."

Darcy forced herself to remain calm. "I'm going to do more than upset them if you don't tell me right now where I can find my child. Mother, what is wrong with you?"

"Nothing. I should be asking you the same thing. Here Jeanette and Freda and Barb and I went to the trouble of pulling this party together on the spur of the moment—"

"I know. While I was in the shower."

"Well, not the whole thing, silly. We worked on it

last night, too. Made all the phone calls. And here you are, not the least bit grateful—''

"Mom, I'd be the most grateful daughter in the world, if you'd just tell me where I can find mine. Please. Call it new-mother panic, if you want, but just produce her, okay?''

Margie Alcott pulled back...and looked offended. "Will you listen to you? You act like I've lost her or something. I've been a parent a lot longer than you have, young lady, and did I ever lose you?''

"At the Grand Canyon. When I was four.''

Margie pursed her lips together. "And I found you, didn't I?''

"No. Dad did.''

"Well...see? It turned out fine.''

"Uh-huh. Where's Montana? I'm just not thrilled with all these people handling her, Mother. She'll be like a little bruised banana. And she's only a week old.''

Margie instantly softened, squeezing Darcy's arm affectionately. "Oh, baby, you're right. I'll take care of things in here. You go on out back and see her.''

Darcy froze. "Out back?'' she croaked.

Margie became the very embodiment of insulted parent. "I swear, Darcy Jean, you must think I'm senile. Yes, she's outside. But, not by herself. Why, some Gila monster could bite her on the head on that soft spot and drag her off under a rock. Or a scorpion with its ugly old tail could sting her. Or a rattlesnake could—''

Darcy didn't hear anymore because, in a full-fledged panic, she forced her way through the crowd of folks who seemed demonically bent on getting in her way, congratulating her and hugging her and tell-

ing her how pretty she was and how pretty her baby
was. Pure evil, they were. But finally, she got to the
door off the dining room that led to the backyard,
ripped it open, and flung herself outside. Behind her,
the door slammed closed. Panicked, her heart thump-
ing, she looked around.

And spotted her daughter, who, as her mother had
said...wasn't alone.

Not by a long shot. No, she was in the shade, in the
swing...in Tom Elliott's arms. In profile to Darcy, his
face shaded by his white Stetson, Tom was chuckling
at the baby who had a hold of his pinkie. He didn't
even look up, or give any indication that he'd heard
Darcy's door-slamming entrance. Darcy stood there,
her heart racing with too many emotions to sort out.

"You may as well come on over, Darcy."

She jumped at the sound of his voice. Still, he didn't
look up at her. Darcy eyed him, then eyed him with
her daughter. Then looking back toward the house and
the crowd inside...she gave up. Feeling suddenly de-
flated, with her adrenaline rush subsiding, Darcy
dragged herself over to the swing.

Tom glanced up at her. Darn, but his eyes were as
blue and as compelling as she remembered them...
from yesterday. Now that was dumb. Of course they
would be. Darcy swallowed, willing her thoughts to
order themselves into something coherent and helpful.

"You look nice," Tom said, stopping the swing's
gentle motion with his foot. "Here. Sit down with
us."

"Thanks," Darcy heard herself say. Tom didn't say
anything else or look at her again. Darcy remained
quiet, too, just staring out into the desert...and feeling

a welcome calm settle over her. "It's nice out here," she said without thinking.

Next to her, Tom nodded. And chuckled at Montana. Darcy looked over at the baby and saw she was trying to stuff his fingertip in her mouth. Darcy smiled. "She must be getting hungry."

"Yep." Tom shifted his weight on the swing. "I expect she'll want her mama here in a minute."

Darcy made a self-deprecating noise. "That's the only time she wants me. She hates me."

"No, she doesn't." He met Darcy's gaze. "She loves you. Very much. Even a week's long enough to know that about a person."

Darcy swallowed around the growing lump of emotion in her throat. She looked away from Tom and held on to the swing's chain. "So. Tom. I thought you'd be on your way home this morning."

"I did, too. But that was before the law paid a visit to my hotel room."

Darcy's eyes widened. "The law? What happened?"

"Bachelor Number Three."

Darcy frowned. "Are you serious? Johnny Smith?"

"Serious as a rodeo clown. The old hound dog just showed up at The Ranch Hotel and said he wasn't allowed back home unless I showed up here with him this morning at a party."

Embarrassed, Darcy put a hand to her forehead. "You poor man." She lowered her hand to her lap. "I just want you to know that I had nothing to do with this. I'm as surprised as you are."

"I expect so. But neither one of us is half as surprised as the folks down in the lobby were when they saw me being escorted by a sheriff out of the hotel. Yep, that was fun.''

''I think you should sue my mother.''

Tom chuckled. ''No good ever comes of suing family.''

Darcy started to remind him that her mother wasn't family to him, then realized to what he must have been alluding. Darcy clamped her lips together. She told herself it was just a Freudian slip on his part—and a line of thought she wasn't touching. Instead, she stood up and turned to face Tom, holding her hands out for her daughter. ''Look, you were a good sport to go along with all this. But you did your part. So if you want to go, I'll take Montana and you can slip out by the gate over there—''

''Do you want me to go?''

Darcy turned away, highly agitated. ''Oh, for God's sake, Tom, this is where I came in. I've already seen this movie.''

''Then tell me how it ends.''

She turned to face him. He hadn't moved from the swing. And Montana still had a proprietary hold on his finger. Symbolic, no doubt. ''I can't. I don't know how it ends.''

''Maybe that's because the true ending hasn't been written yet.'' His blue eyes radiated sincerity...and warmth...and something else equally tender.

Tears threatened to gather in Darcy's eyes. And she didn't like that one bit. No more than she liked him being here now, just when she'd adjusted to the idea that she'd never see him again. To her, it seemed as if she was being given a chance to see again what she'd lost. ''All right, how do you think it ends? Pretend you're writing this romance.''

He nodded, ever calm, ever capable. "Okay. I say the female love interest comes to her senses and realizes that the male love interest is, after all, the right man for her. And they kiss and declare their undying love for each other. And then the male love interest helps the female love interest pack her things, as well as the requisite baby's things. And then they tell everyone at the hastily arranged party meant to bring the two love interests together that they're going to live in some Western state—"

"Like, say, Montana?" Darcy crossed her arms and fought a grin.

Tom nodded thoughtfully. "Okay. It's as good as any."

"Well, don't keep me in suspense. What happens next?"

Tom put Montana to his shoulder, snuggling her securely, and then continued. "Well, the way I see it, they leave amidst a hail of cheering and laughter, with everyone happy for them—"

"In a white pickup, no doubt."

"Well, not all of them. Just the three main characters. And a trailer for all the presents they got at the party."

"I see. And what about the female love interest's career back East? She's invested a lot of effort in that, you know."

Tom nodded. "Good point. That, she has. But the male love interest points out to her that the universities in Montana are just as good and probably need teachers like her. And none of them has her former love interest on campus."

"Oh, excellent point. That should help sway her."

"I'd think so."

"What else? Is that it?"

"No. I'm afraid the male love interest has something he needs to confess to the female love interest."

Darcy's insides quickened. Uh-oh. Just when she'd been getting on board with his movie-scripted version of their lives. "Sounds like a problem. What is it—that he's an alien or an escaped mental patient?"

"Either of those would do, I suppose. But I was thinking more along the lines of a trust-fund thing he was supposed to have corrected."

Darcy lifted her chin. "Oh? And he didn't do it, right?"

His expression never changed. "No. He did it. He just didn't do it exactly the way the female love interest thought he would."

Darcy put her hands on her hips. "Tom, what exactly did you do?"

He shrugged, never looking away. "I put it in your name."

Darcy felt as if someone had whacked her behind the knees. "My name? But you were supposed to—"

"Take it out of Montana's name. And I did that."

Darcy could only stare at him. Words wouldn't come. She truly needed to tell him how she felt. About him. Suddenly the words just tumbled out of her. "I swear, Tom Elliott, if I didn't love you like I do, I'd—"

"What did you say?" He stopped the swing from swinging and stared hard at her.

Darcy frowned. "I said if I didn't—" She covered her mouth with a hand. "I can't believe I just said that."

"I can't, either," Tom said, grinning to beat the band. "I thought sure I'd have to hold your feet to the fire to get you to admit that. Not that I can blame you, mind you, given everything that former love interest dealt you."

Darcy lowered her hand, ignoring the crazy way her pulse was racing. He was right about Hank. And about how she'd been clinging to what now seemed like silly reasons for going it alone. Where was it written that she had to be a martyr? "Well, thank you for that much, anyway."

Then Tom turned serious. "Darcy, come here, please, and hold your daughter. I'd like to talk to you, if I could."

It was a pivotal moment. She glanced around, seeking inspiration. Movement at the corner of her eye had her looking toward the house, to the back picture windows. From inside, about 400 faces were pressed shamelessly against the glass. A few daring souls even smiled and waved, urging her toward Tom. "Oh, for heaven's sake."

"They still there?"

"Yes. How'd you know? You have your back to the window."

"Are you kidding? Who didn't know? Come here. They won't be able to see you if you come sit by me."

That decided it. Darcy took the few steps needed to get her over to the swing and turning, sat down. Tom immediately handed her Montana, who made an awful face, reddened, and drew her legs up. "Great," Darcy said drolly as Tom put an arm around her shoulders.

Completely warmed and happy and falling more and more in love with him with each passing moment, Darcy met his waiting gaze. "Make sure you get that mountain of diapers Mom's bought when you help me pack, will you?"

Tom looked at her as if she'd just said *I do* to him in front of a church full of people. Indeed, she thought sure he was going to drop to one knee and propose to her. Then, it struck her. "Hey, you are going to marry me, aren't you? I mean, someday, right? After everything I've been through, I'm not about to live with a man—"

"Hold on. I'll marry you. But first you have to kiss me."

Darcy shook her head. "No, that's not the way I remember it. The kiss comes at the end of the ceremony."

"Not in Montana."

Darcy pulled back and stared at him. "You are lying."

"Now, is that any way to start a life together? With one of us calling the other one a liar?"

"No, I suppose not. But what about you and what you did with your grandfather's land?"

It was his turn to pull back. "I didn't lie. I took it out of Montana's name, exactly as you asked me to do."

"Yes, and put it in my name."

"Honey, I'm ready to put everything I own in your name."

Darcy shook her head in wonder. "I have never met anyone like you, Tom Harrison Elliott. You make me forget all my doubts. I had good reasons for saying everything I did yesterday, but seeing you, I can't think what they are now."

Tom leaned over and planted a kiss on Darcy's temple. "They're not important, if you love me. Do you love me, Darcy?"

Her insides melted. "I'm afraid I do. More than is good for me."

"I'll take that. You think you could stand to live in Montana? If you don't want to live there, I'll come back East with you. My foreman can—"

"No. That comment about my former love interest convinced me. I'd like to try Montana. Besides, it's closer to my mother than Baltimore is."

"That's true. But, hell, she can move up there, too, with us. I don't mind."

Darcy's expression became plaintive. "Oh, please. Mind."

He chuckled. "All right. We won't mention it to her for a while. And speaking of a trip to Montana, you think you can stand that ride up there right now? I mean, will your doctor let you and the baby travel?"

Darcy grimaced. "I hadn't thought about that. I don't know." Then she realized something else. "Oh, Tom, you're not still planning on leaving today, are you? I'll need time. I can't—"

"No, it's fine. Take all the time you need. I can just make a few phone calls, have my foreman fly the jet down here—"

"*The* jet, Tom? Not *a* jet, but *the* jet?"

He managed to look embarrassed. "Well, it's a small one. Anyway, I'll have Corey fly it down in a couple days. That ought to give us time to make your arrangements and say your goodbyes here. And then I'll have Corey drive my pickup back to Montana. And you and I can fly back with the baby."

"You're a pilot, too, right?" Darcy had no idea who this man was. But she intended to thank God every day for his presence in her life.

"Yeah. Didn't I mention that?"

"No. You omitted that part. What else should I know?"

He looked away, as if giving serious thought to that. Darcy drank in his handsomeness and the strength of his profile. "Well," he said, looking down at her. "I suppose I ought to tell you how this whole party inside came about."

"Please do."

"You see, yesterday in the mail, so your mother told me today, Montana Skye's birth certificate came. And she opened it—"

"And saw your name. I forgot about that. That stinker, she opened my mail. She never said a word to me."

"Don't be too hard on her. She did what she thought was best. Besides, getting us together like she did just made that birth certificate a little easier to explain to Montana later on."

"Well, that's true. I guess I'll let this one pass."

"Good for you." Then, suddenly, Tom stroked her cheek, melting Darcy's insides. "Darcy, I just want you to know that I'll always be good to you. I'll do my best never to hurt you. I'll cherish you and Montana always, I swear it."

The tears gathered in Darcy's eyes. "I know. Say you love me, Tom."

With all due earnestness, he murmured, "I love you, Tom."

Darcy swatted at his arm. "Stop that."

Chuckling, Tom gathered her in his arms, pulled his white Stetson off and held it between their faces and the crowd behind them still clustered in the picture window. He tenderly told Darcy he loved her...and then kissed the life back into her heart and the fire into her soul.

In her mother's lap, with her drive-by daddy next to them, Montana Skye yawned and relaxed. All was well in her little world. Or would be...if only someone had a dry diaper they could loan her.

PATRICIA KNOLL

Calamity Jo

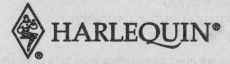

HARLEQUIN®

TORONTO • NEW YORK • LONDON
AMSTERDAM • PARIS • SYDNEY • HAMBURG
STOCKHOLM • ATHENS • TOKYO • MILAN • MADRID
PRAGUE • WARSAW • BUDAPEST • AUCKLAND

Dear Reader,

I have always loved eccentric people, so I thought writing about a townful of them would be a lot of fun. And where else could I set this story, but in an old Arizona mining town. In fact, starting with a couple of unlucky miners and calling the place Calamity Falls seemed right too.

Jo Ella Quillan and Case Houston run afoul of each other when she interferes with an investigation he's pursuing, so much that he begins thinking of her as the biggest calamity in Calamity Falls. Little does he guess that the only casualty will be his heart. I hope you enjoy the sparks that fly between these two.

Happy reading,

Patricia Knoll

Books by Patricia Knoll
HARLEQUIN DUETS
3—MEANT FOR YOU

HARLEQUIN LOVE & LAUGHTER
53—DELIGHTFUL JONES

Prologue

Arizona Territory, 1879

"DOES IT LOOK BAD, Battlehaven?" Rudolph Shipper asked as he bounced on the hard stagecoach seat, flew up and hit his head on the roof, and crashed back again. He was sure he felt some bones snap, but it didn't matter. Since the stagecoach had begun trying to outrun the Apaches a few minutes before, he'd made several such bounces and he figured most of his bones were broken anyway.

"It looks as bad as possible, Shipper," Lord Albert Battlehaven announced as he made a flying bounce of his own. He scrambled to hang on to his porkpie hat as he landed, then slid along the horsehair seat and collided with the door. "I think these aborigines are taking exception to our presence on their ancient habitat."

"Huh…uh?" Shipper hiccuped the word as his head again made contact with the coach's roof.

"They want to kill us for trespassing."

On Shipper's next flying trip past the window, he saw the determined faces of the pursuing Apaches. Fierce black eyes met his, seemingly promising death. He gulped, wishing he'd never left the Iron Range of Minnesota. The Indians there had been tame, pleasant even, he recalled wistfully. They were no longer interested in parting hapless white men from their hair.

"What are we gonna do?" he wailed.

"I think we should encourage the driver to exhort the horses to greater feats of exertion."

"Huh?"

"Tell him to drive like hell."

Grasping the edge of the window, Shipper stuck his head out, being careful to dodge bullets and arrows. When he shouted Battlehaven's instructions to the driver, the man craned his neck around, gave him a wild-eyed look, and released a string of abusive curses that had Shipper ducking back inside. The man riding shotgun and firing desperately at their pursuers added a few curses of his own for good measure.

Shipper bounced back into his seat and reported, "He's doing his best."

"Do you think we made an error in judgment by attempting to ride across Apache territory in this conveyance?" Battlehaven asked. He knew it was inconceivable that he'd made a mistake, but he craved confirmation of his leadership.

"No, I think we made a mistake before we took this stagecoach, when you suggested we try riding across on mules and stopped to ask directions in that village on the reservation. That was where you got the attention of that Indian maiden."

"She was a comely lass." Battlehaven sighed, then took another worried peek out the window. So far, the coach was keeping ahead of the Indian ponies. If they closed the gap, though, he planned to panic. Too bad he didn't have a gun, he thought. Too bad he was such a dreadful shot.

"She was promised to the young warrior who's

leading that pack out there," Shipper snapped, his hand flying upward as he pointed to the rider, who was armed with bow and arrows, two rifles, a six-shooter and several long knives—all of which seemed to have Shipper and Battlehaven's names on them.

"An arranged marriage," Battlehaven answered dismissively, as if such trifles were meant to be disposed of according to his wishes.

Shipper gave him a horrified look, then hunkered down as best he could in the wildly rocking stagecoach bemoaning his fate. Things weren't supposed to be this way. Meeting the English lord in Chicago had been a stroke of luck, or so he'd thought. Battlehaven was a remittance man, paid by his family to stay as far from them as possible. His remittance was bankrolling their mining expedition to the Arizona territory, and Shipper, with his mining background, was to provide the labor and expertise. So far, though, they'd had nothing but trouble.

"Besides, how was I supposed to know she had a fiancé?" Battlehaven asked, pulling his hat down low over his eyes. Maybe if he disguised himself, that Apache warrior would think Shipper was the one who had tried to seduce the girl. "She didn't speak English and I don't speak Apache."

Shipper had no answer to that. He was too busy making his peace with the Almighty.

To his everlasting gratitude, though, the shotgun rider miraculously managed to outshoot the Apaches, who started to fall back. Their leader let out a frustrated and furious yell as he waved his weapons in the air.

Battlehaven breathed a sigh of relief and promised himself to keep his trousers firmly buttoned from now on—or at least when there were Apache maidens around.

Shipper broke into loud prayers of praise and fell back against the seat. He promised the Almighty that from now on he would be the best of men. He gave Battlehaven a sidelong glance, then added a promise only to associate with the best of men.

The stagecoach hurtled forward, straight for the safety of Fort Lowell in the dusty little town of Tucson, out of harm's way. Shipper was grateful that Battlehaven was willing to pay for a hotel, where the two of them had a real bath and several drinks to calm their nerves. They dined out on the story that evening, retelling their adventures over and over.

Shipper realized that with each retelling, their heroic exploits became more and more exaggerated. By bedtime, they'd become the ones rescuing the stagecoach and the driver and shotgun rider had become the ones cowering inside. Shipper knew that the lie should have bothered him more, especially considering his recent promise to the Almighty, but it made him feel so heroic he let it stand.

By the next day, Shipper and Battlehaven had begun exploring the possibilities of prospecting in the area. On Shipper's advice, Battlehaven quickly decided that they needed to head northeast of the town. They bought a map guaranteed to lead them straight to a big gold strike, purchased some equipment, found a few mules, and headed out.

Three days later, they stopped their pack mules at the base of a craggy mountain.

"Do you think this could be it?" Shipper asked. Gratefully, he clambered down from the back of the

mule he'd nicknamed Nutcracker and stood staring upward, his crumpled felt hat pushed back on his head.

Lord Albert Battlehaven swung down from the saddle, looking as elegant as if he were out for a Sunday
afternoon jaunt. He consulted the map they'd purchased in Tucson. The former U.S. cavalryman who
had sold it to them had guaranteed its accuracy.
"Puertas de las Mulas," Battlehaven answered.
"Mule Pass. This looks right." He glanced down at a
shallow creek that glistened at their feet, now only
running because of the heavy spring rains. A dull
gleam caught his attention and he dismounted to investigate. He dipped a careful palm into the creek and
came out with a handful of sand, flecked with gold.
The real thing. He could always tell the real thing.
Hadn't he squandered enough of it to make him an
expert?

"This *is* right, old man," he said excitedly, holding
his hand out to show Shipper. "We've finally found
that for which we came all this way."

On saddle-sore legs, Shipper stumbled to his side.
He had panned for gold—though not very successfully—in California thirty years before and was sure
that he, too, could recognize the real thing.

Battlehaven used a meticulously kept fingernail to
flick out specks of gold and place them in Shipper's
dirt-crusted palm. If he turned his hand just right in
the strong light, Shipper could almost see them.

"We're rich," he said, in awe.

Battlehaven nodded regally. "After the horrors
we've endured, we've finally arrived and we're going
to be rich."

Shipper gazed at his friend with admiration. "Your

family back in merry old England will sit up and take notice of you now, won't they?''

''Without a doubt.'' Truthfully, they'd taken notice of him before, especially after he'd lost a bet and had paid it off by riding buck naked through Regent's Park. That, and his involvement with two lusty actresses, had prompted his family to turn him into a remittance man. Well, he thought smugly, let them say what they would about his behavior, but he'd never known any of the Battlehavens to turn up their noses at gold.

''Yessiree, meeting up with you in Chicago was a stroke of luck for me,'' Shipper said, forgetting his previous laments about that very thing. He could afford to be forgiving. They were going to be rich. ''All we have to do is follow the creek and discover the mother lode. Let's go.''

To Shipper's dismay, they didn't find the mother lode that afternoon or the next. In fact, it took them two weeks of careful searching and wrong turns to find what they were looking for. At last, in an outcropping of rock near the San Pedro River, Shipper discovered a thimble's worth of nuggets. A day of digging convinced them that they had found a rich source of gold. They planned to rush back to Tucson the next day to file their claim. The men solemnly shook hands on their agreement to share everything fifty-fifty, then stayed awake all night, each watching the other for signs of possible treachery.

The next morning, they were up early. They packed their things and eradicated all signs of their occupation of the site, just in case anyone else happened along to jump their claim.

''I say, Shipper,'' Battlehaven called out when he

had meticulously followed instructions to brush out their tracks with a branch of a creosote bush. "Won't *we* have trouble finding this when we return?"

Shipper gave him a pitying look. Didn't they teach these aristocrats *anything?* "Look around, Battlehaven, at the signs that are here; that outcropping of rock, these piles of stones, this empty wash. They'll lead us right to our gold. Don't worry."

Carefully, he folded away the detailed map he'd made of their claim. "Besides, we can't leave any signs of our own to show us the way back here. We don't want people finding it and jumping our claim. If we say anything, people will come rushing in on us just like they did on poor old John Sutter thirty years ago in California."

Battlehaven nodded. "I'll defer to your superior knowledge if not your intellect," he said.

Shipper grinned, pleased that the Englishman knew which of them was smarter.

They finished packing and hurried back to Tucson.

This time, they agreed there would be no dinner with their new acquaintances, no flow of rotgut, because they both knew it would loosen their tongues and reveal the whereabouts of their strike. Nothing was going to jeopardize their claim. Again, they spent a sleepless night watching each other, and filed their claim first thing the next morning. Then they set off for the river again.

When they were fifty yards from the site, the animals started to behave strangely, dancing and rearing back to paw the air.

"What the...?" Even an expert horseman like Battlehaven couldn't hold his animal. He leaned forward and shortened the reins.

Shipper was hopelessly outmatched by the mule he rode. The panicked animal dumped him into a stand of cholla cactus. Shrieking and struggling out of the spiny thing, he shrieked again when he felt the ground moving beneath him in a way he'd known in California. "Earthquake," he yelled.

He threw himself on the ground, only to feel it rippling beneath him, so he staggered upwards and swerved drunkenly from side to side, looking for safety. Battlehaven continued to fight his mule who was crow-hopping around in circles, trying to throw him off.

The tremor lasted only seconds, but it was enough to loosen the outcropping of rock where they'd found their mother lode. Boulders tumbled and crashed down, dumping tons of rock and debris into the stream. Undaunted, the water worked its way up and over, forming a waterfall about ten feet high that splashed merrily down the once-empty wash, sweeping away their dreams of riches.

When the ground settled, Shipper stared at the falls and began to whimper.

"This is a calamity," Battlehaven pointed out unnecessarily.

"Yup," Shipper agreed. "We thought we'd found our destiny, but we all we got was calamity. Calamity Falls."

1

Jo Ella Quillan opened the door of Perk Avenue and stepped carefully inside. Ever the optimist, she hoped that if she didn't move too quickly, her head wouldn't fall off and go rolling across the floor. Behind her, a car backfired and she winced, biting back a moan of pain as the sound seared through her head.

The scent of fresh roasted coffee mingled with baking muffins swept over her in a wave that made her choke. Ordinarily, her taste buds would have sat up and begged, but today her stomach was roiling.

Late-night wine didn't agree with her. In fact, wine rarely agreed with her, so she didn't drink it often. Unfortunately, she'd forgotten that last night when she'd arrived home, depressed over the way her evening had turned out.

She took a quick glance around, saw that the place was almost empty and aimed her bumbling feet toward a chair. Gratefully, she sank into it and draped herself over the glass-topped table. Her chin-length chocolate-brown hair spilled over her face, cutting off her view of the room. That was okay. There wasn't anyone she wanted to see and she was sure that after they'd taken one look, they wouldn't want to see her, either. The glass felt cool on her flushed cheek. Maybe Lainey would let her stay there all day. She opened one bleary, sea-green eye to see where her best friend was.

Lainey Pangburn, the owner of Perk Avenue was

making her way toward Jo carrying a tray that held two large glasses of water and a cup of coffee. Deftly, she wove between the tables, her long, brightly patterned skirt swishing softly as she moved. She sat down with a whoosh of breath, brushed her long, straight, red hair back from her face, and looked at Jo with sympathy melting her brown eyes.

"You're a pal, Lainey." Jo reached for the coffee only to have a glass of water shoved into her hand.

"Coffee for me. Water for you until you wash the lingering alcohol out of your system. How much wine did you have last night?"

"I don't know," Jo answered wearily, gulping the ice water, then laying her head back down on the table.

"I understand you're upset about Steve dumping you over dinner at the Copper Pot last night, saying that he wasn't ready to make a commitment and it was time for him to move on."

"No, I'm not...."

"Yes, you are," Lainey answered breezily. "His timing was pretty convenient, since his surveying job here was finished anyway and he was heading back to Tucson. He's a rat and you're too good for him even if you did love him...."

"No, I didn't...."

"Yes, you did," her friend went on. "And he broke your heart."

"No, actually, he didn't."

"Yes, he did, and..."

"Lainey," Jo said sharply, almost leaping across the table to silence her. She took a breath and waited for her head to stop doing an imitation of a Tilt-A-Whirl. When she could speak, she said, "He didn't break my heart. He didn't even dent its fender. I didn't love him. I'm *not* upset about him dumping me."

"Methinks you doth protest too much," Lainey responded sagely.

Ignoring her, Jo went on, "However, I think he could have found a better place than the Copper Pot on a Monday night, with half of Calamity Falls and a battalion of tourists listening in."

Lainey blinked at her skeptically. "If your heart's not broken, what was that all about when you called me last night after drinking a bottle of wine?"

"I *think* it was only two glasses," Jo admitted. "I have no head for the stuff." She sat up straight, took a deep breath, and said, "I was upset because I wasted four months on Steve Grover. What kind of woman dates a guy for that long when she doesn't even like him very much?"

"You liked him," Lainey insisted. "In fact, you loved him."

Jo waved off that response and answered her own question. "I'll tell you what kind," she said, wagging a finger beneath her friend's nose. "One who obviously needs a major change in her life, and not just in my choice of boyfriends either. I need a new job. A new life. A new home." She gulped down the second glass of water, then frowned. "On second thought, maybe changing my life isn't such a good idea," she said doubtfully. "After all, look what happened last night when I tried to change myself into a drunk."

"One evening of overindulging does not a drunk make," Lainey answered pedantically. "You're a smart, capable woman and a good reporter. If you think you're not satisfied and happy in this town, you probably aren't."

Jo rubbed her palms down the front of her jeans, then straightened the collar of her pumpkin-orange camp shirt. "You're right, of course. So how do I go about making this change?"

Lainey returned to sipping her coffee. "You tell me."

Jo thought about it for a minute, her smooth forehead pleated into a fierce frown. "I like Calamity Falls, for the most part. I love Aunt Millie and Uncle Don and I was glad to come help run the *Ingot* when Uncle Don got sick. Even with modern medicine, pneumonia is still serious. But he's well now, has been for a couple of years."

"So what's your point?"

"The point is that I'm grateful for the experience they've let me have working as a reporter, but I'm not making use of my journalism degree. I want to do something bigger, more important. This place isn't big enough for me." Her hands shot out to take in the room—the whole town, in fact. "I'm a better reporter than they need. Any journalism student at Calamity Falls High School could do what I'm doing. I've tried writing articles and sending them to the Phoenix and Tucson papers on spec, but I get replies back saying 'Thanks, but no thanks'."

"What kind of articles?"

"One on the danger of the unsecured, open underground mines around here. Another about the rising water table in some of the mines, and how it's threatening the infrastructure of Calamity Falls."

"Those sound like newsworthy topics to me."

Jo sighed. "That's what I thought, but the editors only seem to want articles on our local eccentrics."

Lainey rolled her eyes. "You'd think that had been done to death by now. Every newspaper and broadcasting station in the state has been here in the past five years. Some of them more than once."

Jo nodded. "I know. They usually end up at the *Ingot* office to find out what new kook has moved into town."

The two women looked at each other. The influx of odd and eccentric people into Calamity Falls was the idea of Lainey's grandfather, Dr. Julius Pangburn. A retired university chemistry professor, Julius had come to Calamity Falls eight years before and immediately decided it would be a perfect haven for people whose ideas didn't exactly mesh with those of mainstream society. He had put out the word among his friends and colleagues and soon the place had begun filling up with people who had unusual obsessions and hobbies. All of them were harmless, but the townspeople, and especially the city council, had been worried about the reputation Calamity Falls was gaining. Yet another newspaper article on the subject wouldn't make any of them happy.

"I've got to find a new angle, something besides our local eccentrics, a new story or slant on a story that will make an editor sit up and take notice." She glanced around thoughtfully at the few customers in the normally busy establishment. They sat alone or in pairs, reading the newspaper, or just contemplating the coming day. "Slow morning?"

"Not really. You're just later than usual today. This place was packed until half an hour ago, then Charlotte came in and announced that she was ready to give one of her hawk lectures. All the tourists grabbed their coffee and scurried outside."

"At least she's moved to that empty lot across the street and has quit tying up traffic right in front of your shop."

Lainey answered with a rueful grin. "It would be better if she found a lecture hall or something. There are suitable places available in town and she could more than afford it.''

The two women fell silent as they considered ways to change Jo's life. Because she knew her friend so well, Jo knew Lainey was thinking in terms of new clothes, new hairdo, new man. Jo had decided, rather fuzzily, during her night of wine-sipping and self-pity-wallowing, that she really didn't need any of those things. Steve hadn't broken her heart. He *hadn't*. And if she said that often enough, she might actually begin to believe it. What she had just told Lainey was true. She needed a story that would get the attention she wanted. Journalism jobs weren't exactly thick on the ground, so she needed an angle.

Out of the corner of her eye, she noticed a tall, robust man with a mane of white hair jog by. His high-tech running shoes slapped the pavement rhythmically. His paisley-print robe and striped pajamas flapped and fluttered in time to his steps.

Jo straightened up. ''Your grandpa's late for his morning run.''

''He was out late. Had a hot date last night,'' Lainey said.

Dread filled Jo's eyes. ''He and Martha didn't go to the…?''

''Copper Pot. Yes, but probably after you and Steve had left.''

Jo groaned. She loved Julius and his lady friend, Martha Smalley, but they loved gossip. Anyone who didn't already know she'd been dumped would find out before lunch was over. ''My life sucks,'' she moaned.

Lainey reached over and patted her hand. ''Jo, I'm your best friend so I can tell you. Whining doesn't suit you.''

Jo gave her a disgruntled look and went back to wracking her brain for a story idea that would get her the attention she needed.

What could it be, though, here in Calamity Falls? She glanced up idly as the bell on the door jingled with a merry sound. A man entered and she gave him a casual look, then her eyes drifted away. However, when the image her eyes had picked up worked its way through her sluggish brain, her attention snapped back to him.

This was no ordinary tourist. Wind-tossed black hair, dark brown eyes, a smooth, square jaw. His nose was long and straight, the perfect complement to his other strong features. He wore a black Henley shirt, black jeans, and black butt-kicking boots, as if he'd just swept into town on his way to a bikers' convention. He stopped a few paces inside the door and looked around, his midnight eyes taking in everyone there.

Dark, dangerous and…delicious, Jo thought wistfully. Too bad she'd sworn off men last night.

However, her heart thudded, pumping much-needed blood to her brain. Her vivid imagination conjured up pictures of the two of them, wide-open spaces, the back of a Harley. Maybe she had just found a new cure for a hangover.

As Lainey's assistant waited on him, Jo's mental processes began to work a little harder. She'd seen this man somewhere before. Not in person, but somewhere. In print. She frowned. Then she remembered. It had been in an obscure little publication from a Phoenix insurance company. When she made the connection, her eyes widened.

Turning to Lainey, she said, "What on earth is Case Houston doing in Calamity Falls?"

"Case who?" Lainey looked around and spotted the newcomer. "Oh, him. I don't know what he's doing here. He arrived yesterday. He's staying at the Copper Quest Bed and Breakfast. He seems like a nice guy," she added casually.

Jo's attention was still riveted on him. Was Lainey blind? He was more than nice. He was breathtaking, sexy, rugged. Dangerous with a capital *D*.

He placed his order with Lainey's assistant behind the counter, then stood looking around, his dark eyes surveying each person in the room. When his gaze met Jo's, it paused for a second. Did she imagine there was a flicker of interest in his eyes? She hoped so because his look had sent her pulse into a wild flamenco dance. She glanced down at her wrist to see if she could detect the interesting action going on there.

"Do you know him?" Lainey went on.

"One can only hope," Jo murmured, propping her chin on her palm.

"What?"

Jo blushed, realizing what she'd said. Only the most pathetic of women would get dumped on a Monday and start ogling a new man in town on Tuesday. She *wasn't* pathetic. Only somewhat confused.

She cleared her throat. "I know *of* him. He used to work for the state attorney general's office. Remember that insurance scam that was uncovered a couple of years ago? The one that involved a huge group of people filing claims under various false names for work-related injuries that never happened?"

"Vaguely," Lainey admitted, then shrugged. "You know I don't keep up with the news the way you do."

"It was a big story at the time. Anyway, he was the one who exposed the scam by going undercover. He had his life threatened, the whole thing. I'd love to know why he's here.'' Jo fell silent as her mind clicked over various possible reasons for his appearance in town, pleased to notice that her mind finally seemed to be functioning on all cylinders. She was relieved. For a while after she'd first awakened, she'd been afraid she'd permanently pickled her brain.

''Uh, Jo? It's October, the beginning of our tourist season. Could it be that he's simply here on a vacation?''

''Could be,'' she admitted slowly. Heat was tickling the tips of her fingers and moving up her arms. ''Lainey,'' she said. Her voice was faint, her eyes wide. Excited color washed into her cheeks. ''I've got the tingle.''

Her friend's eyes widened. In alarm. ''Oh, no. No. No. It's only your hangover, and...''

''I'm telling you it's the tingle,'' Jo insisted.

Lainey slumped in her chair. ''I hate it when you have the tingle. It always means trouble.''

''You're exaggerating.''

''Exaggerating? I don't think so. You had the tingle just before you talked me into going on that blind date last month with that friend of Ralph Byrdsong's. I should have known better than to date the best friend of a man whose hobby is collecting leg manacles. You said you had the tingle and that you just knew this guy was the right one for me.''

Jo looked away. ''Sal wasn't so bad.''

''He was a *prison* escapee. The sheriff tracked him down right in front of the theater where we had agreed to meet for a movie. It was just like a replay of John Dillinger. I felt like the woman in red.''

Jo winced sympathetically. ''Maybe that wasn't the tingle, after all. Maybe it was a rash or something.''

She shrugged. "Look on the bright side. He said he'd never forget you."

"Jo, my friend, he thought I'd turned him in. That was a threat, not a promise." Lainey gave Jo a fierce look. "So don't go telling me anything about that blasted tingle of yours."

Jo relented. "Okay, I admit I may have been a little off there, but this time, I know it's going to lead to something big."

"Yeah, maybe this time *you'll* be the one trying to escape prison," Lainey said morosely. "Did you ever think the tingle might *truly* be nothing but allergies?"

"Don't be silly. Besides, it's never failed to bring *something* exciting into my life, and you're the one who agreed I need to make some changes."

"I was thinking in terms of a haircut, nail wraps, body waxing, something along those lines," Lainey said desperately.

"I can consider those things, too," Jo answered, giving Case another look. "In fact, it might be a darned good idea." She paused. "He must really like coffee. Either that, or he didn't get enough for breakfast at the Copper Quest."

Realizing she wasn't going to change her friend's mind, Lainey gave her a exasperated look and stood up. "Maybe he heard mine's better."

Case had his coffee and was heading for the door. Her eyes on him, Jo stood up and reached over to squeeze Lainey's arm. "I'll see you later. I've got work to do." She checked her bag to make sure she had her notebook and pen, and hurried away.

Outside, she glanced quickly around to see which way Case had gone. She caught sight of him disappearing up Battlehaven Avenue, his dark head easy to spot above the colorful array of sun visors, baseball caps and cowboy hats that surrounded him. Jo hurried along, trying to catch up, but got caught in the crowd dispersing from Charlotte's lecture.

One shell-shocked tourist was speaking to a companion as they left the empty lot where Charlotte had set up a lectern and some benches.

"Who would have thought the Harris hawk was so *lusty?*" the lady said, fanning herself with a paper napkin.

"Amazing," her friend agreed, looking around. She propped her hands on her hips. "I know it's a cliché, but I need a cigarette."

"You quit smoking ten years ago," her companion chided.

Jo hid a grin as she sidestepped the two women and dodged around those in her path. Case was a block ahead of her. Hurrying to catch up, she started to call his name, but was jerked to a stop by Martha Smalley. Besides being Julius Pangburn's ladylove, Martha was an artist who made her creations out of wrought iron. Since she used a forge and anvil, she had muscles unknown to most seventy-year-old women. When she encircled Jo in a sympathetic hug, Jo couldn't have escaped with a crowbar.

"Jo Ella, Julius and I heard what happened last night, though of course we don't know all the details." She paused, obviously hoping that Jo would share a few. When Jo only answered with a sickly smile, Martha continued. "Steve wasn't good enough for you."

"Tha-thanks, Martha." Jo gasped for air as black dots danced before her eyes. Martha released her just before Jo would have needed smelling salts, and took her hand in a warm grasp.

"All you have to do is let me know if there's anything I can do," she invited. "If you want me and my

group to do something about Steve, we'll be happy
to.''

"No," Jo said, panic shooting her voice up an oc-
tave. Martha and her ''group'' were women to be han-
dled with care. It was rumored around town that they
practiced some form of homegrown voodoo. This
could be proven by the number of their ex-husbands
and philandering men friends who had developed embarrassing illnesses and quirks. Martha's ex-husband,
Lester, had a wandering eye that really did wander
now.

"Really, Martha, it's fine. I'm fine.'' Or would be,
if news of her break up ever died down around this
town.

"Of course you are, dear," Martha said, patting her
arm. "But you can't let a man like Steve treat you
badly. Word will get around and then all men will treat
you badly.''

Jo winced and started backing away. "Thanks for
your concern.''

Martha waved her off and Jo turned, hoping the
embarrassed redness was fading from her face. She
forced herself not to fret over her new status as pity
object of the week. Her heart wasn't broken. Why
wouldn't anyone believe her?

She forgot about Martha when she caught sight of
Case once again.

He had stopped before the large plate-glass window
of Franklin's Emporium. She was about to rush up and
speak to him when the studied casualness of his posture made her pause.

He seemed to be examining a display of antique
kitchenware in the window. Did he collect rusty nut-
meg graters? she wondered. She watched as he turned
his head casually, right and left, then seemed to fix his

attention on someone inside the store, all the while sipping nonchalantly from his cup. Only someone watching very carefully would have noticed his actions. Jo congratulated herself on being that someone.

Smoothly, she moved up the sidewalk and came to a stop near him. She peeked into the store, but could see nothing except a milling crowd of shoppers. Barry Franklin was having a sale on headgear. Jo couldn't tell who Case was watching in that throng. Everyone looked identical, sporting Barry's latest creation, a hat embellished with a two-armed sahuaro cactus. Green heads bobbed throughout the store. She saw one hat that seemed a little different, a dark brown fedora that sported a bright red feather, but it disappeared in the throng. After a few minutes, Case took out a small blue notepad, wrote something down, and slipped it back into his pocket. He gave Jo a sidelong glance, then moved a few steps down the sidewalk, all the while keeping the interior of the store in view.

Since she couldn't figure out who he was watching, she decided to approach him. Turning, she gave him a brilliant smile as she pulled out her own notebook and pen. "Good morning, Mr. Houston. I'm Jo Quillan of the *Calamity Falls Ingot*. Are you in town working on an investigation?"

His head snapped around, his gaze swept over her, his dark brows pulled together. "No," he said.

"A vacation, then?" she asked brightly. "What would you say to giving me an interview about your most famous cases?"

"I'd say no," he answered matter-of-factly, and started walking away.

Undeterred, Jo scurried after him. She had never really dealt with a reluctant subject before. In this town, *everybody* wanted to talk.

"Really, Mr. Houston, the readers of the *Ingot* would be thrilled to learn about the work you've done with the…"

"No, Ms. Quillan," he said, rounding on her. "I'm here on a vacation, not to give interviews. I don't *do* interviews." Then he whirled and stomped away.

2

"WELL, YOU SEE, that's where you're making a mistake, Mr. Houston," Jo said, hustling along beside him. "People are interested in the kind of work you do. In fact, people are actually very grateful that you uncovered that insurance scam. It probably saved the taxpayers and policyholders millions of dollars."

He sent her an annoyed look and kept on walking. His long legs covered a great deal more distance than Jo's, so she had to lengthen her stride to keep up.

"So, Mr. Houston, what brings you to our fair city?" she asked brightly, juggling her bag, notebook and pen as they dashed along the sidewalk. She tried to ignore the fierce look in Case's eyes as he glanced at her.

"And do you think you'll be in town for a while?" Jo gave him a hopeful, if trembly, smile.

"No interview, Ms. Quillan. As I said, I'm in this town strictly on a vacation and I'd like my privacy undisturbed."

Jo started to argue, then thought better of it. If she antagonized the man, she'd never get her interview. She snapped her notebook shut even as she berated herself for giving in so easily. "Whatever you say, Mr. Houston," she said breezily. "Welcome to Calamity Falls. Enjoy your stay."

Her quick capitulation drew a frown from him, as if he didn't trust her. She manufactured a bright smile that didn't seem to convince him either. With a quick nod, he turned and walked away. The powerful momentum of his stride, the set of his shoulders and the expression on his face had the crowds on the sidewalk parting like the Red Sea splitting before Moses. He stopped beside a trash can, threw in the paper cup with his unfinished coffee, and kept going.

"Probably a good idea," she murmured as she watched him leave. "He seems tense enough. Maybe he really *is* here on a vacation."

CASE WISHED he really was on vacation. He stopped at the corner and glanced around. Not that he would have chosen Calamity Falls for a rest cure. The town's offbeat reputation was notorious throughout Arizona. He'd never had a desire to visit the place. He didn't like offbeat. He liked well-beaten smoky sports bars where an occasional fight erupted or a Diamondbacks game with lower-deck seats and a couple of beers. To him, that was heaven.

Give him the rumble and bustle of Phoenix. The scorching heat radiating up from the melting asphalt on a July day, the heady aroma of diesel fumes and car exhaust—all that was the staff of life to him. He avoided anything rustic, rural, quaint or cute, and Calamity Falls qualified in all of those areas.

Case surveyed the rough outline of the Mule Mountains as they punched the sky, and the small town that clung to their foothills. Consisting of many levels of twisting streets strung together by concrete stairs nearly a century old, it looked exactly like the resuscitated mining town he knew it to be. He'd grown up in a place almost exactly like this, and didn't have much desire to go back. Some people were born for cities and he was one of them.

The frantic call he'd received had convinced him to come to Calamity Falls, though, so here he was.

He tossed a look over his shoulder. Just his bad luck that the local paper had an eager-beaver reporter on staff who happened to remember him. When he saw that Jo had turned in the opposite direction, he allowed himself a thorough survey of her.

Smooth, straight hair as rich as semisweet chocolate swung across her neck as she strolled down the sidewalk. Its red highlights glinted in the sun. *Good-looking woman,* he thought, his irritation giving way to admiration. His attention dropped lower, appreciating her long legs and the lush curves of her figure, traveling down her straight back to her narrow waist and softly rounded hips encased in snug, faded jeans.

Nice back view, he thought. Made him think of Marilyn Monroe. He glanced at those long legs again. *On stilts,* he amended.

She bent over to pick up a small, stuffed animal a backpack-riding baby had dropped onto the sidewalk. Case gave a friendly look to the way her jeans stretched across her behind. *Darned nice,* he amended.

Distraction, he thought grumpily, and turned around. He was in Calamity Falls on business and he'd better remember that.

As he'd taught himself to do years ago, he focused his attention for a moment, concentrating on the problem at hand. He'd lost the man he'd been following and needed to pick up the trail again. He could go to the man's house, of course, and wait for him, but that wouldn't tell him where the guy had been, whom he'd talked to and why.

Case let his vision go soft. If he stared too long and hard, his quarry might elude him. Besides, his fixed glare would be noticed and bring unwanted attention.

Across the street an elderly man appeared to be conversing with a lamppost. On second thought, maybe no one here would notice, Case thought, giving the man a wary glance. An unhappy thought had just occurred to him. What if the eccentricity that galloped through this town was catching like the flu or the plague?

Too late to worry about it now. He'd been here for nearly twenty-four hours, plenty long enough for an incubation period. Case assessed the people crowding the street. He caught sight of a flamboyant brown fedora decorated with a red feather. Ah, there he was.

With a glance in either direction, Case checked for moving traffic, then plunged back into the chase.

JO HAD CALLED the few people she knew in Phoenix who might have an idea what Case Houston was doing in Calamity Falls. None of them could answer her questions. She sat at her desk and flipped paper clips into her empty coffee cup as she thought about the problem.

She had been brooding on it for half an hour, ever since she'd returned from her abortive attempt to get Case to talk to her. The floor around her desk was littered with paper clips because she missed the cup more often than she hit it, or they struck and bounced off the rim.

Across the office she shared with the *Ingot*'s editor and photographer, her uncle Don and aunt Millie, Don was busy writing up an account of last weekend's football game between the Calamity Falls Red Devils and the Morenci Wildcats. Millie was cropping pictures of the game to go into the *Ingot*. They had busily discussed the game all morning, fascinated by every detail, proud of the high-school team members and their hard work.

Millie and Don loved their small town paper. Jo loved them and was grateful for the opportunity they'd given her, but she wanted something more.

Like Case Houston and whatever he was investigating. But what was it?

The phone rang and since both of the other people in the room were engrossed in their work, Jo answered.

"Please tell me the tingle is gone," Lainey said, without preamble. "I've been worrying about it all morning."

"You know, experts say that most of the things you worry about never happen."

"None of those experts have ever met you," Lainey sighed. "Did you get an interview with that man you were stalking?"

"I wasn't stalking him, just trying to talk to him. I didn't get the interview yet, but it's just a matter of time. I do have some conclusions to go on, based on facts, though. Fact, Case used to work for the state attorney general and is now on his own. I definitely saw him watching someone through the window of Franklin's Emporium."

"So your conclusion is that he's in town to investigate someone?"

"That's right, but I realize he's not going to let me interview him. It was kind of rash and foolish to think he would."

"Jo Quillan did something rash and foolish?" Lainey said in mock wonder. "Alert the media! Oh, wait. You *are* the media."

"Very funny," Jo said, not the least bit amused.

True, she was occasionally rash and foolish—look

at the number of months she'd wasted dating Steve. She needed to be much more circumspect and professional in her approach if she was to get Case's cooperation.

Jo sat up suddenly and her feet thumped to the floor as an idea broke over her like a dam bursting. "I know what I need to do," she blurted. "I'll talk to you later." She hung up over Lainey's squawk of protest.

All she had to do was offer to help him in his sleuthing in exchange for exclusive rights to the story when he had successfully concluded his investigation.

Delight rushed over her at the rightness of her idea. How could he turn down such an offer? The help of an experienced reporter would be invaluable to him since he seemed to be working on this case, whatever it was, all alone.

Ignoring the small voice that told her he *wanted* to work alone, Jo jumped up, told her startled aunt and uncle that she was going to be gone for a while, grabbed her bag, and rushed out the door. She would go to the Copper Quest and see if she could talk to Case. Confident that she was on the right track, Jo trotted down the street to the base of the staircase that rose two levels to the inn.

The Copper Quest was up on Manzanita Street, a tiny road with only the inn and one other house on it.

Placing her hand on the cast-iron railing, Jo started up. By the time she reached Manzanita, she was winded, but determined to continue. She was pleased when she saw a black four-wheel-drive Jeep in the inn's driveway. It looked like the kind of vehicle Case would drive. That didn't necessarily mean he was there. After all, he hadn't been headed back here when she'd last seen him, and he could easily have taken the stairs anywhere in town. Still, it was a place to start. When she spoke to the inn's owner, Sharon Zonder, she discovered that Case was gone and wasn't expected back anytime soon.

Disappointed, Jo asked to use the restroom and Sharon directed her upstairs to the family's bathroom on the third floor, since she was busy preparing to scrub the family's dog in the tub of the downstairs bathroom.

When she came out of the rest room a few minutes later, Jo started downstairs, then paused and looked back at the guest bedrooms. There were six of them, all named after various minerals found in the area; copper, turquoise, malachite, obsidian, fire agate and tiger's eye. Meandering down the hall, she peeked into the rooms. They were beautifully decorated, each in the color of the mineral they were named after. She wondered which one Sharon had given Case.

Was her friend whimsical enough to give him one that matched his eyes? Perhaps Obsidian? Nah, Sharon was too businesslike for that.

The doors of most of the rooms stood open, telling her they were empty of guests. The door to Tiger's Eye was closed, though. Could that be his?

Jo's hand formed a fist and she lifted it to knock, then paused. She already knew he was gone, so why should she knock? She stared at the door with intense concentration as she debated the ethics of what she was about to do. She wasn't snooping exactly, she rationalized. She was merely curious about what kind of man Case was.

She was only going to put her hand on the knob and see if it was locked. It wasn't as if she was going to go in and rifle through his things. That decided, Jo reached for the knob, then started with a shriek when a hand clamped down on her forearm.

"Miss Quillan, we meet again." Case's voice, low and even, vibrated in her ear.

Jo paled. How did he move so silently in those biker boots of his? She considered running, but his hold on her arm told her what would happen if she tried it. He'd hang on tight and she'd end up with one arm longer than the other. Instantly, she decided to bluff.

She met his eyes and gave him a big smile. "Mr. Houston, I was hoping to run into you."

He lifted an eyebrow at her. She truly admired the way he did that, even while the fierce look on his face had her quaking in her Birkenstocks.

"I'll bet," he said.

"No, really." She nodded as convincingly as possible. "I realize that my approach this morning was all wrong, so I decided...."

"To look for me in my room?"

"Oh, is this your room?" she asked blinking innocently. "What a coincidence."

"Yes, isn't it?" His tone was drier than the desert outside.

He didn't say anything more, only stood and waited for her to go on. She turned up the wattage on her smile. "Well, as I was saying, I wanted to speak to you."

"No interview. I'm on vacation."

"Then I think it must be a working vacation." She tilted her head. "You seemed awfully interested in a certain group of people coming out of Franklin's Emporium this morning." She gave her arm an experimental little tug, but she might as well have saved her energy because he only responded by sliding his hand down to her wrist and encircling it.

"I'm a student of human nature," he continued in that dry tone, but there was a spark of enjoyment in his eyes. "I was trying to figure out what would make people buy a hat decorated with a cactus."

"Uh-huh," she said. "I think you're here on an investigation, and I came to offer my help in exchange for an exclusive interview when the investigation is finished."

He gazed at her for several seconds. "If I was involved in an investigation—which I'm not—I wouldn't need help from you or anyone else. I work alone."

Even though she'd tried to fool herself into thinking otherwise, Jo believed that was his usual way of doing things. She wondered if she could run a bluff. "That probably works well in Phoenix where you know people, but you might want to rethink your tactics here in Cochise County. You know how it is in little towns—it's not what you know, but who you know."

He didn't fall for it, but he did release her wrist. He leaned against the doorpost and crossed his arms over his chest. "In this case, it's neither one. I'm here on vacation. So why don't you go away and let me get on with it?"

Surreptitiously, Jo rubbed her wrist. If this guy ever had to capture a criminal, he wouldn't need handcuffs. She managed to keep from saying that aloud. Instead, she kept her mind on the story she was sure would launch her into the career for which she was so perfectly qualified. "Then why don't I treat you to the best barbecue in Calamity Falls?" she asked brightly. "As a way of welcoming you to town. May Ling Schultz over at the Lotus Blossom makes fabulous spareribs."

"May Ling Schultz?"

"Chinese-German, by way of Dallas."

"I see." His eyes narrowed as if he was debating with himself about taking her up on her offer.

Jo met his gaze and felt the tingle once again. Wait. Maybe it was lust instead. She wondered how good she would be at seducing the story out of him. She dampened her lips and let them fall open in invitation, then allowed her eyelids to droop in a sultry manner.

He squinted at her. "You seem to be breathing through your mouth. Are you having trouble with your adenoids?"

"Certainly not!" What was he, a doctor in his spare time? She tried the sultry look again.

"Is there something wrong with your eyes, or are you trying to fall asleep standing up?"

"Neither," she said, giving up and glaring at him. "I was...thinking. How about that barbecue?"

"No, thank you, Ms. Quillan..."

"Jo, please," she corrected him. "If you change your mind, let me know. I mean, you have to eat. Give me a call. My number's in the book."

He looked relieved to be getting rid of her, but he asked, "Do you invite all newcomers out for meals?"

"No, just the ones I want to interview."

His jaw tightened. "Go away. I have a meeting..."

Her eyes lit up as if someone had set off a roman candle inside her head. "A meeting? Why don't I come with you?"

"Because I don't want you to." he answered firmly. "And because it's for men only," he added, then paused as if he regretted having added that last part.

She latched onto it like a robin on a worm. "A meeting for men only? Where?"

His exasperated gaze swept over her. "In case you haven't noticed, you're not a man. What you are is the most damned persistent woman I ever saw."

"That's what makes a good reporter."

Case reached into his pocket for a key. "Well, Ms. Good Reporter, do you want to know what makes a good detective?"

His question had her scrambling for her notebook and pen. "No, what?"

"The ability to keep one's mouth shut." He said it as if he was reminding himself of that fact, then unlocked the door of the Tiger's Eye room and slipped inside with a wink at her annoyed expression. He shut the door in her face and she stared at it for a second as she resisted the urge to give it a childish kick. It wouldn't do any good and besides, there was no point in marring Sharon's careful paint job.

She turned away knowing the encounter hadn't gotten her anywhere. Maybe she was wrong. Maybe the way he'd been acting on the street today was normal for him, but the way he'd been watching that group of people...

Jo's steps slowed, then stopped. Those people. The man in the dark brown fedora that sported a red feather.

Her head jerked up and she stared straight ahead as it came to her. She'd only seen one person in town with a hat like that. Dr. Harold Purdy. That's what his name was. She didn't know if he was a real doctor or not, but he seemed like yet another of the harmless eccentrics who had gravitated here. He'd moved into a house on Nugget Street and begun cultivating a friendship with some of the other newcomers.

Jo hadn't met him yet, but she knew a number of people who said he was a fascinating man. She'd also heard he was leading some kind of men's meeting up on Rattlesnake Mesa tonight just after sunset—and no women were allowed.

With a speculative gleam in her eyes, she hurried down the hallway. She'd just see about that.

"THIS IS THE MOST INSANE thing you've ever done," Lainey grumbled as she knelt and tried to stitch up the hem of the slacks Jo was wearing. "And where in the world did you get these pants?" she asked as she tried to take up what seemed like yards of fabric at the bottom of the legs.

"The thrift store," Jo admitted. "I thought about simply wearing my own jeans, but..."

"You wear them too tight for them to be able to disguise the fact that you're a woman."

Jo grinned. "Something like that."

Lainey finished one hem and started on the other. "Wouldn't it be simpler to ask this Dr. Purdy to let you observe and report on his meeting tonight for the *Ingot*? After all, it might be of local interest."

"I tried that. Even tracked him down at that house he's rented, but he sent another man out to say no, that the meeting's private."

"Which, of course, made you all the more curious and determined to go, right?"

"You know my motto...."

"'Idiocy Above All Else'?"

"No, 'Obstacles are Made to be Overcome.'"

"I'll remember to suggest that for your tombstone," Lainey grumbled.

"My curiosity's aroused. I tried to talk to this man who calls himself Professor Purdy but he wasn't home."

"Probably out looking for people to attend his rally."

"I went next door to ask Starina Simms if she'd seen anything suspicious, but she said no."

"Starina wouldn't see something suspicious unless it was attached to the end of her own nose. She's too involved in her quest for a perpetual-motion machine. How's that coming, by the way?" Lainey asked around a mouthful of pins.

"She says she's almost got it this time." Jo grinned. Starina had been saying the same thing for years, ever since she'd left her job as an engineer with an aerospace firm and moved to Calamity Falls.

At last Lainey sat back and viewed her handiwork. "This is only tacked up, so don't do anything foolish like try to run in them." She stood and turned Jo around so she could see herself in the mirror. "I don't know about this," she said.

"I do." Jo gave her outfit a critical look. Baggy tweed slacks held up with a belt, a man's dress shirt, several sizes too big, tucked into the slacks, and a loose suitcoat to top the whole thing off. She was grateful that it hid her figure successfully, and that the October evening would be cool enough to give her an excuse to keep the jacket on. She picked up a black billed cap, pulled her ponytail up on top of her head, and settled the cap into place.

"There," she said in a tone of satisfaction. "I did some more checking on Dr. Purdy this afternoon. I think I look exactly like the kind of down-on-my-luck guy who'd be interested in listening to him."

Lainey shook her head as she viewed the mismatched outfit. "*Down* on your luck? You look like your luck packed up and left town."

"Good. That's exactly what I want." Jo leaned close to the mirror and examined her smooth jaw. "Now, how do I make myself look like I haven't shaved in several days?"

"A fake beard?"

"Nah. It might fall off, and besides, where would I get one at this time of day?"

"I read somewhere that Hollywood makeup artists sometimes use glue to apply coffee grounds to the face to look like a beard."

Jo grimaced. "I don't think so, even though you would obviously have a ready supply of them. And wouldn't that give me a rather distinctive odor?"

Lainey rustled in Jo's makeup case. "How about if we resort to the old tried-and-true eyebrow pencil?" Holding Jo's jaw between her thumb and forefinger, she made careful marks, then smudged them with her thumb. "Do you want sideburns?"

"Sure, throw them in, too," Jo said recklessly. In spite of Lainey's skepticism, Jo was sure this was a great idea. She could find out what Case was investigating without him ever knowing it. She could blend in with the other people there and never be noticed. It would work perfectly.

"THIS ISN'T GOING to work," she muttered an hour later, as she finished the climb up to the top of Rattlesnake Mesa and saw that there were only about ten men there. They were backlit by a huge bonfire that had been built in the clearing, so they were easy to count. She had expected to get lost in the crowd, but this "crowd" was more sparse than she'd expected it to be.

Professor Purdy was moving among them, shaking hands, making them welcome. Jo, who'd never seen him up close before, thought he was a handsome man. He appeared to be in his late forties or early fifties and was very self-assured.

"In for a penny, in for a pound," she muttered and started to walk across the mesa, keeping a careful lookout as she went. This place hadn't gotten its name by accident and it was exactly the time of day when the rattlers would be heading back to their nests. She hoped she wasn't walking down the middle of a snake freeway.

Before she reached the light coming from the bonfire, she remembered to stop walking like a woman, square her shoulders, and put some swagger into her step. She planned to get close enough to Case to see if she could discover why he was investigating Purdy, but not so close he would recognize her. That might be a little tricky, but she consoled herself with the reminder that great reporters always took risks.

Her heart was pounding in her throat and her hands were shaking, so she dug them into the pockets of her jacket, told herself that any good investigative reporter would be experiencing the same fear, and kept going.

CASE LOOKED AROUND at the men who had assembled at the bonfire and wondered if they felt as foolish as he did. Most of the men were older, but there were a few who appeared to be in their twenties and had probably come to Dr. Purdy's Way of the Unbroken Man rally purely out of curiosity.

Case could see Purdy on the other side of the bonfire, pressing the flesh and greeting newcomers. He'd shaken Case's hand and Case had managed to present a suitably deadpan expression that hadn't aroused the other man's curiosity. Purdy had a smile that looked genuine, serene and untroubled.

The thought of trouble brought Jo Quillan to mind. Now there was trouble if he'd ever seen it. Too bad she was so blasted appealing. But he wasn't going to think about that right now, he decided, concentrating on the other men gathered around Purdy.

What about that latecomer? Case glanced at the guy who was sidling up to the fire. And why was he walking as if he was nursing a rash?

The guy nodded to the men on both sides of him, then buried his hands in his pockets and his chin in the collar of his jacket. Shy and uncomfortable, Case thought, feeling a spurt of sympathy, and wondering if he would turn and run. In fact, the kid's stiff posture told Case he was one breath away from being terrified.

Against his better judgment, he decided to go over and speak to the guy. Wouldn't do much for the manly image the kid was so obviously trying to project if he fainted dead away from fright. Carefully, Case strolled around the perimeter of the group just as Purdy began talking.

"The modern world has broken men into fragments, tried to make something wrong and ugly of masculinity. This isn't the fault of women, it's our own fault because we let it happen. The Way of the Unbroken Man seeks to reconnect those parts that have been fragmented; body, soul, and spirit pulled back together in wisdom and strength."

He went on, but Case tuned him out momentarily as he concentrated on the most recent addition to the group. He eased up behind him and noticed that although the guy seemed to be listening intently, he appeared to be glancing left and right nervously. In fact, his attention seemed to be focused on the place where Case had been standing.

Puzzled, Case stepped forward and whispered, "Don't worry, buddy. I think this whole gathering is going to be pretty harmless."

Case! Jo jerked and made a sound like a gasp that turned into a cough as she raised her hand to cover her mouth. She reached up and tugged her hat down over her ears. *Now* he wanted to be friendly and chatty. Great!

"Hey, are you okay?" Case asked, then frowned. "Has there been a weather report for a projected blizzard?"

Jo dipped her chin further into her collar and answered gruffly. "I'm okay, thanks…uh, buddy." She tried to edge away into the darkness. Darn! Why had she moved up so close to the bonfire?

Case leaned nearer. "Well, if you think you want to get out of here, go ahead. Nobody'll stop you."

Jo hunched her shoulders up and peered out at him like a turtle from its shell. "I'm staying till the end. I'm interested in what Purdy has to say."

"Suit yourself, but you don't look like you belong here." Case snorted. "Do you even know which end of the razor you use to shave with?"

Jo's harrumph made Case chuckle.

Why didn't he move *away?* Jo thought frantically. Leave her *alone?* It was the worst possible luck that Case would decide to show his compassionate side and try to comfort him. Uh, *her.* She gulped the bubble of hysterical laughter that was threatening to erupt.

She wanted to find out why he was here, what he was investigating regarding Purdy. She didn't want him investigating *her.*

"I've been to one of these before," Case whispered again. "This is the part where it begins to be really interesting."

"Oh?" Her voice shot up and she cleared her throat. "Oh?" she asked in a gruff tone. "What happens?"

Purdy was holding forth on the need for men to retake their rightful place in society, to stop allowing the world, and the opinions of others, to dictate their actions.

"Well, like I said, it starts out pretty harmless, but I think we're probably coming up to the point where we get in touch with our inner Unbroken Man," Case said. "We'll hold hands and walk around the bonfire, repeating chants that Dr. Purdy has designed for that purpose."

Jo sneaked a sideways glance at Case. Was he kidding? Case definitely didn't seem like the type to be holding other men's hands and repeating chants. Still, how well did she know him? Was he investigating Purdy, or joining him?

"Oh," was all she could manage to say. She could do that. The holding-hands part might be a little bit dicey, especially if someone noticed that her hands were softer than they should be, but she could do it.

Purdy's voice rang out over the mesa and the wind began to pick up. The fire shot sparks into the air and the flames bent toward Case and Jo, driving them to step back out of danger.

"That wind's gotta let up a little before we can go on to the next part, though," Case added matter-of-factly.

"Why? What's the next part?"

"As soon as that fire dies down, we'll be walking over hot coals."

"What?" She forgot to keep her voice low, so she snapped her lips shut and stared at him in dismay.

His mouth turned down in a considering frown. "Oh, don't worry. He'll demonstrate first, show us how to go into a trancelike state so that we don't feel a thing. It's amazing. I've seen it before, though I've never seen a group do it the way this one does."

Jo licked her lips and swallowed the cotton bale that

was lodged in her throat. "How does this group do it?"

"Naked."

Her throat squeezed like a deflating accordion. "Na-a-a-a-aked?" she asked.

"You know how us guys like to get together and throw the old testosterone around. Purdy says doing the fire walk naked is the only way to make it authentic."

"What if we don't care about authentic?" Jo asked frantically.

"Then why are you here?"

"I'm beginning to wonder."

Case lifted his hand and clapped her on the back, almost sending her to her knees. He grabbed her elbow and propped her up. "Don't worry, buddy, I'll be right here, glad to give you help and support."

She didn't need support. She needed to run. And this looked like a heck of a good time to do it.

Jo eased her arm out of Case's grip. "After listening to him, I don't think Dr. Purdy's message is for me. I'll just be on my way."

"You can't do that." Case let go of her elbow, but tossed his arm around her shoulders in a companionable way. "This may be your only chance to get in touch with your inner Unbroken Man."

"Mine wants to stay broken," she said, starting to panic when she glanced around and saw that the other men were beginning to form a circle and clasping each other's hands. Her palms began to sweat.

"Nonsense," Case answered heartily. "You'll never be a real man until you have this experience."

"I don't want to be a real man." Jo ducked away from him, turned and fled into the darkness.

3

HE KNEW! Jo dashed across the mesa, tripped over the hem of her pants and nearly went tumbling onto her nose. The action snapped the worn leather belt that had seemed like such a bargain at the thrift store and the baggy pants slipped down her hips. She jerked them up and hobbled away, looking like a little old man with a bad back. Behind her, she could hear Case chuckling.

She turned and glared back at her nemesis. Even in the dim light from the bonfire, she could see him grinning. He gave her a cocky salute indicating that he knew it was her—probably had known all along, the rat—and that he was enjoying her predicament.

Furious and embarrassed, her first thought was to run home—well, hobble home. She couldn't do much running in pants that insisted on trying to head south with every step. The more she thought about running, though, the angrier she got. He'd told her that cock-and-bull story about walking naked over hot coals just to get rid of her.

She floundered across the mesa, away from the light of the bonfire and into the shadows. When she came to a thick stand of mesquite bushes she stopped and glanced once again at the group of men. It would be a shame to miss whatever was going to happen, she concluded. Besides, she'd come all this way and made a fool of herself. So she might as well stick around.

Recently fallen dried mesquite beans crunched and snapped beneath her shoes as she pushed her way in among the gnarled, smoky-smelling trunks and peered out at the group still gathered around the bonfire. She hoped they hadn't heard her noisy entrance, but then, none of them seem to have noticed her flight from the fire, so she probably was safe. Even Case had returned to the group, obviously believing he'd run her off.

She wasn't that easy to get rid of. He should know that by now. Hadn't she been practically stalking him all day? Jo winced at the truth of that statement as she leaned against the mesquite trunk and watched the group gathered on the mesa.

Because she'd been distracted by Case when she'd been near the bonfire, she'd barely noticed that there were a number of men from Calamity Falls in the group. She'd known Purdy's message, whatever it was, would appeal to tourists—after all, they came to town to see what the odd inhabitants were up to. But she saw a number of men from town, as well, including Lainey's grandfather Julius, who looked fascinated by the proceedings.

She noticed Stavros Pappas, who ran a Greek restaurant in town and had a strong interest in astrology. He didn't cook certain dishes on days the stars didn't seem in the proper alignment so the menu at his place was always a delicious surprise. Why would he be interested in Purdy's Way of the Unbroken Man?

Beside him was Cedric Warrender, a wealthy retired British landscape architect who liked to trim the pyracantha bushes in front of his house into the fanciful shapes of characters from *Alice in Wonderland*. He thought they spoke to him and recorded their conversations in three-ring binder notebooks.

Nearby were several other of the town's eccentrics,

mostly newcomers Jo didn't know very well. Jo felt a surge of concern when she saw how eagerly they seemed to be listening to Purdy's message. She thought their interest in him was strange because most of Calamity Falls' oddballs were determined individualists.

They didn't usually follow anyone else's ideas, but tried to get others to agree with their own unusual theories. Something about Purdy must be very attractive to them. Perhaps it was the warm, fuzzy, get-in-touch-with-your-feelings method he was talking about.

The rich timbre of Purdy's voice was compelling. As she listened to the words rolling through the night air, she felt herself caught up in their flowing cadence. She blinked and shook her head. It was almost hypnotizing.

She stood on her tiptoes to peer through the mesquite branches as she searched out Case. He stood with the other men, arms folded across his chest, head bent forward in an attitude of intense concentration.

"Hmph," she said scornfully, rocking back on her heels.

She certainly couldn't imagine Case Houston getting in touch with his feelings, if he had any, beyond irritation with her. She had to gulp down loud laughter when he joined hands with the other men and they began walking in a circle around the bonfire, chanting something that sounded like, "Male Power built the world. Male Power will preserve the world."

"And women had nothing to do with it?" she murmured, peeking out from her perch. Their circling and chanting went on for a while, then Purdy talked some more, then led them in more chants. It was easy to hear him in the still night air, but she couldn't make much sense of what he was saying. "Maybe because I'm not a man," she whispered to herself.

Finally, thinking she wasn't going to see anything worthwhile, she started to creep from the mesquite bush, ready to go home. Small thorns and branches plucked at her loose clothing and it took her a few minutes of grappling with the bush to get herself loose.

Just as she finally staggered out of the branches, however, Purdy once again climbed on top of a small stool and called for the men's attention. Jo paused behind the mesquite to listen.

Purdy lifted his hands into the air and grasped them together so that he looked like a prizefighter proclaiming victory. "I can fe-e-e-e-el the power," he said, his head thrown back, his magnificent voice rolling out through the desert night.

"Yes sir," some of the men answered, nodding solemnly.

"There's power here tonight," Purdy went on, fisting his hands and punching them into the air above his head. "There's something in the air. I can feel it." He waved his hands, paused for effect and turned his head. "I can smell it."

"Maybe it's just that his undcrarm deodorant has failed," a deep voice rumbled above her head.

With a squeak of surprise, Jo jumped and whipped around. Or tried to. Her baggy pants tripped her up and as she grabbed at them and tried to right herself, her elbow connected with Case Houston's midsection.

"Oof," he grunted and rubbed his stomach. "Hey, watch out."

"You shouldn't sneak up on people, Houston," she hissed, giving her baggy clothes a jerk to pull her pant legs out from under her heels. She did a staggering dance around in a circle before she got her feet straight again and her pants out of the way.

"And you shouldn't lurk around in the bushes, Ms. Jo Ella Quillan," he responded, muffled laughter in his voice. "Although in that getup, I can understand that you wouldn't want to be recognized."

"I was merely trying to do my job," she said in a haughty tone. She lifted her chin and gave him a superior look that she knew was a major failure in the darkness.

"You were following me."

No point in denying it. She changed the subject instead. "Aren't you going to stay for the rest of Purdy's talk?" she asked, tongue in cheek. "Or are you fully in touch with your unbroken inner man after all that hand-holding and chanting?"

Case surprised her by leaning close and whispering, "My inner man and I are just fine, thank you."

The scent of his spicy cologne teased her nose and the feel of his breath brushing against her ear was disconcerting—and exciting. She gave him a sideways glance, noting how the moonlight made shadows appear along his high cheekbones and eyebrows. The outer man wasn't bad, either, she decided with a sigh.

She hadn't meant the sound to be audible, but he responded by asking, "Are you annoyed with me? Good, then maybe you'll quit being such a pain in the keister."

"I could be a big help to you, Case, if you'd only let me."

"The day I need help from the Little Tramp is the day I hand in my investigator's license," he grumbled as he gave her outfit a dismissive glance.

Jo's lips pinched together. Did he know that in that insult he'd just confirmed what she'd been thinking all along? That he was in Calamity Falls to investigate something—and now she was almost positive that it was Purdy. "What's Harold Purdy up to, by the way?"

Case's brows drew together in a ferocious frown as if he was regretting what he'd said. "Oh, hell," he murmured. Before he could say any more, though, Purdy's voice boomed across the mesa. "Our inner man compels us to take control once more of our world and to that end, I would like to invite all of you to a lecture on the fascinating subject of cosmogony. You'll find what you're truly looking for," he said in his intriguing voice. "Cosmogony is the story of earth's past and future, a new, but proven, science that tells us exactly what each individual's place is in this universe."

"Cosmogony?" Jo asked.

"Shhh!" Case said, grasping her shoulder and giving her a gentle shake. "I'm trying to hear what he's saying."

"Then why didn't you stay with the group?"

"Because, damn it, I had to come find out what you were up to. I knew I hadn't been lucky enough to get you to leave."

Jo shrugged him off, alarmed by the sudden spurt of awareness that bolted through her. She dragged her attention back to Purdy just in time to hear him say the lecture on cosmogony would be held later in the week at the house he was renting. Jo immediately began making plans to attend, if it wasn't for men only.

"You're not going to that meeting," Case growled into her ear.

"Excuse me," she said angrily. "The last I heard, this is a free country and I can go to that lecture if I choose. Besides, it might be of interest to the readers of the *Ingot*.''

"You're only interested because you think I am.''

"Aren't you?''

Case took her arm and started marching her toward the edge of the mesa and the trail that led down to the road into Calamity Falls. "If you don't stop following me, I'll have you arrested.''

"Oh, I'm so sure you'd do that,'' she responded sardonically. She would have stopped and dug in her heels but she didn't get the chance. He kept hustling her along and she couldn't fight him off and hold up her pants at the same time. Her only defense was to stick out her elbows and try to deflect him, but he responded by grabbing both of them so that he was marching her along like a prisoner heading for a padded cell.

"Don't doubt that I *will* have you arrested.''

"Won't trying to have the reporter for the local paper locked up bring you attention that you don't want?''

Case let go of one of her elbows and from his pocket took a small flashlight to light their way down the path. It wasn't steep or rough, but Jo was grateful to be able to see. She hadn't thought to bring a flashlight.

When they reached the road, Case roughly urged her around to face him. He leaned close and stared into her wide eyes. "Stay out of my way, Jo. Stop following me. I'll do whatever is necessary to keep you out of my investigation.''

The determination in his face had her gulping down a lump in her throat, but she couldn't resist saying, "Investigation? Of Purdy? Why are you investigating him?''

A low sound of annoyance was her only answer. The look in his dark eyes would have been enough to singe her whiskers off if they'd been real. He didn't say anything else, but pocketed his flashlight, placed both his hands on her shoulders, and moved her away from him. "Good night, Miss Quillan. Stay away from me."

Or you'll regret it.

The unspoken threat hung in the air. For all of her bravado, Jo flinched. He sounded like he meant it. If he hadn't been holding her in place, Jo suspected her knees probably would have crumpled. She forced a little starch into them by reminding herself that good investigative journalists didn't back off at the first sign of trouble, that they persevered and didn't become intimidated. Looking into the displeasure in Case's eyes, though, she wondered if any of her hero journalists had ever faced anyone like him.

Without another word, Case set her away from him, turned and strode into the darkness. Jo stared after him in dismay. She wanted to stand still for a few minutes and think things through, but Purdy's audience was coming down off the mountain and she needed to scurry out of the way so she wouldn't be seen.

Holding her pants up with both hands, she scuttled through the dark streets toward home. Fortunately, Calamity Falls was small and Jo knew every staircase and back alley that would lead her to the little house she rented on Cholla Circle, a fancy name for the narrow street that had been built a hundred years ago for carriage and foot traffic.

She fervently hoped that none of her neighbors saw her. Old Mrs. Rios was convinced people were peeping into her windows at night. She kept a ready supply of rocks stacked inside her front and back doors in case she needed to defend herself. If the old lady saw Jo in her tramp's garb, those stones would be zinging through the air in record numbers.

Jo scurried past Mrs. Rios's house and in her own front door. As she shut it behind her, Lainey came out of the kitchen carrying a thick sandwich and a can of diet soda. She looked at Jo's bedraggled appearance and laughed. "What happened to you?"

"The belt broke," Jo answered in disgust.

"Don't say I didn't warn you," Lainey said, sitting down on the couch, propping her feet on a small trunk that Jo used for a coffee table, and taking a huge bite of her sandwich.

"I wouldn't dream of it." Jo hurried into her bedroom and shucked off the baggy outfit, vowing to return it to the thrift store first thing in the morning.

"What happened?" Lainey called out.

As she scrubbed off her fake beard and then donned a nightshirt and fuzzy slippers, Jo reported on the Way of the Unbroken Man meeting.

"Your grandpa was there."

"Oh, great," Lainey muttered. Julius loved checking out any new events going on in town. "And was Case there?"

"Oh, yes." She returned to the living room, took the sandwich from her friend, picked up the uneaten half and sat down beside her. "Hey, that's my sandwich," Lainey grumbled.

"Made from food in *my* refrigerator."

"Mine's always empty."

"Perhaps you should shop for food."

Lainey nodded, considering the idea. "I could, I suppose, when I buy supplies for my shop, but food tastes better at your house."

"A likely story, Lainey."

Lainey grinned. "It was the best I could come up with at the moment. Tell me about Case."

Jo gave her a grumpy look. "It might have been a more effective disguise if I'd stayed away from Case and hadn't let him panic me."

Interested, Lainey sat up. "He panicked you? This is getting good. How'd he do that?"

Jo gave a simplified version of the walking-naked-over-hot-coals story, but it still sent Lainey into peals of laughter. While Lainey howled, Jo chewed and scowled.

When her friend came up for air, Jo said, "He unnerves me. He's not what I'm used to."

"Because most of the men you know in Calamity Falls are either retired, eccentrics, or..."

"Retired eccentrics," Jo finished.

"Or men like Steve who are here on short-term surveying assignments, then break up with their girlfriends, leaving their hearts crushed into itty-bitty pieces just before they breeze out of town."

"It wasn't like that," Jo insisted although the thought of Steve still dismayed her. The previous night's embarrassment had begun to fade. She no longer wanted to crawl under her bedcovers and hide. She could thank Case Houston for that. He'd given her something to think about besides her broken heart.

It *wasn't* broken, she reminded herself sternly. It wasn't even cracked or dented. She had been accustomed to Steve, that was all. They'd gone out for months, had regular Monday and Saturday night dates. They were accustomed to each other's company, and while she hadn't thought of him in terms of a husband, she'd been comfortable with him. She was used to him. True, she'd been in a rut and she supposed she should be grateful to him for catapulting her out of it and into the path of Case Houston and his investigation.

She simply had to remember that Case might be an attractive man, but he was only a source, someone who would help her with the story she needed. The fact that he was dark, dangerous and sexy couldn't be allowed to affect her objectivity.

She couldn't say all that to Lainey, though, she thought, giving her friend a sidelong glance as she got up to rifle through Jo's freezer for ice cream. Lainey would build it up into something it certainly wasn't.

The two of them enjoyed late-night ice-cream sundaes, which Lainey assured her would put her right to sleep with no regretful thoughts of Steve. Jo gave up her efforts to change her friend's mind, realizing she was only trying to save Jo from another evening of wine imbibing.

When Lainey breezed out at ten o'clock, Jo headed for bed. Whether it was the ice cream or not, she didn't spend any time thinking about Steve. Instead, her mind was on Case—his presence in Calamity Falls, his investigation, his dark, glittering eyes. It was disturbing, but better than thinking about being dumped on a busy Monday night at the Copper Pot, she reflected as she drifted into sleep.

TAPE RECORDER in one pocket of her jacket, notebook in the other, dark glasses firmly in place, Jo strolled easily down Battlehaven Avenue. She stopped in front of a plate-glass window to adjust the brim of the low-crowned slouch cloth hat she'd bought last year to protect her from the sun on a trip to the Grand Canyon.

With a satisfied nod, she turned away, sure she blended in perfectly with the tourists. She smiled as she passed a man wearing plaid Bermuda shorts and argyle socks and considered that maybe her jeans and T-shirt were too conservative. On the other hand, she needed to be a little less conspicuous in her efforts to get Case to talk to her, so subtlety would be the best approach.

She had already nosed around that morning and discovered that Purdy had no meetings scheduled for the day. He was often out and about in Calamity Falls, though, and she suspected that where Purdy led, Case was sure to follow. She could observe them both and see if she could discover what it was that Case was investigating. She had to be careful, though, that she didn't follow so closely that she looked like the tail end of a parade.

She made her way in and out of the shops, surprised by the Wednesday-morning crowds, but pleased for the merchants who were doing brisk business. It took her an hour of supposedly aimless wandering but at last she located Harold Purdy at an outdoor café. He was in the middle of a group of people who had pushed a couple of tables together to be near him. He was speaking and they leaned close to hear him.

Jo saw that the group included Charlotte Quail, who appeared to be enthralled with whatever Purdy was saying. Beside her sat an elderly lady Jo didn't know. She seemed to be as enamored of Purdy as Charlotte was. The two of them sat like two white-haired bookends, listening to Purdy as if he were explaining the whereabouts of the Fountain of Youth.

Dismayed, Jo removed her sunglasses in order to see them better. She could only wiggle her fingers weakly when Charlotte looked up and give her a hearty wave.

Purdy glanced around just then and Jo felt the full impact of his attention. She started when it landed on her with an almost physical force. His gaze swept over her from head to toe in a split second, then came up to meet hers. His eyes were a clear, pale blue that warmed and softened when he saw her. It was as if he was asking where she'd been all his life.

Jo gulped, feeling herself being drawn to him as inexorably as energy disappearing into a black hole in space. It was all she could do to nod quickly and look away.

She understood why Charlotte found Harold Purdy enthralling. Being caught in his gaze was like being snatched up by a Harris hawk.

Jo wished she was close enough to hear what he had to say, but she certainly didn't want to look into those mesmerizing eyes again.

Besides, she was determined to maintain her distance so as not to attract the attention of the man who sat not far away, seemingly engrossed in the Phoenix newspaper. Though she had been sure he hadn't spied her, Case folded down one corner of the paper and looked at her over the top. She couldn't read the expression in his eyes because of the dark glasses he wore, but he didn't look the least bit surprised to see her.

Acknowledging that she wasn't much of a spy, Jo shrugged and strolled over to sit opposite him.

"You're late," he said, then indicated the insulated coffeepot in front of him, and the upside-down cup sitting on a saucer at her place. "Want some coffee?"

"I'm late?" she asked, frowning.

"I expected you to catch up with me an hour ago. I knew as soon as I told you to keep away from me last night you'd be stuck to me like flypaper today. Help yourself. I'm paying."

Jo stared at him suspiciously. What was this?

"You see," Case went on. "I've decided that in dealing with you, I need to tell you exactly the opposite of what I want you to do. If I say stay and have some coffee, you're certain to run off and leave me alone."

Against her better judgment, Jo grinned. "Don't you wish." She picked up the pot and poured herself a cupful, happily adding cream and sugar.

"What's with the Mata Hari outfit?' he asked. "Didn't the hobo look work out for you? Do you have a disguise for every occasion?"

Jo studied him for a moment before answering. He was so freshly shaven his jaw glistened. The breeze picked up the scent of his aftershave and sent it swirling through her head. His black hair was ruffled, as if he'd just run his fingers through it, and in spite of her annoyance with him, she had to curl her fingers into her palms to keep from doing the very same thing. Dreamily, she noticed the way his thick lashes lay along his cheekbones as he glanced down to fold his newspaper. *There ought to be a law against a man looking this good so early in the day,* she thought, then snapped herself to attention when she saw that he'd slipped his ever-present blue notepad under the newspaper.

Coffee, she thought, taking a massive sip, *do your stuff.* The sight of the notepad reminded her why she was there and the coffee helped her gain enough presence of mind to ignore his questions.

"So what's Dr. Purdy up to today?" she asked, nodding toward the other man.

"Besides turning the high beams of his charm on you?"

Jo fought a blush and didn't answer.

One corner of his mouth kicked up as if he knew that she was ignoring him. "The usual."

"And that would be?"

"Talking."

Jo stifled a sigh. It was going to be a long coffee break. "You know, if you were a writer who got paid by the word, you'd go broke."

His dark eyes glittered at her. "Fortunately, I'm an investigator who gets paid by the job, so I'm in no danger of starving."

Jo settled back in her chair and sipped from her cup as she watched him. Not a difficult chore. "So you do a lot of this kind of work?"

"Some," he admitted. "What about you? Do *you* do a lot of this kind of work? Is there much call for investigative reporting in Calamity Falls, Arizona or do you spend all your time reporting on the happenings of the local oddballs?" He glanced across the room to a table where a man sat busily sewing what looked like a doll's dress in between bites of toast and sips of tea.

Jo propped her chin on her hand. "They don't much like being reported on. Take Roger, there. He has a huge collection of dolls from around the world that he takes care of as if they were his children. They're worth a fortune, and he's been asked for a number of interviews, but he won't do one."

"Afraid all the attention will go to the dolls' heads? Or is it because you annoyed the hell out of him, too?"

Jo gave him an exasperated look. "No, because he's afraid someone will come and steal them, though, of course, his word is 'kidnap.'"

"Wise man."

"Most of our eccentrics are very intelligent. In fact,

many of them are geniuses. They're not all wise, though." Her gaze rested on Charlotte.

"Did some of them move here because the town already had a strange history?"

"Yes." She told him the story of Battlehaven and Shipper, who had discovered gold only to lose it in the earthquake that created the falls. "They had a number of other adventures that always ended in disaster for them."

"Poor saps."

"Some people say the place is cursed. The town has suffered fires, miners' strikes, landslides, mud slides, mine cave-ins. Calamity Falls is appropriately named."

"It must have been a proud moment when your local representative was elected governor," Case said thoughtfully. "Or at least until he was indicted for fraud and tax evasion."

She spread her hands. "What can I say? The town lives down to its name." Jo gave him a crafty look. "Speaking of that indictment, you didn't have anything to do with...?"

"Who me? Nah," Case denied, but his eyes twinkled, so Jo didn't believe him.

They were playing a cat-and-mouse game, and even though she had the certain knowledge that she was the mouse, she was enjoying it.

"So why the interest in Harold Purdy?" she asked, her gaze settling on the newspaper that hid his blue notepad. What was in it, anyway, and what were her chances of getting a look at it?

Case's eyes flashed with amusement. "You still don't think I'm interested in his Way of the Unbroken Man?"

"No. If you were, you'd be over there at his table,

listening, taking it in," she smiled slyly. "Being taken in."

The two of them turned to look at the man that interested them both. This morning, Purdy was dressed like an English country gentleman, right down to his tweed jacket and the ascot knotted casually at his neck. He was the center of attention, though at the moment he wasn't doing any of the talking. Jo was fascinated to see the way he turned his attention from one person to the other at the table. Charlotte was beaming as she spoke to Harold Purdy, her usually pale face pink with excitement.

Purdy sat slightly forward as he listened to her, one arm on the table, his full attention fixed on her. He dipped his head slightly, then brought his eyes up in full focus, making Charlotte's face pinken even more with delight.

Someone as innocent and sweet as Charlotte seemed wildly out of place with Purdy, and yet she seemed thrilled to be with him, to be the object of his attention.

She glanced at Case, who seemed to be absorbed in watching Purdy. When she looked down at the table, she saw that when Case had turned, he'd bumped the edge of the paper, exposing the notepad. Casually, she laid her hand on the tabletop. Strictly of their own will, her fingertips crept forward.

Without even looking up, Case brought his hand around to clasp her wrist. "Hands off, Quillan," he said, slipping the notebook off the table and into his pocket.

Darn! Thwarted, Jo clasped her hands together.

"Something about Purdy worries you?" Case asked.

"Maybe as much as he worries you?"

"You know we're just talking in circles here?"

"You're right," Jo answered with a firm nod. "Let's change the subject. Why did you leave the state attorney-general's office? Hadn't you been with them a long time?"

Case hesitated before answering. He would have liked to flatter himself into thinking that her interest was in him, but having been followed by her for much of the past twenty-four hours, he knew better. A pity, he thought, watching the way shadows cast by the branches of an overhanging mulberry played over her smooth skin. She had the face and body of a goddess and the mind of a ferret.

"Eight years," he said abruptly.

Her hand edged toward her jacket pocket and he wondered if she was going to whip out her notebook. He saw her struggle, then put her hand around her coffee cup once again.

"Why did you leave?"

"I wanted to slow down, take life at an easier pace, be my own boss, take time out for Suns and Diamondbacks games."

"The work too hard for you?"

Before he answered, he glanced over to make sure Purdy was still busy enthralling his audience. "No. I woke up one day and realized I had nieces and nephews living in Phoenix that I hadn't seen in six months because I'd been too busy. I'd missed Christmas with them, and some of their birthdays. I'm not married and have no kids. Being away from family is no way to live. I love the city, but not the frenetic pace of life there."

Jo felt ridiculously pleased to learn he wasn't married. She glanced up and down the sunlit street. "A slower pace of life isn't all it's cracked up to be."

"Like life in Calamity Falls? Why are you here, then?"

This time Jo was the one who hesitated, but he'd answered her questions honestly, she believed, so she would answer his. She told him about her uncle's illness. "So I've been here ever since," she concluded.

"And you want to leave?"

"It's time I used my education and experience," she answered defensively, because she felt guilty about leaving the *Ingot* even though she knew her aunt and uncle would support her decision. "I'm hoping to get a job on a major newspaper, I need a bigger story than the daily happenings of our local eccentrics, and..."

Case sat forward suddenly.

Too late, Jo realized what she'd said. She stared at him in dismay.

"So that's what this is all about," he said, low and fiercely. "I thought you only wanted a story for the local paper. You want to use this story about Purdy, and me, to get the attention of a big-city editor."

"That depends," she answered in a cautious tone. "What *is* the story about Purdy and you?"

He stared at her for several seconds, then he sat forward. "I have no interest in being used to further your career, or the career you *think* you're going to have."

4

CASE GOT TO HIS FEET and Jo gaped at him as burning embarrassment swept over her. If she hadn't been a complete professional with the highest standards of behavior, she would have tried to crawl underneath the table and hide.

Case was right. She had been following him and watching him. She'd already decided she might be jeopardizing his investigation, but still...

He was turning to stride away, when he came up short, face-to-face with Harold Purdy, who was standing only a few feet away with his group of admirers.

Jo had to admire the way Case could stop so suddenly and completely. He must have great brakes in those biker boots of his. He seemed momentarily taken aback. When a look of annoyance flashed in his eyes, Jo wondered if he was angry with himself for losing sight of Purdy to the point where the other man could come up behind him like that.

Harold Purdy gave Case a friendly nod, then spoke to Charlotte Quail in that easy, flowing voice of his. "Charlotte, why don't you introduce me to your friends?" His smile bathed all of them with so much warmth Jo wondered distractedly if she'd remembered to put on sunscreen that morning.

"Well, I don't know this gentleman," Charlotte answered with a breathless twitter and a coy look at Case. Her long, gray hair floated around her face like pale butterfly wings and her light gray eyes shone. "But this is my friend, Jo Ella Quillan."

Purdy reached out to enclose Jo's hand in both of his. The firmness of his grip seemed to say *trust me.* Those startling blue eyes of his stared straight into hers with supreme sincerity. "How do you do, Miss Quillan? When you walked into the restaurant earlier, it was as if you brought a fresh spring breeze with you."

Eyes wide, Jo felt the world tilt beneath her feet. "Really?" she asked, feeling her jaw go slack. He was so handsome, so warmly earnest. If she could do nothing more than stand here for a few minutes and stare into those mesmerizing eyes, she was convinced that she would be perfectly happy.

Up close, she could see that he was younger than she'd first thought. He was probably in his midthirties, but the confidence and maturity he radiated made him appear older.

"Uh, it's an open-air restaurant," Case said in a nasal tone, moving back into Jo's line of sight. "And it's October and I don't think she brought the breeze in with her."

Jo, reeling from the impact of Purdy's personality, turned her face and blinked at Case. What was this? Case's face had undergone some kind of transformation. His jaw was slack, his eyes dull, his broad shoulders slumped. It was as if he had the words Desperate Loser stenciled on his forehead.

Nothing could have brought her out of her entrancement with Purdy more quickly. She shook herself.

Out of the corner of her eye, Jo saw Purdy frown at Case. "Yes, of course…?" the man said.

"Case Houston," Case said, offering a hand that appeared to be limper than a dead eel.

"Ah, yes." Harold tilted his head back, stealthily

wiped his hand on his jacket, and then nodded. "I saw you last night at our rally, Mr. Houston, but you left rather quickly."

"There was something I had to take care of," Case answered, and let it go at that. He stared at Purdy openmouthed.

Jo fought to keep her own jaw from sagging in amazement. She didn't know quite what Case was up to. He looked as if he was going to start drooling any second. She glanced at the table for a napkin. He might need it.

Harold blinked and seemed a little taken aback by Case's brusqueness. However, he made a fast recovery. It took only a moment for his smile to regain its full wattage. "I was merely complimenting Miss Quillan on the freshness of her beauty."

"Yeah, she's beautiful, all right," Case said, giving her a watery-eyed gaze of adoration. "Smart, too."

Purdy smirked and Jo wondered if he was asking himself how smart she could possibly be if she was hanging out with this dim bulb.

Gathering her wits, Jo smiled at the woman who accompanied Purdy and Charlotte. "I don't believe we've met. I'm Jo Quillan," she said, offering her hand.

The lady, who had been gazing at Purdy with the same dazed expression Jo and Charlotte had shared, turned to look at Jo. After a couple of attempts, she focused. "Oh, hello. I'm Freida Long."

"You're new in town?" Jo asked, though all the while she was aware of Case, who seemed to be gazing blankly into space. No doubt, he was waiting for them to beam him up.

"Yes," Freida said, dragging Jo's attention back to the conversation. "I've heard so much about Calamity

Falls, its charming history, its unusual citizens...."
Her gaze drifted back to Harold. "So I simply had to
come and stay for a while."

"We're happy to have you and your..." At that
second, Jo noticed the woman's jewelry. Diamonds of
at least a carat sparkled in each ear. Around her neck
she wore a simple choker of pearls. Rings festooned
with magnificent gemstones sparkled on her hands.
Even her watchband was encrusted with blazing diamonds.

...*your magnificent jewels,* Jo almost concluded, but
caught herself in time. "You're...you're sure to enjoy
your stay. I...I hope it's a lengthy one," she stammered.

"I think it will be, " Freida answered, then blushed.

Jo's reporter's radar, in the form of the tingle running up her arms, alerted her that there was something
going on she didn't quite understand. Purdy was smiling, beaming in fact. Charlotte and Freida were beaming back at him. Case was in Alpha Centauri somewhere, seemingly oblivious to what was being said.

She *had* to find out what was going on here.

"It was wonderful to meet you, Miss Quillan," Harold said, giving her another enveloping handshake. "I
assure you that it has made my day." He turned the
brightness of his smile on high beam before he went
on. "I'm afraid we have to go now, as we're meeting
some other people." With a terse nod to Case, who
answered with a loopy grin, he shepherded the women
toward the door.

Jo stared after them, then gazed at Case, whose face
was transforming itself back to normal.

"What was *that?*" she demanded.

"What?" he asked, all innocence.

She threw her hand out. "That doofus-of-the-year,

sorry - but - I - accidentally - flushed - my - brain - down - the - toilet act you just put on.''

He frowned. "Oh, that. I didn't want him to think I was too bright."

"You succeeded."

"I may need to talk to him later," Case explained. "And it's better if he can feel superior to me."

"I see," Jo said slowly. "Don't you think you overdid it a little? A garden slug could feel superior to you in that mode."

"I needed to put him off his guard."

She was desperate to know why. Her fingers itched to write all this down. "Is this how you usually conduct investigations?"

"I do whatever is necessary."

"Sort of like I do to get the story I need," she said slyly.

He ignored that. "Tell me about Charlotte."

Sensing she wasn't going to get the answers she wanted, Jo told him about Charlotte and her lectures.

"I...I've never seen Charlotte spend a day away from her lectures. Those talks on the Harris hawk are her *life,* but she seems to have forgotten that completely. And that other lady, Freida—did you see those diamonds?"

"Yeah," Case answered. "And so did Purdy."

Jo immediately snapped around to face him, her eyes huge. "Is he a jewel thief?" she asked breathlessly excited at the idea of actually helping to actually catch a jewel thief. She pictured Purdy dressed all in black, dashing over rooftops with her in hot pursuit. Unfortunately, Case intruded on that exciting daydream, tumbling her off that imaginary rooftop and back to earth.

"Not that I know of," he said.

Suppressing a sigh, she asked, "If you weren't here to catch him, why did you go into the village-idiot act?"

Case's expression cooled. "Catch him doing what? Admiring Freida's jewels? Taking little old ladies to brunch? Telling you you're as fresh as a spring breeze?" He snorted in what Jo considered to be a most ungentlemanly way. "The guy ought to be advertising laundry soap."

Jo tilted her head and gave him a speculative look. "He does seem to have the personality of a great salesman."

"And you were buying."

"I was interested in what he had to say," she defended, glancing away.

"He didn't *say* anything. But you probably didn't notice that, since you were too busy drooling on his shoe shine."

Jo gave him an annoyed look, but kept her temper in check. "I think you're jealous of him."

Case stared. "Jealous?"

"You have to admit he has a certain…charisma that you lack."

Case put his hands on his hips and stuck his chin out. "You don't think I have charisma?"

"No." Inwardly, Jo was flailing away at herself for ever starting this, but she couldn't back down.

"And he does? Let me tell you something, Jo. He works at his charm to get what he wants."

"Well, most people have to, Case. It doesn't come naturally to them." She gave him a pointed look as if to say that charm *certainly* didn't come naturally to him. "Personally, I would have thought that if you were investigating him, you would have reacted in a more…direct manner."

Case met her gaze and one corner of his mouth kicked up. "While *you* looked like you were ready to sign up for whatever he's selling."

A frisson of excitement began to hum through her. She'd been temporarily bewitched by Harold, that was true, but it had been the fleeting interest one would show in any new phenomenon. Case, now, *he* fascinated her with his shifting moods, his quick humor, and his single-minded focus on his goal.

"Is that why he's here? Because he's selling something?"

Case rocked back on his heels and gave her a long look followed by a sly grin. "Try to remember that whatever he's selling, you might want to think twice before buying." He leaned in close and surprised her by running the tip of his finger down her cheek.

This time the tingle had nothing to do with her reporter's radar.

"Guys like that devour little girls like you for breakfast and don't even have heartburn," Case said. "You might want to watch out for him. Now, I have work to do. Don't follow me, don't get in my way, and don't use me to get a story that will advance your career. I'm not your stepping-stone out of Calamity Falls." Sketching a salute in the air, he strolled away, whistling.

Annoyance came, swift and hot as she watched him go. *Pompous know-it-all,* she fumed, and then looked down. To top it off, he'd stuck her with the bill for the coffee.

JO LEFT THE RESTAURANT a few minutes after paying the bill, but Case was nowhere to be seen. It was just as well, she thought. She had lots to think about and didn't need him distracting her.

Her thoughts circled back to Harold. Now that she'd been out of his presence for a few minutes, she could think about him more clearly.

She had to hand it to him. He knew how to listen with the greatest intensity, giving the speaker the impression that every word falling on his ears was pure gold. It was a gift, she'd decided, watching him, one he must have cultivated very carefully.

What did his interest in Charlotte and Freida have to do with "men reclaiming their rightful place in society"? Or this cosmogony idea? She would keep an eye on him and if that meant she got in Case's way, then so be it.

Her conscience prickled with the memory of Case saying that she'd only been using him. Okay, maybe what he'd said had been justified. However, there were other ways for her to get the story she needed without compromising Case's investigation, she thought, cheering up. She knew some of the men who'd been at the Unbroken Man rally. She would ask them what they thought. She wondered if their impressions of Purdy were the same as hers.

Hurriedly, she dodged around people in her path, greeted many she knew, and climbed the steps up to Fallsview Loop to talk to Stavros Pappas. On Wednesdays, his restaurant was only open for dinner, but she knew she'd find him in the kitchen.

He stood before a huge pot stirring something that smelled divine as it heated slowly over the fire. Stavros was a tall, stocky Greek with black eyes beneath bushy gray-salted brows and a head that was as bald as a billiard ball.

When he saw her, Stavros greeted Jo with a beaming grin as he said, "Good news, Jo Ella, my friend. Venus and Mars are correctly aligned for making *ste-*

fado. In fact, they have also ordained that celestial conditions are exactly right for me to become a little daring with the herbs.'' His eyebrows waggled around like a couple of caterpillars playing shortstop and his hand hovered over piles of the fresh herbs he grew in huge terra-cotta pots on the restaurant's patio. ''This *stefado* will be divine, exquisite,'' he declared with fervency. ''It will be so perfect, my own mother—'' he rolled his eyes heavenward ''—my own dear mother, God rest her soul, would weep to see its perfection.''

''That's...that's wonderful, Stavros,'' Jo stammered, taken aback as always, and yet charmed by his enthusiasm. ''What, exactly, is *stefado*?''

''Stew,'' he shrugged. ''Today made with the leanest, freshest lamb, the most exquisite meat for this dish.'' He went on, extolling the virtues of the ingredients in his stew while Jo listened, nodded, and tried to think of a way to work the conversation around to last night's rally.

When she'd first moved to Calamity Falls, it had taken Jo a while to become accustomed to the way the local eccentrics were so involved in their projects, almost to the exclusion of everything else. They were invariably cheerful, friendly and outgoing, glad to see any visitors, eager to share information about their particular area of expertise, but, truly, their own interests excited them as nothing else could.

Stavros himself paid very little attention to anything except his astrological charts and his cooking, which was another reason Jo had been surprised to see him at Purdy's rally.

When she realized she wasn't going to get him off the subject of his perfect *stefado*, Jo simply jumped right in.

"Stavros, were you interested in what that Mr. Purdy had to say last night about the Way of the Unbroken Man?"

Stavros stopped, blinked, and took a few minutes to focus. "No," he admitted. "I thought it sounded like the ravings of a madman."

Jo gaped at him. "Really? Then why did you go?"

He answered with another of those big, extravagant shrugs. "Helen was having some women over for a lingerie party." He nodded toward his wife, who was short, solemn, and as stocky as the butcher-block table where she stood chopping vegetables. She gave her husband a coy flutter of her eyelashes.

"I wasn't invited," Stavros said.

"So you don't think you'll be attending Purdy's next meeting?"

"No, not with all that marching and chanting. I've got bunions. I can't do all that marching. Pah! What nonsense, anyway, to think we have to look inside ourselves to find answers. All one has to do is consult the stars..."

Jo felt her eyes begin to glaze over as he talked. To keep herself from falling asleep standing up, she nodded and smiled her way toward the door.

Just before she could make her escape, though, Stavros looked up and said, "By the way, Jo, Helen and I were sorry to hear of the death of your romance with Steve. Has he left town now?"

Dismayed, Jo stared at their sympathetic faces. "I think so," she answered, barely managing to keep from shuffling her feet and studying the floor in embarrassment.

"Ah, too bad. I was going to offer to have a little talk with him on your behalf." Stavros picked up a knife and examined the blade meaningfully. "He shouldn't have broken your heart that way."

Jo blanched. "My heart's fine, Stavros, but thank you for your concern."

"With your next boyfriend, come to me and I'll help you consult the stars. You shouldn't be choosing a man with no help."

No kidding, Jo agreed silently. "I'll do that, Stavros," she said, and left him to his work.

Fifteen minutes later, she was standing beside Cedric Warrender, who had a small pair of clippers in his hand and was carefully edging the Cheshire Cat's whiskers. Because a large number of tourists crowded the sidewalk in front of his house every day, Cedric kept the pyracantha characters from *Alice in Wonderland* meticulously groomed. When he had heard about Calamity Falls' welcoming attitude toward people with unusual interests, he had rushed to buy this small house with its big yard. Out back, he'd created an English gardener's paradise, though the corner of poisonous herbs he grew might not be what most people would want in an English garden. His pet project, though, was the Lewis Carroll characters. He had struggled for two years to get the thorny, overgrown bushes into their fanciful shapes.

As he'd labored on them, they'd become real to Cedric, which was why he talked to them—and listened to them. When he was finished with the cat's whiskers, he stepped back and smiled fondly. "There. Perfect."

Jo looked on. The cat was, indeed, perfect with his wide grin neatly edged into the thorns and leaves. Even his teeth were trimmed as evenly as shoepeg corn. "How do you do that?" she asked in admiration.

"Just like Michaelangelo," Cedric answered

dreamily. "I simply cut away every part of the bush that isn't cat."

"You're a true artist, Cedric."

He blushed a tide of red that washed up his neck, over his face, and finally faded out at his hairline. Avoiding her eyes, he turned and picked up his three-ring notebook and began fiddling with the pages.

Seeing she'd embarrassed him, Jo hastily asked, "I hear you were at the Way of the Unbroken Man rally last night, Cedric. What made you interested in Dr. Purdy's message?"

"Oh, I wasn't interested, but I saw the notices around town and then I told the crew here about it." He nodded toward the line of pyracantha bushes. "The Mad Hatter thought I should go. He said a person should always be willing to learn new things."

"Did he?" Jo asked cautiously. She had to be careful what she said, because to Cedric they were real. "And what did you think of what Dr. Purdy said?"

Cedric smiled his charmingly innocent smile. "Oh, it was pretty interesting, but I felt there was more to learn."

Uh-oh, Jo thought uncomfortably. "And do you intend to go to his next meeting?"

Cedric looked up and down the line of his *Alice in Wonderland* crew. "I probably will," he said. "If I'm not too busy and if my friends think I should."

Jo knew he was talking about his leafy friends, not his human ones. "I see."

"Charlotte…"

Jo turned back from the gate. "What about her?"

Again embarrassment washed his face beet red. "Charlotte thinks I should go."

Jo didn't know quite what to say. She knew he and Charlotte were close, but the way he was blushing, she wondered if there was more to it on his part. "Charlotte seems to be friends with Professor Purdy, so she probably thinks he's going to say something you'd like to hear," she said, feeling like a hypocrite because of her own doubts about Purdy.

"That's what I thought," Cedric answered.

Jo said goodbye again, and as she closed the gate behind her, she thought that she was one for one now. Although the chef hadn't been interested in Purdy's message, Cedric was, but mostly because of Charlotte's influence. The look of adoration she'd seen in Charlotte's eyes was what really had her worried, though.

The next stop was at Laincy's grandfather's house, but when she swung through the back gate, she saw that someone else had had the idea before her.

Case sat in Julius's backyard. He rolled a frosty bottle of beer back and forth between his palms as he watch the older man tie fishing flies. Fly-tying and fly-fishing were two of Julius's many passions. Everyone who knew him tried to avoid getting him started talking about either one.

She paused when she saw Case there, then decided she had as much right to talk to Julius as he did. More, in fact.

When she walked in, Case looked up and his expression hardened. She ignored him, swinging breezily across the patch of lawn to greet her friend with a hug.

Julius smiled. "Good afternoon, Jo. What's the occasion? You haven't been up here to see me in months. Do you know Mr. Houston? He's new in town."

"We've met." Pointedly, Jo pulled up a chair and joined the two men at the round table where Julius had set up his fishing equipment.

"Ah, well, good."

"That's what you think," she murmured under her breath, smiling at Julius, who was too involved in his fly-tying to hear her.

Case answered with a slow, dangerous curve of his lips. The challenge in his eyes silently reminded her that he'd warned her not to follow him. She gave him a serene stare.

"Would you like something to drink?" Julius asked. "We're having beer, but I could get you some iced tea. I think Martha left some here."

"Only if the tea is decaffeinated. Caffeine impairs her hearing," Case said, pointedly reminding Jo that over the coffee they'd shared that morning, he'd told her to quit following him.

Julius drew back in surprise. "Really?" He gave Jo a fascinated look. "I've never heard of that before."

"Caffeine *doesn't* affect my hearing, Julius," she insisted. "Case was only joking." She gave her nemesis a pointed look. He toasted her with his beer bottle.

"He was?" Julius asked. "Okay. I'll get your tea as soon as I finish this. I know you probably don't want beer," he continued guilelessly as he picked up a small spool of shiny black thread. "Since two glasses of wine send you into a crying jag."

"Julius!" Appalled, Jo stared at him.

"Don't be embarrassed," he answered with a shrug. "All of us have troubles in our love lives once in a while. Lainey says you really loved Steve, but even a heart as crushed as yours will mend if you give it time."

"Oh, really?" Jo decided instantly that she was going to hold a murder-mystery evening that very night starring Lainey Pangburn in the role of the corpse.

"Some guy named Steve crushed your heart?" Case

said, grinning as his gaze swept over the fire in her cheeks. "That's too bad."

"It's none of your business."

"Steve Grover was her boyfriend. He broke up with her over dinner at the Copper Pot Restaurant the other night. Pretty callous of him, if you ask me."

"Nobody asked you," Jo said desperately, clapping her hand down on the tabletop. "And it's no one's business, anyway...."

"Broke her heart," her friend wound up, giving her a look full of love and sympathy.

"It *didn't* break my heart."

Case leaned forward and propped his chin on his fist as he regarded her with devilish laughter in his eyes. "Please go on, Julius. As a friend of Jo's, I'm heartsick that she went through such a trauma."

Julius gave him a big smile. "You're a good man, Case."

"A real peach," Jo seconded, looking daggers at him.

"Some of us were thinking about finding him and teaching him that you can't treat our Calamity Falls women like that. It's just not right."

First Martha and her friends, then Stavros, now Julius. Was it some kind of Calamity Falls vigilante group? While she was glad her friends were concerned, she wished they weren't so outspoken with their interest.

"A crime," Case agreed.

"However, there are some people who say there's a curse on the women of this town, anyway."

"A curse?" This was the first Jo had heard of it.

"Destined to fall in love with the wrong men over and over until the right one comes along. Jo, exactly how many times have you been in love since you've lived in Calamity Falls?''

"None! And could we please change the subject?"

"Now, Jo," Julius said in a sympathetic tone. "You don't have to try and cover up with us. You're among friends here."

"Yeah, Jo," Case said, all but guffawing out loud. "You're among friends."

"If only that were true." Jo rolled her eyes and looked back at Julius just in time to see him giving Case a speculative look. Alarmed, she sat up straight. Whatever he was thinking, she needed to distract him. And quickly.

"Uh, Julius," she broke in desperately. "I need to ask you something about the rally you went to last night."

"The one with Purdy?" he asked. "That's just what Case and I were discussing. How did you know I'd been there?"

Jo smiled straight into Case's eyes. "Case told me."

The devilish glint in Case's eyes deepened in challenge.

"You thinking of doing an article on Purdy for the paper?" Julius asked.

She looked at Case again. "Maybe," she said, pleased to see annoyance flare in his expression. "It depends on how much information I can gather."

"None." Case mouthed the word at her and she smirked at him.

Julius, involved in his fly-tying, didn't notice their byplay. "The truth is, Jo, I went because I'm always interested in the mechanics of a good con game." Carefully, he began winding shiny black thread around a tiny bit of peacock's feather, attaching a small metal eye as he went.

Jo slipped her notebook from her pocket and uncapped her pen. "What made you think it was a con game?"

Briefly, Julius described what had gone on at the meeting, unaware that Jo already knew. She didn't enlighten him that she'd been there herself. "It was all too full of rehashed ideas, but phrased in new, attractive ways. Wouldn't you say so, Case?"

"That's right." Case sat back, picked up his bottle of beer and took a long drink. "Nothing much new in what he had to say."

Julius went on. "That cosmogony idea of his. He says it's science. *Pah.* He seems to be trying to present himself as a holy man, but a true holy man doesn't have to seek out followers like Purdy's doing. They find him."

"Holy man?" Jo asked, disturbed. "You don't think he's trying to start some new religion, do you?" First jewel thief, now religious leader. What next?

Julius shrugged. "I don't know what he's trying to do, but I don't think he's here to learn the charming history of the town or to become part of the eccentric population."

"He's not eccentric," Case said quietly.

"What is he?" Jo asked the two men.

Case didn't answer, but Julius glanced up. "Time will tell."

It was certain that Case wouldn't tell, she thought, annoyed with him for perhaps the hundredth time in the past twenty-four hours.

ONE WAY OR ANOTHER, Case thought, he and Jo had spent a lot of time annoying the hell out of each other since they'd met. Case took a sip of his beer and turned his attention to watching Julius's patient work.

She was a thorn in his side, he thought darkly. Getting in his way, making him think about dealing with her rather than his investigation of Purdy. It had nearly knocked the pins out from under him today when he'd turned away from the table and run right into Purdy. That never should have happened. It never *would* have happened if he'd kept his mind where it belonged.

He glanced across at Jo, saw the way her shiny, swinging cap of chocolate-brown hair shone in the sun, how her green eyes went dark and thoughtful as she listened to Julius, the erotic way her full lips pursed in concentration.

He hadn't been the only one to notice those things. Harold Purdy's tongue had been all but dragging the ground as he'd looked at Jo. And she'd been equally enthralled with him.

What was it with women, anyway? he wondered irritably. Couldn't they see Purdy for what he was? Jo was trying to be an investigative reporter and even *she* couldn't see Purdy for the confidence artist he was.

"There is one way you can find out what Purdy is really doing," Julius said. He finished the fly he was tying, stood and stretched.

Jo sprang up straight, her face lively with interest. "How?"

"Martha tells me he's speaking to the women's club tonight. Their scheduled speaker had to cancel, so he volunteered. Oh, speaking of Martha, I forgot to bring you your iced tea. I'll be right back." He headed for the house.

Case could tell from Jo's bright, fixed gaze that a thousand possibilities were flying around inside her head. He pointed a finger at her. "Don't even think it," he commanded.

Jo ignored him. "The women's club," she said. "I could go to that, see what he has to say."

"The hell you will," Case growled.

5

JO GAVE HIM an annoyed look. "Unless someone re-wrote the Constitution while I wasn't looking, this is a free country, and…"

"You are bound and determined to mess up this investigation for me, aren't you?" he asked. He was beginning to count the moment she'd spotted him as one of the unluckiest of his life. And to make him even more crazy, the memory of the way Purdy had cast a spell on her while trying to look down her cleavage had jealousy exploding inside his head like fire-crackers.

"How can attending a women's-investment-club meeting possibly do that? And besides, how can I know that I'll be messing up your investigation if I don't know what you're investigating?" She leaned back and spread her hands wide in an obvious attempt to look like the most reasonable of women. "Now, wouldn't it make more sense if the two of us worked together? After all, you want to know what Purdy's up to, you're not a woman, and I don't think you'd be willing to borrow one of my dresses in order to attend the meeting."

"I'm not interested in using your techniques. I have no intention of taking up cross-dressing this late in my career. I work alone, Jo."

She rolled her eyes. "Oh, for crying out loud. Even the lone wolf needs a mate once in a while.…"

Jo stopped, consternation filling her face, then turned her head, paying a great deal of attention to a patch of dandelions sprouting in Julius's lawn. Case fought not to grin. "Honey, I don't think we're quite to that stage in our relationship yet, but I'll keep you in mind."

He watched her, enjoying the expressions flitting across her face as she mentally backpedaled her way out of that blunder. In a few seconds, she came charging back.

"Never mind that. I'll bet I could get an interview with Professor Purdy, get the information you need, write it up as a story later."

"No!"

"You have to admit that I could be of help."

He ran his hands through his hair. "Yeah, if I ever need a pit bull."

She was preparing to blast him for that unflattering statement when Julius returned with her tea.

"Here you go," he said, handing her a frosty glass embellished with both lemon and mint. "Now, what were we talking about?"

Neither of them enlightened him, and he gave them a surprised look before launching into a description of his favorite fishing places in the area, adding that he would be pleased to have Case join him.

"That's a great idea, Julius," Jo said. "In fact, you two should go right now." She gulped her tea and bounced to her feet. "I've got work to do. Bye, Julius, thanks for the tea," she said, swinging out the gate. Case almost stuck out his foot to trip her because their discussion definitely wasn't over, though she seemed to think it was. She paused on the sidewalk and wiggled her fingers at him in farewell, then headed off, hair bouncing beneath that floppy hat, back straight, walk saucily declaring that she'd had the last word.

"That's what you think," he murmured.

"Did you say something?" Julius asked, then followed Case's gaze with his own. "She's a good girl," he said, drawing Case's attention back to him. "She didn't have to tread water in this little burg for three years, but she did it to help her uncle out. It was probably career suicide for her, but she did it. A good, well-written story that she could add to her portfolio would go a long way toward helping her get a job that's worthy of her talents."

Case turned his head and squinted at his new friend. "Were you eavesdropping?"

"Of course. How else could I find out anything?" Julius tipped up his beer bottle and drained it. "I love eavesdropping," he said. "It gives one such insight into the human spirit."

Case grinned. "You don't believe that old saying about eavesdroppers hearing nothing good about themselves?"

"Nah," Julius said, waving that notion away. "What bad thing could anyone say about me?"

Case chuckled, finished his beer, and stood up. "That you're an eavesdropper?" he suggested.

While Julius laughed, Case thanked him, waved goodbye, and started after Jo. There was no need to hurry. He knew exactly where she was going. With a snort, he acknowledged that she'd turned the tables on him. Now *he* was the one following *her*.

"ALL RIGHT, I'm throwing in the towel."

Startled, Jo looked up to see Case standing over her desk, arms folded across his chest, unhappy scowl on his face.

Hurriedly, she blocked her computer screen with her body as she frantically worked the mouse to hide the request for information she'd put out on Purdy, and the one on Case.

"Throwing in the towel?" she asked. "Why, what do you mean?"

"You know what I mean," he growled.

"Yes," she admitted, sitting back, resting her hands behind her head, and smiling up at him. "But I want to hear you say it."

"I could use your help in investigating Purdy," Case answered, each word sounding as if it was being dragged from him.

"I'd be happy to help," she responded, joy and excitement bubbling through her. "What do I need to do? Will I need to wear a wire? I have to find my tape recorder." She opened her desk drawer and began scrambling for it. "I had it a while ago, but I put it in here, and…"

A firm hand clamped down on the desk, making her jump. "No wire, no tape recorder, no secret passwords or magic decoder rings. All you're going to do is go to this meeting and listen to what Purdy has to say."

Looking up, she swallowed her disappointment, then reminded herself she was a professional or would be, after this story.

"Okay. What else do I have to do?" Unable to resist, she glanced around surreptitiously to see if anyone was listening. She needn't have worried. Her aunt and uncle had gone home, the bookkeeper was closed up in her office, and the advertising department, which consisted of Faye Owen and two high-school kids, was involved in its own projects.

Case pulled up a chair, twirled it around, then seated himself in it, arms propped along the top of the back.

It was a distinctively masculine way of sitting and something about the way Case did it made it seem even more manly.

Focus, Jo, she told herself. *Focus.* Now that she finally was on the verge of getting what she wanted, she couldn't afford to let her attention stray. Okay, she thought, one quick peek at the way those black jeans stretched over his thighs. In spite of the way he annoyed her, she had to admit that he had what it took to fill out those jeans.

"Are you listening?" Case asked abruptly.

She started and her gaze swung back to his stormy, dark eyes. "Of course," she said, lifting her chin. She folded her hands on the desk top. "You were about to tell me what I have to do to help you out."

He gazed at her for a few seconds before he answered. "A few days ago I got a call from a lady in Chicago named Estelle Long."

"Long? You mean like the lady we met this morning...?"

"Freida. " He nodded. "Estelle is her daughter."

Jo rubbed her hands together. "This is getting good,'' she said breathlessly.

"How do you know? I haven't told you anything yet."

"Anticipation is often better than the real thing."

Jo saw something dark and humorous flash in his eyes. For some reason, it made heat wash up her face and sizzle in her ears. She cleared her throat. "You were saying?"

"Freida is originally from Chicago and has been living in a retirement community in Phoenix for a couple of years. Two weeks ago, she came to Calamity Falls on her first visit, stayed a few days, during which

she apparently met Charlotte, and Harold Purdy, then
went back home, packed up and moved here.''

"And her daughter's worried, no doubt.''

"Yes, plus the fact that she seems to be withdraw-
ing a great deal of money from her bank lately.''

"What's she spending it on?''

"She won't say.''

Jo sat back and frowned. She reached into her desk
for a handful of paper clips, positioned her coffee cup,
and began flipping the clips into it. "Do you think
she's giving it to Purdy?''

"Could be. One look at that jewelry-store clearance
sale of gems she wears was probably all it took to get
his attention.''

"Do you think he's going to rob her?''

"It wouldn't be robbery,'' Case answered. "She
looks so enthralled with him she'd probably hand them
over in a heartbeat, which her daughter thinks is what
she's already doing.''

"So you're trying to see if he's doing anything il-
legal?''

"Yeah, and not succeeding very well due to certain
distractions.'' He gave her a pointed look.

The paper clip she'd been about to dunk into the
cup wobbled as it left her fingers, skated across the
rim, and landed at Case's feet. He picked it up, flicked
it with his thumbnail, and directed it straight into the
cup.

"If you're going to help me with this, you've got
to be a partner and not a distraction,'' he told her.

"A partner,'' she said, nodding vigorously. She
liked the sound of that.

"All you have to do is listen to Purdy tonight. He
may be giving Freida financial advice and scamming
money from her that way.''

"Why does it have to be a scam? Couldn't she simply be investing the money legitimately?"

"If she was, don't you think she'd tell her daughter about it?"

"Unless the two of them don't get along and the daughter is afraid Freida is spending her inheritance."

"Estelle says they had a good relationship until a few weeks ago, when her mom suddenly became secretive. Also, Estelle owns a car dealership and is married to the owner of a successful electronics manufacturing plant, so I don't think money is the issue." Case shook his head and leaned forward until the chair was on two legs. "No, from what I've been able to find out, this seems to be the way Purdy operates. He gets chummy with someone, usually a little old lady, then her money starts disappearing."

"He's done this before then?"

"Yes, at least twice, though the ladies were too embarrassed to press charges. Also, he may have pulled this scam before, but using a different name. If so, he's gotten away with it because there are no charges pending against him and he's spent the past few years meandering around the western states. He's been a little hard to track."

"What about that rally last night, though, and all that Unbroken Man stuff, and the marching, and whatever else was going on?"

Case shrugged. "I don't know yet. It appears to be some new twist he's adding. Julius didn't seem to be taken in by it, but maybe some of the other men were and want to go to his next meeting."

"Cedric was," Joe answered, and told him about her friend the gardener. "I think he's a very lonely man. I know he's shy and doesn't talk much." She gave Case a sideways glance. "Well, except to his plants. I stopped by and complimented him on his yard a dozen times before he'd even acknowledge me with a nod. Do you think that could be another part of Harold's plan? To get money out of lonely people like Cedric?''

Case answered with a considering frown. ''Could be.''

''Then if Purdy's caught and is prosecuted, embarrassed little old ladies wouldn't testify against him, and if someone like Cedric did, the jury wouldn't believe him.''

''Because he's crazy? Talks to his plants?'' Case suggested.

''No, because he's eccentric.''

Case snorted. ''We don't know any of that yet. You're getting way ahead of yourself.'' He took a deep breath. ''Now, do you understand what it is you're supposed to be doing tonight?''

Jo nodded. ''I have the full picture. I'll go to the meeting tonight, take notes on what he has to say, watch him, see how he operates, then invite him out for a drink and ask him for more details.''

''Whoa!'' Case's chair thumped onto the floor.

''Actually, I could ask him up to my place,'' she said, brightening, then shook her head. ''No, that might not be...''

He held up his hand as if trying to stop traffic. ''Hold it right there, Mata Hari. What did you think you were going to do? Slip truth serum into his drink and have him confess all?''

Her eyes wide with excitement, Jo said, ''Do you think I could?''

''No!'' he roared, springing to his feet. ''You're not going to do any spying, any prying, or any—''

''Denying?'' she teased. For some reason, instead

of being annoyed at his insistence, she was ever so slightly flattered. Was it possible he was uncomfortable with the idea of her being alone with Harold?

"Look," he said, leaning over her desk. "If you're going to help me, you've got to do exactly, and I do mean *exactly,* what I say."

The firmness in his voice and face finally got through to her. "Well, all right, Case, you're the boss...."

"If only that were true," he muttered, sitting down again. He ran his hands through his hair and gave her a baleful look. "You're to do nothing except report back to me on what he talks about. Got it? You can do that, can't you? Report and nothing else?"

Jo gave him an insulted look. "Of course. I *am* an experienced reporter, you know."

"Remember that. And another thing, there's got to be strict confidentiality in this. You don't report a word of it, or even breathe a word of it until the investigation is all wrapped up. Otherwise, no story."

"That goes without saying. I would never risk your investigation."

He treated her to the skeptical look that deserved. "You're not even to tell your best friend, who I assume is Julius's granddaughter, right?"

"That's right, and no, I won't even tell her."

"Because otherwise it'll be all over town."

"Lainey wouldn't tell!"

He snorted. "Like she wouldn't tell about you getting snockered on two glasses of wine and bawling because your boyfriend dumped you over dinner and broke your heart?"

"He didn't break my..." She waved a hand at him. "Oh, never mind." She was getting sick of repeating that, and besides, nobody seemed to believe her, anyway.

Case gave her a slow, even smile that said he didn't believe her, either. "So, are we straight on what you're going to do?"

Dutifully, Jo repeated his instructions back to him word for word.

When she was finished, Case sat back and nodded. "It sounds like you've got it all down."

"Try not to sound so dubious," she advised. It was on the tip of her tongue to ask why he was letting her help if he truly didn't think she could do this, but she didn't want to put any ideas in his head.

"He's going to find out pretty quickly that you're a reporter, so he might not talk to you. How will you handle that?"

She gave him a sly look and stood up, striking a seductive pose. "I've got a slinky black dress that's got a slit on the thigh clear up to..."

"No." Again he was on his feet. This time he added emphasis by stomping around the room. "You don't get it, do you? You just don't understand...."

Jo giggled, then bit her lip. When he whipped around to glare at her, she said, "Gotcha."

Case stared at her for a few seconds, then his right eyebrow went up, his lips came together, and he sauntered over to stand before her. He crossed his arms over his chest and tilted his head. His gaze touched on her face, on the color riding high in her cheeks and the bright mischief in her eyes. "You know, Miss Quillan, for a reporter, you've got kind of a frivolous attitude toward investigations."

"Really?" She could feel the rhythm of her heart picking up to a quick patter in her chest. Casually, she leaned against the corner of her desk. "You mean I'm not serious and sober enough?"

"No, you're not." A grin played at the edges of Case's mouth. "And you tend to think that you're in charge."

"That is kind of a bad habit of mine. I guess it goes with the territory. After all, I'm the only hard news reporter on the *Ingot,* so I can pretty much run my own show."

He nodded. "And in Calamity Falls, that show would be, what? Reporting on a chicken that laid an egg with a double yolk?"

"No, my uncle handles those stories. He loves oddities like that. Aunt Millie takes care of social happenings in town. Yours truly is responsible for all the really hard news around here," she said importantly.

Jo was amazed at her own delight when she saw the interest in his eyes. This was much better than arguing with him, and much more intriguing. Looking into those deep, dark eyes of his made her forget all about Steve's perfidy. Case looked so good, in fact, that her gaze dropped to his lips. She wondered how they tasted.

"What kind of hard news?" those lips asked.

"What?" She blinked and focused. "Oh, hard news." She cleared her throat, ignored his blossoming grin, and said, "Did you know they're going to re-surface the parking lot over at the supermarket? Painting new stripes and everything."

"Fascinating. Have the major wire services picked that up?"

"Not yet. I'm keeping it quiet for the moment." Her smile flickered then she grew serious. "This investigation of Purdy is the first really serious story I've worked on in a while."

"In a while?"

She rolled her eyes. "Okay, in a *long* while. But it won't be the last one," she added quickly. She straightened, neatened her collar and pretended to brush dust from her shirt cuffs. Smiling impishly, she said, "I'm going to be really good at this investigative-reporter job."

"Oh, yeah," he said, his face going cool. "So you can get out of Calamity Falls and onto the fast track."

Remembering how he felt about the fast track, and his relief at having escaped it, she said, "I know it wasn't for you, but that doesn't mean it's not for me."

Case's eyes were steady on hers. "That's right." He looked at her mouth, which for some reason began to tingle. "And I've got to remember that, too," he finished.

He stepped away from her abruptly. "I'll need to talk to you after the meeting tonight."

Jo felt a keen sense of disappointment at his brisk tone. For a moment, she was at a loss. "My place," she said. "Here, I'll write down directions."

"No need," he said, starting toward the door. He turned and gave her a cocky grin. "I'm an investigator. I can find it."

Jo watched him stride out, her disappointment warring with her good sense. It was better if they were cool and strictly professional with each other. Getting involved in anything even remotely personal would be a big mistake. She knew that. She didn't have time for anything personal. She wasn't going to get involved with a man, even one as interesting and compelling as Case Houston. She didn't have time for it.

She sure was curious about how those lips tasted, though.

HE'D PROBABLY MADE the biggest mistake of his career. Case sat stretched out in a chair, legs extended, boot heels digging into the plush carpet of his room at the Copper Quest.

He *never* involved nonprofessionals in an investigation. And why this girl, of all people? She was maddeningly persistent, completely sure she knew exactly what she was doing when it was obvious that she was clueless.

"Great," he muttered, sitting up and resting his head in his hands. He was partnering up with a clueless reporter. She was eager, he had to give her that.

Eagerness was in her words, in her voice, in everything she did, from making friends with the town's odd citizens, to seeking out a story that could get her out of this little place and into the high-profile, high-powered, high-stomach-acid career she thought she wanted.

Talk about clueless. Case stood and began prowling the room, stopping occasionally at the window to gaze down Manzanita Street at the cozy little town.

Jo had no idea what she was letting herself in for, the kind of stress she would have to endure, the millions of details that would demand her attention. The memory gave him a sickening punch to the gut.

He'd hate to see that happen to her. She was too soft for that life, despite her desire to be a hard-driving investigative reporter. Too soft.

Case's eyes lost focus as he gazed out the window. Too soft. He thought about the way her hair belled around her face, the gentle curve of her cheek, her lush mouth, that Marilyn Monroe body with extra leg length added.

"Oh, hell!" He whirled away from the window and paced the room like a caged lion.

He was the one who was soft. Soft in the head.

Somehow he'd lost the good judgment he prized in himself. In doing so, he'd gotten tangled up with Jo, who wasn't a model of good judgment, either.

He'd given her careful instructions, but would she follow them? Panicked doubts sent him hotfooting it toward the door.

He'd better go find out.

6

"I WANT TO SEE what you're going to wear tonight."
Case stood on Jo's tiny front porch, rocking on his
heels and trying not to look like as much of a fool as
he felt.

Jo gaped at him. "What I'm wearing?"

Actually, what she was wearing wasn't bad; a lacy
robe in stop-your-heart red, no shoes, hot pink polish
on the nails. He should have known she'd be the kind
of woman who'd paint her toenails. Somehow that
made her even more enticing.

She'd had a bath. The scent of roses swept out to
greet him and lure him in. Her soft, smooth cap of hair
swung in a chocolate-brown wave. Her lips were
touched with pink. She looked like a woman getting
ready for a hot date.

He'd arrived exactly in the nick of time.

"I thought we were going to join up later," she said
pointedly, crossing her arms at her waist as she
blocked the door. "*After* the women's-club meeting."

"Yeah," he said, picking her up by her shoulders
and moving her out of the way so he could get into
her house. She gave an outraged squeak, but he ignored her. "I decided I'd better come check out what
you're going to wear. You can't look too attractive to
Purdy, or too much like a reporter." He turned and
gave her another up-and-down look.

Those sea-green eyes of hers asked if he'd lost his

mind. *Yes,* as a matter of fact. He'd already established that. He scowled, trying to pretend he was a sane professional—or at least a professional.

"Case, everyone in town knows I'm a reporter. It won't matter what I wear."

"Then go get dressed, show me what you've picked out and I'll tell you if I approve."

Jo's hands rose to her hips and she looked him over as if he was some form of mutant insect species. "If you *approve?* Case, you left me only an hour ago. Did you spend that time listening to a tape on how to be an ape-man?"

"No. I spent the time thinking I've made a big mistake and that you're much too likely to fall under the spell of Harold Purdy, the King of Charisma."

"Well, thanks for the vote of confidence!"

He didn't answer, hoping that his silence would convey the idea that what he'd said made perfect sense.

He glanced around her living room, which he thought he could cross in exactly five steps. Through one open doorway, he could see her kitchen, and through another, the hallway to the bathroom and bedrooms. It was like a doll's house, decorated in what he assumed was aunt-and-uncle cast-off chic. A small faded sofa that he figured he could fit into his back pocket was covered with a bright, knitted throw. Print pillows were scattered around, tabletops were covered with pictures and knickknacks. It was warm, cozy and inviting, and he didn't know what the hell he was doing there.

He ignored her irritation, then chose a chair that he thought might not break beneath him and sat down.

"Make yourself at home, Case," she murmured, closing the door—but not until she'd stuck her head out and taken a quick look up and down the street. Probably worried about what the neighbors would think.

He frowned. She could tell her neighbors that this was strictly business. Maybe she should tell him that, too. "Thanks, I will. Why don't you get dressed?" When she opened her mouth to argue, he held up his hand. "I'm the boss, remember? We both agreed that I'm the boss and you're going to do exactly what I say."

She stared at him for a couple more seconds, then dropped her hands in defeat, shook her head, and left the room. He heard the door close, then another click, which told him she'd locked the door.

Smart girl. Case leaned forward to crane his neck and peer down the hall so he could see which room was hers, then sat back with a sigh. Okay. He'd come this far. He could justify this whole exercise in stupidity by saying that he'd never worked with a partner before and wanted to make sure she knew what to do. Or he could say he didn't trust her. Or he could simply tell the truth and admit that he was spooked by the idea of her listening to Purdy.

Jo was back in a few minutes, dressed in a knee-length sleeveless dress of lemon yellow. She looked casual, cool, and as tartly sweet as a lemon drop. He could feel his mouth puckering.

"Too much leg showing," he croaked, then cleared his throat. "You don't want to get Purdy's attention on a personal level." Never mind that she'd already done that this morning.

"Case," she said, her voice dripping with patience, "there'll only be half a dozen women there—older women, with blue hair and polyester pantsuits. I'm certain he's going to notice me, no matter what I wear.''

Exactly what Case was afraid of. "Do you have anything...longer?''

"Oh, this is ridiculous. I don't..."

"Want this story?"

She met his eyes, turned, and headed back to the bedroom, emerging a few minutes later wearing a full-length evening dress. It was a shimmering black, had a high neck and long, tight sleeves.

"Will this do?" she asked sweetly, and did a slow pirouette in front of him. That was when he saw that the thing had no back. His mouth went dry as he counted her vertebrae. Funny, he'd never known how wildly erotic a woman's back could be.

He told himself not to have a heart attack and managed to wheeze, "Do you know that thing's got a gaping wound where the zipper ought to be?"

She looked at him over her shoulder, a move that had all kinds of sexual connotations he didn't even want to consider right now. The puckering effect in his mouth seemed to be sweeping through his whole body.

"It's long," she said. "It covers my legs." She wrinkled her nose at him. "I lied about the slit up the thigh. Isn't that what you wanted?"

He looked at the determination in her eyes and felt admiration sparking in his own. "Got any pants?"

"Why, yes, I believe I do." The sweetness in her voice could have caused cavities.

As she swept out of the room, Case found himself standing on tiptoe to see exactly how far south that slit went.

Damn. He'd almost seen the top curve of her derriere. He should be struck blind for what he was thinking. Sitting down, he tried to bring his imagination back under control.

In a few minutes she stood before him in dark green slacks and a white sweater set. "This is it, Houston. Take it or leave it. The fashion show's over and I've got to go."

She looked cool and virginal. Oh, hell. He nodded, stood up and gave her a close inspection. Deciding she probably wouldn't like it if he reached over and tugged up the gentle V-neck of the sweater, he finally said, "Looks fine. Remember you're observing and taking notes, and…"

"I *know* how to make a report," she said, taking two steps in so that they were standing inches from each other. "I told you that already and if the way I'm doing this doesn't please you, then you can just…"

"Okay, you're on your own." He knew when it was time to quit talking and start walking. He headed for the door. "I'll be back later and you can give me the report."

He scurried out before she could throw something at her.

INFURIATING MAN, Jo fumed as she trotted down the street, descended two sets of stairs, and landed, breathless, at the front steps of the women's club. The only good thing this had done was keep her mind off this meeting so she wouldn't get nervous. She was wildly excited about the chance she was being given, but also determined to be professional. It wouldn't do to show her unsureness, and in the sparsely populated room it would be even more obvious.

On the dot of seven o'clock, she swept in the door and came to a screeching halt.

The place was packed.

Jo stared. She wouldn't have to worry about standing out in the group. She wouldn't even be able to *move* in this group. She sincerely hoped the fire marshal didn't hear about this. The room, which had been built to hold one hundred, was jammed with twice that many chairs and more were being passed hand to hand over the heads of the ladies present.

"Oh, hi, Jo," Martha said as she squeezed between two other ladies. She stopped to fan herself with a printed program. "Better find a seat quick or you'll have to stand. I stood up to adjust my girdle—they can call these damned things body-shapers all they want, but they're still girdles to me—and I lost my chair in the front row to Melba Parker. I never knew she had such a vicious right elbow," she complained. "She nearly broke my rib."

Still awed, Jo nodded. "Martha, where did all these people come from? They're not members, are they?"

"Lots of tourists heard that Dr. Purdy was going to be here. Charlotte announced it at her lecture this afternoon." She stood on tiptoe and scanned the crowd. "Also, I think several cars full of ladies came over from Bisbee, Douglas and Tombstone." She shrugged. "It seems he's got a message people want to hear."

"No kidding." Jo quickly found a seat at the edge of the back row. She couldn't see very well because of the press of people in front, but by nearly climbing into the lap of the lady next to her, she managed to get a view of the podium.

When Dr. Purdy stood and began to speak, a hush fell over the group. As he talked, he seemed to cast a hypnotic spell over his audience. They were silent, respectful, and listening intently, though, from what Jo could understand, he wasn't saying anything new in regard to investing money. Now that she knew he was a con man, she thought it odd that he'd be counseling people to invest prudently. Why wasn't he asking them to give their money to him? Isn't that what con men did?

By the time he finished speaking, she could feel the restiveness in some members of the audience. Apparently, their interest didn't stretch to listening to his advice about what to do with their retirement checks. In fact, when the meeting broke up, Jo heard several women say they'd only come to hear him talk.

"He sounds so refined," one woman sighed. "Just like Cary Grant or Ronald Coleman."

"He doesn't have a British accent," her companion said.

The first lady snickered and fanned herself with her hand. "No, but he's so debonair, so suave. I overheard him say a few words in a restaurant this morning, and I just knew I had to come tonight if only to listen to that man's voice."

"Mabel, you've been divorced too long. I thought we only came tonight because there was nothing good on television."

"Well, yeah, that too." She looked around at her friends. "Anybody want to stop by the Copper Pot and have a piece of pie?"

As the women trooped out, Jo edged closer to Purdy, who had several women grouped around him including Charlotte Quail and Freida Long. Now that Jo knew Freida's story, she was even more wary, but she hid it with a warm smile.

"Dr. Purdy," she began, and he immediately turned his clear blue eyes on her and bathed her with that warm smile. He stepped forward and took her hand, though she hadn't offered it. "Your talk was very...enlightening. Is your background in banking? You certainly seem knowledgeable.'' She hoped she didn't sound like a twit, but there was something about being near him that made her feel as if her brain cells were clicking into sleep mode and only banal chatter could come from her mouth. It made her think of the old thirties radio show *The Shadow,* about a character who clouded the minds of men.

That voice washed over her in a warm, resonant wave. "Why, Miss Quillan, thank you, but no, I'm only telling my friends about the strategies I've picked up over the years.'' His gaze traveled over her obviously checking out the V-neck of her sweater and the swell of her breasts.

Darn, she thought. Case had been right. Remembering Case made her focus on why she was there.

"There is a subject, though, that I've studied in great detail,'' he said, giving them all a serious look.

Jo's familiar tingle ran up her arms. *Uh-oh,* she thought. *Here comes the pitch.*

"It's called cosmogony and it's a pure science, one that other scientists have ignored.''

So now he was a scientist? Interesting, but she still didn't quite catch on to how it tied in with his Way of the Unbroken Man and his investment counseling, or why it held such appeal for Charlotte, who seemed to be responsible in large part for the big crowd tonight.

He continued to talk. Jo found herself so caught up in it that she forgot to be wary. For a few seconds his whole idea of earth and space seemed to make sense. It wasn't until after he stopped talking that she wondered what he'd actually said. Trying to pin down the truth and the science in his ideas was like trying to hold a soap bubble in place by driving a nail through it.

The others gathered around seemed to feel none of her qualms. Somehow he'd managed to say something that would be of interest to some of the ladies. Many of the true eccentrics had interests in science, though they usually skewed the facts to suit themselves and their own theories and they preferred to be the ones on the giving end of scientific information. In fact, they insisted on it.

"I'm having a meeting for my new friends at my house tomorrow evening. Anyone who would like to come is welcome." He beamed that two-hundred-watt smile at them all.

Many of the women nodded to each other and began making plans to attend as they walked away. Freida and Charlotte departed as well, though somewhat reluctantly, leaving Jo and Harold standing with Martha and Jo's aunt Millie on the front steps of the building.

Martha looked at her two friends and said, "Jo, Millie, maybe you should write up an article for the paper about the meeting."

Beside her, Jo saw Harold start visibly.

Millie said, "I'm afraid it's too late for the *Ingot* this week, Martha."

Harold recovered himself smoothly and asked, "The paper?"

Jo could tell that he wanted to sound interested, mildly amused, but she heard a note of worry in his tone. She tried to smile in a reassuring way while thinking, *Yeah, buddy, you should be worried.*

"Millie and her husband publish it and Jo is their star reporter," Martha said, beaming at her young friend. "Why, it was only last week that she wrote an excellent report on the repairs to the high-school roof.''

Smiling weakly, Jo said, ''Thanks, Millie. I'm glad you liked it.''

Harold looked at her as if he'd just received a gift. The edge of worry in his voice melted away. That all-enveloping smile of his reached out to wrap around her. ''You write about local happenings, then? How sweet.''

Sweet? It was on the tip of Jo's tongue to say that she was on the verge of a career as a hard-news reporter, that she was going to blow the lid off stories that would rock the world of journalism. However, she thought better of it when she recalled that *he* was the story she was currently working on.

Instead, she gave him a fatuous smile and tried an out on him. ''I try,'' she said, simpering the tiniest bit.

Martha and Millie exchanged puzzled glances while Harold gave her a long, slow look, all but licking his chops as he examined her. Jo did her best not to shudder too visibly.

''Perhaps you'd allow me to take you to dinner tomorrow evening before the meeting at my house?'' Harold suggested. ''I would love to hear all about your little job.'' He took her hand again. ''Although I doubt that you'll want to write about me and my humble efforts to help people find the truth in themselves and their place in the universe.'' The heat in his eyes willed it to be so.

Jo almost spat the words ''little job'' right back at him, but thought better of it. He was very anxious to make sure she didn't write about him and he thought he could charm her into agreeing with him. That was a challenge she couldn't ignore. Before she could respond, she heard a soft, deep voice behind her shoulder. "You ready to go home, Jo?"

She glanced around, and then down. Case stood on the steps below her, looking up with adoration in his eyes.

Uh-oh, she thought. He was in doofus mode again. How *did* he make that killer jaw of his go slack like that? And that vacant look in his eyes clearly said, "nobody's home."

He ducked his head and asked, "Are you ready, Jo?"

Knowing she had to play along with this, she finally found her voice. "Yes, Case, I am."

To gather her thoughts and stall for time, she introduced him to Martha and Millie.

He came up the steps eagerly, gave them a toothy grin, and his sack-of-wet-laundry handshake as if he was pathetically grateful for any crumb of attention.

This guy is wasted as an investigator, Jo thought. *He should be an actor.*

"Well," Case said, doing that chicken-pecking-for-grain dip again. "I'm here to walk Jo home. I mean, if that's all right. You know, a beautiful girl like you shouldn't be out by yourself."

No kidding, she thought. *Not with guys like you running around.*

"Now see there, Jo," her aunt broke in with a beaming smile. "You don't have to worry about no one wanting you, not with two nice men like this begging for your attention. I know you loved Steve and he broke your heart by dumping you the other night at the Copper Pot, but you can't stew about it. You're still young and beautiful."

"Thanks, Aunt Millie," Jo said weakly. She looked from Millie's loving smile to Martha's interested eyes, to Harold's speculative expression, then back to Case's vapid and adoring gaze. *Get me out of here,* she thought.

Harold pushed himself forward and took her hand. Once again she was on the receiving end of his intense blue gaze. "Shall we say tomorrow evening for dinner at the Lotus Blossom? I hear the food there is exceptional."

"Yeah," Case broke in. "Especially their barbecue."

Harold gave him a look that asked why this goof was interrupting, but the good-natured blankness of Case's smile seemed to reassure him. He turned his attention back to Jo and he took her hand once again, pressing it to show her how interested he was.

Her smile felt frozen. What kind of signal was Case trying to give her? Should she go out with this guy? Was she willing to do so only to get a story? What if he had more on his mind than talking about investments? It was obvious he did. *Oh, help.* She took a deep breath and hoped she was doing the right thing.

"I'd love to, Dr. Purdy," she said, tittering brightly. "That would be so...exciting. I'll meet you there. Shall we say at six, since your meeting begins at eight?"

His eyes flared with interest, then his expression settled into smugness as if he were congratulating himself on his persuasive powers. "That would be fine," he purred.

"Gee, mister, you're really lucky to have a beautiful lady like this go out with you," Case said, but Jo, who was beginning to know him, heard an edge to his voice. "I feel honored that she'll let me walk her home."

Harold gave him a when-you've-got-it-you've-got-it look, kissed the back of Jo's hand, then placed his jaunty hat on his head and strolled away.

Millie and Martha gave simultaneous sighs of delight. "What a gentleman," Martha said. "If my ex-husband had been such a gentleman I wouldn't have had to get rid of him. See, Jo, not all men are cads like that worthless Steve who—"

"Broke my heart." Why did she even fight it? And why did everyone insist on feeling sorry for her? "Yes, I know." She cast a sidelong glance at Case. "Some men are not at all what they seem."

Case grinned as if she'd paid him a vast compliment. He ducked his head and gave her a shy look. She rolled her eyes at him then said good-night to Millie and Martha and, taking his elbow, started up the street.

When they were out of earshot, she tried to pull her hand away, but he clamped it close to him, and closed his own hand over it. "Now, now," he said, his voice returning to normal. "We can't take a chance that someone will see you trying to get away from me. Paying attention to someone like me will make you look good. After all, I'm a pathetic loser, grateful for your attention."

"And I'm a brainless twit who has a date tomorrow night with a con man." As they walked beneath a streetlight, she glared at him.

"Hey, that was your idea," he protested. "I didn't tell you to accept."

"Then what was all that stuff about the delicious barbecue at the Lotus Blossom?"

"I was only quoting what you'd told me."

Horrified, she stared at him. "You mean you weren't sending me some kind of signal telling me to go out with him?"

"Hell, no. Why would I do that?"

Jo took him by surprise by jerking her hands away and throwing them in the air. Then she punched him. Hard.

"Ow." He rubbed his arm. "Why'd you do that?"

"Because we're having a serious communication problem here. You're supposed to be the boss, remember? You insisted on it. I'm supposed to be following your orders exactly and that's what I thought I was doing."

"Well, I didn't mean you had to go out with the guy." Uncomfortably, Case stared at her. He didn't want her to go out with Purdy. Purdy worked some kind of magic on people, especially women, and he didn't want to see him work it on Jo. He didn't want Purdy *near* Jo. The thought gave him heart palpitations.

"Does he have a phone at that house he's renting? You can call him up and cancel."

"I'll do no such thing." She turned and began stomping down the street once again. Maybe she was being ridiculously stubborn, but now that she'd made the date, she was going to keep it. Her professionalism was on the line.

Genius, he thought. *Now you've made her mad.* He'd be darned if he was going to go chasing after a woman, one who'd agreed that he was the boss, one who was supposed to do what he said.

"Great," he muttered, and loped along behind her until he caught up. She started up the steps, but he whipped around in front of her and stopped one step above, blocking her path.

"There's no need for you to go out with him to help in this investigation."

Jo pushed past him and paused on the next step so

that they were at eye level. "There's every need. I can learn something useful. I do have *some* skills as an interviewer, you know."

She hurried up a few more steps, but he barreled around her again and stopped her. "I'm not questioning your skills as an interviewer. I'm saying you don't need to do this. We can get the information we want without letting that smarmy jackass ply you with barbecue."

Even in the dim glow from nearby streetlights, he could see the anger flashing in her eyes. She brushed past him, moved up a couple of steps so she was once again in the dominant position. She leaned toward him until they were nose to nose.

"Maybe it isn't simply the interview I want. Maybe I'm interested in more than finding out what con game he's playing. Maybe I'd like to go out with a refined gentleman..."

"He's a con man! Which you acknowledged not five minutes ago."

"...or at least one who *pretends* to be a gentleman," Jo shot back. "Some people can't even pretend." With a toss of her head, she started away, but he reached up and whirled her around, tumbling her into his arms and fastening his mouth on hers.

7

HE DIDN'T BOTHER with seduction. This kiss came out of nowhere, straight into the moment. It exploded between them.

"Gentleman?" he muttered, his mouth hot on hers. "I'll show you a gentleman." Only he didn't. This kiss was raw, powerful, pulling her into a vortex. No gentleman would kiss like this.

"Case...I..." She gasped for air.

"Shut up," he growled, pulling her more tightly against him "Just shut up."

For once, she obeyed, clinging to him. But that was like trying to grasp fire in order to be protected from the heat.

With his mouth on hers, Case ran his hands around her waist, up and under the edge of her sweater. He had to touch her skin, to make her feel what he was feeling; the hunger and need that had been prickling at him for two days now. He had to taste her, so his lips crushed hers, his arms pulled her flush against him. Vaguely, he thought she must be as stunned as he was, her arms stiff as if she'd received a shock and couldn't move. After a moment, her hands came up to cup his jaw and hold him in place. Her mouth ravaged his. Desire, hot and hard, linked with exultation that she wanted him as badly as he wanted her. It was maddening. *She* was maddening.

Jo's breath was clogged somewhere between her

chest and next week. She couldn't remember how to breathe, couldn't even recall why she'd want to. The only thought in her head was to prolong this kiss.

He tasted wonderful, exactly as she'd suspected he would; warm, enveloping, sensual.

Delightful. If she wasn't so annoyed with him, she might actually enjoy this, she thought dizzily, standing on tiptoe, kissing him for all she was worth.

"You irritate the hell out of me," he murmured against her mouth, then nipped at her lips until she opened for another kiss.

"I...ca-can't stand you, either," she responded, wrapping her arms around his shoulders and spiking her hands through that sable-soft hair of his to hold him still for her enjoyment.

"You don't do what I tell you to." His lips skated across her jaw and his teeth nipped at her ear.

"You're so darned bossy." She turned her face so that his lips couldn't avoid hers. How could he be soft and hard at the same time? she wondered. How could he be so delicious that she wanted to pull him inside her and so aggravating she wanted to kick him down the steps?

Excitement vibrated through her even as she thought that this was crazy. They were standing on the stairs between two streets. Anyone could walk by and see them, be shocked by them.

"You're not going to dinner with that jerk," Case growled. He'd tugged her sweater up and his hands encircled her ribs. Her skin was the softest thing he'd ever touched. He was desperate to touch her all over.

"Yes I am." She shuddered with longing and her own hands dove down his back and began tugging his shirt out of his jeans. *Just a moment,* she thought desperately. Just a moment more and she'd touch him the way he was touching her.

When she tangled her hand in the hairs dusted across his stomach, then looped her fingers in the waistband of his jeans, he groaned as if she were killing him, gulped for air, branded her with his mouth once again, and then panted, "I'll bet you throw a baseball like a girl."

"Wha-a-at?" Stunned, she stared up at him.

"Sorry," he wheezed, fighting for air, blinking and shaking his head as if he was coming out of a fog. "I had to say something to stop this."

"Oh! Well, *you* started it!" Realizing where her hands were, she snatched them away, stepped back, and began straightening her clothes. Appalled, she looked around. What had they been thinking? What had they been *doing?*

She cleared her throat, and quickly scanned the staircase and the streets above and below them.

Case smoothed his hair. He could still feel her fingers entwined there. For a minute, he'd forgotten why he was in Calamity Falls at all. He'd forgotten what they'd been talking about. Oh, yeah. They'd been arguing. No surprise there.

He took her arm and propelled her up the steps. "Come on. I'm taking you home. We'll finish this conversation in private."

He was hustling her along so fast that Jo's feet only touched the ground about every third step. She didn't have enough breath left from the kiss and the dash toward home to tell him to slow down.

When they finally reached her house, Case waited impatiently while she unlocked the door and then he hurried her inside.

She stopped in the middle of her pocket-handkerchief-sized living room, turned to him, and said, "We're going to argue, aren't we?"

He released a frustrated breath, ran his hand through his hair once again, and said, "Yeah, we are."

"Well, that's fine," she muttered. "That's just fine. In that event, I need food." She tossed her purse down on the sofa, kicked off her shoes, and went into the kitchen.

She could cook, she thought furiously as she started searching for the ingredients for brownies. It always soothed her to mix up huge batches of something deliciously sweet.

That phrase made her think of Case's mouth. *No.* Sweet wasn't good. She slapped the cupboard door shut.

"What are you doing?" Case asked, watching from the doorway as she banged pots and pans around, then slammed the cupboard door shut.

"I was going to bake brownies," she said, lifting her chin in a way that dared him to make something of it. "I always bake when I'm mad."

"You do?"

"Yes." She nodded, then paused. "Or at least I used to. The last time I did it, though, I nearly set the kitchen curtains on fire."

"Baking brownies?" Now laughter was edging his mouth.

She waved a hand at the antiquated range. "It's a gas stove, okay, and the burner wouldn't light, so I was trying to light it with a candle, and I set it on the stove top for a minute, and the flame got too close to the curtains, and..."

"I get the picture," he said, moving into the room. "So, I guess you didn't do this the other night when Steve..."

"Dumped me while we were having dinner at the Copper Pot and broke my heart. Only he *didn't* break my heart." She paused. How odd that mention of Steve didn't give her that sick little twist of the stomach she'd been feeling since Monday night. Was it possible that Case's kiss had done that? No, that wasn't possible. Forcibly, she got her mind back on track. "No. I maintained my dignity. I came home, had some wine and decided to change my life."

Case leaned against the doorjamb, shook his head, and said, "You've succeeded in doing that, all right. And it looks like the changes have just begun."

"And don't you forget it," she retorted as she went back to rattling pots and pans.

"If you're hungry, why don't you settle for a sandwich?" Without waiting for an invitation, he pulled out a chair, twirled it around, and sat. For some reason, he was getting a kick out of this. He didn't mind seeing her thrown off-kilter, especially since his kiss was what seemed to have done it to her.

She leaned against the counter, folded her hands across her waist, and said, "All right. Would you like one?"

He thought she probably didn't have a clue about the way that pose pushed her breasts up and out, and he wasn't about to spoil the view. However, he was hungry, so he said, "I thought you'd never ask. What can I do?"

Jo directed him to the bread and the sandwich makings while she found cans of cola and filled glasses with ice. Once they had everything set out, they sat on opposite sides of the table, made their snack, and ate in a more amicable atmosphere than Jo would have thought possible.

"There's one thing we've got to get clear between us," she said firmly, waving a pickle spear at him.

He liked the way she ate, with a careless kind of passion, snagging bits of lettuce and pickle from her turkey sandwich and nibbling them with gusto.

He made himself focus on the challenge in her eyes rather than the softness of her lips. "What would that be?"

"That kiss was a mistake. It...it only messes things up."

Yeah, like his mind. He nodded slowly as he wondered where she was going with this. "I see."

"We're going to be working together. Partners, and nothing else."

He could barely hide his amusement. "Nothing else?"

"That's right. It's a well-known fact that partners in investigations are at risk for affairs because they're in a dangerous situation. I'm informing you right now that isn't going to happen to us."

Case listened without interrupting. When she finished, he only stared at her.

Why didn't he say something? When Jo couldn't wait any longer, she stumbled back into speech. "I'm one to give credit where it's due. You're an attractive man."

He lifted an eyebrow at her.

That sardonic gesture kicked her nervousness up a few more notches. He was a very attractive man. Not to mention sexy and dangerous to her peace of mind. "And your kissing technique is very...acceptable."

He was laughing at her now. His eyes sparkled and his lips twitched. "Thank you, Jo. Yours isn't bad, either."

Jo didn't particularly like having her own faint

praise turned back on her, but she forged ahead anyway. "So, what I'm saying is that we can't have a repeat of that kiss."

Case leaned forward, gazed directly into her eyes and said, "Then don't provoke me."

She narrowed her eyes at him and swallowed a sharp retort about exactly who had been provoking whom. However, she felt foolish enough, so she said, "I won't."

Not bloody likely, he thought, but he only gave her a bland look. It wouldn't do for her to know how she'd gotten under his skin. He didn't like to admit that, but since he had changed his life a few years ago, he had become a man who never lied to himself.

He liked almost everything about her from that beautiful, smooth hair to those sea-green eyes to that killer mouth. She was smart and quick and stubborn and he knew she'd do just fine when she got where she wanted to be—working on a major newspaper, covering the kind of stories she thought were what she wanted. Dangerous ones, no doubt. The thought had dread fisting his guts into a knot.

There wasn't much real danger in the situation with Purdy, but he wasn't going to tell her that. Call him old-fashioned, but he liked the idea of having her depend on him a little bit.

Her future, the danger she might face, the stress, loneliness, overwork. All were her choice. He watched the way she pinched off a corner of bread and scooped it into her mouth. Her choice, and his misery.

He finished his sandwich, stood abruptly and began putting everything back where he'd found it. Jo gave him a surprised look and said, "You'd be really handy to have around the house."

He shrugged. "I live alone and I don't like mess, so I clean up after myself."

He lived alone. Somehow she'd known that. He'd said didn't have a wife. He must not have a live-in girlfriend, either. That was good.

He lived in Phoenix. He thought she was pursuing the wrong goal with her desire to have a faster-paced life and career. That was bad.

Sometimes life just sucked.

"Besides," he went on. "I've got three older sisters. They trained me the way they wanted their husbands to be."

Jo, an only child, stared at him, fascinated. "Did it work?"

"I can cook. I can clean. I can even change diapers."

Jo rested her forehead on the back of her hand. "Give me strength," she moaned. "I've met the man of my dreams."

He chuckled, and then sobered. That man-of-her-dreams part sent a shock wave rocketing through him. Better get this back on track. He returned to the table and sat down opposite her.

"There's no need for you to go out with Purdy," he said, proud of himself for his calm, reasonable tone of voice.

"I might learn something important."

"We can both learn what we need to know at the meeting he's having at his house tomorrow night. I suggest we go as a couple, listen to what he has to say, and act interested."

She shook her head. "Why would he think we're a couple? Most people there will know you just arrived in town and that we're not a couple because Steve and I only broke up a few days ago."

''That's the beauty of it, Jo. You're heartbroken because you were dumped. Fortunately, I was right there to comfort you.''

''Uh, yes, Case, but you seem to be playing the part of a doofus.'' She grinned suddenly. ''Is he going to believe that a smart woman like me would be interested in you?''

He leaned across the table and looked into her eyes. ''I've got news for you. He thinks you're not too bright, or why would you be living in this little hick town writing up newspaper reports on the repairs to the high-school roof? Remember, he said it was 'sweet'?''

Case must have been eavesdropping when Harold had said that. ''Nevertheless,'' she responded grimly. ''If I break the date now he might get suspicious.''

Case threw his hands in the air. ''Of what?''

She didn't know, so she bluffed. She picked up a paper napkin and began pleating it between her fingers. ''That maybe...maybe I've learned something about him that would cause me to break the date, that I've learned he's a con man.''

''That's so transparent I could read the *Ingot* through it,'' Case scoffed. ''It's more likely that *he'll* have second thoughts and decide you're trying to pump him for information and that you might blow his scam even though he seems bent on assuring you that his humble little story would be of interest to no one. He'll probably be relieved if you call off the date.''

''Perhaps,'' she admitted. She folded her hands on the top of the table and gave him a straight look. ''I'm going to do it, though.''

He pushed his chair back, stomped around the room, and growled, ''God, you're stubborn.''

"Which is why I'm good at my job," she said.

At least, she fervently hoped she could be good at this. How did she know? She'd never been in this situation before, never been on the verge of a big story. Couldn't Case see that she was worried? The butterflies in her stomach were whirling around like the blades on a food processor. It would be so easy for her to back down, to forget this whole thing, to go right back to reporting on parking-lot and roof repairs. She was struggling to get out of her rut and she felt like he had one of his biker boots planted on top of her head.

She wanted him to approve of what she was doing, Jo thought uncomfortably. It was important to her.

Good grief, she thought as she watched him pace around her tiny kitchen. If she wasn't careful, she could fall in love with him.

He stopped, leaned against the sink, and glared at her.

Impossible. She couldn't fall in love with a man she'd known three days. Besides, she wasn't over Steve yet. Was she?

"Well, hell," Case finally muttered. "It looks like I'm not going to be able to talk you out of this, so we might as well decide how you're going to play it." He pointed a finger at her. "And don't start getting any ideas about wearing that slinky black dress with air molecules where the back should be."

Relief washed through her that he'd agreed to her plan. "That dress would hardly be appropriate for dinner at the Lotus Blossom."

"Good. Where'd you get that thing, anyway?"

"Bought it at a thrift store," she said with a grin. "I wore it to a Halloween party. I was the Mistress of the Dark."

"Yeah, well, don't wear anything that will give Purdy the idea that you're going to be *his* mistress."

"Oh, don't worry," she answered demurely. "I don't think things will go that far." She paused and gave him a sly glance. "I don't suppose I'll be wired with a microphone to record what he tells me, will I?"

"No. I don't have that kind of equipment with me."

"Well, what kind of investigator shows up without electronic bugging devices?"

"One who doesn't want to get arrested."

"Then I'll have to take my tape recorder along, and...what's the matter?"

Case was shaking is head. "Do you think Purdy's going to let you record him?"

"Well, sure. I'm a reporter, I'm interested in what he has to say and I might want to write an article about him."

"He's not taking you out to get interviewed. He only wants to romance you to keep you from writing about him. Do you think he's stayed out of jail this long by giving interviews to reporters? Even a reporter he thinks isn't very bright because she works on a little hick-town newspaper?"

"I can at least ask if I can record him. I won't know unless I ask."

"Stubbornness, thy name is Jo Ella," Case groaned.

Jo didn't answer because it would only prolong the argument. Besides, in spite of her qualms, and his, she was beginning to get excited about this. "And where will you be while I'm having dinner with him?"

Hanging around outside plotting his murder if he touches you, Case thought, but he only answered, "Oh, I'll be around. I'll see you at the meeting at his place."

"You can do your lamebrain act. I can take pity on

you, and we can sit together,'' she said impishly. ''Everyone will think I'm a true humanitarian.''

His smile kicked up one corner of his mouth. ''Just you wait. My dimwit persona might come in handy.''

Case stood and started for the door and she followed him. With his hand on the knob, he glanced back at her and said, ''Remember, though, that what you're doing is only an act, as well.''

Jo heard the same edge in his voice she had heard when they'd been talking to Harold Purdy, and it still puzzled her. It couldn't be jealousy, but it almost sounded like it. She smiled to herself. She wasn't the type of woman who inspired jealousy.

''I'll remember, Case,'' she promised faithfully.

He paused for another few seconds as if he had more to say, his dark eyes fixed on her.

''What?'' she asked.

''Be careful,'' he said. ''Purdy may be more than we expect him to be. He hasn't stayed in this business for as long as he has by being stupid. And Jo...''

''Yes?''

''Remember, don't wear anything too sexy tomorrow night.''

She stared at him. Did he really think she was going to vamp the professor? ''Except for my Mistress of the Dark number, I don't *have* any sexy clothes, Case.''

He opened his mouth as if he was going to argue, but instead, he said, ''Good. We don't want to give him the idea that he's going to get you between the sheets to finish off the evening.'' Then he swept out the door and was gone.

''O-o-o-o-oh.'' Jo jerked the door open and shouted after him. ''I can take care of myself, you know!''

There was no answer. He'd disappeared into the

darkness. Frustrated, she closed the door and locked it. She was glad he'd gone. Otherwise he might have learned that his last words made her nervous. She didn't know what to expect, but she didn't want to spend the evening fighting off Purdy's advances. Nor did she want to spend it figuring out ways to stay out of danger. In fact, despite her babbling remarks to Case about their kisses being a reaction to a dangerous situation, she really didn't think she had much to fear from Harold. He was a talker, not a fighter. Still, now she wished Case was going to be there. Even in his doofus mode, she knew she could depend on him.

She took a deep breath to steady herself. This was what she wanted, she reminded herself fiercely. Hard-nosed investigative reporters didn't turn and run at the first sign of danger. They didn't need backup in the form of smart, well-muscled, and sexy investigators.

And if she kept saying that, she might actually begin to believe it sometime before six o'clock tomorrow evening.

"OF COURSE, during my time with the Institute, I studied under Dr. Ralph Twicklesworth, whose ideas on time and space are well-known."

"Really, Harold? How fascinating." Jo smiled serenely and sipped her tea. So far the evening was going well. In spite of her annoyance with Case's bossiness, she'd taken his suggestion and dressed demurely in a black skirt and a white silk blouse with small pearl buttons that fastened almost to her throat. She had met Harold at the restaurant as planned and so far he'd been an impeccable host.

Everything about this man should have been perfect, Jo thought. Harold's clothes were well-made and understated. Even though he affected an ascot instead of a tie, it somehow suited him. He didn't have a hair out of place and looked as though he tweezed his eyebrows to get them in shape, as well. His hands were manicured and unblemished by hard work. He wore exactly the right amount of cologne. The second hand on his Rolex watch swept smoothly from one second to the next without the jerky movement of a fake. His conversation was sophisticated and witty. Delivered in that awesome cadence, it was irresistible.

So why was she fighting the urge to lay her head right down on the table and go to sleep?

"I haven't heard of Dr. Twicklesworth's theories before, Harold," she said, stifling a yawn. "Why don't you explain them to me?" She reached into her purse to remove the small recorder. "And I'm sure you won't mind if I tape what you say, will you? You've given me so much to think about this evening that I'm quite certain I won't be able to keep it all straight in my head."

He paused, his blue eyes narrowing for a second at her guileless smile. She put every ounce of warmth she could muster into that smile. It should have boiled the soy sauce he was sprinkling on his extra spicy beef and broccoli.

Then he smiled, replaced the soy-sauce bottle on its saucer and reached smoothly across the table to take the recorder from her hand.

Surprised, she stared at him as he said, "Oh, let's don't do that." He leaned forward suggestively and looked at her as if the two of them were the only ones in the room. "Having that little electronic tool out will spoil the intimacy between us."

Intimacy? Yikes. Jo gulped and smiled sweetly as she took the recorder back and put it away. "Of course you're right, Harold. You're so wise."

He preened and sat back, continuing his monologue about Dr. Twicklesworth's theories while Jo gnashed her teeth. Resigned, she ate her lemon chicken and made appropriate remarks whenever he paused for breath.

To his credit, when she did speak, he paused as if he was hearing pronouncements from Mount Olympus and gave her his full attention. It was very flattering, but she kept wishing he'd make a pitch for money so she would have something to focus on. But oh, no, he'd talked about his education, his travels, asked about her job, smirked at the stories she'd covered. She wanted to kick him under the table even though she knew it was hypocritical to poke fun at the *Ingot* herself and then become incensed when someone else did it.

Case had been right. Harold thought she wasn't exactly overburdened with brains and she had to continue with that boring act or risk giving away her secret agenda.

A disturbance at the table next to them caught her attention and she glanced over to see a little old man being shown to his seat directly behind Harold. With a shaking hand, he pulled out his chair and sat heavily as if his tired legs were giving way beneath him. It took him a few minutes to arrange himself, first removing a musty old coat, then smoothing his long gray hair and beard. Finally, he settled down and picked up a menu the waitress had left him. Squinting, he struggled to read it. When the waitress returned, he gave his order in a creaking voice, then sat sipping from his water glass.

Jo smiled sympathetically at the old gentleman, but he didn't see her. Harold, involved in what he was saying, didn't even notice.

"I have to admit it's a somewhat lonely life, Jo," Harold was saying. "I've spent many years on the road, working to help people."

"You mean with financial advice?"

"That and other things I've learned from years of scientific study."

Her expression full of melting warmth, Jo said, "Please tell me about it." There was something odd about that old man, she thought, but she couldn't quite put her finger on it. His long hair and flowing beard looked like the latest word in rat's-nest chic. His clothes could only be described as scruffy, but in a place like Calamity Falls, a man of his appearance wasn't an unusual sight. In fact, it seemed she was the only person in the place who had even noticed him.

She pulled her attention away from him and focused on Harold. After all, he was her story. "What places have you visited in your efforts to help people?"

He talked while she listened and tried to remember all the places he said he'd been so she could follow up and find out if he'd pulled any cons in those places, but it was hard to remember them all without her recorder or her notebook.

She was concentrating on Harold as she forked up some grains of rice, but her attention strayed when she saw the scruffy old guy at the next table pull a small blue notepad from his pocket and open it before him.

"Oh!" Jo gasped, got a throatful of rice, and began to cough. Grains of rice spewed across the table just as Harold leaped to his feet and swept his plate out of the way.

Hurriedly, he checked to see if she'd managed to soil his jacket, or his dinner, then he glanced at her. "Jo, are you all right, my dear?"

Jo, choking for air, swiping water from her eyes,

and grabbing for her cup of tea, could only nod and croak, "Fine, Harold. I'm fi-fine."

Belatedly, he came around the table to lean over her and pat her solicitously on the back. The people nearby were staring, including the grizzled old guy at the nearest table, who gifted her with a wink from one of his dark brown eyes.

While Harold was patting her back, Jo lifted her head and glared. Case Houston. She didn't know why she was surprised. He'd been worried that she couldn't do this, so he'd shown up to keep an eye on her.

Well, that was fine, she thought furiously. That was just fine. He had his little notepad out and he could take notes to his heart's content while she pumped information out of Harold for all she was worth.

But later, Case had better be ready for an earful!

Harold reassured the people around her that she was all right, but he paused when he saw Case and gave him a long look.

Case responded to Harold's scrutiny with a slow nod, hid his small notepad with one hand, and reached for his water with the other. Still, Harold stared at him.

Alarmed, Jo patted her chest and by some odd quirk, several of her buttons came undone. "Thank you, again, Harold," she said in a breathy tone that pulled his attention away from Case.

At the next table, her partner's eyes narrowed, but when Harold sat down across from her, his widened appreciatively.

"My goodness," she said, batting her eyelashes and fanning herself with her napkin. She tilted her head and smiled her most winning smile. "I don't know what came over me. Thank you, Harold, I think you probably saved my life. I might have choked to death if you hadn't been there to save me."

He lifted his hands as if to deflect her gratitude. "Think nothing of it, Jo. I'm honored to be the one here to help you out when you need it."

"Yes," she sighed as if he was a gift straight from the gods. "I was wondering, though, if you could do one more tiny favor for me?"

"Anything. Anything at all."

"Could you ask the waitress for some more ice water? With lots of ice? I feel quite...*flushed*." She ran her fingertip down her throat and into the V created by the open buttons. Another worked itself free.

Harold's eyes nearly popped from his head. "Certainly." He nodded and signaled for the waitress. While his head was turned, Jo wrinkled her nose at Case, who lifted a dusty gray eyebrow at her. Grumpily she wondered if those were his eyebrows or if he'd given a trim to someone's sheepdog.

When the ice water arrived, she drank some, then fished a piece of ice out of the glass and popped it into her mouth. Pursing her lips around it, she said, "Now, what were you telling me about all the places you've been, Harold?"

8

WHAT MAN COULD RESIST such an eager and appreciative audience? Jo knew she was hitting the right note with him when he launched into a travelogue of the places he'd been. Behind his shoulder, she glimpsed Case busily writing down everything Harold said.

She hoped it helped in the investigation, and she knew the information would be helpful for her as well when it came time to flesh out her story on Harold.

Still, it rankled that Case had followed her and was actually getting the information that she, the reporter, was supposed to get.

Jo and Harold both finished their dinners during his monologue. She was amazed to see that anyone could talk, eat, and project that much charisma all at the same time. She thought it must have taken years of practice before a mirror.

For her part, she'd had no practice in the art of being a brainless femme fatale, so she had to constantly remind herself to look absorbed by what he was saying, moisten her lips occasionally with her tongue, suck provocatively on ice from her water glass, and give him occasional glimpses of her peekaboo buttons. It was exhausting. If she had to do this every evening, she would need a nap each afternoon. However, it was worth it because it kept Harold's attention firmly fixed on her and he didn't notice what the man behind him was doing.

Case was going to owe her big-time for this one.

As they sipped green tea, Harold turned his laser-blue eyes on her. "What about you, Jo?" he asked. "It must be hard for a woman of your obvious intelligence and talent to stay here in this little town."

"Oh," she said breathlessly. "It is."

"I doubt that there are many men who appreciate what a treasure you are." His eyes were all but glued to her cleavage, telling her exactly what treasure he meant.

She lowered her eyes demurely. "You have no idea, Harold, how difficult it is, but it's wonderful to have someone like you to appreciate me."

Case looked up and rolled his eyes. Jo ignored him.

"Especially after that cad, what was his name? Steve? Yes, Steve, after he dumped you so callously."

"It did hurt, Harold," she admitted, tightening her lips in a show of bravery and batting her eyelashes.

Case held his nose. She looked away. Harold reached to cover her hand with his. "You have such courage," he said. "What about that rather dim-witted young man who seems to be so taken with you?"

She gave a theatrical sigh. "As I'm sure you've noticed, we have many odd characters here in Calamity Falls, with strange and unusual interests. Case's is the strangest of all and many of us are trying to help him overcome his obsession with..." She stopped as if she were embarrassed.

Harold began to stroke her hand. "What is his obsession?" He leaned forward, projecting warmth and inviting her to confide in him.

Jo sighed. "You see, he's afraid he's never going to measure up." Feigning embarrassment, she looked away. "He's heard that there are certain things a woman wants in a man and well, frankly, he just doesn't have what it takes."

Harold was all but kneading the skin off her hand. "Most distressing."

"Oh, you have no idea." Her free hand fluttered up to cover her eyes. From beneath its protection, she could see Case glaring at her in outrage.

"You're a good woman to take on his worries and try to reassure him. But, you know, my dear, sometimes there are things that can be done. Medical procedures and such."

She turned grateful eyes on him. "Do you really think so, Harold? That's comforting because so many of us are worried about Case and his obsession with…" She rolled her eyes apologetically.

Case nearly fell out of his chair in his effort to hear her breathy response. She kept her eyes firmly fixed on Harold's as she said, "Facial hair."

Harold stared. Case gave her a dirty look. Jo smiled sweetly.

"FACIAL HAIR?" Case was seething. "You told him I don't measure up in the area of *facial* hair?"

He'd accosted her as soon as they met outside Purdy's house. Several people had been waiting for Harold when they had arrived, and he had hurried to invite them inside. Jo was following them into the house when Case slipped out of the darkness and pulled her aside.

He'd ditched his dirty-old-man disguise, probably in the nearest trash can, she thought, and was dressed in his usual black outfit, biker boots and leather bomber jacket. He'd combed his hair by running his fingers through it several times so that it looked ruffled and messy and infuriatingly irresistible.

She shrugged innocently. "I was sitting there looking at that dog's ruff of hair around your face and it was the only thing I could think of."

"Next time, think harder." He ran his hand over his smooth jaw and said, "I told you he wouldn't talk into that tape recorder. He doesn't want to leave a trail of information behind him anywhere he goes. That's how he's stayed in business, by leaving as little evidence behind as possible."

"So you felt like you had to show up and take notes?" she whispered. She'd been put out with him almost constantly since they'd met. Now she was incensed. Grasping his arm, she pulled him into the shadows at the corner of the house and said, "I was handling things just fine, thank you. I didn't need you to cover me."

"Oh, really? You were able to instantly memorize everything he said?"

Jo didn't answer since they both knew she hadn't, but she lifted her chin anyway, thinking that if all else failed, she at least had bravado. "I was doing my best."

Case tapped the front of his jacket to indicate where he kept his notepad. "I'm sure you were, but now I've got a list of every place he's been in the past few years, so I can check out what he's been doing."

"*We've* got the list," she said pointedly. "If you think you're going to keep me out of this story now…"

"No, I'm not going to do that," he answered with an impatient little slicing gesture of his hand. "Not now that we're getting close to the truth."

"If he was *telling* the truth." That had occurred to

her while she'd been breathlessly questioning Harold and he'd been ogling her.

"Honey, no man could lie when faced with the possibility of getting you to sleep with him," Case said dryly, and even in the near blackness of the shadows she could see his ferocious scowl.

She clapped her hands onto her hips. "Sleep with him? Oh, please! That is so lame."

"Is it? Then what was the signal you were trying to give him by airing out your cleavage for him?" He did an imitation of her fanning herself and his voice took on a falsetto note. "'I feel so flushed, Harold, darling. Could you pour some ice water right here between my breasts?'"

Heat rushed into her face. "I said no such thing. For your information, I was trying to distract him from looking at you and seeing who you really were."

"He wouldn't have known. It was a good disguise."

"Yeah, if you can believe anyone would actually choose to look like a sheepdog."

"It was the best I could do on short notice, and it was all the thrift store had on hand. Apparently, you shop there on better days than I do."

"Well, here's something you can take back to them," she said, reaching up and tugging at his eyebrows, which were still frosted with gray.

"Ouch!" His hand grabbed for her wrist.

The stuff wouldn't come off. "Case, what did you do? Glue something to your own eyebrows?"

"Yeah, I trimmed that fake beard I got and used rubber cement to stick it on my eyebrows," he said. "Worked pretty good, too."

"Except that you didn't get it all out and everyone's going to see something's fishy once we get inside."

"Nah," he answered in a peeved tone as he brushed at his eyebrows. "They'll just think it's all part of my obsession with facial hair."

Jo fought a grin. "Since I'm the one who's supposed to be helping you learn to control the obsession, lean down here and let me get that stuff out."

Reluctantly, Case lowered his head so she could pick out the remaining fragments of artificial hair and glue. His breath hissed in with each bit she pulled. "Ow! Hey, I think you're enjoying this too much."

"Oh, quit being such a baby," she scolded. "I thought investigators like you would know how to do a better disguise than this."

"What the hell makes you think I've ever needed a disguise before? This is new for me. Everything's new for me since I met you."

"I'll take that as a compliment," she said, finishing the trimming job.

"Jo, is that you?" A cautious voice spoke in the darkness, followed by scurrying footsteps. A small woman dressed in mechanic's coveralls came out of the darkness. She was a fierce-looking little thing with short white hair that stood up around her head in a crazed sort of halo.

"Starina," Jo said, startled. "Hello."

Starina came up close and squinted at them. "What are you doing to this guy? Is he bothering you? Need some help taking care of him? I've got a monkey wrench that'll put a goose egg on his head the size of Nebraska." She hefted it and waved it menacingly.

Case held up his hands and stepped back. "Whoa, there. Jo, call her off."

"It's okay, Starina, he's a friend of mine—in a manner of speaking," Jo murmured. She introduced the two people who regarded each other warily.

"Hmph," Starina said. "You here to listen to what His Royal Fakiness has to say?" she asked, nodding toward Harold's house.

"Yes." Jo exchanged a glance with Case. "What makes you think he's a fake?"

"I've tried to have a few conversations with him, but he doesn't have anything to say worth listening to. Doesn't know beans about science. He travels light, too. Doesn't even own so much as a hammer." Her voice was ripe with disgust.

Case looked to Jo for an explanation, but she held up her hand to forestall his questions. "I see. Starina, what else have you noticed about him?"

"I've heard strange noises coming from this place late at night."

"Strange?" Case asked. "In what way?"

"Sounded like ripping wood." She leaned close. "And I say, why's he working with wood over here if he claims not to have any tools? He had to come over and borrow my crowbar."

Case and Jo exchanged glances, but before they could ask any more, Charlotte Quail called from the front porch steps.

"Jo?" The older woman squinted into the shadows, searching for them. "Are you and your friend coming in?"

"Uh, yes, Charlotte," Jo called back. "We'll be right there. We wouldn't miss Professor Purdy's talk for anything."

Starina snorted derisively and headed back to her own house next door. "Darned fools," she muttered as she went.

Jo and Case hurried around to join Charlotte.

"I wouldn't miss it, either," Charlotte twittered as she rushed back into the house. "Isn't this exciting?"

"Riveting," Jo agreed. She gave Case a quick look to see if his eyebrows appeared to be back to normal. They looked a little sparse in places, but she thought no one else would notice. "We'll talk to Starina some more later. You'd better pull your feeble-witted look out of your bag of tricks now."

He grumbled something under his breath, took her arm, and hauled her up the front steps and into the house.

If they'd hoped to get lost in the crowd, Case saw right away that wasn't going to happen because there wasn't much of a crowd. In spite of the number of men at the Unbroken Man rally, and the throng at the women's meeting, the only ones who were present were Purdy himself, the two of them, Charlotte, Freida, Cedric, and about half a dozen others he didn't yet know.

Maybe that was all Purdy needed, though, Case thought as he donned his eager, good-old-boy expression and found seats for himself and Jo in the sparsely furnished living room.

Purdy didn't seem dismayed by the small number of people his message had attracted.

Case thought it was odd that Purdy hadn't rented a nicer house. This one was in a nice setting, near the top of the falls themselves and near the old mine offices, but the house was rundown and dismal inside.

In his experience, Case had known confidence men to use only the best they could afford in order to project a well-off, and therefore trustworthy, image. Purdy had that part of the con down perfectly with his clothes and his manner.

This house didn't fit the image at all. He still wasn't precisely sure what kind of con Purdy was working, but it was related somehow to money. It always came down to money.

Case knew for sure that Freida, Charlotte, and Cedric had money. If the others did, too, then it was possible that Purdy only needed a few followers who were willing to give him what he needed.

He would have to share these thoughts with Jo once the meeting was over. Case gave her a sidelong glance. If she was speaking to him, that is. It was just barely possible that he'd been wrong to disguise himself and follow her on her date with Purdy. He'd been able to justify it by telling himself that Purdy would never agree to their conversation being taped.

In truth, he'd been worried all day, an emotion he hadn't felt in years. He'd left that kind of thing behind when he'd quit the attorney general's office and started working on his own. Three days of knowing Jo Ella Quillan had brought it all back.

He shifted in his seat so that he could look at her. She was busily glancing around, studying the people who were there and talking to Charlotte, who was seated on her other side.

She'd buttoned her blouse, he noticed thankfully. Seeing her slip those buttons open had nearly given him a stroke, even if she did claim that she'd done it only to help keep Harold's attention on her and away from him. At one point, he'd thought he was going to have to grab Jo's ice water and pour it down Purdy's pants. Remembering it made him grind his teeth together. He couldn't believe she'd resorted to using an enticement like that.

He vowed that the two of them were going to finish their conversation about that subject as soon as they got out of this meeting. He'd add a few choice words regarding his "worries" about not measuring up in the area of facial hair.

Purdy was standing in front of them now with his arms upraised and his beneficent smile in place. "The universe is not what you've been lead to believe it is," he began. "There's much more to it, and to yourselves, than mankind has yet dreamed."

While Harold spoke, Jo secretly watched the reactions of the others. As he poured forth his pseudoscientific theories, Cedric and Charlotte, and a few other people, appeared to be more and more intrigued. She thought it was interesting that they were all people she knew to have an interest in science, they each had their own area of expertise, some as odd as the ideas Harold was presenting.

"The earth is not round, or as the ancients believed, flat, but concave."

Jo stared at Harold when he made that statement. Beside her, Case appeared to be swallowing a laugh. Several other people looked puzzled, but interested. Freida looked, quite simply enthralled with him. Anything he said would have intrigued her.

Freida's expression made Jo especially uncomfortable because she recognized it as that of a woman in love. She wondered if she'd ever gazed at Steve like that. Or if Case had ever looked at a woman like that.

Maybe. A man didn't usually reach the age of…what?…thirty?…without having experienced being in love. What was Case like when he was in love? Did he send flowers? Romantic gifts? What kind of lover was he? Slow, thoughtful and considerate, or quick and careless?

Nah, she didn't think so. He seemed to be careful about everything. Suddenly she became aware that he was staring at her.

He mouthed the words, "What's wrong?" at her.

Appalled at her thoughts, she shook her head quickly and fixed her attention on Harold.

That was what a professional investigative reporter did, she scolded herself. They got all the information possible on the subject of their investigation. They didn't sit and moon over their fellow investigators.

It was hard to listen to Harold, since his theory of how the earth was formed seemed to make little sense. She fought to keep the skepticism from her face, maintaining a fascinated and enthralled expression.

To her surprise, the pitch for money never materialized. Harold wound up his remarks by inviting them back again the next afternoon to hear more on the subject. He then swept into the small audience, shaking hands, hugging those who already seemed to believe him, like Charlotte and Freida. He seemed to know exactly the right thing to say to everyone, even Case, whom he clapped on the shoulder in hearty welcome.

"I'll hope to see you here tomorrow, young man," he said smiling warmly. "You look like someone who would want to learn as much as possible about how to be a real man and about man's place in the world." He leaned in close and said, "And don't you worry, you'll be able to grow a beard one of these days."

Jo had to stifle a laugh when she saw the way Case's eyes narrowed and his jaw worked as if he wanted to spit bullets. She was ready to jump in and intervene when he got his reaction under control and grinned his foolish grin. "Thank you, Professor," he mumbled, ducking his head humbly. "How nice that someone as smart as you are would want to encourage me."

"And lovely Jo Ella." Harold's voice hit its lowest, most engaging, sexiest register as he took her hand, turned it, and suavely kissed the back of it. He lifted his eyes to hers. ''Thank you for a wonderful evening. I'll be looking forward to many more in the future.''

Although she was taken aback, and fully aware of Case standing beside her, giving her that patently fake gaze of adoration, she managed a welcoming smile and said, ''Harold, I don't know when I've enjoyed an evening more. The conversation was so stimulating.'' She took a deep breath so that her chest expanded and her buttons strained as if they were about to pop open. ''I truly don't think I'll be able to sleep a wink tonight. You've given me so much to think about, the ideas are simply *pounding* through my brain.'' She reached up and trailed a finger down her cheek provocatively. ''I'll see you tomorrow. I'm eager, absolutely *eager,* to hear more.''

Behind Harold, she saw Freida Long watching them with a stricken expression in her eyes. Jo felt terrible because she knew the older woman was in love with Harold. Charlotte put a protective arm around Freida and gave her a hug. Jo wanted to say something reassuring, but knew she couldn't. What could she have said, anyway? Freida seemed like a nice lady and didn't deserve someone like Harold.

''We'd better go, Jo,'' Case said in his wimpy tone. Only she could hear the edge to it. ''The professor is probably tired and would like to have some time alone.'' He started pulling her toward the door, but Harold still had her hand, so for an instant there was a momentary struggle she feared would jerk her arms from their sockets.

Case won the tug-of-war, though, and quickly hustled her out the door. Jo had the presence of mind to give Harold a fleeting smile of regret as she went.

Once they were outside, Case put his right arm

around her waist and his left hand on her arm and frog-marched her toward home.

"His ideas *pounding* through your brain?" he grumbled. "You're *eager* to hear more?"

"What else was I supposed to say?" she demanded, trying to jerk herself free of his grasp before he cut off all circulation to her arm and lower body. She finally managed to stumble away from him as they reached the stairs leading to her street. She grabbed the handrail and scurried up. "Should I have told him we know he's a con man and we're going to do everything possible to put him in jail?"

"Don't be ridiculous."

"I'm not being any more ridiculous than you are right now," she shot back, even as she acknowledged the childishness of that response.

They made the rest of the trip to her house in grim, seething silence.

Once they arrived, there was no question about whether or not Case would come inside. She had a few things she wanted to say to him, so she unlocked the door and swept into her house, then looked back at him, eyes wide and commanding.

He lifted an eyebrow at her silent command, but he strolled in behind her. "Are we going to argue?"

This time, he was the one asking the question and she was the one answering, "Yes."

"Neither of us is hungry, right?" he said in a wary tone.

"Not tonight." She folded her arms in that provocative way she had and Case had to fight the grin that wanted to surface. It made him think of a wife taking her husband to task. *Wife?* he thought as a jolt went through him. The grin died.

He cleared his throat. "Or we could skip the fight and decide what we're going to do next."

"We?"

"Yes, *we*. I felt like it was the right thing to do to disguise myself, follow you, and take notes of what Purdy said, but I admit I should have told you what I was going to do. I'm sorry."

Jo blinked. He was apologizing. Yet another surprise.

"So, I'll forget what you said about my obsession with facial hair, but you've got to promise me one thing."

For some reason, happiness was bubbling away inside her. "What's that?"

"No more femme-fatale routines, okay?" he grumbled. "No more displays of your…female qualifications."

Jo grinned. For some reason, this absolutely delighted her. He was scowling at her, his jaw was set, his eyes dark and stormy, but she was delighted.

"Agreed," she said with a nod and was rewarded by the relief she saw sweep through his eyes. She sat down and motioned him to a seat.

He stared at her for a few seconds as if there was more he wanted to say, but he finally nodded and sat in the same chair he'd used the night before. "We've picked up a lot of information tonight and from what Starina told us, there's a lot more to learn."

"We can talk to her in the morning and find out all she knows."

"What about Harold's meeting tomorrow?"

"What about it?"

Jo paused, took a deep breath, and said, "Even though he invited you specifically, which means he's probably not suspicious of you, I think I should go alone.''

He jerked upright. "The hell you say."

"Now listen to me," she said, waving him back to his seat. "The one thing my little performance did this evening was to put him off his guard. He thinks I'm a bimbo he can influence as he chooses." Jo leaned forward excitedly. "What if he thinks I'm a wealthy bimbo?''

"One who lives in Calamity Falls, Arizona?" Case scoffed. "Why would he fall for that?''

"I already told him that I came here to help out my uncle Don. I've been to the women's club meeting where Harold talked about finances. I don't think it would be that hard to convince him I need his financial advice. And I think he would be more forthcoming if I went alone tomorrow.''

Case regarded her for a long time. Unfortunately, what she was saying made sense. Still, he shook his head. "I don't like it. We still don't know what his con is.''

She threw her hands in the air. "Well, do you have an alternative suggestion?''

Case brooded on that question for a few seconds, turning various possibilities over in his mind. "No," he finally admitted. "I don't.''

Jo waited for him to add something, but he remained silent, his feet stretched out before him, examining the toes of his boots. She tried to study his face and comprehend what he was thinking, but he gave her no clues.

Disappointed, she said, "We can do the same thing we've been doing—meeting up afterwards—and I can tell you what happened.''

Case nodded, stood, and started for the door. "Will

you be at the *Ingot* office tomorrow, or shall I come by here to pick you up for our talk with Starina?''

"Here," Jo answered. "I've told Uncle Don that I'm working on a special story and I'll be out of the office for a few days."

Again, Case nodded as he reached for the doorknob. Jo stared at him, uncertain of what to say. She trailed him to the door, watching in puzzlement as he lingered there.

"Case?" she asked. "You do agree that it's best if I go alone tomorrow, don't you? Even though Harold doesn't think you're very bright, he'll probably be more willing to talk if you're not around."

"Yes." He glanced at her from beneath his brows. "What are you going to wear?"

She threw her hands in the air. "Why are you so obsessed with my clothes?"

"It's not your clothes," he growled. He abandoned the door, turned suddenly, and swept her into his arms. "It's your body."

His lips met hers in a kiss and Jo felt her bones disintegrate and slide right out of her body. Somehow, she found the strength to put her arms around him and kiss him back, though.

"I don't want Harold looking at your body," he said, sliding his kiss over to her cheek, then her ear. His breath puffed warmly against her earlobe as he said, "I don't want anyone looking at it except me."

Heat exploded inside her. "Case? What do you mean?" She had a pretty good idea, but she wanted to hear him say it. While she waited, she got in a couple of good kisses of her own.

"Don't be dense. You're a hotshot reporter. You must know I want to make love to you." His mouth was scorching her. And not just once. Over and over again.

Jo was flattered, delighted. Yet confusion and longing buffeted her. This couldn't be love. A week ago she'd thought she was in love with Steve. She'd only known Case a few days. Wanting wasn't the same as loving him.

"And until I can make love to you, until you're ready for me, I don't want Purdy looking at you."

She turned her face to meet his lips with hers. "Case that's a...a very unrealistic way of..."

"So call me old-fashioned," he said. "Do you think that favorite thrift store of yours has a nun's habit around somewhere that you could wear? You could tell Purdy that you've decided to join up, and..."

"You're crazy," she murmured, putting her hands on each side of his head and holding him still so she could get the full impact of his kiss.

"I could say 'You make me crazy, baby,' but that's too much of a cliché. Too bad it's true," he grumbled.

"I find that flattering," said, smiling up at him. "And I could say 'Your kisses drive me wild,' but that would be a really sickening cliché, too."

"Yeah, but is it true?"

Jo sighed against his lips. "O-o-oh, yeah. You're really good at this. I could write a newspaper article on kissing techniques. Yours rates a ten."

"Better than Steve?"

"*Much* better."

"Good. I don't want you finding out how Purdy kisses, though."

"Oh, really?"

"It would completely cloud your reporter's objectivity."

She started to answer, but he groaned and covered

her mouth with his once again. "This whole thing worries me, Jo. I've never worried about someone like this. Oh, man," he said, pulling away and running his hands through his hair. "I've lost *my* objectivity. That's never happened to me before. Why does it have to be with you?"

Jo stood, rocking slightly on her unsteady legs, unsure whether to take his statement as a compliment or an insult. "Case, I..."

"Our lives are complete opposites," he said in a fierce tone. "Or they will be when you get all you want out of this story."

"Case, it's not like you think it is..." she began, but he cut her off once again.

"You've got to do whatever is necessary to stay safe in your dealings with Purdy, and I've got to make sure that you're safe and that we're able to put him away to protect people like Freida and Charlotte from him. That's my obligation. That's all I have to do." He headed for the door. "I'll see you in the morning," he said, stalking out.

"But I..." Her hands fell helplessly to her sides and she muttered a very unladylike word under her breath. He was an impossible man, thinking that there could be no future for them because they were pursuing different things, different life-styles.

A *future?* Slowly, Jo locked the door and started for her bedroom. When had she begun thinking in those terms? She'd certainly lost her objectivity, but it had nothing to do with Harold Purdy.

Jo reached up and covered her eyes with her fingertips. She might as well stop fooling herself and admit she was in love with Case, even though she barely knew him. She knew the important things about him.

He wasn't going to try to coax her into bed purely for sexual gratification, even if her tingling body told her it would, indeed, be *very* gratifying. Case wasn't going to make her any promises he couldn't keep.

She also knew that she wasn't going to be able to convince him that her idea of a fast-track career wasn't the same as what his had been. Her only hope was that somehow she would get the opportunity to show him.

9

In this town of oddballs and their kooky ideas, Starina Simms might just win the award for the most whimsical invention, Case decided. He and Jo stood side by side in Starina's workshop and stared in awe at her perpetual-motion machine.

Along the back wall marched a row of stainless-steel cylinders that resembled oxygen tanks. From each one, long, plastic tubes extended upward to a central tube where they all emptied various colored liquids into a huge vat. To this was attached a dizzying array of geared wheels, gearboxes, switches, levers, and overflow tanks.

"Wow, Starina," Jo said in a hushed tone. "You've really expanded it since the last time I saw it. It looks marvelous."

Case gave her a baffled glance. She sounded as if this thing looked normal. He was no mechanic, but even he could tell that this Rube Goldberg contraption was all form and no substance.

He wondered which of those flowing liquids was flammable—or if they all were.

"Not only expanded it, but perfected it." Starina, dressed once again in her coveralls and sporting tools in every pocket, lifted her hand and held her thumb and forefinger a fraction of an inch apart. "I'm this close to applying for a patent. The patent office demands a working model, and when I've got this one right, I'll just make a scale model and send it in, along with the instructions.''

"Uh, Ms. Simms, you do realize that only about one percent of patents are ever actually awarded?'' Case cautioned.

She resembled a perky little white-haired bird as she looked up at him. "I know."

"And that no one's ever made a successful perpetual motion machine.''

"Until now,'' she said proudly. From her back pocket, she pulled a rag and began polishing the spotless surfaces of the smaller metal tanks.

"They've failed because the parts wear out...''

"Due to inferior lubricants,'' she answered blithely. She pointed to the tubes of liquid. "As you can see, I've invented my own lubricant as well.''

"Well, what about...?''

"Case,'' Jo said, laying her hand on his arm. "Starina knows all that. She's heard it from her colleagues a million times.''

He blinked at her. "Colleagues?''

"Starina holds doctorates from M.I.T. in both mechanical and electrical engineering,'' Jo said, smiling proudly at her friend. "And she was an engineer at an aerospace firm before she came here.''

He looked at the sprightly little woman, who was returning Jo's grin. "But the people I worked with were so closed off to my ideas, I left the engineering world and came here as soon as I heard about Calamity Falls. I belong here,'' she concluded happily.

"Well, I'll be...speechless,'' he said. There was obviously more to these quaint people than he'd thought.

Jo smiled as if she understood exactly what he was thinking and turned to Starina. "We're interested in hearing more about Professor Purdy. What have you heard going on over there besides the sound of ripping wood?''

"That's all, and I don't know what he's tearing apart with my crowbar, but I can guarantee you that the owner of that house, Rick Morales, isn't going to be happy about it. Rick doesn't do much to fix the place up, but he doesn't want anyone else to either for fear he'll have to pay for it.''

"You don't think he's got permission to do some work there?'' Jo asked. "Sometimes landlords will let people make improvements on their own.''

"Sounds like he's tearing down walls. I don't think Rick would see that as an improvement,'' Starina answered tartly. "I tried a week ago to call Rick and tell him what's been going on, but he's off on a fishing trip somewhere. He's as crazy about fishing as Julius is.''

Case walked over to the workshop window and looked out. The two houses were set at such an angle that there was a clear view of the front door and all the windows on the east side of Purdy's house. He turned thoughtfully and said, "Starina, Jo's going to another meeting at Purdy's this afternoon. I'd like to keep an eye on things from a distance. Mind if I come over here and just watch?''

Jo frowned slightly and he knew she was wondering why he hadn't discussed this with her, but it had just come to him as he'd seen the vantage point from Starina's window. He gave Jo a little shrug to acknowledge her puzzlement.

Starina's eyes brightened. "Sure. You've never seen my machine in action. I'll set up a little demonstration for you while you're here.''

Jo's face blanched. "Wouldn't it be better if you waited a little while before you do another demonstration? After all, the volunteer fire department was just out here last month.''

"Fire department?" Case asked. Apprehensively, he glanced around. Maybe his idea wasn't such a good one.

"Starina's machine exploded one time," Jo explained.

"Well, twice," the quirky inventor corrected.

"Yes, but that second fire was such a small one, it hardly counted."

"That's true." Starina nodded. "I don't know why the fire chief felt he had to drag everyone out here. I could have put that one out with my fire extinguishers." She pointed to a row of the bright red extinguishers that Case hadn't noticed in his enthrallment with the machine. There were six of the largest type available, lined up and ready for action. His mouth went dry.

"The only thing I lost in that one was a table full of beakers."

"And your eyebrows," Jo added, giving Case a sidelong glance that hinted at mischief when she saw the horrified awe on his face.

"They grew back, though," Starina said cheerfully. "And that little explosion showed me exactly where I'd been going wrong with the air-intake valves, and now I've got it almost ready to go." She turned away, effectively dismissing them.

"Case will see you later, then," Jo said, taking his arm and heading him toward the door farthest from Purdy's house. Starina waved them off, already forgetting them as she pulled a screwdriver from her pocket and returned to her project.

"I think I outsmarted myself," Case said once they were on the street again.

"Probably. Starina will bend your ear about her work, but her window will make the perfect spot to watch the house." She glanced at him, her green eyes smiling. "And please note that I'm not annoyed with you for deciding to observe this afternoon."

He gave her a cautious look. "And why is that?"

"You've got an investigation to conduct, just as I have. We may be working together on this, but really, we have different goals."

In this case, and in life, he thought, feeling disappointed even though he knew what she said was true. He'd made a fool of himself last night; kissing her, wanting her, and pushing her away.

"Yes," he said, trailing along behind her. "That's right."

"So it's all settled, then. Same investigation, same conclusion, but different goals." Breezily, she started up the nearest set of stairs. Today she was wearing a blouse of deep rusty brown and a matching print skirt. As she trotted up the steps, the skirt bounced around her calves with a soft rustle that made him think of bodies sliding over crisp percale sheets.

Oh, hell. He had it bad if he was loping along behind her in the bright morning sunlight thinking about her and bedsheets. Did she ever have those kinds of thoughts? She kissed him as if she wanted to crawl right inside his skin and make him part of her. The memory of it gave him sensual shivers.

He had to get his mind back on track. After all, in spite of everything, he was still the one who'd been hired to find out what Purdy was doing. So far, he had very little to tell Estelle Long except that her mother was in love with a con artist and that the money Freida had given him was probably gone for good.

Maybe today, with Jo's help, he'd know more, find out what he needed to know in order to stop Purdy.

He had talked to Rex Killian, the city police chief, who said he'd had no complaints against Purdy, and that even if his message and scientific theories about the universe seemed strange, they weren't out of the ordinary by Calamity Falls' standards. Case hadn't found that to be the least bit encouraging.

"You're not worried, are you?" Jo asked, pulling him out of his morose thoughts.

He caught up to her and they finished the walk to her house together. "About Purdy? No, I don't think he's actually dangerous."

"I meant worried about watching from Starina's workshop," Jo said, giving him a dry look.

He shook his head. "Nah. I'm strong. I can take it."

"Yeah, but are you fireproof?"

He grinned and as they reached Jo's house, he said, "Now, show me what you intend to wear this afternoon."

"AH, HERE YOU ARE." Harold Purdy hustled down the steps of his house, placed his arm around Jo's waist, and took her hand in his. He gave it a fervent kiss as he said. "You're the last to arrive, but in this case it is true that the best has been saved for last." He glanced around. "Your friend Case isn't with you?"

Jo fought the urge to roll her eyes at him. "Oh, Harold, thank you for the compliment. No, I think perhaps that your message isn't for Case." She gave him a look full of what she hoped was innocent sexiness. "I encouraged him to stay home."

Lust flared in Harold's eyes. "Did you, my dear? That was probably wise."

Jo sighed. "I just have to tell you that the last few days have been so exciting. Since I've met you, I have a whole new understanding about, well, about men." She dropped her gaze demurely "I was so heartbroken over Steve, you know? And you've renewed my faith in what a true gentleman is like. I mean, I just know you would never take advantage of me like he did."

"Certainly not." Harold's hand inched up her waist and over her ribs, aiming for her breast.

One more inch, she thought, *and I'll break every one of his fingers.* She kept her smile in place, though. "I was wondering if we could get together this evening, Harold. I was so impressed with what you had to say about investing money at the women's club meeting. I only have a few thousand to invest, but I'd like your advice on where to put it."

His blue eyes fairly glowed, he licked his lips. "Oh, my dear, I can tell you exactly where to put it."

She gave a tittering little laugh she'd once heard Marilyn Monroe use in a movie. He hustled her up the stairs and into the house.

OBSERVING from Starina's workshop window, Case couldn't decide whether he wanted to kill Purdy first, or spank Jo. He'd have some time to ponder it while he waited for her to come out.

"I'll have this ready in just a few minutes, Case," Starina called out. "There are only a few more calibrations that need to be done."

"Great, Starina," he answered absently, his mind on the couple next door. "Can't wait to see it."

"It's like nothing that's ever been invented. It's going to revolutionize industry as we know it."

Case nodded and returned to his vigil.

JO WAS AMAZED to see that only she, Charlotte, Freida, and Cedric were in attendance. Harold noticed her surprised look. "I've decided to concentrate on the true believers," he said. "Only those who are open to new truths have been invited today. I'm hoping that those dear souls will help me spread the message of cosmogony."

There was an air of suppressed excitement about the other three, although Freida was giving Harold troubled looks. Jo moved away from him and tried to give Freida a smile that told her she had nothing to worry about, that she had no personal interest in Harold. Freida answered with an unhappy frown.

"If you all will come with me," Harold said. "I have something exciting to show you." He lead the way down a short hallway, past small bedrooms and a bathroom. Jo had only a quick glance in each room and was struck with how bare they were. She saw no personal items in any room.

In the farthest bedroom in the corner of the house that backed directly into the mountainside, Purdy turned, made a sweeping gesture, and said, "This is it. This is the very place I've been searching for during many years of traveling around the country, learning all I can, sharing my message with believers like you." He beamed his generous smile on them and then he grew serious as he said, "And at last I have found it, right here in Calamity Falls, Arizona. Right in this room."

While his small audience gaped at him, he strolled across the floor and pointed to a door.

"It's a closet," Freida whispered in awe.

"Not just any closet, my clever and generous Mrs. Long," he said. "It leads to our future."

With that, he threw the door open dramatically. A

dank mustiness swept into the room. Jo and the others crowded forward. The back of the closet had been ripped away to expose a black opening. From his pocket, Harold pulled a small, powerful flashlight.

Jo stepped back and looked at her friends, who were shivering with excitement, then at Purdy. It was getting harder and harder to maintain her ditzy role, but she said, "It's a tunnel. Isn't it part of the old Skinner mine?"

"Yes. I did careful research all over this country and I found that this spot in this house is the exact center of a powerful vortex that will protect us when the world collapses in on itself."

"Really?" Freida and Charlotte whispered in unison.

"Well, I say," Cedric breathed, his Adam's apple bobbing violently.

"Oh, brother," Jo muttered under her breath.

"WHAT THE HELL are they doing?" Case grumbled. "How long does it take for him to give his pitch for money and for them to get out of there?"

"How long?" Starina asked. "Oh, not long. I'm almost ready."

Frowning, Case glanced over his shoulder and saw that she had pulled out a crank of some sort, had inserted it into the front panel of her machine, and was busy giving it a whirl. Her face was red with excitement, her hair stood up as if she was receiving an electric charge, and the tip of her tongue protruded from the corner of her mouth. She was involved in a massive effort. The motor caught, coughed, and began to turn over with a clank and a whir. The tubes of lubricants pulsed to life, the liquid running toward the machine in a gurgling rush.

Starina fairly danced with delight.

Case decided she wasn't really paying any attention to him, but he gave her machine an unsure look. He hoped she knew what she was doing.

"THERE IS ONE major drawback, though," Harold announced in a deadly serious tone.

"What?" his believers echoed.

Here it comes, Jo thought.

"We do not own this property." Harold looked around at his tiny flock, lifted his hands, palms upward, and let them drop dramatically. "I have searched this world over, and not only myself, but many others who believe as we do have been searching. I want to let them know that I have found the place." He lifted his hands skyward and looked up toward the cracked and stained ceiling. "The very place for which we've searched so long, the place where men will no longer have to apologize for being men, where women will know themselves and their strength for who they really are."

Jo rolled her eyes. She'd known all along that Harold's con was something outrageous, but she hadn't imagined anything this silly. The enthralled look on her friends' faces alarmed her. "Wait, a minute, Harold, I don't think I quite understand...."

"Oh, yes, you must let everyone know," Freida interrupted fervently. "The location of this place is too important to keep it to yourself." Charlotte and Cedric nodded their agreement.

"But, alas, I cannot bring my friends here. We can't use it as our base of operations from which true, righteous believers like you will go out and spread the word."

Cynically, Jo wondered what the word was, besides money.

"Why not, Harold?" Charlotte asked.

"I'm sorry to say that we can't build this property into the shelter it needs to become because I don't, I mean, *we* don't own it."

"I could give you money, Harold, dear," Freida said. "You know I've got money. I've offered it to you before." She turned to Charlotte and Cedric. "I think he was too proud to take it, but now I think he should, don't you?"

They added their encouragement to hers while Harold attempted to look suitably humble.

Jo was relieved to hear that Estelle's fears were unfounded and Freida had not yet given Harold any money.

"In fact, I have money with me." She gave Jo a quick look and Jo immediately understood that Freida had been feeling jealous and had brought the money to regain Harold's attention. "How much would it take? I knew, I just knew this was going to be the day you would allow me to give you what you need, Harold. You're such a good man, so caring and full of truth, your message mustn't be delayed any longer."

"I've got money, too," Charlotte said, catching the enthusiasm. "I've been saving it up. It's under my mattress. It won't take me any time at all to get it."

"Sir," Cedric said, "if you will allow me, I would be happy to help out with your costs. This sounds like something that would be worthwhile, a help to mankind."

As Freida reached for her shoulder bag and the other two started to scurry home to get their life savings, Jo spread-eagled herself in front of the door. "Wait,

Frieda, everyone, don't you think you should learn more about this before you give Harold your money?''

The older lady blinked at her. "What more is there to learn?''

"Whether or not he's telling the truth, for one thing.''

Harold's eyes narrowed. "My dear, you know my truth is self-evident.''

"I don't know any such thing," she shot back. She turned on him. "This is a scam, Harold. You've enticed and enthralled these three into thinking that you've got a message that will change the world. All you have is a desire to line your own pockets.''

"Jo!" Charlotte gasped. "That's not true. ''

"Certainly not," Freida added, outraged. "If he'd wanted my money, he would have taken it before now.''

"Obviously, he wanted more than just yours," Jo said desperately. "Freida, Charlotte, Cedric, don't you see that he's only been setting you up?''

"That's preposterous," Harold scoffed. His tone was firm, but in his eyes she could see fury beginning to spark, telling her he wasn't as benign as he'd pretended to be. Not that she was surprised. Nothing about him was turning out to be true. "These three pure souls are giving me their money out of kindness and a generous spirit of which you know nothing.'' He held up his finger and pointed it at her. "You *tricked* me," he roared. "You let me think you were a true believer, but you're nothing but a fraud, determined to catch me in some lies of your own making.''

Outraged at the way he was trying to turn the tables on her, Jo said, "Don't listen to him, please.''

He ignored her and turned his kindly smile on her friends. "I will be happy to take your funds and I will rush right away to the owner's home to give him the money and buy this house.''

"Property sales don't happen that fast!'' Jo said desperately. "You know they don't, Cedric. Remember when you bought your house? Didn't it take a while for the paperwork and the title search, and—''

"I've already spoken to Mr. Morales about this,'' Harold thundered. "It's all set.''

Jo clapped her hands onto her hips. "How is that possible, since he's off on a fishing trip?''

CASE PACED by the window. "I'm going over there,'' he muttered. "I'm giving them about three more minutes, then I'm going over there. I've got a bad feeling about this.''

"Oh, don't worry. It's working perfectly,'' Starina sang out. "Look.''

Case took his eyes off the window for a minute and swung around to see what she was doing.

The machine was beginning to rumble and shake. Sparks shot out of one of the gears as it whirred and meshed with another. Starina grabbed an oilcan and rushed forward to squirt it with lubricant. "Only a minor problem,'' she shrieked over the din. "Isn't this wonderful? It's working perfectly.''

Alarmed, Case yelled, "Are you sure? Is it supposed to be making that much noise?''

"Well,'' Starina shouted happily. "It might need a few minor adjustments.''

"I SPOKE to Mr. Morales only this morning…'' Harold began.

"That's a lie.''

Harold's benevolent persona fled as he stepped forward threateningly. "*You're* the liar. You're determined to make these fine people think that I'm a villain." He looked at them with an appeal in his eyes. "I spoke to Mr. Morales. He's going to sell me the house as soon as I give him the money, which will then be put into an escrow account at the bank until the paperwork is done."

"Don't believe him, Freida. He's going to take your money and run. Look at this place," Jo said, spreading her hands to take in the room and the house. "It's bare. He has no intention of staying. If you give him your money, he's going to be out of town with it in a few minutes. His car is probably all packed."

"Lies! Outrageous lies!"

"In fact, this whole idea is something that he's probably cooked up on the spur of the moment." She pointed toward the closet. "Somehow he found out this house hooked up to the old mine and he tore out the back of that closet to confirm it. He didn't even have any tools. He had to borrow a crowbar from Starina."

Harold paused, turned, and glared at her. "So you've been asking about me, have you, missy? I think maybe *you're* not all you pretended to be."

"No, but at least I wasn't doing it to steal someone's money."

Harold looked from her angry face to the other three, who were beginning to draw closer to each other and, Jo saw, away from him.

Charlotte frowned. "We believed in you, Harold. We brought people to hear you."

"But what did he actually *say*, Charlotte?" Jo asked desperately. She looked at Freida. "What is this message of his that he wants you to spend money on?" She pointed toward the closet. "And using that mine tunnel is ludicrous. The owners would never allow it, and…''

''Shut up,'' Harold shouted. His eyes hardened and his mouth curled into a sneer. ''I've spent weeks on this deal,'' he snarled. His refined tone had disappeared, to be replaced with venom. ''You don't have any idea how hard I've worked on this deal. Finding this place, kissing up to people who're too stupid to know what's going on.'' He turned to Freida, whose face had fallen into a horrified and disillusioned frown. Tears filled her eyes.

''Well, old girl,'' Harold said. ''It's been fun, but I've gotta go. You don't mind financing my trip, now do you?'' With that, he grabbed her shoulder bag with one hand. ''And this will help, too.'' He snatched her diamond-encrusted watch as well, then gave her a shove, knocking her into Cedric and Charlotte. The three of them went down in a heap.

He shoved past Jo, who made a grab for him, but he wrenched himself free and charged toward the front of the house, out the door, and down the steps.

Jo checked to see that her friends were all right, and helping each other to their feet, then she rushed after him. By the time she got out front, he was running to his car, Freida's bag clutched to his chest.

''Case!'' Jo shrieked, waving toward Starina's window for attention. ''Case! He's getting away.''

There was no answer, but she heard Harold's car starting with a roar. With a squeal of tires, he started to back up. She had to jump out of the way to avoid being hit. She made a grab for a door handle, but missed.

He spun the steering wheel and started forward, but he'd judged the distance wrong, had to back up and try again in order to miss the corner of the house. Again, Jo tried for the door, but it was locked.

"Stop!" Jo shrieked. "Case, help!"

Purdy had the car clear now. The tires spat gravel as they spun. He gave Jo a vicious look and aimed the vehicle straight for her.

She started to scramble out of the way when she felt the earth buckle beneath her feet.

That was when the roof blew off Starina's workshop.

10

JO WAS KNOCKED OFF her feet. Stunned, she sat on the pavement for a moment trying to clear her head and catch her breath, then lifted dazed eyes to look around.

Harold's car was stopped a few feet away. A huge chunk of roof had crashed onto the hood and he had careened into a light pole. The impact had crumpled the fender and burst the radiator, which was leaking a stream of water. Behind the wheel, he sat rubbing his head while feebly trying to push the air bag off his lap and find the door handle.

Jo blinked and focused on the chunk of roof, then everything came rushing back and she staggered to her feet. "Case!" she yelled. "Oh, no! Oh, no!"

She started for the workshop, saw Cedric, Freida, and Charlotte stumbling from Harold's house and yelled, "Find a phone. Call 911!"

Cedric nodded, shepherded the two ladies ahead of him and the three of them started off down the street at a trot.

Sick with dread, Jo dashed to the corner of the building, but was met by Case, who lurched out to meet her. Under one arm he had a fire extinguisher and under the other, he carried Starina, who was struggling and shouting in protest. "Put me down, you young turk. I'm not hurt!"

When he saw Jo, Case set Starina on her feet and dropped the fire extinguisher. Starina immediately hurried out to the street to look at the damage from a distance, then strolled over to check on Harold.

"Oh, God," Jo sobbed, throwing herself into Case's arms. "You're all right. I was so afraid." Tears of relief poured down her face as she ran her hands over his arms and shoulders. She would have checked out his legs, too, if he hadn't grabbed her and kissed her hard.

"What happened?" he asked in an agitated voice.

Didn't he remember? She reached up and touched his face. "Why, Starina's machine blew up again and blew the roof off—"

"No," he said. "I know about that part." His eyes searching her face, then standing back to make sure she was all right. Relieved, he kissed her again. "I mean what happened with Purdy? Did he try anything? Because if he did..."

Shakily, Jo lifted a hand and pointed. "He stole Freida's money and tried to escape." Hurriedly, she explained what had happened. "What about you, though? You're really all right."

"Yeah." Case shook his head in disgust. "I wasn't watching what she was doing because I was looking for you. The machine caught fire, so we both grabbed fire extinguishers, but when I saw it was going to blow, I grabbed Starina and dragging her out of there."

All the starch was draining out of Jo's knees. She leaned on Case for support. "Thank God you did."

Case was no better off than she was. Propping each other up, they walked over to where Starina was pulling Harold from the car and checking him over.

"Wait a minute," he was saying, groggily. "Don't you know you're not supposed to move an injured man. I could sue you..."

"Try it, buster," Case growled.

"I'm a doctor," Starina said bluntly, though she didn't tell him what kind of doctor. "And all you've got is a little bump on the head."

Sirens were wailing in the distance and within minutes the fire trucks had arrived. While the firemen rushed to put out the blaze, the fire chief climbed out of his car with his assistant and the two of them stood before Starina in their heavy gear, hands on hips, disgruntled scowls on their faces.

"You did it again," he said.

"You *promised* you wouldn't do this anymore," his assistant scowled.

"Oh, hello, Julius, Lainey," Starina answered brightly. She dragged Harold over and sat him on the low stone wall that edged the street in front of her house. "Yes, I'm afraid I did. Too bad, too, because I almost had it this time. I know exactly what went wrong, though, and I know how to fix it."

Shaking his head, Julius took Starina's arm and pulled her away. Lainey spotted Jo and, forgetting her role as assistant fire chief, rushed over to hug her and make sure she wasn't hurt.

"I'm okay, Lainey," Jo said, trying to duck Lainey's firefighter's hat.

"You said you wanted to change your life," Lainey said tearfully. "You didn't say *anything* about blowing it to pieces."

"Lainey, I wasn't in the blast." Jo explained what had happened. She looked over at Case. "We're both okay."

He grinned back, put his arm around her waist and drew her over to lean against him. Finally reassured, Lainey looked from one to the other of them and said,

"There's more you need to tell me," then went to help the volunteer firefighters.

The police arrived as Cedric, Freida, and Charlotte reappeared at the scene. With Jo and Case's help, they explained what had happened and Harold was taken away, but not before Freida had snatched her purse back from him and clobbered him with it. Walking bent over, Harold held his head with one hand and his crotch with the other. Groaning as he fell into the back of the police car, he seemed glad to be in the safe custody of the police.

Freida found her watch in his car, snapped it onto her wrist, then marched along behind with another officer, eager to swear out a complaint against him. Cedric took Charlotte's hand and followed. Jo smiled, glad to see that her friends were completely disillusioned with the charlatan.

Case put his arm around Jo and said, "Can we go home now?"

She looked up at him and grimaced sympathetically. "I think we'd better. Case, you're not going to have to worry about that facial-hair obsession of yours for a while."

"Why's that?"

"Your eyebrows are gone."

His hand shot up to swipe across his face. "Well, I know where to get some more," he said, and gave her a lopsided grin.

Shaky with gratitude that he'd survived, Jo wrapped her arm around his waist and pushed through the crowd that was gathering. Paramedics insisted on checking them out, and they had to go to the police station to make their official statements, but they were finally released to go home. They accepted the offer of a ride from a police officer and were back at Jo's house by the time dark was falling.

They walked inside, took turns in the bathroom to clean up and then they collapsed together on her couch. For several minutes, they sat that way, their heads together, both of them emotionally drained, staring up at the ceiling.

Jo reached over and took his hand, still amazed and grateful that he was all in one piece. "I still don't understand exactly what Purdy was doing. Why did he have that Unbroken Man rally and speak at the women's club and all the rest of it? Those things had nothing to do with his cosmogony idea."

Case turned his head and looked at her. "It's always about money, Jo. For these guys it's always about money. In this case, Freida's money, which was something we actually knew all along. She fancied herself in love with him, and offered him money, but he held out for the biggest possible payoff. Somewhere along the line she told him about the odd and interesting religious and scientific ideas that interested her..."

"Which was why she was attracted to Calamity Falls. We have an abundance of that kind of thing here," Jo added.

"When she told Harold that, he came up with the Unbroken Man idea, and if you'll remember, the women's club speech was a last-minute thing. He was pretending to cast as wide a net as possible for his 'true believers,' but really, I think all that cosmogony nonsense was desperation. The focus was always on Freida. Still, she wouldn't let go of her money, but when he started being interested in you, she got jealous and decided to buy back his attention."

"I thought it was something like that. How much money did she have in that purse, anyway?"

"Almost a hundred thousand dollars."

"Good grief!" Jo sat up. "You're kidding."

Case lifted his hand. "It's the truth. She made several withdrawals, always intending to give it to him, but even though she was in love with him, it wasn't until she got jealous of you that he was finally able to shake it loose from her." Case looped an arm around he and drew her close. "And then you messed it all up for him so he did a snatch-and-grab. Might have been able to get away, too, if the roof of Starina's workshop hadn't gotten in his way."

"I wonder why he was in Calamity Falls in the first place?"

"Probably hiding out from his last scam. No doubt he was looking for a nice, quiet place."

"He just didn't know this wasn't it, and that Calamity Falls would live up to its name and land on his head," Jo said. "He'll have time to think about it while he's serving time in jail for theft and assault and destroying private property. Rick Morales isn't going to be pleased that he ripped out the back of that closet."

"So, that's enough about Harold Purdy. In my opinion, you've spent way too much time thinking about him this week," Case said. His hand was softly stroking her arm.

"He was my first big story," Jo said impishly, then she started laughing.

"What's so funny?"

"Think about it," she hiccuped. "I was following you…"

"Stalking me," Case corrected, a grin tickling at his lips.

"Okay, stalking you. You were following Purdy, who was following Freida to get her money, then I pretended to be a bimbo to get his attention, while he was using me to make Freida jealous.''

"It boggles the mind,'' Case agreed, then he scowled at her. "I didn't like the amount of time and attention you gave him.''

That little hint of jealousy delighted Jo. She gave him a demure look. "I had to give him all my concentration.''

"So I noticed, but since the investigation is over, it's time you changed your focus.'' He picked her up and turned her so that she lay across his lap.

"To what?'' she asked, looping her arms around his neck. The love she felt for him was flowing in a warm, sweet wave.

"To a guy who's facial-hair challenged,'' Case said. He lowered his head and kissed her.

"Only in the eyebrow department,'' she answered, kissing each singed place. "I like it, though. It gives you a really streamlined look.''

His laughter puffed against her lips. "I'll think of them as battle scars won in the battle to get Jo Quillan the story of her career.''

That statement bothered Jo, but she didn't have time to think about it because he was kissing her again—a long, warm, sweet meeting of lips that had desire rushing through her.

"The first time I saw you, I thought you were a dangerous man,'' she said softly.

"I am.''

"Your kisses are certainly dangerous,'' she said, looking up at him with warmth and sincerity in her eyes. She wasn't going to tell him she loved him. His job was done. He was going to be leaving Calamity Falls very soon, probably tomorrow, maybe tonight, and she could see no reason to cloud things with an admission like that. She slipped her arms around his shoulders and played with his thick, sable-dark hair. "They make me forget things I should remember."

"Like what?" He brought his mouth to hers once again, touching and tasting, trying to tease the answer out of her.

"Like the fact that you're going to leave now. Your job is done, and you're…going to leave." She had to stop and swallow a sob.

"I'm flattered that bothers you." Caso didn't know why he felt as if a giant hand was squeezing his chest, grabbing his heart and wringing the life out of it. Something about the look in her eyes was scaring him, making him think that a secret lurked there. He didn't have the words to ask her, though, and maybe he didn't want to hear the answer.

She touched him inside, in a place that no one had ever touched. He couldn't tell her that because he already knew he was going to lose her. The future she planned for herself loomed and he wasn't part of it.

So he didn't ask about her secret. Instead, he placed his mouth on hers, letting her warmth seep through him. "You taste so wonderful," he murmured, eyes closed, kisses filling his mouth, his senses. "In all those years on assignment, I was all over the country, sometimes the world. I looked for something, someone like you, and you were here in Calamity Falls all along."

Jo didn't know exactly what he meant, but his word made her happy. His mouth fit hers perfectly, it was like rejoining herself to a lifeline—safe, secure, but an invitation to pleasure.

"Jo," he whispered. "This little house of yours has a bedroom, doesn't it?"

She paused, looked up as happiness flooded through

her. "Yes, it does. And a bed. Would you like to use
it?"

"Uh-huh," he answered, kissing her as he stood
with her in his arms.

The bedroom wasn't hard to find and he had her
there in about twelve strides. Outside, the streetlights
had just clicked on in the gathering dark. In its faint
yellow glow, he could see an old-fashioned iron bed-
stead standing against a wall with blue striped wall-
paper. The spread was blue and the bed was puffed
with a feather comforter and mounds of pillows.

Smiling at the sensual delights with which she surrounded herself, he said, "Jo, do you want to turn
down the bed?"

He was giving her a choice, she knew, and she was
glad for it. They were partners in this and if this was
going to be the only night they had together, she
wanted it to be perfect.

"I want to turn down the bed," she answered,
speaking softly into his ear as she nuzzled it. "I want
to light candles and put on soft music and open a
bottle of wine."

"All right," he whispered back. "But later. I want
you, Jo. I think I've wanted you from the minute you
accosted me on the street and demanded an interview."

"Then for right now, I'll only turn down the bed."

He set her on her feet and watched while she folded
the comforter and set it aside, slipping her hands
smoothly over the roundness of it in a way that had
his pulse pounding. She stacked up the throw pillows
and set them on a chair, then pulled back the coverlet
and the sheets.

The way she moved—with smooth, clean, feminine
motions—made his mouth go dry. She was sexy and

innocent all at once. As she finished turning down the bed, the scent of vanilla drifted upwards to entice him.

"There," she said, and came to stand before him. Her heart was pounding madly, and for some reason, her throat was full of tears. She loved him so much, wanted him so much, but her hands hung at her sides, afraid to reach out and grab what she wanted.

"Case," she said hesitantly. "There is one thing... protection."

"I have something with me," he reassured her, then grinned. "Even in quaint little Calamity Falls, you'd be amazed at the full line of condoms available at the drugstore."

She smiled, glad that he had planned for this while she had only hoped.

They paused, looking at each other, and then Case reached for her, and she came to him in a rush. The banked-down heat of her desire flared and she welcomed him with a groan of desire.

Kissing her, Case began to unbutton her blouse and push it off her shoulders, following the sliding fabric with his lips. "You're so beautiful, Jo. That's why I wanted you."

She laughed at him as she unbuttoned his shirt, too. "Not for my curious mind?"

"Uh-uh," he said. "And not for your sassy mouth, either." He kissed her sassy mouth, slipped off the rest of her clothes, then his own, then picked her up and laid her on the bed.

"I'll never smell vanilla again without thinking of this," he murmured against the velvety softness of her skin. "Without thinking of you. I'll probably get turned on every time I pass a bakery."

She laughed, then gasped when his lips teased her

breast, then eased the heat he was creating by taking it in his mouth.

"Oh, please, Case," she moaned, then she reached for him and surrendered her sanity.

They touched each other and gave each other pleasure, rolling across the bed in a hot, devastating flood of desire. Within her, everything tightened so that when he slipped inside her and wrapped himself around her, her body bucked, welcoming him.

Within moments, they reached a peak, shuddered together, then slipped down quietly, still joined.

Case's lips roamed her face, caressing her cheeks, her eyelids, dropping kisses in the hollow of her throat. She arched to him and was amazed to feel him stirring inside her.

"Case?" she murmured.

He chuckled, which made the feel of him even more exciting. "You may have to forget about lighting those candles for a while, Jo. I don't think we're going to get off this bed for a while."

"That's okay," she murmured back, smiling at him. "I didn't want to go anywhere, anyway."

And they didn't. The night was a long, slow loving that didn't stop until they fell into an exhausted sleep in the smallest hours of the morning.

JO WOKE to his kisses and reached for him. "You're insatiable," she mumbled. "Thank God."

He chuckled. "Insatiable or not, Jo, I've got to go."

"Go?" Her eyes popped wide open and she struggled to sit up. She shoved her hair out of her eyes and saw that he was fully dressed. Darn it. "Go? Go where?"

"Home." He sat on the side of the bed and took her hand, linking his fingers with hers. "I've got to make a report to Freida's daughter in order to get paid, and there are other things pending.''

He was leaving. Fear turned ashen in her mouth. ''What's the rush? I…I thought you were the guy who took life easy.''

''That was before I met you,'' he teased, but she saw sadness lurking in his eyes. ''Jo, I've got to get back to my life in Phoenix, and you've got to get back to changing yours.''

She was fully awake now, sitting up and facing him. ''And we have to do all this today?''

Case leaned in and kissed her. ''If I don't go today, I'll be in your way.''

''No, that's not…how?'' She was babbling but fear did that to her.

''You want to write the article about Purdy, to get it published, work for a major newspaper. You've got a whole set of goals and dreams that don't include me.''

He was so kind, so understanding, so reasonable, she wanted to kick him, except that she was barefoot. She snatched her hand away from his and climbed to her knees in the center of the bed. ''How do you know about my hopes and dreams? You haven't even asked much about them, because you've been so sure you know exactly what it is I want. You're such a stubborn know-it-all. Did you ever think that maybe my idea of a fast track wasn't the same as yours?''

His calm, composed manner disappeared in a scowl. ''There's only one track, Jo and it only goes at one pace. Sure, maybe you'll start out slow, but the more you get involved in your career, the more other things get left behind. It's like a treadmill that gets cranked faster and faster. I know that, Jo. I did it, remember?''

''You don't know beans,'' she fumed.

He shook his head, stood, and reached into his jacket pocket. "I have something for you."

Though she'd had no hope that he was going to pull a diamond engagement ring from his jacket, she was startled when he drew out his small blue notepad and handed it to her.

"What's this for?" she asked, taking it from him.

"Research for your article. I don't need it now."

He didn't fully agree with what she planned to do, but he was making it possible for her to do it. Jo stared at the book until tears began to swim in her eyes, then she looked up at him. Tears spilled over her cheeks.

"Case," she whispered. "No, don't do this. We can…"

His face was grim, sick with distress. He leaned in and pulled her to him, wrapping his arms around her so that the breath was pushed from her lungs in a rush. His mouth ravaged hers, kissing her again and again. Finally, with a wrenching groan, he pulled away. "I've got to go, Jo." He placed one last kiss on her cheek. "Have a good life."

Turning, he left her crumpled in the middle of her bed. It took her a moment to untangle herself from the sheet, grab her robe, and dash after him, landing on the front porch in a rush.

It was too late. He was already in front of Mrs. Rios's house, striding away as fast as he could. Mrs. Rios was sweeping her front lawn, her bright old eyes going from Case's disappearing figure to Jo's devastated face.

"You wanna borrow some of my rocks, honey?" she asked sympathetically.

With a shake of her head, Jo went back inside and shut the door. He'd left. She couldn't believe it. He wouldn't even listen to her. She'd never had a chance to tell him she loved him—not that he deserved to hear such words, anyway. The more she thought about it, the angrier she got.

She stomped to the phone, snatched it up, and punched out a number.

"Perk Avenue," Lainey sang out.

"Lainey," Jo said on a sob. "It happened again. I've been dumped twice in one week! And I re-really loved him."

"Steve?"

"No," Jo wailed. "Case Houston."

A long pause followed, punctuated only by Jo's sobs. "You don't have any more wine around, do you?" Lainey asked.

HIS HOUSE WAS LOVELY, set back from a shaded street in a section of Phoenix where the houses dated from the twenties; bungalows that had seen hard times and then harder times, and were now working their way back. The entire neighborhood seemed to be under reconstruction, with scaffolding around many of the structures. Paint and construction crews swarmed over them. The whole street had an air of busyness.

Except Case's. It had a party atmosphere.

Jo stood on the front walk and surveyed the place with apprehension. A fistful of helium balloons were attached to the porch posts and the front door. Was it his birthday? she wondered.

It stunned her to realize she was in love with him and didn't even know his birthday. She didn't want to intrude, and yet, she'd come so far, she couldn't turn back now.

It had taken her a month to work up her courage to make this trip. She wasn't going to back out.

Tucking her purse under her arm, she made her way

up the walk and onto the porch. When she neared the front door, she heard screaming. It took her a few seconds to realize it was children, and that they were also laughing.

Now she knew she was really intruding. She decided to come back later. She was turning away when the door was thrown open and a woman came barreling out.

She had thick black hair that curled around her face in gypsy waves and olive-dark eyes. She gave Jo a startled look and then broke into a huge smile that looked very familiar. "Hello! Oh, please tell me you're here with the jumping castle."

Jo blinked. "The jumping...?"

The woman slapped her hand to her forehead. "Oh, why today of all days would those people be late? Don't they have any pity for a woman with a houseful of small children?" She shrugged. "Well, there's nothing else to do but call them again and make threats." She focused on Jo. "Sorry. Can I help you?"

"I was looking for Case, but if this is a bad time..."

Leaning in to gaze at her, the woman broke into a wide grin. "Are you the one who burned his eyebrows off?"

Jo laughed. "No, that was Starina Simms. I'm Jo Ella Quillan."

"All I can say is that Calamity Falls must be a hell of a place. Case hasn't been the same since." She stuck out her hand. "I'm his sister Jessica. He's inside with my kids and about six others. It's my son Ryan's birthday, and we're having it here because Case has a backyard big enough for a jumping castle. You know, one of those huge, air-filled things where kids get in, jump around, get sick as dogs and throw up cake and ice cream all over each other."

Drowning in this torrent of words, Jo could only shake her head. "No, I..."

"Wait'll you have kids," Jessica said, reaching out to pat her arm. "You learn all these things very quickly." She looked up to see a truck pulling a small trailer down the street. "Oh, thank goodness. There they are. I'm going to go flag them down." She waved toward the open doorway. "Go on in." Before Jo could do so, she leaned in and yelled. "Case! There's someone here to see you. She's gorgeous and if you let her get away, you're a sap." She turned, gave Jo a sweet smile, and said, "Go on in."

With an introduction like that, Jo didn't think she could do anything except follow the sound of the shrieking children. She took a good look at his house as she went, noticing natural woods, warm earth tones, an open, airy feeling that welcomed her.

Butterflies churned away in her stomach. She hoped Case welcomed her.

She found him in the dining room, down on his hands and knees, with a small boy on his back. He was making wild-bull noises while the boy clung to the neck of his shirt and shrieked with joy.

"My turn, Uncle Case," a tiny girl insisted. She tried to shove the boy off, but Case reached behind and rescued him.

"It's not your turn yet, Samantha," he said. "Just a..."

His gaze landed on Jo's shoes, then traveled up her legs, over her pale yellow sheath dress, and stopped at her face.

Joy and fear circuited through her when she saw the stunned amazement on his face. He slipped the little boy to the floor, but before the girl could climb on his back, he said, "Let's take a break, kids. Uncle Case needs to talk to this lady."

Jo looked at him, and then down at the children, who were regarding her with curiosity. "The jumping castle's here," she said.

That cleared the room instantly. Ten small children raced from the room leaving Case and Jo standing, facing each other.

"You came," he said, his voice full of wonder. Then he strode forward and grabbed her around the waist, crushing her mouth beneath his. "You came to me."

"We didn't finish our last argument," she said, holding his face in that way she loved to do and kissing him fervently. "You didn't listen to me."

"I was an idiot."

"Yes, you were."

They stood in the middle of his dining room, which was scattered with confetti, balloons, and a couple of stray child-size shoes, and feasted on each other. Her breath was clogged in her throat and her knees were shaking.

"You've got to listen to me, Case," she said.

"I read the article," he responded, drawing her away so he could look into her eyes. "It was great. You caught the right tone for all the people involved without making it sound like a silly Calamity Falls adventure." He paused. "I guess this puts you on the road to where you want to be."

"Only if it gets me here with you," she answered. Everything rested on this. She'd rehearsed this speech for days now and it was slipping from her mind.

"Did you get a job offer from the newspaper here in town?"

"Yes. And I turned it down."

He jerked. "Turned it down. Why? I thought that was what you wanted."

"I thought so, too, but I realized I like being on my own." She gulped. "I'm going to be a freelance writer. I know I can do this, and I'll be good at it. It'll be hard. It'll take commitment, but I know I can do it, and..."

"I've got an office here that you can use."

Her words stumbled over each other and died. "What?"

"I love you, Jo." He kissed her fervently. "I love you and I want you to marry me. Live here, work here, do whatever you want, but don't leave me."

"You're the one who left," she pointed out, laughing. "I tried to tell you that my idea of a fast-track life didn't mean I was going to be gone all the time, chasing stories around the world. I only wanted to use my education and experience."

"I was an idiot to leave," Case said. "But I was coming back." He dragged her to a small closet off the living room. He threw the door open. "See?"

On the floor rested a black duffel bag. "It's packed," he said. "I was coming back to you right after Ryan's party." He wrapped his arms around her. "Have your life on whatever track you want," he said. "Just make sure it's with me."

Jo stood on tiptoe and kissed him, putting all of her love into it, filling it with promises.

"I'll marry you, Case, as soon as I can, but it'll have to be in Calamity Falls."

He gave her a wary look. "Why is that?"

"Stavros Pappas says he'll make the cake just as soon as the stars tell him what kind, Cedric and Charlotte will do the flowers—they're getting married, too, by the way—Lainey's dying to wear a hot pink brides-maid's dress, and…''

"I get the picture. We've got to get married there or have the whole town mad at us."

She leaned back and laughed into his eyes. "And if there's one thing we don't want, it's to have that town mad at us. It could be a disaster."

"A calamity," he added, and winced at his own corny joke. He swept her into his arms and kissed her again. "Nah. Our calamities are over with. Aren't they, Jo?"

She answered him with a sly smile.

"Jo?"

Reaching out, she took his hand and rested it low on her stomach. "Case, I don't think Calamity Falls is where we ought to be buying condoms from now on."

Confused, he stared into her eyes until the impact of her words hit him. "You mean?"

Her lips trembled. "I guess we'd better start learn-ing about things like jumping castles, Daddy."

"Jo?" he gulped, then he swept her into his arms and danced her around the room.

"You're going to make me a father." He stopped, swiped his hand over his face, and said, "Well, why not? You've already made me into a babbling fool."

She laughed with him, and then hugged him, secure in his love.

"That's the last surprise you have for me, isn't it?" he asked.

Her lips curved in a secretive smile.

"Jo?"

Return to the charm of the Regency era with

GEORGETTE HEYER,

creator of the modern Regency genre.

Enjoy six romantic collector's editions with forewords
by some of today's bestselling romance authors,

**Nora Roberts, Mary Jo Putney,
Jo Beverley, Mary Balogh,
Theresa Medeiros and Kasey Michaels.**

Frederica
On sale February 2000
The Nonesuch
On sale March 2000
The Convenient Marriage
On sale April 2000
Cousin Kate
On sale May 2000
The Talisman Ring
On sale June 2000
The Corinthian
On sale July 2000

Available at your favorite retail outlet.

HARLEQUIN®
Makes any time special ™

Come escape with Harlequin's new

Series Sampler

Four great full-length Harlequin novels bound together in one fabulous volume and at an unbelievable price.

Be transported back in time with a Harlequin Historical® novel, get caught up in a mystery with Intrigue®, be tempted by a hot, sizzling romance with Harlequin Temptation®, or just enjoy a down-home all-American read with American Romance®.

You won't be able to put this collection down!

On sale February 2000 at your favorite retail outlet.

HEART OF THE WEST

Every Man Has His Price!

Lost Springs Ranch was famous for turning young mavericks into good men. So word that the ranch was in financial trouble sent a herd of loyal bachelors stampeding back to Wyoming to put themselves on the auction block!

HARLEQUIN®
Makes any time special ™

Visit us at www.romance.net

PHHOWGEN

MONTANA MAVERICKS

Big Sky Brides

Legendary love comes to Whitehorn, Montana,
once more as beloved authors

Christine Rimmer, Jennifer Greene and Cheryl St.John

present three brand-new stories in this exciting anthology!

Meet the Brennan women:

SUZANNA, DIANA and ISABELLE

Strong-willed beauties who find unexpected
love in these irresistible marriage of
covnenience stories.

Don't miss
MONTANA MAVERICKS: BIG SKY BRIDES
On sale in February 2000,
only from Silhouette Books!

Available at your favorite retail outlet.

Silhouette®

Coming in February 2000
WHO'S AFRAID OF A BIG BAD WOLFE?

Not the special ladies who tame the remaining
Wolfe brothers in these sensuous love stories by
beloved author **Joan Hohl.**

Available February 2000 at your favorite retail outlet.